Miss Julia's Marvelous Makeover

Miss Julia's Marvelous Makeover

ANN B. ROSS

VIKING

VIKING
Published by the Penguin Group
Penguin Group (USA) LLC
375 Hudson Street
New York, New York 10014

USA | Canada | UK | Ireland | Australia | New Zealand | India | South Africa | China
penguin.com
A Penguin Random House Company

First published by Viking Penguin, a member of Penguin Group (USA) LLC, 2014

Library of Congress Cataloging-in-Publication Data

Ross, Ann B.
Miss Julia's marvelous makeover : a novel / Ann B. Ross.
pages cm.
ISBN 978-0-670-02611-1
1. Springer, Julia (Fictitious character)—Fiction.   2. Cosmetics—Fiction.
3. Self-realization in women—Fiction.   4. Domestic fiction.   I. Title.
PS3568.O84198M5655 2014
813'.54—dc23
2013041161

Printed in the United States of America
1 3 5 7 9 10 8 6 4 2

Set in Fairfield
Designed by Alissa Amell

This one is for the multitalented and multitasking Valerie Wellbourne, professional land surveyor and superb bookseller, with appreciation for her help with this book and with all the others as well. Thanks, Val!

Chapter 1

I didn't see it at the time—how many of us do?—but it all started back in January, a few days into the new year, when I felt compelled to sit down and take stock as, on occasion, I feel the need to do. So with the house quiet that morning—Sam off meeting with some local businessmen, Lillian at the grocery store, Lloyd in school, and me with time on my hands—taking stock was exactly what I was doing.

Now, I'm not talking about counting up assets and debits in a portfolio—I let Binkie, my curly-headed lawyer, take care of that—but rather, totting up the pluses and minuses of my life while hoping that they'll balance out in the final accounting. Admittedly, I have a lot of pluses: Lloyd, Sam, Lillian, Hazel Marie. I could go on and on, but I also have a lot of minuses, like stubbornness, self-centeredness, a tendency to jump into the problems of other people—all for their own good, but still—and a certain impetuosity when action is called for.

I would like to report that, at the time of which I speak, I dwelt on the pluses and how thankful I was for them, but I didn't. I was in a critical frame of mind, and all I could think of were the numerous times that I'd overstepped myself, blithely confident that I knew best and acting on that certainty.

Even as I inwardly cringed at the remembrance of some of my rasher moments, I could also comfort myself with the fact that only a few of them had actually made things worse. I will concede, however, that my recollections can on occasion be a tiny bit selective. But that in itself is a gift, an asset if you will, for who among us could live with our character defects constantly in the forefront?

I know I couldn't face a day with mine uppermost in mind.

I have to keep them safely stored in a mental box, opening it only when I feel the need to take stock, then quickly storing them away again.

So that's what I'd been doing the morning after Sam had told me in no uncertain terms that he was tired of taking trips by himself and that, furthermore, he had no intention of giving up his trips. In other words, he meant for me to go with him, and right there I had to add another minus to my debit list: I was too self-centered to put his desires above my own, but I'll tell you the truth, I did not want to go traipsing all over the world.

"But you'd love it, Julia," he'd said. "Think of all the places we could go—Ireland, for example. Wouldn't you like to go there? Or we could do a cathedral tour in Europe or a tour of the great houses of England. Or what about Rome or Paris?"

"Yes, and what would we have when we got back? Aching feet and a bunch of pictures with nowhere to put them."

"Memories, honey. We'd have memories, and we wouldn't have to take any pictures."

"I should say not," I said. "The thought of walking all over creation with a camera around my neck is not my idea of fun. Besides," I went on, "I don't fly."

"We wouldn't have to fly. We could go by boat. You'd like it if we went first class—dressing for dinner, strolling on the deck, meeting interesting people."

"And suffering from seasickness the whole way, too. Oh, Sam," I said, immediately contrite at the disappointed look on his face, "I'm sorry. It's just that I have no desire to see the world. I like it right here, doing the same things every day. The daily routine ressures me, while constant change disturbs my equilibrium. But I know you love to travel and I wouldn't discourage you from it for anything."

"I know you wouldn't, but I'd enjoy it so much more if you were enjoying it with me. And I think you would, if you'd just try it. We could start with a few short trips to get you used to being away. We could take the Amtrak Crescent to New Orleans, for instance, or take it the other way and go to New York. See some Broadway shows, go to museums, do a little shopping."

"You're getting closer," I said with a smile to show I was teasing. "What about a Sunday afternoon drive? Wouldn't that suffice?"

"And see what?"

"Oh, there're waterfalls around and fruit stands and motorcycle convoys. Maybe a fireworks stand. And we'd be home by dark."

Sam laughed. "You just don't want to leave home."

"That's right. I like it here."

"Well, I like to travel and I'd really like you to go with me."

"I'll think about it."

That had been the end of the conversation, but I knew it wasn't the end of the matter. But, I declare, I didn't want to take off for parts unknown and leave the people who might need me. Why, what would happen to Lloyd without me around to watch over him? And what if Hazel Marie needed help with her twin babies? And what would Lillian do if trouble descended on her or Latisha, her great-granddaughter? To say nothing of the Abbotsville First Presbyterian Church. If I were gone any length of time, there was no telling what Pastor Ledbetter would get in his mind to do. He might change the order of worship again—something that he seemed to do just to keep us off balance. Or to keep us awake, but who knew?

The last time I'd been out of town for a few days—the time I chased jewel thieves all the way to Florida—you wouldn't believe what had happened while I was gone. I'd been elected treasurer of the garden club, president of the Lila Mae Harding Sunday school class, and leader of the book club for a whole year. And on top of that, I'd been volunteered to host a Christmas tea and to help with Vacation Bible school the following summer.

No, it wasn't safe to leave town. I needed to stick around to protect myself. Sam, of course, didn't have that problem. If he returned from abroad or wherever and found himself in an office he didn't want, he'd just smile and say, "Thank you all the same, but I think I'll pass on that." And he'd stick to it, whereas I would be so riddled with guilt for turning down an elected honor that I'd accept it and hate every minute of it.

So the days and weeks passed with no further mention of the wonders of travel while I put aside my stock taking since I couldn't remedy or rectify any lapses of the past anyway. I noticed, however, a few travel brochures left lying around the house—on the hall table, for one, in the kitchen by the phone, and even next to the sink in our bathroom. It seemed that Sam had in mind a boat trip down the Rhine—or up it, depending on which way it flowed. And all I could think of was how could he expect us to spend a week or more on the high seas just to get to the Rhine, then spend more time on water once we got there.

Looking back now, though, I should've jumped at the chance to fill our summer with a globe-trotting trip. I should've realized that my husband's inquiring mind would not be content without something new and intriguing to occupy it, but I made no mention of the brochures nor did I ask about Sam's plans. I just let things ride while hoping that his wanderlust would wear itself out or, if it didn't, that he'd get over wanting me along. Neither happened, but a few things came up that took their place, and I'm still not sure which would've been for the best.

Chapter 2

"Julia," Sam said with a little smile pulling at the corners of his mouth as he snapped open the newspaper, "I've decided not to take a trip this summer. It looks to be so busy that I won't have time to get away." This was on an evening a few weeks later while we relaxed by the fire in our new library at the end of a blustery day in February.

I looked at him in the other wing chair, taking note of his carefully averted eyes, and knew that something was afoot. "Is that right," I responded. "Well, I'll be glad to have you home. What changed your mind?"

"Oh, I've just realized that there're a lot of interesting things to do closer to home. I don't have to go halfway around the world to keep myself entertained."

He was being entirely too noncommittal, deliberately holding back on something.

"You're not planning a camping trip in Pisgah Forest, are you? Because if you are, I don't sleep on cots or in tents."

He laughed. "Not my cup of tea either." Then he made a great show of concentrating on an article in the paper—a patent attempt to engage my curiosity.

"May I ask what it is you've found that'll keep you too busy to float down the Rhine? And, yes, I've noticed all the brochures you've left lying around."

"Thought you would," he said without looking my way. "They didn't tempt you, did they?"

"No," I said, shaking my head. "They didn't." Then waited to hear what he'd come up with to replace his travel plans. And kept waiting, while he read the want ads, the sports page, the editorials, a columnist with whom I knew he didn't agree, and the letters to the editor. At this point, I realized that I had another character defect that would go on my list of minuses the next time I decided to take stock: lack of patience.

"Well," I demanded. "What is it? What do you have up your sleeve that you're dying to tell me about, but not before I have to drag it out of you?"

He frowned and pursed his mouth, as if he were giving it some deep thought. "Well, it's like this. It might involve a little travel—not far—just around a couple of counties, as you suggested, but still you might not be interested. I can probably handle it by myself, but if not, there'll be plenty of volunteers to help out."

"For what? I never heard of having volunteers to travel around a few counties. And who would volunteer, anyway?"

"Oh, a lot of folks, all eager to do whatever I want. I'll have my pick, but don't worry. No overnight trips as far as I know."

"Well, that's good," I said, thinking that I'd figured out his plans. "Sounds as if you've found some fishing buddies. You'll be floating around on water even if it's not the Rhine, and you'll probably catch more, too."

"Nope, won't be any time for fishing. The French Broad and Mud Creek will have to do without me this year."

"Sam Murdoch," I said, fully aroused by this time, "put down that paper and tell me what you're doing."

He lowered the paper, smiled at me, and said, "I've decided that you're right—home is where I want to be, too. So tell me, how would you like to be the state senator's wife?"

"*Jimmy Ray Mooney's?* Sam, he's married."

"So are you," he pointed out, laughing at the shock on my face. "But no, you won't have to change husbands. The one you already have has been asked to run for the senate of the North Carolina General Assembly."

"The state senate," I murmured, as if it was a new concept, which it was. "In Raleigh?"

"Where else?" Sam asked.

"Well, I guess I'm just surprised," I said, running over all the ramifications in my mind. "I didn't know you had political ambitions. How long have you been thinking about this?"

He looked at his watch. "About two hours," he said with a straight face. Then he put aside the paper to give me his full attention. "Here's what happened: I was approached about running several weeks ago, but I had my heart set on taking a trip with you this summer. So I turned it down, but then Frank Sawyer had to drop out—you heard about that?"

"He had a double knee replacement, didn't he?"

"Yeah, and not doing very well, I understand. The party was counting on him to run against Jimmy Ray again, but he's not up for campaigning all spring and summer. Look, Julia," Sam said, leaning forward, "the deadline for filing is at the end of this week, so if you have any hesitation about this, tell me now. I'll turn it down with no regrets. In fact, it'd give me a good excuse to go fishing instead."

"Well, I guess that's better than going down the Rhine, but I don't know, Sam. You're not giving me a whole lot of time to think. Would we have to move to Raleigh?"

"No. The Assembly is in session only a few months a year. We could get a small apartment there, and you could go with me or I'd come home every weekend. They close up shop on Thursdays, so we'd have three-day weekends at home."

"It's a long drive, though."

"About four and a half to five hours." He raised his eyebrows and smiled. "Depending on how often we stopped."

I smiled back. I didn't let many rest areas go by without dropping in. Then I gazed into the fire for a while, thinking over what a political campaign might mean to our comfortable way of life. Then I looked up at him and said, "This may sound as if I'm trying to talk you out of it, but I'm not. I just want to know what we'd be getting ourselves into. You've retired from practicing law, do you really want to take on another job? And what about your book— the one you've worked on so long? Would you just put that aside?"

"As for taking on another job, the beauty part of this is that I would be a one-term senator—I've made that clear. The party is grooming an up-and-comer, but he's too green this year. In two years in the next election he'll be ready or Sawyer will be healthy enough to run again. Frank knew he was having surgery, but he assured the party he'd be able to run, but, well." Sam stopped and chuckled. "He didn't take into account some complications he's having. I understand he's cussing his surgeon up one side and down the other. Fact of the matter is, Julia, I'd be a stopgap, which is fine with me. Two years of politicking is enough, and besides, it'll give me more material for my book."

The book of which we spoke was a history of Abbot County's legal community—the lawyers, judges, defendants, and so on—which Sam had been working on during his retirement.

"But," he went on, "if you're against it, I won't do it. The only reason I'm even considering it is because I'm a firm believer in the two-party system. To let Jimmy Ray run unopposed goes against the grain. He's been in the senate long enough." Sam stopped and thought for a minute. "And there is this: I may have no choice. I might not win."

"Oh," I said, waving my hand to brush that possibility aside, "you'll win, all right. Everybody knows you and respects you. I have no doubt you'd win."

He laughed again. "Thanks, but I'm not so sure. There's an ingrained group that's controlled this district, county, and town for years—it's a tight network of old hands, except they've been careful to bring in newcomers so that the same faces don't appear over and over. But they know what they're doing. They pretty much stack the town council, then they take turns standing for mayor. And they do pretty much the same with state and federal offices—that's why it's such a blow to lose Frank Sawyer. He was the best one to take on Mooney. He almost beat him two years ago."

"So you'd be running against Jimmy Ray?"

"Right, and he'll be hard to beat with that crowd behind him."

As I thought this over, I realized that a lot of underhanded things must've been going on that I—and a lot of others—hadn't known about.

"That just burns me up," I said, somewhat hotly. "Do you mean to tell me that our elections have all been rigged for years?"

"Not rigged exactly, no," Sam said, shaking his head. "Just that they've been able to preselect the candidates who run, and with this district being mostly a one-party district, voters have little choice. And they put up enough new names now and then to give the appearance of real change. They're all alike, though, and they all have the same agenda."

"And what agenda is that?"

"Knowing ahead of everybody else which industry plans to expand, where a new business or a government building will be located, what roads the DOT will widen and where new ones will be constructed—just a few minor things like that. Then they form a corporation to buy up land before any of it is made public."

"I don't think that's legal, and who are they anyway?" I demanded, riled up now at the thought that I'd been freely exercising my right to vote all these years without knowing that I'd not been so free after all.

"Well, look who's on the town council and on the county commission, and look at our representatives and senators—state and federal. They're all part of it. But voters might be ready for a real change this go-round. Take Jimmy Ray, our current state senator . . ."

"I don't have to take him. Every time I hear his name, I feel so sorry for that daughter of his. Jimmie Mae Mooney—who in their right mind would saddle a child with a name like that? He should've just named her Junior and been done with it."

"Oh, he's all right," Sam said, thinking the best of people as he usually did. "In fact, they're all decent enough. But Frank Sawyer was our best bet to take on Mooney and break that stranglehold. I'm trying to consider it an honor that the party asked me to take his place." Sam grinned in that self-deprecatory way of his.

"Well, *I* consider it an honor, as well as an indication of the party's good sense in selecting you. But, tell me something, Sam—were you never interested in being a judge? You would be such a good one—you're so fair-minded and you certainly know the law."

"I thought about it a couple of times," Sam said, shrugging. "But I was caught up in writing my book, then I got a bee in my bonnet about a certain widow lady, and the interest faded away. Now, though, learning and doing something new is very appealing, especially if it appeals to you, too. I think we'd have a good time, Julia, doing this together and doing something good for the district, as well. But," he said, raising a finger to emphasize his point, "I'm not going to do it without you. We'd be making a two-year commitment if I win, and that would be it. And if I do win, it'll mean going back and forth to Raleigh when the Assembly is in session, and keeping an office open here for constituents during the off-season. But keep in mind that it's very likely that I'll lose, and I don't want you to be disappointed. As for me, I can take it or leave it."

As I studied the matter, I realized that I, too, could take it or leave it. However it turned out, I was not so invested in a senate race that I'd be thrilled on the one hand or devastated on the other. Of course, though, it never entered my head to discourage Sam from doing anything he wanted to do, but it was clear that he wanted me to want what he wanted. In fact, it sounded as if he wouldn't do it at all if I was the least bit hesitant about it. I'd already disappointed him by turning down a globe-trotting trip, but this I could do without having to pack a suitcase.

So I thought about it, and the more I thought, the more appealing it seemed. I thought about those long drives to and from Raleigh—just the two of us in the car alone, the talks we could have—why, we'd have more time together than we'd ever had at home. And the thought of being the representatives of all the people in the district—working for them, improving conditions, speaking for them—I just got all patriotic and shivery at the thought. Well, of course I knew that it would be Sam who'd be their senator, but I, too, would have a small part in sacrificing for my country.

"One question, Sam," I finally said. "Would I have to make any speeches?"

"Oh," he said offhandedly, "maybe one or two. Maybe to your book club or to other small groups, that sort of thing. We'd work up a little ten-minute talk, and you'd give that over and over." He arched one eyebrow at me. "All about how wonderful I am."

I laughed. "That would be no problem, except I'd probably make every woman in the district jealous."

"And," Sam went on, "during the campaign we'd have to show up at every pig-pickin', barbecue, watermelon cutting, parade, VFW meeting, and civic event around. Your job would be to stand there and gaze adoringly at me."

"Oh, Sam," I said, laughing, "you make it sound like fun. And we could take Lloyd to some of the events. He could meet people and learn all about politics. But," I went on, getting serious, "there's one thing I want you to promise me. Please, please don't use the word *fight* in your speeches or advertising or anything. It just turns me off to hear a candidate—even a sweet, grandmotherly type— say, 'Send me to Raleigh or Washington, and I'll *fight* for you,' as if they can't wait to get into a brawl with fisticuffs and hair pulling."

"Okay, I agree—no fighting. You want to do this?" He leaned over and took my hand. "Are you with me?"

"I'm always with you, and, yes, I do want to do it, because you're the best one for the job and," I couldn't help but add, "it beats floating down the Rhine any day."

He laughed, then said, "One thing you should be aware of— there'll be people who'll be working against us."

"Like *who*?"

"Well, like Thurlow Jones for one."

"*What!* Why, Sam, you are without doubt the best-qualified, the most experienced, the fairest, most honest, and best-liked man in town. How could anybody be against you? And Thurlow?" I waved my hand in dismissal. "Nobody pays any attention to him."

"That's not exactly true, sweetheart," Sam said, his voice taking on a serious tone. "Thurlow is the money behind the ones in office now. He's the one who makes the decisions for the other party—he'll be against us. Not many people know it, but he pretty much runs this town."

Well, that was a shocker if I'd ever heard one. Thurlow Jones was an unshaven, disgraceful, and disreputable excuse for a man who delighted in showing his contempt for women in general and for me in particular. If you didn't know him but happened to see him on the street, you'd think he was a tramp down on his luck. There was no way to tell from his appearance that he could buy and sell half the town.

And to think that *he* was the power behind the thrones of the county and the district—it beat all I'd ever heard. Until the mail came one sultry morning a few months later.

Chapter 3

"Sam?" I called, tapping on the door of his office as soon as I'd scanned the letter in my hand. Hearing his response, I walked into my former sunroom—the one Deputy Bates had rented after Wesley Lloyd Springer left me a somewhat bereaved widow and before Deputy Bates married Binkie—the sunroom that I'd made into Sam's home office. I was loath to disturb him, because this was one of the few free days he'd had to work on his book since winning the primary the previous month. Of course, having been the party's only candidate, winning the primary had been a foregone conclusion. "If you're busy," I said, though not really meaning it, "this can probably wait. We can talk later."

"Never too busy for you. Come on in." Sam had risen from his creaky executive chair behind the desk and pulled a wing chair closer. "Sit down and talk to me. I'm stuck in the year 1966, trying to decide how much to reveal about Judge Alexander T. Dalton. You may remember him better as Monk Dalton."

"Vaguely," I said, sitting down and trying to show a little interest in the history he was writing about the shenanigans of the local legal community. "Didn't he have two wives at the same time?"

Sam laughed. "Yeah, they had him on a bigamy charge until one of the women, the one he'd lived with for years, told him that if he'd make a hefty settlement on her, she'd testify that they'd never had an actual ceremony, and she'd move to Florida. He did and she did, and the charges were dropped."

"Oh, well then. Tell it all, Sam. That's the kind of book people will buy. But listen, the mail just came and I need your advice." I held up the letter—written in pencil on lined notebook paper—that I'd just received.

"Who's it from?"

"Elsie Bingham. You don't know her, but she's my half first cousin or half cousin, first removed, or something. Her father was my father's half brother." I stopped and thought for a minute. "Or maybe his stepbrother, which would make her no kin at all to me. Wouldn't that be nice."

Sam smiled at my sarcasm. "Not good news, then?"

"About as far from it as you can get. Listen to this." I began reading.

Dear Julia,

Haven't heard from you in so long you might be dead as far as I know. But in case your not, guess your still living high on the hog like you always did.

I let the letter fall to my lap in disgust. "Wouldn't that just frost you! A nice way to start a letter to someone you haven't had contact with in forty years."

"Kinda puts you off, doesn't it?" Sam agreed.

"I'll say. But she was always like that. Well, listen to the rest of it." I lifted the letter and began again to read:

I know you remember the summer you spent with us on the farm which is gone now and good riddance I say, except we're on another one just as bad. Or worse. Anyway your mother was sick and died from whatever she had so that's why we had to take you and your sisters in and feed and cloth every one of you all summer long cause your daddy was to broke up to lift a hand for his own children.

"I say, feed and clothe us! That was the worst summer of my life. And I happen to know that Papa sent money to Uncle Posey

to take care of all our needs. What he actually did with it is another matter because we ate a lot of corn bread and buttermilk and
you wouldn't believe the amount of beans. And as far as clothing
us is concerned, by the time we were sent home we'd outgrown
everything we owned. Papa had to send Pearl downtown with us
to buy school clothes. You should've seen what we ended up with,
but Elsie's right about one thing. Papa was out of his mind with
grief and not responsible, which was when I as the oldest began
to take over."

"And did an excellent job of it, I'm sure."

"I don't know about that," I mused, recalling the problems of a
young girl taking charge of a motherless home. "Did the best I
could, I guess, although my sisters wouldn't think so." I sighed and
took up the letter again, reading aloud:

> *Anyway, when things get binding* families *do what*
> families *ought to do. There is such a thing as* family *ties*
> *and* family *responsibilities and so on you know, which is*
> *the reason to remind you of what my* family *did for your*
> family.

"Can you believe this!" I demanded, waving the letter.
Sam smiled and shook his head. "She wants something."
"She sure does and you won't believe that either."

> *Anyway living out here in the sticks our Trixie don't*
> *have a way to meet nice people and learn that a high-*
> *school dropout wont do more than pump gas the rest of*
> *his life and not even that with all the self-serving stations*
> *we got nowadays. She's Doreen's girl, but Troy and me*
> *had to take her and raise her long after I thought I was*
> *through with all that and I wont the best for her. So Im*

sending her to you for the summer so she can get spruced up and polished and learn what high living is like and meet somebody willing and able to support her like you did. I thought you'd never get married but you finally did pretty good at it.

"The *nerve* of the woman!" I exclaimed. "Does she think I run a finishing school? But, listen, Sam. It gets worse."

So don't tell me you cant do it because I happen to know you took in a woman no kin to you and one who had done you dirt to boot. Trixie has never done a thing to you and she wouldn't for the world—shes real sweet and good company cause she dont talk a lot and worry you half to death. And Julia dont tell me you cant afford it. I happen to know you married above yourself with that little banty of a man that owns a whole bank by hisself so if you got the money to take in his floozie then you got the money to feed and cloth your own kin for a few months like we did you. And your sisters to. We had a good time playing under the scuppernong vine that summer.

"Sam," I said, closing my eyes and leaning my head back against the chair. "I am simply speechless. I don't know how she knows anything about me—she doesn't even know that Wesley Lloyd Springer is dead, and she doesn't know about you. But she obviously knows about Hazel Marie."

"Where does she live? Way off somewhere?"

I turned the envelope over and read aloud. "Route one, Vidalia, Georgia. That's near Savannah, I think, but too close as far as I'm concerned. But you haven't heard the worst of it yet." I read the next paragraph to him:

So Im putting Trixie on the Greyhound real early Thurs. morning and she will get there about noon for you to meet her. You want have no trouble with her. Shes good as gold and likes chickens if you keep any she will look after them for you and earn her keep. Just tell her what to do and she will do it without a lot of backtalk.

"They Lord!" I cried. "Does she think I keep chickens? The woman is crazy. What're we going to do, Sam?"

"Looks like we're having a guest for the summer. She'll be company for you while I'm out campaigning."

"You're taking this entirely too complacently. Besides, I intend to campaign with you and I already have all the company I want. I won't have time for any more."

"Well, maybe we can introduce her to some young people around town—keep her busy and entertained that way."

"I don't *know* any young people, and I heartily resent the high-handed tone of this letter. She doesn't even *ask,* just tells us she's sending this Trixie!" I had to grit my teeth to calm myself down enough to read the rest of it to him:

Anyway you can send her back at the end of the summer when I especk her to know all the ends and outs of all that la-de-dah living you do. I dont want her marrying a gas-pumper or a farmer like I did. I give you credit Julia for picking a man with money even if he don't look like much. You cant eat looks anyway. Take care of Trixie. Shes a real good girl. Your cousin, Elsie Bingham.

P. S. Troy says to tell you not to spruce Trixie up to much. He dont wont her coming home with her nose in the air like you always had yours. But I say if she finds herself a decent husband up there she can get as stuck up as she wonts to.

I let the letter fall to my lap and leaned my head on my hand. "This is too much, Sam—too much to ask of anybody. Not that she's asking. I don't know this girl. I never knew her mother—this Doreen—and barely remember Elsie herself. I am just not going to do it."

"Well, call her up and tell her it's not convenient at this time . . ."

"Actually at *any* time," I mumbled.

"Anyway, as Elsie is prone to say," Sam said, "it doesn't seem to have occurred to her that you might have plans for the summer."

"That's the truth." I stood up, folded the letter, and put it back into the envelope. "Thanks for listening, Sam. I'm glad you agree that we can't do this. I'd better go ahead and try to get Elsie's phone number from information—you'll notice she didn't give it in the letter. I'm going to tell her not to put Trixie on that bus."

"Julia," Sam said as I turned to leave, "what day is it?"

"Thursday, why?" I suddenly stopped in my tracks, snatched the letter out of the envelope, and scanned it again. *"Thursday! That girl's been on a bus all morning! And it's almost noon when she'll be here."* I couldn't believe Elsie had so effectively trapped me. Because without a doubt in this world, she'd planned her letter to arrive just as it had—too late to keep Trixie at home. It was just as I remembered Elsie—sly, crafty, and determined to have her way.

But I wasn't yet outmaneuvered. With a glint in my eye, I said, "Sam, about that trip down the Rhine—it would pretty much take up the whole summer, wouldn't it?"

Chapter 4

Well, of course it was too late to plan a summer voyage on the ocean or a river, but, believe me, I regretted having been so adamant about staying home. Now, of course, Sam would be too busy campaigning to go anywhere, but Elsie didn't know that and neither did Trixie. I drove to the Greyhound bus station on the edge of town, still simmering at the high-handedness of them both. I'd already decided that as soon as that girl stepped off the bus, I was going to put her right back on.

Actually, I'd probably have to wait with her for the next bus going south, but I was determined not to leave the station with Trixie in tow. Fuming, I decided that I'd sit there with her if it took all day for the next southbound bus to come in. Let her surprise her grandmother instead of me by showing up out of the blue. And it would be a surprise because I'd been unable to get a phone number for Elsie—either because she didn't have one or her last name was no longer Bingham even though that was the way she'd signed her letter.

She could've just signed it that way, I mused, so I'd know who she was. But then again, she'd mentioned Troy, so she was still married to the same man she'd started out with—Troy Bingham. Maybe, I thought, they used only a cell phone like a lot of people were doing. In which case, their number wouldn't be listed. The possibility still existed, though, that they simply didn't have a telephone—Troy hadn't been that good a catch to begin with.

I let the car idle at a red light, remembering the handwritten wedding invitation we'd received from Elsie the year we'd both turned twenty-one—the year I'd resigned myself to spinsterhood. But not Elsie. She'd been looking for a husband since she'd been sixteen, and apparently Troy Bingham had been the first one to take her up on it. The invitation had been no more than a long boastful dig because she was getting a husband and I wasn't.

Of course she changed her tune a few years later when Wesley Lloyd Springer came into the picture. Although she didn't want him—and I didn't much either—he *was* a financial catch, as no one knows better than me. Well, Sam and Binkie know, but that's beside the point.

When that invitation had come, Elizabeth, my youngest sister, said, "I wouldn't go to her wedding for all the tea in China." And Victoria had added, "I still have nightmares about that summer. How Papa could've sent us to that family is beyond me." Then they reminded me of the time that Elsie's mother had chased down a chicken, wrung its neck, and fried it up for Sunday dinner. She'd put a wing on each of my sisters' plates, looked at me, and said, "Too bad hens don't come with three." Then put the boney back on mine. Elsie had come by her meanness naturally.

Except for several preprinted birth announcements from Elsie—for which I'd sent gifts that had never elicited thank-you notes—that wedding invitation had been the last personal contact between us. Until now.

When I reached the bus station, I pulled in and parked. Then just sat there deciding how I'd tell Trixie that she wasn't welcome. I could tell her that we were facing a terribly busy summer with plans to go abroad—I couldn't flat-out lie and say we were definitely going—and her grandmother hadn't given us enough time to change our plans. And besides, I didn't have room for a guest. With all the remodeling I'd done—changing the sunroom into an office and the downstairs bedroom into a library—the only room available was the small one next to Lloyd's room that Lillian and Latisha used when the weather was too bad for them to get home. It just wasn't right to give their room to Trixie even though a snow-fall was highly unlikely in July.

I glanced at my watch—a few minutes past twelve, but I'd

called the station and the bus wasn't due until twelve-thirty. Another thing Elsie had been wrong about.

Gritting my teeth as I thought about dashing a young girl's hopes for the summer, I determined to be kind but firm. We just could not have her, that's all there was to it. I'd have to be strong even if she teared up with disappointment—I was sure that Elsie had filled her head with unrealistic visions of my la-de-dah living, as she'd called it, so the girl was probably looking forward to a round of parties, teas, and dances all summer long, ending up with an engagement ring. Well, if that was the case, she might as well cry with disappointment now as do it at the end of the summer when none of that had come to pass.

Wonder, I thought, *if every family has some Binghams around somewhere on the outskirts of their lives. Probably so,* I decided, *they just don't let on about it.*

Then I began to wonder what Trixie looked like and how I would recognize her. Sam had said that with a name like Trixie, she was probably an outgoing, perky little thing. "The only Trixie I've ever known," he said, "was a cheerleader." But the name conjured up a different association for me. I rubbed my neck where the only Trixie I'd ever even heard of had almost pinched my head off. Lillian, however, when I moaned to her about unwanted guests, said, "The onliest Trixie I know is my neighbor's ole dog that sleep under the porch. The girl got to be better'n that."

Looking at my watch again, I got out of the car and went into the small bus station. It was almost empty—only a few tired-looking travelers sitting in the rows of plastic chairs. I sniffed at the sight of ticket stubs and candy wrappers littering the floor and walked over to the ticket window.

"Could you tell me, please," I asked of the man behind the grate, "when the next bus to Vidalia, Georgia, comes in?"

He smoothed his thin mustache as his eyes traveled up and around the window—thinking, I supposed. Then he cleared his throat. "That would be your Jacksonville bus. Twelve-forty-five."

"Really!" I exclaimed, pleased beyond words that I could put

Trixie on a southbound bus as soon as she stepped off the north-
bound one.

"A.M.," he said, and I had to hold on to the ticket shelf to steady
myself.

More than twelve hours to wait. I couldn't believe it. Well, nothing could be done about it—I'd have to take her home, give her
dinner, and bring her back in the middle of the night.

I turned to walk away, disappointed and about half angry, wondering if I could put Trixie on a plane or hire a car service—
anything to get her on the way out of Abbotsville.

The roar of a heavy motor and the screech of brakes announced
the arrival of a bus. I walked outside to see a cloud of black smoke
issuing from the rear of the bus as it pulled in and parked. When
the door opened, passengers began to descend the steps to the
platform—mothers with babies, a soldier, two unkempt men with
paper sacks rolled up under their arms, an old woman with a scarf
around her head, a heavyset girl with a shopping bag, and two
attractive young women who didn't seem to be together.

I walked over to the most likely one, smiled, and asked, "Trixie?"

She gave me a scornful look and said, "I don't talk to strangers,
especially in a bus station." And walked away.

Just as the public address system came to life, announcing,
"Bus for Asheville, Knoxville, and points in between now loading
at Gate Three," I approached the other teenager, who was struggling with a large suitcase.

"Trixie? Are you Trixie Bingham?"

"No, ma'am," she said, hefting the suitcase from one hand to
the other, "but I wish I was. I need help with this thing."

Hope sprung in my breast—maybe Elsie had changed her
mind and kept Trixie home. Turning away, I started for my car,
thinking that I'd done my part by meeting the noon bus. It wasn't
my fault that Trixie wasn't on it.

"Uh, ma'am," a voice said to my back. "I'm Trixie."

It's a good thing that I'd had so much experience in handling
sticky social situations—you know, the kind that embarrass or

shock you, but which have to be managed without letting your true feelings show. This was one of those situations that demanded careful control of my face and voice, because Trixie turned out to be a short, stocky, almost muscular, and not-so-young woman with stringy hair and a sweating face that flushed bright red when I turned to look at her.

"Trixie?" I said, almost strangling on the word.

She ducked her head and clutched a wrinkled Target's shopping bag closer. "Yes'm, that's me."

Lord, even if I'd been looking forward to giving the girl a social whirl in Abbotsville society—such as it was—this was impossible. I glanced down at her hairy legs and large toenails—painted purple—sticking out of dusty sandals, taking in her bitten fingernails on my way, and realized that this situation called for every iota of self-control and social poise that I possessed.

"How do you do, Trixie," I managed to get out. "I'm Julia Murdoch. You may address me as Miss Julia while you're here. But speaking of that, let me say that I'm sorry that you've made such a long trip in vain. Ordinarily, we would be happy to have you, but unfortunately, it seems that our plans for the summer call for us to be away. I'm afraid your visit will be an abbreviated one, and you'll have to return home tonight."

She shrugged her shoulders, mumbled, "Okay," and looked from side to side—anywhere but at me.

Well, that was easily done, I thought, as she seemed unruffled by the prospect of a quick round trip. To be sure that she understood, though, I went on. "Yes, as much as we'd like to have you, our summer is completely taken up. But you'll have dinner with us, then I'll bring you back about midnight. I expect you can sleep on . . ." I stopped as the girl shifted from one foot to the other, then bent over, shuddering ever so slightly. "My goodness, are you all right?"

"I got to pee real bad."

"Oh," I said, my eyes widening. "Well, run into the station. There'll be a ladies' room there."

"Meemaw said they's nasty people in 'em. I can wait till we get to your house."

Meemaw? That, I supposed, would be Elsie, but, I declare, I could think of half a dozen more acceptable names for a grandmother—Nana, Grandmommy, Grandmom, Grammy, even Granny—but Meemaw? Thank goodness, I didn't have the problem, having had no children. Therefore, no grandchildren.

"Well, come on then. Let's get you home." I led her toward the car, wondering why she'd brought up the subject if she was able to wait. Then, stopping, I said, "Your luggage! Is it still on the bus?"

"They's a suitcase somewhere," she said, making no move to retrieve it. Then she swung the shopping bag around. "My good stuff's in here."

"That's all? For the *summer?*" I couldn't help the surprise in my voice.

Never meeting my eyes, she mumbled, "Meemaw said I'd need different clothes up here, and you'd know what to buy."

"Get in the car then," I said, opening the door and thinking that her Meemaw probably expected me to buy the clothes, too. "I'll see about your suitcase." Walking back to the bus where the driver was emptying the baggage compartment, I found Trixie's huge, Samsonite suitcase—the kind with no wheels—among several others. When I tried to drag the thing to the car, the bus driver took pity and put it in the trunk for me.

With that done, I rounded the car to the driver's side, steeling myself for several afternoon hours of Trixie's company, while looking forward to the time I could put her on that midnight bus to Georgia.

Chapter 5

As I pulled away from the bus station and headed for home, Trixie sat slumped in the seat beside me, her straight hair falling over the side of her face. I glanced surreptitiously toward her several times, thinking that if I were to take her on for the summer, the first thing I'd tackle would be the state of her posture. I wanted to say, "Head up, shoulders back. Sit up straight and act like a lady," but I didn't. She was not my problem.

Making an effort to assume the role of hostess, regardless of how brief the role, I tried to draw her out, asking about her trip, her family, her interests—all to no avail. She answered with a mumbled "No'm," "Yes'm," or "I guess." It was enough to make me want to shake her and forcefully say, "Speak up!"

But to tell the truth, the girl needed more than a pep talk, and I was more and more relieved that I wasn't the one responsible for providing what she needed. Take that hair, for instance. It wasn't just that her dark roots were showing, it was that the roots had grown out some five or six inches, leaving the bottom five or six inches a brassy blond shade with an undertone of—would you believe—pink.

She took a sudden sharp breath, then crossed her legs, giving me a sudden sharp fear of possible damage to my leather seats. I turned into a Shell station and parked at the side.

"Go use the bathroom, Trixie," I said. "The door's unlocked."

She squirmed, an agonized expression on her face. "Meemaw said—"

"And *I* say go use the bathroom before you ruin your kidneys."

That was all she needed. She was out of the car in a flash, scuttling toward the ladies' room door, while I waited and waited. I sat, hoping that relief would loosen her tongue and brighten her outlook, neither of which occurred.

When she came out of the ladies' room, I watched as she hurried—no, scuttled was the correct word—back to the car, her shoulders hunched over and her eyes darting fearfully from side to side. What in the world had her grandmother put in her head?

Maybe she was shy and self-conscious—painfully so, from the looks of her. It could be, though, that she only needed a little self-confidence, which she would gain from having a complete make-over. I'd start with hair restoration and styling, professional makeup, manicure, pedicure, more appropriate clothes than the baggy sheath she was wearing, posture and elocution lessons, a book on manners and etiquette, a low-calorie diet, an exercise regimen, and a Lady Schick razor. But she wasn't my problem.

When I turned into the driveway at home and stopped the car, Trixie stared out the window. "This it?" she asked in the same flat tone she'd been using.

"Yes, of course," I said. "That's why we stopped." Then regretted my sharp reply.

"I thought it'd be bigger," she said, and I stopped regretting anything but bringing her home.

"Well, come in and meet everybody," I said, getting out of the car. "We usually go in the back door because we park near it. You can leave your things in the car, since we'll be going back in a few hours."

"Meemaw said not to leave this," she said, hefting herself out of the car, carrying the sack with her.

"Then bring it," I said, shrugging as I led her to the door. The girl had barely said two dozen words, and already she'd rubbed me the wrong way.

She followed me into the kitchen, stopped short at the sight of Lillian at the counter, and whispered, "That your maid?"

Ignoring the question, I said, "Lillian, this is Trixie Bingham, who is visiting for a few hours. And Trixie, this is Lillian, house-keeper and friend."

"We glad to have you, Miss Trixie," Lillian said, drying her hands as Trixie frowned and turned away without responding.

"Trixie's a little shy, Lillian," I said, giving her a roll of my eyes. "Is Sam in the library? He'll want to meet her."

Trixie, still clasping her sack, followed me into the library where I introduced her to Sam. He, of course, was his usual courteous self, standing to greet her and extending his hand.

Misunderstanding the gesture, she mumbled, "It's not heavy. I'll hold on to it." At which, Sam's eyebrows shot up.

"Well," he said, "it's nice to meet you, Trixie. I expect you've had a tiring journey, would you like to rest a while?"

"I wouldn't mind," she mumbled.

"Come then," I said. "I'll take you upstairs where you can freshen up. We'll have lunch in a few minutes, then you might want to take a nap."

Even though Sam and I usually had lunch in the kitchen, Lillian had set the table in the dining room. When I saw the crocheted place mats and the centerpiece of fresh flowers, I knew that she had taken extra pains in honor of our guest. The first course was cups of chilled strawberry soup. After Sam said grace, Trixie— without following the lead of her hostess—picked up a teaspoon, took one taste, and screwed up her mouth. Then she put her spoon back on the place mat.

"Don't you care for it?" I asked. "I think it's nice on such a hot day."

Trixie shook her head. "Mine didn't get heated up." And she cast a sullen glance in Lillian's direction.

"Oh, well," I said, as Lillian brought in plates filled with curly lettuce and fruit, covered with poppy seed dressing. "Perhaps you'll like the fruit plate better. Oh, look, Lillian has made cream cheese and pecan sandwiches on date-nut bread. This is a treat, Lillian. I feel as if we're at a ladies' luncheon, don't you, Sam?"

"I do, indeed," he said, his eyes twinkling. "I love ladies' luncheons. I go to them all the time."

"Oh, you," I said, laughing, but Trixie just stared at him.

She played around with the canteloupe, strawberries, melon, and kiwi slices on her plate, taking tentative bites now and then, but clearly not enjoying her lunch. All I could think of was how glad I was that I would not be taking her to any real ladies' luncheons in Abbotsville. If she didn't like fruit, she probably wouldn't care for quiche, so what would she eat?

Finally I took pity and asked, "Is there anything you'd rather have for lunch?"

"You got any Doritos or Fritos? I could eat that and maybe some onion dip."

Lillian's mouth dropped open.

I quickly said, "I'm sorry, but no, we don't have anything like that. In fact, we rarely have snacks in the house. What about a peanut butter sandwich?"

"A 'mater sandwich would be better," Trixie said, "but I'll take it if that's all you got." As if we were woefully deprived of food.

So Trixie had a tomato sandwich for lunch, carefully prepared by Lillian but for which she received no thanks. In fact, when the plate was set before her, Trixie eyed both the sandwich and Lillian as if she suspected some lurking trickery somewhere.

After that unsuccessful luncheon, I suggested that Trixie might like to rest for a while. I made the mistake, though, of mentioning that the room was kept for Lillian and Latisha on the rare occasions they couldn't get home, hoping to subtly indicate that I was unprepared for an unexpected long-term visitor. Trixie stopped short in the middle of the room, staring at the bed.

"Meemaw said you'd have a guest room," she mumbled.

"This *is* the guest room," I replied, holding back the sharp retort that almost got away from me. "And occasionally Lillian is our guest."

"You mean your *maid* sleeps in the bed?" Trixie asked.

"Well, she certainly doesn't sleep on the floor," I returned sharply. Then taking a calming breath, I went on. "Now, Trixie, I assure you that the linens are fresh and you can either rest on the bed or in the easy chair, whichever you prefer. After all, it's only for a few hours, then you can sleep on the bus where all kinds of people—washed and unwashed—have been before you."

Holding on to my temper as best as I could, I left Trixie still deciding between the bed and the chair. Silently fuming, I wondered if she'd prefer Lloyd's bedroll that still had a rank smell from his last camping trip.

"Sam," I said, finding him waiting for me in the library, "that girl is impossible. I've a good mind to take her back to the bus station and let her sit there till the bus comes in. She can buy Doritos from the vending machine for dinner."

"Only a few hours more, Julia," Sam reminded me.

"I know," I said, sighing as I sat beside him. "But if she doesn't start showing some respect to Lillian, I'm going to let her have a piece of my mind. The idea! Do you know that she didn't want to sleep in the bed that Lillian has slept in?" And I went on to tell him of the conversation upstairs.

Sam frowned, then said, "I was inclined to pity her, but we can't have Lillian's feelings hurt. I tell you, Julia, the girl appears backward to me."

I looked at him in surprise. Sam rarely made critical judgments about people. He could always find reasons or excuses for untoward behavior, which if uncorrected, he simply ignored. I, on the other hand, always felt I had to do the correcting, but not in this case—I wanted Trixie gone. She was not my problem or my responsibility.

Chapter 6

When Lloyd came in from school that afternoon, he was in high spirits—it was the next to last day of his freshman year and, as he said, he had survived undamaged and unbowed.

I laughed, having had no doubt that he would not only survive but prosper in high school. Then I delicately explained to him the presence of Trixie, for whom he was unprepared, since she'd been sprung on us that very day while he was in school.

"Oh, good," he said. "Now I'll have somebody to bum around with. I hope she plays tennis."

"I wouldn't count on it," I said. "She doesn't seem the athletic type. But Lloyd, I want you to know that I'm sending her home tonight, so let this be a lesson to you. Don't ever impose on people by just showing up somewhere, expecting to be welcome. I'm trying my best not to blame Trixie, although she seems old enough to know better. It's really her grandmother who's at fault. So let's just be considerate of her while she's here."

"Okay, I can do that. How long is she going to rest? I want to meet her." Then his eyes lit up. "The pool's open. Maybe she'd like to go swimming."

We both looked up as a low rumble of thunder sounded overhead. "Uh-oh," Lloyd said. "Sounds like swimming's out. I better think of something else. Maybe she'd like to play some computer games."

I was walking a fine line speaking of Trixie to him. I didn't want to express my true feelings and influence his opinion of her. On the other hand, I could not, in good conscience, pretend that Trixie was delightful company.

"I wouldn't count on that either," I said, then sighed. "The fact of the matter, Lloyd, is that Trixie is not, well, very outgoing. I think we'll have a hard time finding anything she'd like. I haven't had much success so far."

He nodded as if he understood. "She's probably just disoriented, don't you think? Everything's new to her—the town, the house, all of us—and now she has to turn around and go back home. If she stayed long enough to get used to us, I bet she'd like being here. I feel kinda sorry for her."

"You're a good boy, Lloyd," I said, feeling somewhat ashamed of my own assessment of Trixie. Not enough, though, to change my mind about sending her home.

A soft summer rain kept Lloyd in the house the rest of the afternoon, and he wandered around thinking up things to entertain Trixie. He got out a thousand-piece puzzle—a sailing ship of some kind—and set it up on the mahogany card table in the library, then enticed Sam to help him start it. I occupied myself by writing out different slogans for Sam's campaign. He had to decide in a few days how he wanted his yard signs to look so they'd be ready to distribute.

"Sam," I said, "what're you thinking about the colors on your signs? Everybody and his brother uses some combination of red, white, and blue, but I think you'd stand out more with something different."

"Whatever you think, honey. Just so it's eye catching. Lloyd, try this piece on that corner."

"Well, I'm thinking a navy blue background with your name in white with some bright green somewhere. What about that?"

"Sounds fine to me. We can have the sign company work up some mockups, then decide what we like the best."

"Work up some mockups," Lloyd repeated, laughing. "Sounds funny. But, Miss Julia, you reckon Trixie's all right? She sure is resting a long time."

I looked at my watch, realizing that it was almost time for dinner. "She probably got up in the middle of the night to catch her bus, so maybe a long rest is what she needed. I'll go up and see about her."

———

Unhappily, though, Trixie's long rest had not improved her disposition. She came reluctantly downstairs after I roused her from her nap—on the bed, I might add—and continued to act half asleep the rest of the evening. Lloyd tried his best to engage her interest, but received only monosyllables in return.

By the time the four of us sat down at the dining room table, which Lillian had set beautifully, we were about at our wit's end. Lillian had again gone to extra trouble for our guest, having lit the four candles on my silver epergne and filled the bowl with roses and greenery. Sam complimented her on how lovely the table looked, then walked over to help Trixie to her chair. Trixie, however, looked so startled by the courtesy that he quickly backed off.

After Sam returned thanks for our food, he began to talk easily about the day's events, and Lloyd and I kept up our end, each of us trying to draw out Trixie. She would not be drawn, keeping her face down as she moved the food around on her plate.

I was about to lose patience with her. I mean, who doesn't like a standing rib roast with oven-baked potatoes and fresh asparagus? I thought of offering her something else, but it was past time for her to learn to eat what was put before her and be thankful for it. Besides, to draw attention to her lack of appetite would just embarrass her more than she already seemed to be. I was beginning to think that the only way she would be comfortable was to let her curl up in a ball and huddle in a corner.

As our conversation began to die out, having gotten little response from Trixie, Lloyd looked around the table.

"Oh, there it is," he said. "Trixie, would you pass the butter, please?"

A deer-in-the-headlights expression passed over her face, her eyes widening as if she'd been called on in class, but then they lit upon the silver butter dish next to her plate—right where it had stopped instead of having been passed on. She picked it up, looked at Sam at the head of the table and me at the end, then as if undecided of which way to pass it to Lloyd, she stood halfway up and thrust it across the table toward him. Her arm, however, went right over the flame of a candle.

She screamed, dropped the butter dish, which splattered in Lloyd's plate, breaking it in two, then careened against his water glass, knocking it over. He pushed back his chair and sprang up. Sam and I both rose and Lillian came running from the kitchen, while Trixie held her trembling arm and wailed her head off.

"What is it?" Lillian cried. "What happened?"

"A burn, Lillian," I said. "We need the first-aid kit."

As Lloyd began picking up the remains of his dinner and the fragments of his plate, Lillian brought the first-aid kit from the pantry. I got up from my chair and went to Trixie to see how badly she was burned.

She jerked her arm away from me. "Don't touch it! Don't touch it! It hurts, oh, it hurts!"

"I know," I said soothingly. "But we have to see how bad it is."

"Here," Lillian said, rummaging in the kit for a tube of Neosporin. "Let's put some of this on it. It'll stop the hurtin'."

"No!" Trixie screamed. "Don't touch it. Get some ice for it!"

By this time, in spite of Trixie's jerking her arm around, I'd gotten a look at the burn. From the way she was carrying on, trembling and crying and moaning, I'd expected to see blisters at least, but it was a quickly fading red spot about an inch in length. My sympathy was fading as fast as it was.

I clasped her arm and held it still. "Calm down, Trixie, and let Lillian put some salve on it. Ice is not the proper treatment."

"But Meemaw always—"

"I don't *care* what Meemaw does. Hold still. Lillian, smear some on."

She did, and Trixie almost immediately dried up, amazed at the soothing quality of the salve. Lillian then put a gauze bandage on the area and held it on with adhesive tape, while Trixie sniffled and wiped tears away with her other arm.

"There now, Miss Trixie," Lillian said. "That'll help it heal real quick."

With a long, wet sniff, Trixie said, "I got to go lay down."

And away she went without a word of thanks to Lillian or an apology for disrupting the meal to the rest of us.

Lloyd and Sam had been quiet during this medical procedure, Sam helping Lloyd wipe up the spilled water and clean the table of the remains of his meal. In fact, Lloyd had gotten another plate, refilled it, and sat now calmly eating his dinner.

I thanked Lillian as she repacked the kit, and she and I exchanged wry glances. "I guess," Lillian said, "she don't want no dessert either."

"Well, I do," Lloyd said. "It's all so good, I could eat second helpings of everything, which is what I'm doing."

We all laughed and the tension eased. "I'm sorry that she got burned," I said, almost whispering in case my voice carried up the stairs, "but who could imagine she'd reach over a candle?"

Lillian turned at the door. "I won't light the candles no more, jus' in case she forget."

"No need for that, Lillian," I said. "She won't be here long. Besides, I like candlelight."

After dinner, dreading every step, I walked upstairs to see about Trixie. As undemanding a guest as she was, she seemed to be taking up all my time.

I tapped on the door of her room, but, getting no response, I eased in. "Trixie? How are you feeling? How's your arm?"

She was not on the bed, but in it, her dress thrown over the chair and her sandals left in the middle of the floor. She moaned, pulled the covers over her head, and turned away from me.

"Trixie?" I said, sitting on the side of the bed. "You need to wake up now. I think we can go on to the bus station in a few minutes, so we'll have plenty of time to get your ticket. You might want a snack from the vending machines before the bus comes, too. Let's get on up now."

"I can't," she mumbled.

"Does your arm still hurt? We can put more salve on it if it does."

She shook her head against the pillow.

"Well, is there anything else wrong? Tell me, so we can fix it before you start your trip."

She buried her face in the pillow and began sobbing. "I wanna go ho-o-ome."

Well, I wanted her to go, too, so I said, "Then jump up, so you can catch your bus."

She turned to lie flat on her back, a look of pure misery on her face. "I can't!"

"Of course, you can. The burn is not that bad. It won't keep you from traveling."

"No!" she yelled, as if I were hard of hearing. "I *can't* go home. They's nobody there! They went off and le-e-eft me up here."

"What? I don't understand. Aren't your grandparents at their farm in Georgia?"

"They *sold* it!" Trixie almost screamed, behaving as if she were reminding me of something I already knew and was too dense to understand. "They sold the farm and moved to *Florida!*"

"When?" I asked, almost as befuddled as Trixie thought I was. "I just got her letter today and Elsie didn't say a word about moving."

In between sobs, Trixie told me that they'd closed on the farm the first of the week, packed the Yukon, put her on the Greyhound, and left from the bus station for Florida.

"Meemaw said," Trixie said, hiccupping between the words, "she said she aimed to live in Florida if it, if it hare-lipped her, and Pawpaw said, 'Then I guess we better go on and, and move down there.' And that's what they did."

"Well, Trixie, that's a little, ah, unusual, but all we have to do is buy a bus ticket for wherever they've moved to and you can join them there."

Trixie's face screwed up tight, as tears streamed from her eyes. "I can't! I don't know where they are. *They* didn't know where they was goin'! They was just gonna keep drivin' till Meemaw said stop."

I was almost speechless, but not completely. "What were they going to do about you, Trixie? I mean, what if Sam and I hadn't been home?" Visions of floating down the Rhine sprang to mind.

"They're gonna write me a letter when they get settled," Trixie said, wiping her face with the edge of the sheet. "But Meemaw said it'd be a coupla months 'cause she wants to see every bit of Florida. So I got to stay here," she wailed, getting louder by the minute, "and I don't *want* to!"

What she would've done if we'd been away wasn't answered—probably because it hadn't even been considered. Stunned by the lack of forethought and the abundance of gall of both her and Elsie, I patted her shoulder, unable to offer any words of comfort or reassurance. Then I rose from where I was sitting, turned like a zombie, and half stumbled toward the door. "Sam," I mumbled. "Sam?"

Chapter 7

Too stupefied by what I'd just learned to watch my words in front of Lloyd, I told it all as soon as I got back to the library. It was not my usual practice to discuss sensitive matters in front of the boy, yet there I was, pouring out my outrage as he sat with widening eyes and intense interest, absorbing every word out of my mouth.

"So we're *stuck* with her, Sam," I said, so offended by the effrontery of the Binghams that tears filled my eyes, "for the whole summer, and who knows but that we'll have her forever!"

"You mean," Lloyd asked, his eyes big at the thought, "they just went off and didn't tell her where they'd be? They just *abandoned* her?"

"Not exactly, Lloyd," I said, wiping away angry tears. "They made sure that *we'd* take care of her—whether we wanted to or not."

Sam got up from the puzzle table and came over to me. Putting his arm around me, he said, "Come on, honey, let's think about this." He led me to the Chippendale sofa and Lloyd followed us. "Look," he went on, "if there's nowhere for her to go, then she has to stay here, whether it suits her or us. And it sounds as if she's as unhappy about it as we are. We'll all have to make the best of it."

"Well," I said, as Lloyd's eyes flitted from Sam to me, "the best thing I can think of is to call the highway patrol and have them put out an all-points bulletin on the Binghams. She's their responsibility, not ours. To my mind, they ought to be arrested." I stopped to calm myself, then said, "What it comes down to, though, is this: she ought to be able to take responsibility for herself. We should just put her on that bus back to Vidalia, Georgia, where she came from. Surely she has friends there or even family on her grandfather's side."

"Think about that for a minute," Sam said. "How old is Trixie anyway?"

"Why, I don't know. From Elsie's letter, I assumed she was young—you know, sixteen or so. But she looks older than that."

"She sure does," Lloyd said, nodding solemnly. "But she acts like she's about ten."

"Yes," Sam agreed. "So I'm not sure we can just send her off and let her fend for herself. We'll have to come up with something better than that."

I sat up straight. "I don't know what that would be, but she is certainly old enough to take care of herself. So I say we let her decide. If she doesn't want to stay, let's just send her on her way."

"Julia," Sam said soothingly, "if she's not competent, we can't send her off on her own."

"So," I said, realizing how effectively Elsie had left us so little choice in the matter. She had counted on my good nature and Christian compassion, some of which I was now scraping the bottom of the barrel to come up with. "So, what you're saying is that we don't have a choice. And I guess you're right, but I'm not constitutionally able to spend the summer humoring her. She'll have to fit into our schedule just as any other long-term guest would."

"It probably won't be so bad," Lloyd said. "I think she just hasn't had our advantages." And this from a child who'd had no advantages at all until he'd come to live with me.

I looked at him, amazed that he recognized and appreciated his good fortune. The maturity of his perceptions made me begin to feel slightly ashamed of myself. "You're right, Lloyd," I said, reluctantly giving in to the inevitable. "She certainly hasn't, so allowances must be made. But it's evident that Trixie is not in any shape or state of mind to have a debutante summer as her grandmother envisioned. I mean, in looks and attitude, she's, well, unfortunate. We'll have to think of something else to fill the summer."

"Maybe she'd like to find a job," Sam suggested. "I don't know what she's qualified for, but a job would give her something to do and a little independence, too."

"That's a good idea," I said, my spirits reviving somewhat. "I'll ask her what experience she's had, and maybe we can steer her to something similar. But first, from the looks of what she's wearing, we may have to refurbish her wardrobe. Lloyd, would you mind bringing in her suitcase? It's in the trunk of my car, and I can only hope there's a better selection in it." I stopped and thought for a minute. "Maybe Hazel Marie will help with her hair. I just don't feel I can take her to Velma with the way she's been acting. If she were to scream and cry in the shop the way she's carried on here, the whole town would know about it and that would be the end of any job possibilities."

"It'll work out, honey," Sam said, trying to reassure me, but falling short. "She'll calm down, and we might end up enjoying having her around."

I just looked at him. "And what are your plans for tomorrow?"

"Oh, I'm meeting with my campaign folks in the morning, then I'll be speaking to the Rotary Club at lunch. There may be a committee meeting afterward." Then he got a sheepish look on his face. "Shall I guess what you'll be doing?"

"No guessing about it. I'll be entertaining Trixie all day long."

When we went upstairs to bed, Trixie's door remained closed, and I didn't disturb it or her. I did not, however, rest well. As the clock approached, then passed 12:45, I visualized the bus that should've been carrying Trixie back to Georgia and felt that a golden opportunity had just passed in the night.

The three of us—well, the four of us counting Lillian—had little to say at breakfast the next morning. We were all awaiting Trixie's appearance and the beginning of her summer with us. She didn't come down, so we ate without her.

"Just carry on with whatever you've planned for the day," I said to Lillian. "It's up to her to fit in with us, not us with her."

"Miss Julia," Lloyd said as he finished his breakfast, "we get out about noon today, so I'll come by and see if Trixie wants to go to the pool or the tennis courts."

"That's fine, honey, and thoughtful of you. I doubt, though, that she'll want to do either one. So don't change your plans if she doesn't."

As Sam and Lloyd prepared to leave for the day, Sam took me aside and said, "I'm sorry that most of this is going to fall on you, but I'll do what I can to help. Why don't you see if Hazel Marie will spruce her up a little, and I'll be asking around about job openings." He hugged me and I hugged back. "We'll get through this, sweetheart, and if we don't, just think—if I get elected, we can move to Raleigh."

I laughed and sent him off, but I was thinking that, even if he got elected, I could still be stuck with Trixie the rest of my life.

Nine o'clock, then ten, came and went, and still Trixie did not come down. Lillian kept looking at me, as if to ask if I were going to wake her, but I'd decided to let sleeping dogs lie.

"Miss Julia," Lillian finally said, "I need to vacu'm upstairs. You reckon the noise bother Miss Trixie?"

"You go right ahead, Lillian. Do whatever you need to do."

Lillian gave a worried glance up the stairs. "You don't reckon she sick or something, do you?"

"I think we'd have heard from her if she was. No," I went on, firmly determined to remain coolly detached, "let's just go about our business and let her go about hers."

When I heard the vacuum cleaner turn on upstairs, I went into the library to call Hazel Marie, confident that my conversation would not be overheard.

"Hazel Marie," I said when she answered, "if you have time to talk, I have a monumental problem and I need your help." Then I went on to explain what had happened and what we had on our hands that had to be put up with for the foreseeable future. "So, what I'd like from you is some help with improving her appearance. The only relief I can foresee is for her to get a job so she won't be on my hands all day every day."

"Oh, I'd love to," Hazel Marie said. "You know how I like to fiddle with hair and makeup. The babies will be down for a nap about two this afternoon. Why don't you bring her over then, and I'll make an appraisal."

I happily agreed and thanked her for her willingness to take Trixie on for some external modification by the application of brushes, paints, and hair curlers. My job would be to set an example of gracious acceptance of what apparently could not be changed.

Chapter 8

I lingered at the desk after hanging up the phone, listening to the household sounds Lillian was making upstairs while trying to come to terms with Elsie's finely tuned takeover of our summer.

I tried to pray about it, asking for a change of attitude and a willing heart to accept what I was unable to change. Except I kept thinking of ways I could change the situation into something more to my liking. In other words, I was not content in whatsoever condition I found myself—I wanted out of Elsie's trap; I wanted rid of Trixie; I wanted our summer back just the way we'd planned it.

With all of that running through my mind, I worked up a tear or two of pure frustration, as well as an increasing anger from being at the mercy of someone I couldn't get back at.

Then, like a bolt out of the blue, I realized that this was not the first time that I'd had these exact same feelings. I clutched the edge of the desk as a wave of memories washed over me, bringing back the time years before when I'd had the same frustrated anger toward someone who had put me in an untenable position.

Wesley Lloyd Springer, my late unlamented first husband, had done the same thing to me when his mistress and their bastard son had shown up on my front porch, announcing themselves two weeks after he was dead and buried, too late for either recrimination or revenge.

Burying my face in my hands, I recalled the depth of anger and humiliation I'd experienced at the revelation of his breach of marital faith, particularly since he'd demanded so much of me. Even worse, I remembered how I'd despised the very sight of that child, looking as he did so much like Wesley Lloyd. The boy was proof positive—if I'd needed more than his mother's testimony—that my marriage had been a mockery and I was the town's laughingstock. I don't know how I'd lived those weeks so burdened with fury at the unfairness of it and my inability to exact revenge on a dead man.

I took it out on the child—I know I did. At the time I couldn't seem to help it, for I paid back the unfairness done to me by being unfair to him. I ignored him. I held my head up in unbending aloofness, both to disconcert the town's wagging tongues and to indicate my feelings toward that innocent child. I was awful to him, and the terrible memories brought me figuratively to my knees— which was the best I could do, given the state of my aging joints.

It was only the sweetness of that little boy, as well as the need that was so obvious as his eyes followed my every move, that finally thawed my frozen heart. From the very first, Little Lloyd adored me, craving my approval and emulating my actions until such unadulterated—and I use that word advisedly—need to please broke through my defenses, working a miraculous makeover from the inside out, and I became a different woman.

And here I was, not so different after all, having the same anger and bitterness toward another innocent person. Of course the situation wasn't the same—Elsie had broken no vows, and Trixie was hardly a child—but my feelings of outrage were the same.

So, I asked myself, if my feelings toward Lloyd had changed so drastically, couldn't my feelings toward Trixie change as well? Probably not, I answered, because Trixie wasn't Little Lloyd. She had no desire to please me or even to be in my company. She wanted to go home, which should've made us allies, because I wanted the same thing.

The fact of the matter was that I couldn't do anything about what Trixie wanted or how she felt, I could only manage myself. I might not like the situation, but I was stuck with it. There was no alternative but to make the best of it.

Having made that decision, I made another one—to lay down the law to Trixie. If we had to put up with one another, she would have to conform to our routines. No more lying in bed all morning—here it was past eleven o'clock and still no sounds of rising from Trixie's room.

I went upstairs, bypassing Lillian with a dustcloth in her hands, and walked straight to Trixie's door. Knocking loudly, I opened the door, saw her suitcase open with clothing strewn around the room. She was still in bed with the covers pulled over her head, so I marched over to her and firmly said, "Get up, Trixie. I want you dressed and downstairs in fifteen minutes."

She moaned and flapped her hand at me to go away. I stepped back, overcome by her audacity. I was accustomed to having even my suggestions immediately obeyed, so being flapped at as if I were a nuisance just flew all over me. But what to do? Drag her out of bed? Threaten her—with what? I'd heard mothers complain about the difficulty of getting teenagers out of bed, but Trixie was no teenager.

This, I decided, was a battle of wills, and if I didn't win the first battle, I'd have no hope for the rest of the summer. I walked over to the television set across the room, turned it on, then turned the volume as high as it would go. Going back to the bed, I leaned over Trixie and said, "In fifteen minutes, I'm coming back with a pan of water. If you're not out of this bed by then you'll sleep in a wet one tonight."

Then I stomped out, unsure as to whether I'd established my authority or lost it entirely.

Passing Lillian again as I headed for the stairs, I just barely heard her say, "Guess the vacu'm won't bother her none now."

Twelve minutes later, I heard Trixie shuffle into the kitchen. I followed her and, pretending that all was well, greeted her warmly.

"I'm hungry," she mumbled.

"I expect you are," I said breezily, "but it's so close to lunchtime that you'll have to wait. I'll be having tuna fish salad, but I'll ask Lillian to make you a peanut butter sandwich. But, Trixie, around here and from now on, we all eat whatever Lillian serves. I know that will probably take some getting used to, but she's not a short-order cook. We either eat it, fix our own, or go without. I'm sure you'll fit right in once you understand the way we do things."

She glanced sullenly at me from behind a fall of stringy hair that tended to hide her face. "I can fix me something."

"Not today, we have other things to do. While we're waiting for lunch, run back upstairs and comb your hair. And," I went on, taking note of the same dress she'd worn the day before, "you might want to change. We're going visiting in a little while."

"Don't want to." Mumbling again.

"Of course you do. We're going to see Hazel Marie—you'll love her. She is beautiful and just as sweet and kind as she can be. We're going to begin doing what your grandmother sent you up here to do—fix you up and get you beautified."

She covered her face with her hands and started bawling. "I don't want to," she wailed. "You can't make me, and I want to go ho-o-me! I want my Meemaw!"

That's when my patience ended. *"Stop that!"* I yelled, startling her so bad that she stopped crying and glared at me. "Listen to me, Trixie," I said in a softer tone, "you don't have a home to go to and that's your Meemaw's doing. Now the sooner you reconcile your-self to the facts, the better we'll get along. So go upstairs, wash your face, comb your hair, change clothes if you have anything to change into, and come back down for lunch. We are going to visit Hazel Marie and see if she can get done what your Meemaw wants done. In other words, we are following *her* orders for you, and, believe me, it's not something I want to do either."

Surprisingly, she wiped her face with her arm, whispered, "Yes, ma'am," then turned and shuffled off to do what I'd told her. *So,* I thought, *bullying works better than kindness,* and I was moved by a tinge of pity. Maybe being told what to do while having her own wishes ignored was what she was used to. Well, maybe gradually we could change that, but for the time being, I now knew how to deal with her.

Chapter 9

After lunch and after Lloyd came in saying he was putting away his book bag for the duration, Trixie and I walked the four blocks to Hazel Marie's house. Trixie was not happy about it, complaining that her feet hurt and mumbling that she didn't know why people had cars if they weren't going to use them.

"The exercise is good for us," I replied, thinking that she needed much more than four blocks' worth. "In fact," I went on, "I'll sign you up for a fitness class at the Y. You'll feel so much better for it."

She didn't respond, just plodded on as if each step was a misery to her. I had begun to notice, however, that she had a habit of grinding her teeth when things didn't go her way. I expect there were words she wanted to say, but dared not, and I also expect that she'd formed the habit from dealing with her grandmother. So I didn't take it personally, just worried about the condition of her teeth.

Things changed, though, when we got to Hazel Marie's house, for Trixie was immediately entranced with her. Hazel Marie had undergone a transforming makeover herself now that the babies were toddling around on their own and James was back in the kitchen and Granny Wiggins had become a household fixture. Hazel Marie now had time to keep up her appearance and I no longer had to worry about Mr. Pickens looking for greener pastures. She had gained some weight so that her curves were more in evidence, and her hair was back to the color it had been for so long that everybody assumed it was what she'd been born with, and she was back to using the lavish amount of makeup on a daily basis so that no one was startled to see her without it.

James was back to his usual complaining self, except now he

had set himself up as the local weatherman, saying that the wrist he had broken could predict rain and that his sprained ankle told him when snow was on the way. Granny Wiggins just cackled when he came out with some of his portentous pronouncements, telling him that her arthritis, or arthuritis, as she called it, could outpredict his old bones any day of the week.

When we got there, Hazel Marie took us into her living room and immediately began an appraisal of what Trixie needed in the way of polish and sprucing up. I was afraid that Trixie might resent it, but she was so taken with Hazel Marie that she just sat there with her mouth half open, following every move that Hazel Marie made.

"I think a haircut is in order," Hazel Marie said. "With maybe some layering so all you'll have to do is wash and dry it. It may be thick enough to go right back into place if you have the right cut."

Almost starry-eyed at the attention she was getting, Trixie mumbled, "I was lettin' it grow out, but whatever you think."

Hazel Marie, with a finger on the side of her face, stood in front of Trixie studying the situation. "We'll need some foundation with, I think, a yellow base to cut down on some of the redness. But, Trixie, you'll have to remember to clean your face real good every night. You have very sensitive skin, so we want to take good care of it."

I didn't say anything during all this, just sat and marveled at Hazel Marie's tact as she complimented Trixie when she could and offered suggestions for improvement when she couldn't.

Throughout the appraisal, Hazel Marie spoke in such a sweet and caring manner that Trixie was not in the least offended. In fact, she seemed grateful for it, except when Hazel Marie said, "Now, Trixie, you should make it a habit to shave your legs and under your arms at least once a week. That's what fastidious young ladies do, although we can try some of the hair removal products if you'd prefer."

Trixie immediately took umbrage. "Meemaw said only loose women do that."

"Do what?"

"Shave theirselves."

"Oh, no," Hazel Marie said. "Keeping yourself free of unsightly hair is part of every woman's beauty routine. You want to have good hygiene and that's part of it."

"Well," Trixie said, her lip beginning to poke out, "Meemaw—"

"I tell you what, Trixie," I said, unable to stay out of it, "let's keep in mind what your Meemaw sent you up here for and forget about everything else she said. If she thought she was doing such a good job of it, she'd have kept you home. Listen to Hazel Marie and forget Meemaw."

When Hazel Marie began to go over Trixie's diet, telling her to eat lots of vegetables and drink lots of water, I began to get restless. There were things to do at home, and just sitting there while Hazel Marie explained what most children learned in grammar school was driving me up the wall.

I gathered myself when Hazel Marie began making out a shopping list for Trixie's new clothes—things she obviously needed because she was still in the same ill-fitting sheath. As I moved toward the door, I said, "Hazel Marie, if you have time to do this, I'll leave you with it. Call me when you're through, and I'll come get Trixie." And I took myself off, breathing a little easier to be on my own for a while.

I wasn't breathing easily for long, though, and neither, apparently, was Sam. As soon as I stepped in the house, Lillian came running toward me, her eyes wide and frightened, a dishrag flapping in her hand.

"Oh, Miss Julia," she cried, "they bringin' him home!"

"Who?"

"The amb'lance folks an' whoever take him to the hospital—I don't know who all they are—them folks workin' on the 'lection."

"You mean *Sam*? Sam's been to the hospital? What's going on, Lillian? Why didn't you call me?"

"Yes'm, Mr. Sam who I mean, an' I don't know what's goin' on, and I didn't call you 'cause they jus' call me an' say they on the way home with him. That's all I know."

The bottom dropped from under me and I had to grab the back of a chair to stay upright. Fear and panic filled my mind with a white haze—I couldn't think, I couldn't plan, I didn't know what to do. My precious Sam in the hospital!

"But they're bringing him home?" I asked, struggling to make sense of what had happened—whatever it was.

"That's what they tole me. Listen!" Lillian turned away and headed for the front door. "I think they here."

I hurried after her, dreading what I'd see—Sam bundled up on an ambulance stretcher, white-coated attendants by his side, campaign workers wringing their hands as they followed him in.

It was nothing like that at all. Sam came walking in on his own two feet with his campaign manager, Millard Wilkes, telling him to take it easy as he turned back to his car.

"Where's the amb'lance?" Lillian asked.

I didn't give Sam a chance to answer, just flung myself at him, crying with relief. "Oh, Sam, what happened? Are you all right? Did you get hurt? Come sit down."

"I think I better," Sam said as he took the first chair he came to in the living room.

I noticed that his tie was off and stuffed in his coat pocket and his face was almost as white as his shirt, but his deep blue eyes were as bright as ever.

I pulled an ottoman up close beside him, took his hand, and tried to appear calm and collected. Lillian had about wrung the dishrag in two as she twisted and turned it in her agitation.

"Tell us, Sam," I urged, desperate to know what had happened, yet not wanting to know.

"Well," he said, leaning his head against the wing of the chair, "I guess I had a little episode. I was at campaign headquarters and we'd just finished making out my schedule. I hadn't been feeling well all morning—a little indigestion, I thought. I'd taken something for it, but the pain kept getting worse. I wanted to just come

home, but everybody got concerned, and before I knew it they'd
called an ambulance." He straightened up and gave me his twinkling smile. "And once the EMTs are called out, there's no turning
back. They trundled me off on a stretcher and I ended up in the
emergency room."

"Oh, my word," I moaned. And there I'd been, using the time
I could've been with him looking after that unappreciative and
sullen girl who'd been foisted on us.

I stuffed those uncharitable thoughts to the back of my mind
and asked, "What did they say it was? I mean, the episode or the
spell or whatever you had. Did they call Dr. Hargrove?"

"Yes, he came, took one look, and called a surgeon."

"A surgeon! Oh, Sam, why?" I nearly crumpled up inside. The
thought of Sam being cut open scared me so bad I could hardly
stand it. Calling a surgeon meant that something needed to be cut
on or out or into. I mean, that's what they did.

"Well, he's not sure yet, honey. Dr. Allen wanted to admit me
to the hospital right then and start some tests. But I had to come
home first and get some things arranged."

"Sam Murdoch! Nothing's more important than your health!
What do you mean—things to arrange?"

Lillian chimed in. "If you got your health, don't matter whatever else you don't got."

"That's right," I affirmed. "Listen to her, Sam. Now tell us what
all you have to arrange and let us to do it. You can just sit here and
rest, or maybe you want to lie down?"

"No, I'm all right here for a few minutes. Then I need to go
upstairs and pack something for the hospital, then get on the
phone and try to get some substitutes for all the events on the
schedule."

It wasn't like Sam to want to sit for a few minutes, especially
when he thought he had things to do. I'd also begun to notice that
he seemed to be short of breath—no way, I determined, was he
going to climb the stairs or get on a telephone. My fear was beginning to turn to anger—he should've stayed at the hospital,

should've let them admit him and let the doctor get started on the tests and whatever treatments that would cure him.

"You're not going to do anything," I told him, getting to my feet. "Lillian, you know what to pack—his shaving things, some pajamas, and a robe and slippers. While you do that, I'll make the calls for him." I started to the kitchen to get the portable phone. "Where's Lloyd?"

"He at that country club, playin' tennis or swimmin' or something. You want me to get him home?"

"No, I guess not. I'll take Sam to the hospital, and when he gets home, you can tell him what's happened and . . . oh, my Lord, I've got to get Trixie home. She's at Hazel Marie's and probably doesn't have a clue of how to get back. Well," I said, throwing up my hands, "maybe Hazel Marie can bring her or Granny Wiggins can walk her home. I can't worry about that now."

Lillian stopped on the stairs and looked back. "You go on an' take care of Mr. Sam's 'lection bus'ness. I'll tend to the rest."

"Yes, thank you," I said, nodding in relief and wondering, as I often did, how I could ever manage without her. In many ways, Lillian and I were alike. We both had a tendency to lose our heads in the first flush of a panic situation, but we also tended eventually to calm down and get done what had to be done.

And, although my heart was still racing and my hands were trembling, that's what we started doing.

Chapter 10

I didn't like leaving Sam alone even for a few minutes, but I took the time to call Dr. Hargrove while I was in the kitchen. Of course I had a hard time getting him on the phone—that snippy receptionist of his thought it her bounden duty to protect him from anyone who needed a word with him.

"Just tell him it's Julia Murdoch," I told the receptionist. "Tell him it's an emergency." And continuing under my breath, "If you understand the concept."

And finally I heard him answer. "Miss Julia?"

"Yes, thank you for taking my call. I am worried sick, Dr. Hargrove. What happened to Sam? Is he going to be all right?"

"Well, right now, I don't know what happened. That's why I called Dr. Allen. It could've been nothing—indigestion, as Sam thought, or an early indication that something else is going on."

"Like what?"

"Ulcers are a possibility, but most likely it's an inflamed gallbladder. We'll run some tests and have a better idea when the results come in. But he needs to get to the hospital so we can get started."

"I understand, but I don't know why you didn't keep him there when you had him."

"Well, you know Sam." Dr. Hargrove chuckled, which under the circumstances I didn't appreciate. "It's hard to keep a good man down."

I didn't see any humor in the situation, nor did I think that platitudes were a bit of help. "That's all well and good, but what do you think? Is he going to be all right?"

"It's like this, Miss Julia: he seemed fine after a little while—his blood pressure and heart rate were normal, and he had no fever. But it's only sensible to do some tests as a precautionary measure. You know, at his age . . ."

There it was again: *at his age,* or as had been said to me so many times, *at your age,* and I was sick and tired of it. Why did one's age have to qualify everything? And have you noticed that you can't turn around nowadays without someone asking for your date of birth? It doesn't matter where you are—in a doctor's office, a lawyer's office, a bank, or a place of business—some little twit a third of your age thinks it her right to demand your birth date. At least, though, they've stopped asking how old you are, having discovered that if they're rude enough to ask for a specific number they're likely to get a nonspecific and ever-changing answer. I finally figured out that they're using your birth date to identify you instead of your Social Security number. Which doesn't make a lick of sense because there's only one Social Security number to a person, yet there must be hundreds, even thousands, of people who have the same date of birth. They'd be better off if they required something like fingerprints that can't be duplicated or stolen, which, come to think of it, will probably be the next step.

Only partially reassured by Dr. Hargrove, I decided to focus on the surgeon—when I could catch him—who would know more than Dr. Hargrove anyway. I took the portable phone to Sam, swinging through the library on my way, to pick up his address book.

"Now," I said, retaking my seat on the ottoman, "who do you have to call?"

"I need my calendar," Sam said, beginning to rise. "It's in the library."

"No, don't get up. I'll get it." And back to the library I went for his calendar.

"Well, actually," Sam said, pulling a folded page from his coat pocket, "I'd better enter these events on the calendar first. Then we can decide who to ask to go in my place."

"Why can't you just reschedule them?"

"I don't think I can—the next few weeks are booked solid. And if somebody doesn't show up for some of these events, why, the party's likely to think they have another Frank Sawyer on their hands."

"Maybe his knees are well enough to take over for you," I

suggested, wondering if Sam should be doing any campaigning at all. And wondering also if the episode he'd had was a sign that the Lord wanted Sam out of politics. Having Trixie on our hands could be another sign, as well. I was becoming less and less enamored of Sam as a potential senator—not that I'd been all that enthusiastic in the first place—but that was something he would have to come to on his own. I wasn't about to suggest it.

"No chance of that," Sam said, responding to what I'd said, not to what I was thinking. "He's still having trouble, so, no, I've got to meet my commitments one way or another."

"Wait a minute, Sam," I said, becoming more alarmed. "Is there something you're not telling me? Just how long are they planning to keep you in the hospital?"

"Oh, I don't know. A couple of days, I guess. And no, I'm not keeping anything from you. But the next few days are packed with campaign events, and I can't just not show up without somebody in my place. Let the word get around that I'm unable to meet my obligations, and Jimmy Ray will have the election sewn up. He's going after me hot and heavy as it is—he's running a television ad against me next week."

"Why, the nerve of him! Make your calls, Sam, then let's get you to the hospital. I don't want you lying up there worrying about Jimmy Ray Mooney."

But after six or seven phone calls, he was having little luck in getting substitutes for a VFW meeting in Brevard the following morning, a speech at the Kiwanis Club luncheon, a Polk County neighborhood meeting in the afternoon, and a local roundtable forum that evening—all on the same day. And in the coming days, a neighborhood barbecue, the Rotary Club again, a street dance in Polk County, a local gathering at the party headquarters, a panel discussion at the League of Women Voters, and I don't know what all.

"I thought," I said after the latest turndown, "that you said you'd have plenty of volunteers. Don't they realize that you can't do everything? Especially from a hospital bed? What're you going to do, Sam?"

"I'm going to turn to the one I can count on—you."

"Me? No, oh, no, I can't do that. You said I wouldn't have to make any speeches." I looked at him, wondering which would be worse—having him in the hospital or me on a stump—and it was looking as if I would have both. "Well, you said not many, anyway."

"But you'd be the best one," Sam said, smiling and drawing my head toward his shoulder. "Who better to represent me and sing my praises? And, honey, I'd rest so much easier in the hospital if I knew you were out carrying on the campaign."

That was a low blow, because of course I wanted him to rest easy in the hospital. He didn't need to be lying in bed worrying and fretting about his commitments to the campaign, even if he had said he didn't care whether he won or not. And of course, as his wife, I'd do any and every thing I could to ease his mind, even though I'd lost that loving feeling about a senate race. But make speeches? I wasn't sure that was covered under the heading of wifely duties.

"Well, we'll talk about it, but right now let's get you on over there," I said, knowing that the best way to avoid a commitment of my own was to change the subject. "Here's Lillian with your bag. Do you want to take something to read?"

"Yes, there's a stack of magazines I haven't gotten to yet and the Gibbon book on top of them—they're all by our bed. Lillian, if you don't mind . . ."

"No, sir, I don't mind," she said, turning to go back upstairs. "Be good to move 'em so I don't stump my toe anymore when I make the bed."

I almost had to fight Sam for his suitcase when we started out to the car. He couldn't stand for me to be carrying it, but I just walked out with it and let him follow behind. Lillian had the worst of it—she'd packed his books and magazines in another bag and it was all she could do to lug it out.

We finally got Sam officially admitted to a private room on the third floor of the hospital with a penthouse view of the parking lot and the spire of the First Methodist Church peeking over the trees. I did nothing for the next hour but sit and watch as one nurse or technician after another came in to fill out forms or draw blood—I didn't watch that—or to check on Sam's comfort. But no doctor came around—the only way I knew one existed was by seeing phoned-in orders being carried out. At least I hoped they were following orders from someone who knew what he was doing. "Just routine for a new admittance" was the only response I could get to my questions. Oh, except one nurse said, "You'll have to ask the doctor." Something I would've gladly done if he'd ever shown up.

When we heard the rattle of supper trays being trundled down the hall, Sam said, "Why don't you go on home, honey. Lillian will have your dinner ready and Lloyd will be coming in. As soon as Dr. Allen comes by, I'll make it an early night. It's been a long day."

Suddenly fearful again that he was sicker than anyone was telling me, I suggested that I spend the night in the one easy chair in the room. "I'd like to speak with that surgeon anyway, and it looks as if the only way to do it is to stay right here."

"No, ma'am," Sam said in a mock-forceful way, "you are not going to do that. I want you to go home and reassure Lloyd and Lillian that I'm all right. Besides, you have Trixie to see to, too."

"Oh, my word," I said with a sinking feeling. "I'd forgotten about her. For all I know, she's lost somewhere between our house and Hazel Marie's. Or else, Hazel Marie is ready to shoot me for leaving Trixie with her all day."

"You run on then," Sam said, taking my hand. "Just, if you have time, would you call around some more? Call the same ones again and see if you can find anyone who'll fill in for me, at least tomorrow and the next day. I should be able to manage after that."

Well, right there I knew what I had to do. "Stop fretting about the campaign, Sam. I'll do it—not as well as you, but I'll go to every one of those events and if my speechifying doesn't suit the party, why, they can just do it themselves. Which is what they ought to be doing anyway."

Chapter 11

As soon as I got home and stepped into the kitchen, I heard voices and laughter coming from the living room. Raising my eyebrows at Lillian, I wondered who was visiting.

"They all in there," she told me. "Miss Hazel Marie an' the babies an' Lloyd an' Miss Trixie, too. They all worried 'bout Mr. Sam an' waitin' to hear how he is. And me, too."

As a burst of laughter emanated from the living room, I frowned, thinking that they didn't sound too worried to me. But to answer Lillian's implied question, I said, "He's doing all right, I guess, if he can do without all the blood they've drawn. But of course I haven't seen his doctor yet. I think they all make rounds when family members are unlikely to be there, and do it on purpose, too. I'll go back over after supper. Maybe somebody can tell me something then."

As I pushed through the swinging door into the dining room, the sounds of revelry increased in the living room. Vaguely wondering why Lillian had not been with them, I walked into the living room to find Lloyd and Trixie on the floor playing with the babies, while Hazel Marie sat smiling at their antics.

"Oh, hey, Miss Julia," Lloyd said, immediately rising and coming toward me. "How's Mr. Sam? Boy, it sure knocked me for a loop when Lillian told us he's in the hospital."

"Yes, how is he?" Hazel Marie rushed over to me, and I just managed to avert a comforting hug. "We've been so worried. What can I do to help? Do you need anything?"

"Just to sit for a few minutes," I said and found a seat in one of the wing chairs. Trixie, I noticed, had remained on the floor, neither greeting nor speaking to me. "I wish I could tell you more, but I don't know anything. There've been people in and out of his room all afternoon, but not a doctor among them. But Sam's in good spirits. The only thing he's worried about is his campaign, so that's why I came home—to make plans to carry out his immediate commitments. That seems to be the only thing I can do that will ease his mind."

"I'll help you, Miss Julia," Lloyd said. "Whatever you need, just tell me."

"Oh, I expect I can . . ." I started to say, then stopped. "Well, yes, maybe there is something you can do."

"And me, too," Hazel Marie said. "I'm just so worried about Mr. Sam. You know that J.D. and I will do whatever we can to help."

"Yes, I know, and I do appreciate it, and Sam will too." From the corner of my eye, I noticed that Trixie had stopped playing with the babies and had scooted over against the sofa, sitting on the floor with her knees drawn up and her face against them. She was watching me with a sullen stare. "Hazel Marie, the next few days are going to be really busy. Besides seeing to Sam, I have to fill in for him on the campaign trail, so if you're planning to go shopping with Trixie tomorrow, that would be wonderful help. If you don't mind doing it without me."

Trixie's expression changed as she shifted her gaze to Hazel Marie, waiting with obvious hope to hear what she would say.

"Then that's what we'll do," Hazel Marie said, and I almost hugged her in spite of my antipathy toward such public displays. "Trixie, I'll pick you up at nine o'clock, and we'll get in a full morning's worth of shopping. I'll need to be back to help Granny Wiggins feed the babies at noon, but we'll make a real dent in our shopping list, and finish up the next day if we have to." She bent down to pick up one fat baby, plopped it in the twin stroller that I'd almost tripped over, then reached for the other baby. "Now, I'd better get on home before Granny comes looking for us."

After Lloyd helped her lift the awkward, baby-filled stroller down the front porch steps, Hazel Marie turned to me and said, "I'll be praying for Mr. Sam, Miss Julia. And for you, too."

"Thank you, Hazel Marie, but hold off on starting the prayer chain—once a request goes out on the phone lines, things get blown all out of proportion. Sam will be done in if word gets around that he's incapacitated—no telling what that would do to his election chances. Besides, he's convinced the doctors will send him home with a clean bill of health in a day or two. Probably just tell him to take an aspirin and elevate his feet. Oh, and maybe you'd better not say anything to James for the time being—you know he can't keep anything to himself. So, just private prayer for now, if you don't mind."

Hazel Marie frowned, then whispered, "Would it be all right to tell J.D.? He won't tell anybody."

"Oh, of course, do tell him, and ask him to visit Sam in the hospital. He'd be good for him, he's so entertaining." Entertaining, yes, because Sam enjoyed Mr. Pickens's company, but I wasn't too sure of the efficacy of his prayers. Still, whatever Mr. Pickens could manage in the way of spiritual pleading would be most welcome.

I walked back into the house to find Lloyd waiting, eager to hear what I needed him to do. "How can I help, Miss Julia?" he asked. "You said there'd be something for me to do."

"Well, Lloyd, I'd really appreciate it if . . . but wait, aren't you helping with the tennis clinics again this summer?"

"Yes'm, but they don't start for a couple of weeks. I'm as free as a bird till then, so tell me what you need."

"That's a relief then," I said, sitting down to gather my thoughts. "Because to tell you the truth, I really do need some help. Sam has me doing something I've never done before and I am lost. I don't even know where to start." I propped my elbow on the chair arm and leaned my head on my hand, simply overcome at the thought of what I'd let myself in for. Especially now that I'd realized I'd just as soon that Sam lost the election rather than expend himself chasing something that he'd said he could either take or leave.

"It's all right, Miss Julia," Lloyd said, pushing an ottoman close to my chair and sitting down, eager to help. His earnest little face gazed up at me with complete confidence. "If Mr. Sam thinks you can do it, and I think you can do it, then you can. Now tell me what you need."

"Ah, Lloyd, just wait till you hear. You may not be so sure when you do. The first thing I need is a speech, and I don't know what should be in it. But you've done so well on all your English essays this year that I'm hoping you can write a speech that will say what Sam would say—except, you know, kind of in my words so I won't sound like a recording. Then," I went on before he could say, as I feared, that such a thing was beyond his skills, "then I would love to have you go with me to these events—just until Sam's out of the hospital and just for the company and for, well, the encouragement."

"Oh, sure," he said, "I can do that. I'm a pretty good speechwriter anyway. Remember I took a political science course last year and I won the election for sophomore class treasurer. Everybody said it was my campaign speech that won it for me."

I had to laugh, because I did remember about his speech. Of course I hadn't heard it, because the election had been limited to the student body and he'd not even told us that he was running for office. Grinning and exceptionally pleased with himself, he'd come home the evening after the election and told Sam and Lillian and me about his victory.

After we'd praised and congratulated him, Sam said, "I want to hear your campaign speech. Let us hear what won it for you— maybe I'll get some ideas for my speeches."

Still grinning, Lloyd had shrugged as if there'd been nothing to it and that giving speeches was all in a day's work. "I just got up and said, 'I'm Lloyd Pickens, and I'm running for treasurer. You should vote for me because I'm good with money.' Then I sat down."

We'd just stared at him for a minute, then we all burst out laughing. Short, sweet, and to the point, as well as being true. He *was* good with money—I'd taught him well.

"Well, Lloyd," I said now, "I expect they'll be wanting a little more than that from me, but not much more. Remember I'll be speaking for Sam, telling about him and what a good senator he'll be. But if you could put all that into a ten-minute or so speech, I would be eternally grateful."

"Okay, I'll do a draft, then you can look it over, then I'll rewrite it, and we can keep doing that until we get it right. You think I could use Mr. Sam's office and his computer? I can hear Trixie's television in my room."

"Of course you can. Use whatever you need," I said, then, looking around, asked, "Where is Trixie, anyway?"

"Oh, probably watching Judge Joe or Judy or Jeanine, or whatever's on." Lloyd got up, a determined look on his face. "I'm going to write you a humdinger of a speech, Miss Julia. Between us, we're going to get Mr. Sam elected, see if we don't."

Chapter 12

As soon as Lillian put supper on the kitchen table—she'd stopped treating Trixie as a guest—I sent her on her way. She had to pick up Latisha from after-school care, but even so she was hesitant about leaving with Sam's condition still up in the air.

"I'll be going back over there in a little while," I told her. "If there's any change, I'll call you."

I had little appetite, being too wound up with anxiety to want much of anything, and Trixie and Lloyd seemed to be in the same condition. I didn't offer Trixie anything else to eat—she could afford to miss a few meals anyway. Lloyd had a blank look on his face as if he had more important things on his mind than eating a healthy meal. And, finally, he let me know what those things were.

"Miss Julia," he said, putting down his fork, "I think I better go with you to see Mr. Sam. I need to ask him what his campaign promises are so I can put them in your speech. And he ought to have a campaign slogan, too, so that needs to be included. You reckon he'll feel like talking about it?"

"I think he'd feel a whole lot better knowing that you're on the job. So, yes, let's hurry and get over there. Trixie, do you want to go with us?"

She jumped when I spoke her name, but then shook her head. "Don't like hospitals."

"Well, neither do we, but sometimes they're necessary. But there's no need for you to go. You can stay here."

"By my*self*?"

"Why, yes, we'll lock the doors, and it won't be dark until almost nine. We'll be back by then. But if you don't want to stay by yourself, you can go with us and stay in the car. Or in the lobby, whichever you prefer."

Her mouth poked out just a little—I could hardly see her face for all the hair that hid it. "Guess I'll stay here then," she mumbled.

I quickly put away the food, but left the table as it was, expecting that Trixie would step up to the plate, so to speak, while we were gone.

She didn't, and when Lloyd and I returned hours later, we were greeted by the table in the same state that we'd left it, only with food dried on the plates. On top of that, it was all I could do to restrain my anger at Trixie's unwillingness to help in a crisis. Assuming that she'd gone to bed, I worked out my ire by clearing the table and filling the dishwasher, but from then on, I determined to let Trixie know what was expected of her. I was through depending on her to see for herself what needed to be done. But I'll tell you this, I would never in this world get up from someone else's table without at least offering to help. Unless, of course, I was at a dinner party where the hostess would be mortified at the thought of guests working in her kitchen.

Lloyd had wiped the table while I'd scraped plates, and now he had the notes he'd taken spread out before him. When we'd walked into Sam's room at the hospital, we found him lying in bed instead of sitting in a chair as I'd expected. His face lit up when the two of us walked in, while mine had darkened at the sight of an intravenous tube stuck in the back of his hand but not hooked up to anything on the other end. And I was not reassured by the sight of Sam in a hospital gown instead of his own pajamas. Yet he quickly switched off Shepard Smith, which he hadn't been watching anyway, and eagerly welcomed us.

"Glad you got here," he said. "I was about to nod off."

"What is that, Sam?" I asked, pointing to the clamped-off tubing.

"Oh," he said, holding up his hand and looking somewhat blearily at it "They're going to give me something else, I guess. In a little while. But we've got to get your speech written. Glad to see you, Lloyd. We can use your help."

And, while I wondered about an intravenous night medication, he began to discuss with Lloyd the points he wanted to make. I mean, that he wanted *me* to make. I just sat and listened and watched, for Sam seemed peculiarly buoyant for a man in the hospital.

"The first thing I think," Lloyd said as he opened a notebook and poised a pen, "is for you to tell me what sort of platform you're running on. That means your campaign promises, I guess."

"Yep," Sam said airily. "The first thing I'm promising is to let all my constituents know exactly what I do and how I vote—no behind-the-door deals, everything out in the open for everybody to see. Julia, honey, you don't need to worry about me. I'll do fine."

"I know you will," I said, wondering if he'd forgotten that I'd be making the speech, not him.

"Could I just say transparency?" Lloyd asked, which sounded good to me. I nodded, pleased to hear evidence that he'd learned something in his political science class.

"Better not," Sam said with a lopsided grin. "That word's taken on a cynical cast here lately. Let's keep a casual tone and word it as if Julia is just talking to friends. Okay, the next thing is a promise to respond to anyone in the district when they need help of some kind, especially with foreclosures. Something's got to be done about that. So say I'm having an open-door policy—my office will be staffed at all times both here and in Raleigh. You need me, I'm available."

"Oh, that's good," Lloyd said. "We might work that up into your slogan. Something like, 'You need me, I'm here,' or 'I'm on the job,' or 'I'm your man.'"

"Okay, whatever, but before I forget it, be sure to take that box of pamphlets—it's in my office at home. You can leave a stack wherever you go. Now, Lloyd, let's get into the particulars. I'm for widening the interstate—you know the one. The only one we have. I know there's a vocal group that's against it, but there's too much traffic and too many accidents on it to put off doing what's needed. Well, wait a minute," Sam said, stopping to yawn, then going on. "We need to say early on that bringing jobs to the district is right up there at the top of my list. I'll go to China if I have to. And say something about how concerned I am about those who've lost jobs and those who might. I'll work as hard as I can to bring in some manufacturing jobs to replace what we've lost."

Lloyd scribbled furiously, then looked up. "Okay, got it."

"Education," I reminded him, noticing that he seemed awfully drowsy. "We're for it."

"Well, yes," Sam said, widening his droopy eyes. "We need to fund our schools, cut class size, and . . . and, Lloyd, here's a biggie: put down that I intend to meet with dairy farmers and nearby homeowners to work out an agreement they can both live with."

"What's that about?" I asked, concerned that somebody might ask a question I couldn't answer.

"Smell," Sam said, frowning at the severity of the problem. "Developers have built houses right up against dairy farms, and now the homeowners are complaining about the smell."

"Cow manure?" Lloyd asked, looking up from his notes. "Didn't they know cows were in the pasture when they moved there?"

"And," I added, "that cows make manure?"

Sam laughed. "Yeah, but it's a problem. Dairy farms in this area and pig farms down east are creating odors that don't sit well with nearby homeowners. Developers and homeowners have joined forces to petition the Assembly to do something about what they're calling air pollution. But most of the farms were started years ago before any of the areas began filling up with housing developments."

"So," Lloyd said, "you don't want to commit to either side yet?"

Before Sam could answer, I spoke up. "I don't think that's right, Sam. I think you should come down on one side or the other, and I'm for the cows. After all, they were here first. Tell the homeowners to close their windows and turn on the air conditioners."

"Julia, honey," Sam said, laughing, "I want to get elected. I have to look at both sides. It may be that the farmers are piling up manure too close to the houses, and all they'd have to do is move the piles to the south forty." He yawned again. "Or somewhere."

I sniffed. "Sounds like shilly-shallying to me."

"Okay," Lloyd said, ticking off the points he'd jotted down. "We've got an open-door policy, new jobs, widening the interstate, and finding a solution to the manure problem. What else?" He looked up at Sam, then suddenly said, "Oh, I have an idea. Mr. Sam, you need to be on Facebook—that's a good way to keep in touch with the district when you're in Raleigh. I can do that for you."

"Good idea, Lloyd," Sam said. "At least I guess it is. I'm not up to speed on social media, but Millard Wilkes, my campaign manager, is adding me to the party's website."

"You might want to have your own site. But I'll see what he does, and if it's not much we'll set one up just for you."

"I declare, Lloyd," I said, "Sam should've made you his campaign manager. But back to my speech—you two have about covered what he's going to do, but what about what he's already done?"

"Oh, yeah," Lloyd said. "We have to have some background, though I expect everybody already knows all about Mr. Sam. But I don't. Where'd you go to school, Mr. Sam?"

"Grew up and went to school right here in Abbot County, graduated from Carolina and went to law school there. Went into the army, then came back and practiced law here for over thirty years. That's about it." He yawned again and lay back on the bed with his eyes closed.

"And," I said, gathering my things so we could let him go to sleep, "helped thousands of people, not just in Abbot County but all over the western part of the state, with their legal problems. And think of all the offices you've held in the Rotary Club, on county commissions, in the state bar association, and on and on. Oh, and don't forget the church. You've been an elder several times, a deacon, taught Sunday school classes, and you've been on pastor-seeking committees." Then I said under my breath as I thought of Pastor Ledbetter, "Too bad you weren't on the last one."

"Yeah," Lloyd said, writing as fast as he could, "and you were on the board of the Boys and Girls Club, too. And the United Fund. Shoo, Miss Julia, you're going to have more to say than you'll have time for."

"Well, write it all down," I said. "I don't want to have to depend on my memory. Oh, Sam, I'm getting nervous about this. I wish I could just say that you're the best of all men, and if they know what's good for them, they'll vote for you."

Sam and Lloyd laughed as if I'd made a joke, but I hadn't. My fear was that my poor and untested speech-making skills, far from helping Sam, would be the very thing that kept him out of office, even if he—or I—didn't care one way or the other.

"Lloyd," I said, getting to my feet, "let's be on our way. Sam needs his rest, and he's about to fall asleep anyway."

"Yes, go on home," Sam said, yawning again. "I'll be all right."

Just as I walked to the bed to kiss him good night, the room door banged open and an orderly and a nurse pushed in a stretcher.

"They all ready for you, Mr. Sam," the orderly said, as a nurse followed him into the room. "Now, ma'am, if you'll just move out of the way, we'll get him to the operating room."

"The operating room!" I cried, aghast at the thought. "At this time of night? Nobody told me he was going to be operated on. Are you sure you have the right room?"

"Yes, ma'am," the orderly said much too cheerfully as he swung the stretcher next to Sam's bed, backing Lloyd into a corner. "Right as rain. They gonna get that mean ole gallbladder out lickety-split."

"Sam! Why didn't you tell me? Oh, my goodness, we were about to go home without knowing a thing."

Sam looked as stricken as I felt. "I thought you knew. Didn't they call you?"

"Nobody called me! And if they didn't do that, what else didn't they do?" All I could think of was how Lloyd and I had peppered Sam with questions about a campaign that I could've cared less

about and all the while Sam was mentally preparing himself to go under the knife. And on top of that, I'd not laid eyes on the one who was preparing to wield that knife. It was a poor way of doing business, if you ask me.

Nobody did, however, but the nurse assured me that nothing else had been forgotten, that Sam would go to the operating room, then to recovery, then be back in his bed in a couple of hours. "It's a fairly simple operation," she'd said. "He'll be out of bed and on his feet in the morning."

"Not after being cut wide open, he won't." I wrung my hands as they rolled my long-suffering husband down the hall out of the room.

"He won't be cut open," the nurse said. "It'll be done with a laparoscope, and you'll be surprised at how quickly he recovers."

"I can't stand many more surprises," I said, somewhat tremulously.

"It won't take long," the nurse said in an attempt to ease my concern. "Dr. Allen and his team are very good."

"But not so good," I said, putting my hand on Lloyd's shoulder to steady myself, "at notifying the next of kin."

Chapter 13

With the events of the past few hours still coursing through my mind, I started the dishwasher, then sat at the table with Lloyd. Calming myself with effort, I watched as he worked on my speech. It was late, closing in on midnight, and after anxiously waiting at the hospital while Sam was operated on, we'd not left until he was brought back to his room and he, himself, had assured me of his well-being.

"Go on home, sweetheart," Sam had said as I stood by his bed clasping his hand. "You have a big day tomorrow and you need to rest." Which just goes to show what was foremost in his mind, regardless of how befuddled he was from the remnants of anesthesia.

Even so, I hadn't wanted to leave him, and my heart was still torn between being with him and preparing for my first foray into the world of politics. And, I'll tell you the truth, if I'd been hesitant about that world before, I was downright positive now that I wanted nothing to do with it.

Nonetheless, a promise is a promise, so I sat down beside Lloyd and looked at all the pages he was working on.

"Don't make it too long, honey," I said. "I want to get in and out of those events so we can go back to the hospital."

"I'm trying to condense it but it's hard to do." He suddenly looked up at me. "You remember who it was that said in a long letter to a friend that he would've made it shorter if he'd had more time?"

"No, I don't believe I do."

"Might've been Samuel Johnson."

"I don't think I know him."

Lloyd grinned. "Probably not. He lived in the eighteenth century. Anyway, if I put all this in, it'll be longer than ten minutes."

He stood up and began gathering his papers. "Let's get on my computer and see what we can do."

That's what we did, and I found myself hunched up next to him, trying to see the screen from the side as he typed away. There is nothing more boring, in my opinion, than watching someone fiddle with a computer. Besides, my mind was filled with concern for Sam one minute, and the next with trepidation for the morrow.

"Hm-m-m," Lloyd said. "That's kinda strange."

"What is?"

"Oh, it's all right. It just looks likes somebody's added some bookmarks, but you never know. They may have popped up automatically. I'll get out of here and go to Word, get everything we want to say entered, then we can begin cutting."

As several pages were filled, I became more and more anxious about the length of the speech. My neck was getting a crick in it, too.

"Lloyd, it's too long. I'll never be able to stand up in front of a bunch of people and say all that. And if you and Sam expect me to memorize it, we'll have to rethink the whole thing." My hands were getting sweaty just thinking of it.

"Yeah, you're right," Lloyd said, leaning back in his chair. "It's too much. Tell you what, though. Why don't you tell me what you'd feel comfortable saying."

I thought about it for a minute, going over in my mind all the points that Sam had mentioned in his hospital room. Not a one of them, I had to admit, was anything I knew about or had ever even been interested in. If making all his points had to be the purpose of my speech, everybody would know I didn't know what I was talking about. And in just a few hours, I would be trying to convince audiences of strangers that I did.

I pressed my fingers to my temples and moaned. "Oh, Lord, Lloyd, I could really do without this."

He watched me awhile, then asked, "How would you answer if somebody just came up to you and asked why they should vote for Mr. Sam?"

"Why, I'd tell them that he cares about people and tries to help whenever he can, that he's spent his life doing just that. That he's easy to get along with, always listening to all sides of a question, that he's invested his life in this district and that people every-where know and respect him. And I'd say that he's the best man I've ever known and that I'd trust him with my life—as indeed I have—and that the people of the district could do no better than to have him as their state senator. They'd never regret voting for him."

By the time I finished my spiel, Lloyd had already begun typing.

"That's it, Miss Julia," he said. "That's the kind of speech you ought to give. It's right down your alley, because everybody'll know you mean it. I mean, who knows better than you what kind of man Mr. Sam is?"

"Why," I said with a dawning wonder, "it'll be like giving a personal testimony, won't it?"

"That's right. And you've heard a million of them."

And didn't believe half of them, I thought, then quickly put that aside. My testimony for Sam would be believable because it was true.

"So," Lloyd said, "let's just leave the promises and positions for him to bring up. They're all listed in his pamphlets anyway, and you can just tell what you know about him."

Well, that was a relief, because I felt I could at least stumble through something I knew. "But, Lloyd, what will Sam think? He's expecting me to talk about all his plans and ideas. Maybe I ought to call and ask him."

"I bet he's asleep," Lloyd said, frowning in thought, "which is where we ought to be, too. Let's go ahead with doing it our way, at least for that first speech in the morning. We'll see how it goes over with the audience, and we'll have time to change it if we have to. But I really think it ought to be what you want to say, don't you?"

"I know I'd feel better doing that instead of reading what Sam would say. Oh, my," I said, glancing at my watch, "it's past midnight. We need to get to bed or there won't be any kind of speech in the morning. It's an hour's drive just to get there."

"Okay, let me print this out. If you'll just read it over right before you go to sleep and then again when you wake up, it'll stay with you."

I glanced at the single printed page he handed me. "This is what I said I'd say?"

"Yes, but have a pen handy, and while you read it over, jot down anything else you think of. I'll print it out right before we leave, and put it in a large font so you can see it at a glance."

Thanking him, I wandered out of his room and headed across the hall, glancing at Trixie's closed door on my way. I'd tried to call her from the hospital to tell her we'd be later than we'd thought, but she hadn't answered. Hoping that she was sleeping well, I was just as glad not to have to put up with anything from her. I had enough to deal with already.

As I began to prepare for bed, I realized that I was feeling much better about speech-giving, now that I could talk about Sam in my own words. But then I had a sudden sinking spell—what in the world should I wear?

I woke up at five o'clock, wide-eyed and scared to death that Sam had not survived the night. I immediately dialed the hospital and was transferred to the nurses' station on his floor. After being assured that he'd had a comfortable night and that it was too early to disturb him, I snatched the speech off the bedside table, switched on the lamp, put a pillow behind my back, and started reading. Lloyd had been wrong—not one word of it had stayed with me, and in only a few hours I'd be standing in front of who-knew-how-many people who were expecting Sam Murdoch and getting me.

And at that thought, I nearly threw up. How were we going to explain his absence and my substitution? We hadn't even thought of that, which meant to me that Sam could be sicker than I'd been led to believe. It wasn't like him to overlook the most obvious question all those people would ask—where was he?

I turned the page over and started scribbling possible explanations for a strange woman standing in his place. First of all, the truth: *He had emergency gallbladder surgery last night.*

No, no, no. They'd think they had another Frank Sawyer on their hands—somebody too sick to run, much less to tend to their business in Raleigh. And, I declare, mentioning gallbladders, or any kind of bladder for that matter, just wasn't an appropriate subject for a lady to bring up in a public setting. As were words like, for instance, *crotch*—a perfectly legitimate word, but one best avoided. I recalled the time I'd taken Lloyd to Belk's to buy some trousers. The saleslady kept referring to the nice fit in the *crotch*, making me cringe each time and confirming to me her common background. How much more tasteful it would've been if she'd noted that they fit well *in the seat*.

If there was one thing I was known for it was the avoidance of discussing indelicate topics in mixed company. I scratched out the reference to Sam's missing gallbladder.

His schedule got mixed up, and he had to be somewhere else at this time. That wouldn't do either—they'd think it showed poor planning on Sam's part, even if I told them his campaign manager did it. Besides, they'd think they were taking second place to something more important. I marked through that one, too.

He was on his way, but had a flat tire, or a fender-bender, or something, and called me to fill in for him. Well, that was a flat-out lie and easily discovered, so I scratched through that one, too.

Then I had a bright idea: *Just as he started out, he got a conference call from party headquarters in Washington and had to take it.* That might work—who would know any different?

But it didn't feel right, so I reluctantly drew a line through it. What could I say instead? How would I explain his absence—the one they had come to hear—and my presence, the one they didn't know from Adam?

By six o'clock, I decided that it wasn't incumbent on me to

explain or apologize for my taking Sam's place. They ought to just be grateful to have somebody instead of nobody. So, hands shaking and about half sick, I got on up and began to dress. Hearing Lillian come in downstairs, I was clearheaded enough to realize that I hadn't called her to tell her about Sam. But that was about the last clear thought I had.

Half dressed and still undecided about explaining Sam's absence, I picked up the phone and called his room. I hoped he'd be awake enough to give me the perfect thing to tell those people who were even then getting dressed to go hear what he had to say. Except he wouldn't be there.

"Hey, honey," Sam said, somewhat hoarsely. "I was just about to call you. You getting ready to go? Got your speech and everything?" Which just showed what was uppermost in his mind, and him lying up there minus his gallbladder.

"Everything's fine here," I said, lying through my teeth because I was a nervous wreck. "How are you feeling this morning?"

"I'm fine. I've had breakfast and now I'm about to get out of bed. They want me to walk around a little." That made me even more agitated—I should've been over there with him instead of heading off on a campaign trail with an upset stomach.

Sam just laughed when I asked him how I should explain my presence at a podium. "Tell 'em the truth, and don't worry about it. This is not going to slow me down. I'll be back to campaigning before you know it."

I wasn't too sure about that, but I assured him that I'd see him between events and let him know how the day was going. Taking my speech, I went downstairs, pushed through the swinging door into the kitchen, and came up short at the sight.

Trixie was already there, hours before she usually got up, but *how* she was there was another matter entirely. I nearly lost my breath as my eyes lit on more than I or anyone else would ever want to see. Trixie was wearing a white T-shirt that looked like one of those old-fashioned undershirts that some men wear—you know, the kind with straps and no sleeves. But that wasn't the worst of it. She also had on a pair of shorts—cut-off jeans with frayed ends. Even that wasn't the worst. The absolute worst was that they weren't just short—they were *too* short with too much of Trixie bulging out around the edges. I had to avert my eyes when she leaned over to adjust her sandals.

"Uh, Trixie," I said cautiously, "I thought you were going shopping with Hazel Marie this morning."

"I am," she said, tight-lipped, as if I were questioning her. Which I was, and which I had every right to do.

"Then I hope you'll be wearing something more appropriate than that."

She whirled around to face me. "What's wrong with it? We're just going to that dinky little Main Street, and Hazel Marie said she's wearing shorts, so why can't I?"

"Because Hazel Marie wouldn't any more wear something as revealing as that than she'd fly. They're entirely too short and your shirt is too tight. Go upstairs, please, and put on something more suitable."

Trixie's face turned red, her lips poked out, and she glared at me until I thought she would simply refuse. I stared her down until she stomped out of the kitchen, pushing through the swinging door so hard that it was still swinging as she clomped up the stairs.

"Lord, Lillian," I said with a huge sigh. "What're we going to do with her? If she doesn't know any better than to dress like a . . . well, I don't know what, then what are we to do?"

"I don't know, Miss Julia, but she showin' too much of what ought not be showed." Turning back to the stove, Lillian asked, "How Mr. Sam feelin'?"

"Oh, Lillian, I forgot to call you. I'm so sorry, but it was so late when we got in, and we still had to write this speech, that I just didn't think about it. They took out Sam's gallbladder last night."

Lillian whirled around to stare at me. "You don't mean it! He got operated on? They Lord, what gonna happen next?"

"He says he's feeling fine, but would you believe they're making him walk around this morning? Years ago, they'd have kept him in bed for a week, then just let him dangle his legs for a day or two. I have to trust that they know what they're doing—though I sometimes doubt it."

"Law, Law," Lillian said, shaking her head in commiseration. "Ever'time I go home, I never know what gonna pop up here while I'm gone. You sure he's all right? Maybe we oughta go see about him."

"I can't, Lillian. He's bound and determined not to disappoint the people coming to hear him speak today, and not at all concerned that they'll be disappointed anyway when they have to listen to me instead."

Lillian stared at me. "Don't tell me he want you givin' speeches to them folks."

"That's exactly what he wants. And don't look so surprised. It's the only way I can help him get well. If I didn't do it, he'd probably have a relapse. I tell you, it's a burden being married to a man of his word—he's determined not to disappoint anybody."

"Uh-huh, what you want to eat?"

"Not much of anything. My stomach's rolling around as it is. And seeing Trixie in that revealing outfit didn't help. But, you know, Lillian, I probably shouldn't have said anything to her. That girl doesn't take correction kindly at all, especially from me. Hazel Marie could've handled it much better."

"Uh-uh. No, ma'am, I don't think so. Miss Hazel Marie have a conniption if she have to take her downtown lookin' like that."

"Well, anyway," I said with a sigh as I sat at the table. "I have more on my mind this morning than Trixie's exposure. Sooner or later, though, I'm going to have to have a heart-to-heart talk with her. The idea of a girl raised on a Georgia farm calling our Main Street dinky!"

"Huh," Lillian said darkly. "You got more'n dinky to talk about. That way down on the list."

Chapter 14

How I wished Lloyd was old enough to drive. Instead of being at the wheel, I could've been going over my speech a few more times as we sped toward Brevard. Public speaking! Lord, my stomach was roiling, my hands slippery on the wheel, my heart fluttering, and absolute terror washed over me in waves. It was a wonder that I kept the car on the road.

Lloyd had set the GPS to take us right to the small brick building on a side street in Brevard that housed the local VFW, although I jumped in surprise every time that woman's voice told me where to turn.

"Lloyd," I said, as I parked the car and made no effort to get out although my hand was clamped on to the door handle in case I had to throw up. "I don't think I can do this. Just look at all these cars—people have come to hear Sam, not me."

"Yes, you can. Look, Miss Julia, I retyped your speech and included everything you changed. All you have to do is stand up there and read it. And don't worry about explaining why you're here and Mr. Sam's not. Whoever introduces you will probably cover that."

As if in a trance, I walked with Lloyd into the large meeting room where military flags stood in stanchions, and service emblems, along with pictures of presidents, generals, and Medal of Honor winners, hung on the walls. Men and a few women of all ages, but mostly elderly, milled around the room, drinking coffee from Styrofoam cups and eating glazed doughnuts. As we entered the room, every one of them turned and looked us over. I thought I would die or maybe faint.

A slender man with a full mustache broke away and greeted us, but I declare, I couldn't tell you his name. My hearing was gone and my vision, filled as it was with that huge crowd, was fading in and out of some kind of fog.

Lloyd spoke with him—I could only nod my head—then Lloyd took my hand and led me to a low platform in front of the room. "Just take one of the chairs, Miss Julia," he whispered, "and get up when he introduces you. I'll be in the audience. Here, let me hold your pocketbook. You have your speech?"

I nodded, although by this time the paper was wadded up in my sweaty hand. I sat down, tucked in my skirt tail so I wouldn't shock the audience, and saw a podium with a microphone stuck on it. *Oh, Lord, spare me.*

The man with the mustache went to the podium, told the crowd to quiet down and sit down, and took a few minutes to go over some items of interest to everyone but me. I didn't hear a word he said, but then before I knew it and long before I was ready, he called my name.

I rose unsteadily, then teetered to the podium, looked out over a haze of faces, and wished for the Rapture. Then one face stood out in the fog—Lloyd's, several rows back but smiling with encouragement.

I leaned toward the microphone, took a deep breath, blew it out, and was startled to hear it reverberate around the room. Moving a few inches back, I smoothed out my speech, determined now to read the thing and get it over with.

I couldn't see one word. Every one of them had disappeared or else I had gone blind, and the crinkled page itself seemed to go and come in my shaking hand. Even worse, I knew my skirt was trembling along with my knees and I was just before heaving in front of all those veterans of foreign wars.

But then I heard myself speaking. I mean, I just opened my mouth and words came out—not the words on the paper, because I couldn't see them, but words—if they would just keep coming, that would get me through the next few minutes, then out of that place.

"I know you were expecting Sam to be here," I started off, "and, believe me, you aren't the only one." I paused as a low murmur rippled across the room. I sought out Lloyd's face, the only one I could discern, and he gave me an encouraging thumbs-up even though he knew I wasn't following the script. I opened my mouth again.

"But don't give up on him," I went on. "The next time he's scheduled to be here, he *will* be, because if I get through this today, you can be sure I won't." Another murmur, louder this time, swept the room, unnerving me to the point that I knew I'd better hurry and finish—you never know what an unruly crowd will do.

"However . . ." I stopped, cleared my throat, and wished I'd gone to the bathroom before speaking. "However, I expect many of you already know Sam Murdoch, especially those of you who've been in trouble with the law." A ripple of laughter interrupted me, so I ran my hand down the bodice of my dress, making sure that a button wasn't undone. Disregarding such rudeness, I pushed on, aiming toward a stopping place. "And the fact that you're here today and not in jail or fighting foreclosure proves that you know what a good lawyer he is. Was, I mean, because he's retired, which is why he's able to run for office. He'll be just as good a state senator as he was a lawyer—looking after your interests in Raleigh. I mean, looking after your interests *here* while *he's* in Raleigh— bringing in jobs, widening the road, doing something about taxes, opening his door—his *office* door, not the door to our home—to everyone, and I assure you that he will not forget to pile up manure in Raleigh. I mean, in the south forty. Wherever that is."

Out-and-out laughter stopped me in my tracks. One man slapped his thigh and another nearly fell out of his chair. I ignored it all because I didn't know what was so funny and, even better, I could see the end in sight. And when I reached it, I intended to head for the car and the road home, never to return.

"So if you want the best man to represent you, to speak for you and to you, you will vote for Sam Murdoch. He is without doubt the best man for the job, and I ought to know—I live with him every day."

I stepped back, folded my unused speech, and was struck still by thunderous applause. Before I could get off the platform, people surrounded me, shaking my hand, telling me I could come back anytime, and that it hadn't mattered what I said, they'd already planned to vote for Sam.

"Oh, Lord, Lloyd," I said when we were finally back in the car. My hands were still so shaky I could hardly get the key in the ignition. "It was awful, just awful. Let's get away from here."

"No, it wasn't awful," Lloyd said, staunchly supportive as he always was. "I'm telling you, they loved it, especially the pile of manure. They've heard so many political speeches saying the same ole things that you just blew them away."

I pulled out onto the highway, wanting away from that place as quickly as I could be gone. "I heard them, Lloyd. They were uneasy, whispering and murmuring, wondering what in the world I was saying. There must've been a hundred people there, all of them ready to tell me to shut up and leave."

"No'm, I counted. There were twenty-six, counting you and me."

"Is that all? Seemed like more to me."

"And all that murmuring you heard? They were smiling and grinning and enjoying what you said. And that's the truth, because I was right there with them."

"Well, it didn't sound like it. But I'm just glad it's over. I've always been glad when anybody's speech is over, but I never knew what a relief it is to finish one of your own."

Lloyd grinned. "Keep that thought, because you have to do it three more times today."

"How can I?" In my agitation, I let the car drift onto the dirt shoulder. Swinging it back onto the road, I moaned, "I don't even know what I said!"

We got back to Abbotsville just in time to go to the Kiwanis luncheon, the next stop on our itinerary for the day. I don't want to talk about that except to say that I might've been able to eat something if they'd had the speeches before the meal instead of after. As it was, I could hardly manage a bite for fear of leaving something between my teeth and for getting more and more frightened of standing up in front of that crowd—much larger than the VFW group—which was accustomed to hearing well-delivered oratory.

And on top of that, their business meeting went on and on interminably, so as I noticed several yawns and lots of droopy eyelids throughout the audience, I decided to do them and me a favor. I would cut my speech to the bone.

"I'm here," I said when I was finally introduced as Sam Murdoch's "better half," "to urge you to vote for Sam Murdoch for the state senate. There are some pamphlets by the door for you to pick up as you leave, so you don't need me to tell you what you can read for yourself. Let me just assure you that Sam will represent you with honesty and integrity. Thank you for my lunch, your time, and your vote. Good afternoon."

"How did it go, Lloyd?" I asked as we got into the car to travel to the next event.

"Well, it probably could've been a little longer. You know, to mention the things Mr. Sam wants to do. But I heard several people say they were glad they didn't have to listen to a long speech."

"That's okay then," I said, "because I didn't want to give one. Most of them were half asleep by the time they got to me, anyway."

"I guess, but maybe you ought not cut it down much more. Pretty soon you'd be saying, 'Vote for Sam Murdoch,' and nothing else."

I smiled at him. "That's a thought."

After driving down the mountain to Polk County, depending again on the electronic voice from the GPS to get us there, I parked in front of a brick ranch-style house in a hilly residential area.

"Lloyd," I said as I tried to do something with my hair using the mirror on the visor. "I'm hoping this will be easy. The hostess is an active party member, and she's invited some friends and neighbors, hoping to interest them in volunteering."

"That's good," Lloyd said as we got out of the car. "You're used to talking to ladies. You want me to stay in the car?"

"Oh, no. I want you with me in case I lose my eyesight again. Don't forget the pamphlets. They'll cover whatever I happen to leave out."

Virginia Case was a well-girdled woman with a hairdo that featured a jaunty flip on one side of her head. She welcomed us into her home and led us to the living room where everything was beige except the eight or nine ladies sitting around and the abundance of crocheted doilies on every piece of furniture. She introduced me, pointed me to a straight chair, and asked Lloyd if he'd like to go outside and play on the swing.

"He hands out Sam's pamphlets," I quickly said. "I need him to stay." She frowned, but brought in another chair which she put out in the hall for him.

"Ladies! Ladies!" Mrs. Case said, clapping her hands to get the attention of the group, none of whom were talking. They were too busy staring at me. "Ladies, we have a treat this afternoon. This is Sam Murdoch's wife, who is helping him in his campaign for the state senate. She is a helpmeet in every sense of the word and a wonderful model for us to emulate as we all get behind our husbands and walk hand-in-hand toward success."

And then that woman proceeded to list off every one of Sam's campaign points. I mean she didn't miss a one, including the woes of the dairy farmers. I sat and listened, wondering what would be left for me to say. And the longer she talked, the madder I got. Why had I suffered agonies of stage fright on the way down the mountain to never have the stage? And why had my time been taken up that I could've better used to visit my hospitalized husband? Which of course I didn't want to mention.

"In conclusion," she said, for which I thanked the Lord, "we're disappointed not to have the candidate himself, but please welcome his wife. I promise you that the next time I invite you over, that handsome Sam Murdoch will be here."

By the time she finally stopped and turned to me with a peremptory wave of the hand to get up and do something, I was seething. With an effort of will, I said, "Thank you for having me. As Mrs. Case has so ably pointed out, Sam Murdoch is the ideal candidate and I hope you will vote for him. Your help will be greatly appreciated. Thank you."

And that was the end of that. Mrs. Case was somewhat offended that I declined the offer of tea and Pepperidge Farm cookies, but pleading another stop on our schedule, I ushered Lloyd out and hurried to the car.

"Have you ever seen such a bossy woman?" I fumed as I turned the ignition. "I thought she'd never stop talking. We could've stayed home for all the good coming down here did."

"She was something, all right," Lloyd agreed. "I wouldn't have minded a few of those cookies, though."

"We have a couple of hours before the next event, so let's go by the hospital and see Sam. We can stop in the snack shop on our way. I'm a little hungry myself."

Chapter 15

We hurriedly had toasted pimento cheese sandwiches in the hospital snack shop, although I took time to call Lillian to tell her we wouldn't be home for supper.

"Just leave something for us," I told Lillian. "I'll warm it up when we get in. You go on home, and . . . oh, wait, Lillian, how's Trixie? Did she get some shopping done?"

"Yes'm, but I don't know what she bought. Miss Hazel Marie brought her back 'bout lunchtime, an' she been upstairs ever since. She don't like my comp'ny."

"She doesn't like mine, either, so just overlook her poor manners. We're going up now to see Sam, then on to give the last speech. We'll see you in the morning."

I was so glad to see Sam and to see him looking well and especially to hear that he would be discharged the next morning, which I could hardly believe. He was fully dressed, minus only a tie, and sitting in a chair reading the newspaper. When Lloyd and I walked in, he gave us a broad smile and I gave him a kiss, then collapsed into a chair, suddenly overcome with fatigue. Giving speeches takes an enormous amount of energy and I had none left.

"How'd it go?" Sam asked eagerly, reaching for my hand. "Don't leave anything out. Tell me everything."

"I don't think I can," I said. "The whole day went by in a haze of strange faces and all kinds of voices. Except mine. Sam," I went on, feeling about ready to cry, "I may have hurt your chances, and I'm so sorry."

Lloyd piped up. "Don't believe her, Mr. Sam. She did great every time. Everybody loved her."

"Virginia Case didn't," I reminded him.

"Well, phooey on her," Lloyd said. "She just wanted to take over."

"Yes, and she was expecting my *handsome husband* but didn't get him."

Sam and Lloyd laughed, but I was still stewing over how Sam's chances would be affected by my poor performance as a speaker. Instead of getting better with practice, I had gotten worse. And I still had to get up in front of another group that night.

But that was going to be the last one. "Sam," I said, "you might as well call Millard Wilkes and tell him to cancel everything on your schedule tomorrow. If you're coming home, I intend to be there with you. I haven't been able to be at your bedside today, but I aim to nurse you at home. After tonight I'm through giving speeches."

"That's fine, honey," Sam said. "I've already talked to Millard and he has tomorrow covered. I should be able to do a little the next day, but I can't drive for a few more days. So, would you mind being my driver?"

Relief flooded my soul at the thought of no more speeches on the horizon. I smiled at him. "I feel as if I've just gotten a promotion, so, no, I wouldn't mind at all."

But as Lloyd and I drove downtown to the next and final event of the day, I couldn't help but reconsider my flat refusal to give any more speeches after that one. I could've said, "I'd rather not," instead of "I'm through." Because the fact of the matter was that if Sam asked me again, I would do it, regardless of any disinclination. And the more I thought about it the more I realized that there is no virtue in doing something for someone else when it's something you also want to do. That's merely being helpful, but it's hardly commendable. The real virtue is in doing something you don't want to do, but doing it because someone else wants it. And who better to do that for than Sam?

After the last speaking event of the day, Lloyd and I got home about eight-thirty. I was beyond tired. Four times—*four times*—that day, I had stood in front of a group of people and groped for words that I could neither read nor even see on the paper. Don't ask me what I said—I don't know.

All I could remember was Lloyd telling me right before each speech after the first one, "Don't forget the pile of manure. Everybody loves that."

And I guess they did, because each of those crowds—except the ladies at Virginia Case's house—practically laughed me off the platform whenever I remembered to mention it. As images of the day flashed in my mind, I recalled the woman who'd grabbed my arm as I was going out the door of the VFW hall that morning to tell me she'd enjoyed my speech. "You're better than Wanda Sykes," she'd gushed. Not knowing any women politicians, much less Wanda Sykes, I just thanked her, hoping she meant it as a compliment, and went on my way.

Lloyd had assured me after each speech that I was doing fine even though I'd not followed the written script. My eyesight had kept getting worse as the day progressed—something to do with the lights aimed at the platforms, I thought, because I had no problem with my vision once a speech was done.

But I will tell you that as poorly as I felt I'd done at each event, the one that evening was by far the worst. The meeting was held in a private room off the main dining room of the S&W cafeteria in downtown Abbotsville. Lloyd and I arrived at six-twenty-five—right on time—only to learn that the group had just finished dinner, to which we had not been invited.

And what a group it was. Lloyd told me later that there were nine men, each one taking care to tell me that he was a retired executive from some major company, and to intimate that his former level of employment gave him unique insight into every field known to man. They all sat back around the table, their arms folded, and awaited my presentation. I felt like a new employee whose job depended on the grade they gave me.

They unnerved me to such an extent that I started with Sam's background, then quickly swerved to list his plans for the future—widening the interstate, reforming taxes, bringing in jobs, and so forth. Then just as I said, "Relocating manure piles," they began to interrupt me with questions and comments.

"What kind of jobs? Where's he going to get them?"

"Where's the money to widen the interstate coming from? The DOT has already spent what was allocated."

"Reform taxes? Sounds like a tax increase to me."

"What about education? Where does he stand on technical schools? And what about home schooling? How do those kids compare to the ones in public schools?"

"First it was Sawyer dropping out, now Murdoch doesn't show up. How healthy is he, anyway?"

"And what's he going to do about zoning wind farms? I sure don't want to hear *whup-whup-whup* all night long."

My head was swiveling from one to the other, unable to answer one question before another took its place. And, actually, I couldn't have answered any of them if they'd come at me one at a time.

So after a brief, embarrassing pause during which I strained for something to say, one man laughed and said, "I believe you mentioned something about manure. I'm not particularly exercised over that, except it sounds like a typical pile of it showing up in Murdoch's campaign."

That just flew all over me. It took an extreme effort of will not to lash back at him, but I restrained myself for Sam's sake. "Gentlemen," I said, "it's obvious to you all that I am unable to speak in detail about the plank that Sam is running on. But he can and will, so if you will write down your questions, I'll see that he gets them. And if you'll invite him again, I know he'll take great pleasure in answering every one of them." And then, to make those know-it-alls feel ashamed of themselves, I went on in a quavering, piteous voice, "I'm not qualified to speak with authority on the questions you've raised. I can only speak to Sam's character—the kind of man he is. He is both wise and knowledgeable, kind and decent, a hard worker, and he's dedicated to serving this district to the best of his ample ability. And furthermore," I said, gaining just enough strength to ride roughshod over my aversion to mentioning distasteful subjects in a public arena, "I assure you that he's in the best of health, because he's just gotten rid of his gallbladder."

Well, that brought a smattering of laughs, then they began discussing their own cholecystectomies, stress tests, CAT scans, and cholesterol counts. When one of them brought up his problems with an aging prostate, I knew my time to go had come. Thanking them, I motioned to Lloyd, and off we went.

Lloyd and I were at the hospital by eight-thirty the following morning, ready to take Sam home. I still could hardly believe that he'd be discharged so quickly after having had major surgery. Obviously, somebody had consulted a list from either the government or an insurance company which decreed that a gallbladder patient deserved only two nights of hospital stay. What would've happened if he'd had complications, I shuddered to think. Still, he was ready to leave, having no complaints other than the fact that his belt rubbed against his stitches. "Soon as I get home," he said, loosening his belt, "I'm taking this off and putting on suspenders."

"What do you want to do with all these flowers, Sam?" I asked, looking around at all the floral arrangements and pot gardens that had flooded in the day before while we were on our speaking tour. One thing you can say about small towns: word gets around whether you want it to or not.

"See if there's anything you want to keep," Sam said. "The nurses will distribute the rest to patients who don't have any. Oh, and there's a list there on the table of everybody who sent something. I'll need that for thank-you notes."

I smiled at my gracious and socially correct husband, thinking that I should've included in my speeches what a gentleman he was.

We finally, after waiting two and a half hours, got Sam out of the hospital and into my car. The wait was because a number of patients were also being discharged and there was apparently a dearth of wheelchairs and orderlies to push them, both of which were required by the hospital in order to avoid liability for any mishaps betwixt bed and vehicle.

Lillian hurried out to the car as soon as I pulled into the drive-way. "Oh, Mr. Sam," she cried, "you all right? We been so worried. What you want to eat? You got some kinda special diet? The bed already made up, jus' waitin' for you. Can you walk? What can I do?"

She reached in and practically lifted Sam out of the car with him laughing and protesting that he could walk without help. Which he did, despite our hovering around every step he made, but I noticed that he was ready to sit in an easy chair by the time he got to the library. Lloyd brought in the bags and the two pot gardens—one from the Ledbetters and the other from the campaign workers—that I'd decided to keep.

In spite of my and Lillian's urging him to rest, Sam spent the afternoon on the telephone catching up with how the campaign was progressing. Which proved again how important the race was to him, even as I was less and less inclined to continue with it.

Lillian, bless her heart, kept interrupting the calls to offer healthy snacks and drinks and asking if there was anything special he wanted for dinner.

"Anything you make will be fine," Sam assured her. "No dietary restrictions at all, so I'll eat what everybody else eats."

" 'Cept Miss Trixie," Lillian murmered to me, as we carried Sam's suitcases upstairs to unpack. "She don't eat nothin' anybody else is eatin'."

"Speaking of Trixie," I said. "Where is she?"

"I don't know, Miss Julia. She come an' go, an' don't say nothin' to me. I hear the front door slam an' off she go somewhere."

"Um, well, maybe she's taking Hazel Marie's advice and getting some exercise. Let us hope, anyway." I glanced at Trixie's closed door as we crossed the hall, wondering if she was behind it or not. "You'd think, though, that she'd at least want to welcome Sam home. Not just ignore a momentous occasion like having survived major surgery and all."

Later in the afternoon after Sam had finally been talked into lying down for a rest, I sat in the library doing a little resting myself. It had been a busy and worrisome few days, and I was hoping for the return of some of the daily routine that I'd told Sam I preferred.

"Miss Julia?" Lloyd whispered from the door. "You asleep?"

"No, honey, just resting my eyes. Come on in, and let me thank you again for all the help and support you've been. I would not have gotten through all those speeches if it hadn't been for you."

He grinned and shook his head. "It was fun, and I was glad to do it. We did have fun, didn't we?"

"I guess we did," I agreed, "now that it's over and I don't have to do it again. But what're you doing at home? I thought you'd have time for a tennis game this afternoon."

"No'm, I wanted to stay close in case Mr. Sam needed anything. And, Miss Julia," he said hesitantly, "well, I wanted to run off some tennis pointers for my first class next week, something for the little kids to take home and study about etiquette on the courts. You know, like not slinging your racket when you miss a shot, or how you ought to shake hands after a match whether you win or lose. Things like that."

"They probably need to be told. Some people don't know how to behave on or off a tennis court."

"Well, but," he went on, "I hate to say this, but I think somebody's been fooling around on my computer. Actually, I *know* somebody has. And it wasn't Miss Lillian, and Latisha wouldn't, even if she'd been here. And it couldn't have been Mr. Sam—he has his own and he hasn't been here, and I kinda doubt it was you."

"Believe me, it wasn't."

"Not that I would've minded if you had. In fact, anytime you want to learn . . ."

"Thanks, but I think not."

"Anyway," he said, frowning, "it's just strange, because nobody's left but Trixie and I hate to say anything to her. And you know, I wouldn't care if she'd ask or even just tell me she wants to use it."

"Absolutely. I can't imagine going into somebody else's room and using things as if they were one's own." I stopped before becoming too agitated at Trixie's audacity. A more hopeful thought had occurred to me. "But, you know, maybe she used it to look for a job, which Sam has urged her to do. That doesn't excuse her by any means, but it would be encouraging to the rest of us. And, of course, honey, you could be seeing something you used for a school report and forgot about."

Lloyd shook his head. "I don't think so, Miss Julia. I found a lot of sent emails that went to strange addresses, and they don't look like places where you'd get a job. I mean, hotstuff@aol.com? Or lookinforlove@yahoo.com? And it's a settled fact that I've never been on Match.com or eHarmony. Or on ChristianMingle, either."

Chapter 16

"Oh, my," I said, as images of the starry-eyed, two-stepping couples I'd seen on television bloomed in my mind. "They're . . ." I stopped as the full implication of what Trixie might be dabbling in hit me.

"Yes, ma'am, they're online dating services. They match you up with people that fit your profile, then you meet and get to know each other, then you marry and live happily ever after. Though I kinda doubt it works out that way every time."

I sat up straight. "You mean to tell me that Trixie has been advertising herself as available to any Tom, Dick, or Harry who's looking for a wife!"

"Well, maybe not a wife, but at least a date. I'm pretty sure they meet first, like for lunch or something, to see if they like each other."

"Well, now it makes sense. Lillian said that Trixie has been going in and out a lot. I thought she was getting some exercise or maybe looking for a job. Instead, it looks as if she's been meeting men she doesn't know. But, Lloyd, how many men in this town would bother trying to meet somebody that way? All they have to do is go to church and they'd find all the decent women they could handle."

Lloyd shook his head. "Not in this day and age, Miss Julia. How many young, unmarried women are there in our church? Or young, unmarried men, for that matter?"

"Well, there's . . ." I stopped as several men and women came to mind, then were discounted for one good reason after another. "I guess things have changed, haven't they? But I can remember when church was the place you went when you wanted to meet people of like mind."

A fleeting smile crossed Lloyd's face. "Sounds like church was the old-timey dating service to me. I guess it worked pretty good though."

"Not always," I said, somewhat grimly, recalling that I'd met Wesley Lloyd Springer at a Sunday morning church service. "Well, be that as it may, what're we going to do about Trixie?"

"First thing I'm going to do is put a password on my computer, and on Mr. Sam's, too, just in case. I'd sure hate for him to have some of these sites pop up. That way, she'll have to ask when she wants to use mine or his."

"Good idea, although I hate the thought of having to lock things up when a guest is in the house. But, Lloyd, if she's already going out to meet who-knows-what kind of men, what do we do about that? She could get into all kinds of trouble—something that Sam does not need, especially at this time. He needs a peaceful recovery, and he doesn't need any kind of unsavory gossip swirling around his campaign."

"I know, Miss Julia, and it worries me, too. There're all types of men on the Internet who're looking for easy marks, and to my mind, Trixie is as easy as they come." Lloyd's eyes got wide as he realized what he'd said, surprising me that he recognized that the term had a double meaning. "I mean, she may not be able to tell that some people aren't who they say they are."

"Yes, I'd say she's quite vulnerable, but one thing we can be sure of: if they're looking for money, they're out of luck. She doesn't have any. Well," I said, standing and smoothing out my skirt, "this business has to be nipped in the bud. I'm going to put my foot down and tell her it has to stop."

"Why don't you get Mama to help you?" Lloyd asked. "Trixie listens to her."

"That's the best idea you've had yet," I said, "and you've had some good ones. That's exactly what I'll do, and between the two of us, maybe we can get Trixie straightened out. In the meantime, Lloyd, if you can think of any unmarried men we can introduce her to, I'd be grateful. Surely there're a few gentlemen we know who wouldn't take advantage of her."

"Only one I can think of is Mr. Jones."

"*Thurlow?* He's too old, and he's not a gentleman. And as far as his being unmarried, there's good reason for it. Nobody would have him. Come to think of it, though," I mused, "Trixie must be fairly desperate if she's looking for love on all those Internet places."

"Lillian," I said, passing through the kitchen on my way to Hazel Marie's house. "I have to have a quick visit with Hazel Marie. Sam should be up in a little while, so please tell him I won't be long."

Lillian banged a spoon on the edge of the pot she had on the stove. "Yes'm, I tell him soon as I hear him stirrin'. And, uh, Miss Julia?"

I turned, my hand on the doorknob. "Yes? What is it?"

"You know what Mr. Sam gonna do with his stones? He brought 'em home, didn't he?"

"His *stones?*"

"Yes'm, his gallstones. Lots of people bring 'em home in a little bottle, like a keepsake or something."

"Well, Law, Lillian, I don't know. I unpacked his suitcase, but I didn't see anything like that." And, without saying it, I hoped I never would. "Why?"

"I jus' thought if he don't want 'em or if he get tired of lookin' at 'em, Miz Pearl Mebane—she a lady in my church—would sure like to have 'em."

My hand fell from the doorknob as I turned to her, intrigued now by someone who craved gallstones. "May I ask why in the world she'd want somebody else's gallstones?"

"Oh, she got her own, but they not enough. She got her heart set on a necklace an' all she got is enough for a bracelet. 'Course," Lillian said somewhat wryly, "she still got to figure out how to string 'em, 'cause ever' time she poke a hole in one, it end up in pieces."

"My word," I said, leaning against the counter, "who would want such a thing? Oh, well," I went on with a sigh as I turned back to the door, "I guess wearing gallstones around your neck is no worse than advertising yourself on a public website."

"Ma'am?"

"I'll tell you later. Listen out for Trixie, if you will, Lillian, and tell her not to go anywhere. I want to talk to her."

"So," I said, preparing to sum up my sorry tale of modern romance to Hazel Marie. We were sitting in her living room watching the twins play with blocks on a pallet on the floor. Lily Mae had just stacked three teetering blocks when Julie reached over and knocked them over, eliciting a piercing squall from Lily Mae that frayed my already tender nerves.

Hazel Marie slid from the sofa to sit between the two little girls. She made a stack of blocks in front of each one and far enough away that they could only knock over their own.

"So what else, Miss Julia?" Hazel Marie asked.

"So, I don't know what to do with her. Hazel Marie, there's no telling what kind of men she's meeting, and I do feel somewhat responsible for her welfare. She's living under my roof, after all, and her grandmother put her in my care, whether I liked it or not. And somebody has to be responsible for her because it's a settled fact that nobody else is. Including Trixie herself."

Hazel Marie frowned. "Yes, and what she's doing does seem like risky behavior. But you'd think by twenty-four she'd know to be a little more careful."

"*Twenty-four?* Is she that old? My word, Hazel Marie, she doesn't act it." I stopped speaking in order to rearrange my thinking. "That puts the situation in a different light, doesn't it? She's an adult, which means I have no real control over her. I can't forbid her to go on computer dates. I can't ground her if she keeps on. And I can't send her home because she doesn't have one. The only thing I can do is appeal to her finer nature, and I'm not sure she has one of those, either."

"I don't mind talking to her, Miss Julia, but I don't know how much influence I'll have. She was really upset with me for not letting her buy what she wanted on our shopping trip." Hazel Marie smiled, a little sadly, I thought. "She said she thought she could do what she wanted up here, but we're worse than her Meemaw ever was."

"Ha!" I said with a delicate snort. "From what I know about her Meemaw, that's a compliment to us."

"Well," Hazel Marie said, "maybe between us we can warn her that she could get into real trouble dating men she doesn't know. I wish there was someone we could introduce her to, but I don't know a soul."

"I don't either. This is a terrible thing to say, but even if I knew someone who was suitable, I'd hesitate to aim Trixie at him. I was hoping that you could work some cosmetic magic on her and at least make her a little more presentable."

"I'm still trying to work with her," Hazel Marie said, smiling. "But she doesn't follow through with what I tell her. She's decided she doesn't want her hair cut, yet she won't do anything with what she has to make it look better. I made up her face, too, and bought her some cosmetics, but she says she doesn't want to use it up. She's saving it for special occasions."

"That beats all I ever heard. What other special occasions does a young woman have than going out to meet someone?"

Hazel Marie made two more stacks of blocks, then looked up at me. "Did you see the clothes she bought?"

"No, I've barely seen her the last couple of days. Between giving speeches and bringing Sam home, I've hardly given Trixie a thought. Why, what did she buy?"

Hazel Marie laughed. "Well, not what she wanted to. I was finally able to talk her into a couple of sleeveless blouses and a skirt or two. Oh, and some intimate garments. After I saw those raggy cotton things she had on, I figured I'd better. Remind me to give you your credit card back before you leave."

"Just keep it. Sounds like she'll be needing more than you got. But don't let her have it. No telling what she'd come home with."

"Believe me, I know. Everything she liked was clingy nylon or polyester, both of which are fine in their place, but not for her, and not cut as low as the ones she picked out. And, Miss Julia, she wanted a strapless sundress that was a good two sizes too small and a bikini, of all things. I mean, bikinis can be very attractive on slim girls, but on Trixie? I had to wrap a skirt around her when she pranced out of the dressing room!"

"My word. Can the girl not see in a mirror?"

"She kept telling me that Kim Kardashian wears tight, low-cut things, so I guess she thinks she looks like her."

"Well," I said firmly, "she doesn't. And if she did, I still wouldn't approve."

"Me, either. But, Miss Julia, back to the problem of her dating strangers. What about if you went at it another way? You know, instead of telling her that she can't do it, maybe you could encourage her to bring her dates home. Or at least have them pick her up at your house. Of course, you'd have to act like you're pleased to meet them. I think that way if any of them have designs on her, they'd think twice after meeting you and Mr. Sam. They'd know that Trixie has people who look out for her, and that she's not some out-of-control girl looking for a good time."

I thought about that for a minute. "You know, Hazel Marie, that just might work. At least we'd know who she was seeing and be able to give the police a description if something happened to her." I shook that thought out of my head. "Heaven forbid. But what you're telling me is to use reverse psychology—kill her with kindness instead of criticizing her. Well, that's probably a better course of action than what I'd like to do, which is to ship her to Florida or wring her neck, one or the other."

Chapter 17

So I walked home with a renewed determination to change my tactics with Trixie. Change them *again*, I realized, because I had already changed from making polite suggestions to telling her firmly, even harshly, what to do. Now here I was, planning an even more radical change, smothering her and her young men with kindness. I intended to take Hazel Marie's advice and graciously welcome into my home whatever strange men Trixie took up with by way of the Internet. No telling who would soon be sitting at my table.

It happened to be Sam who was sitting at my kitchen table, drinking coffee and talking with Lillian, when I walked in. He looked rested and well, not at all like he had just had an internal organ removed. I mentally thanked the Lord that we lived in an age of medical miracles like laparoscopes, lasers, anesthesia, antibiotics, and a number of other things of which I knew nothing but which had obviously restored my precious husband to health.

"Come in, sweetheart," Sam said, struggling just a little to stand. "We're discussing the size and quantity of gallstones."

"Sit down, Sam, for goodness sakes. You don't need to be jumping up and down in your fragile condition." I quickly sat so that he would, too. "Gallstones? Wait till you hear what I have to talk about." And I proceeded to tell them both about Trixie's penchant for online dating, my fears that she would meet a con man or an axe murderer, and Hazel Marie's suggestion that we joyfully open our door to any and all ragtag males that Trixie wanted to drag in.

Lillian and Sam took a minute to absorb the implications of Hazel Marie's suggestion, then Lillian said, "Miss Hazel Marie a smart woman. That do the trick, all right."

Actually, I'd never thought of Hazel Marie as a smart

woman—sweet, kind, the best of friends, yes, but not especially intellectually astute. Yet thinking of the many times when she'd surprised me with her keenness of insight, I had to concede that there was something to Lillian's pronouncement.

"I think so, too," Sam said. "It'll be interesting to see who Trixie invites to dinner, won't it? And, Julia, you'll be happy to know that I've just had a talk with her and she's on her way to a job interview."

"Really!" As my heart lifted at the news, a fleeting thought passed through my mind that I should leave the house more often—no telling how many problems would be solved in my absence. "What kind of job? How did you hear about it?"

"One of the nurses told me about her sister who's just opened a fitness center and needs a couple of helpers. And, Julia, it's at the end of Main Street where that little filling station once was, if you remember, so it's a walkable distance from here. Trixie wouldn't have to be driven back and forth."

"Well, that is remarkable news." I leaned back in my chair, feeling as if a great burden had fallen away. "Maybe she'll be too busy to fool with strange men. But, Sam," I said, "what experience does she have? From Trixie's looks, she doesn't know a thing about exercising or being fit for anything."

"That's the beauty part of it," he said, smiling as if he knew a secret. "The woman—Susan Odell—who's opening the business wants somebody she can teach, someone she can use as an example or role model for the young women who sign up for membership. The nurse told me that her sister's plan is to keep a record of the helper's weight and fitness regimen so the members can see how effective Ms. Odell's methods are."

"Well, I declare," I said in awesome wonder. "That's certainly a new twist. From all I've heard of those fitness centers, everybody who works in them are so trim and athletic that they intimidate anyone who isn't." I thought it over for a second or two. "The only thing wrong with it is if Trixie doesn't like it and won't do it. She just seems averse to extending herself in any way at all." I thought of the pile of dirty dishes left on the table last night.

"Then our part will be to strongly encourage her to do it," Sam said. "If she's offered the job, that is. And I think she will be. I know Susan Odell—I helped her close on her house a few years back, and of course a phone call made at an opportune time always helps." He smiled at me.

"Oh, you," I said. "You have it all set up, don't you?" I leaned over to give him a kiss. "Thank you, Sam."

Trixie came bouncing in, slamming the front door and acting more ebullient than I'd seen her—she had just been hired as an assistant fitness trainer, or, from Sam's description of the job, an assistant fitness train*ee*. I refrained from asking about her working hours, her salary, her duties, and so forth, for fear that she'd take them not as signs of interest but of criticism. As it was, she was just in time to sit down with us at the dinner table, where she frowned at each bowl and platter passed to her.

"What's this?" she asked as I passed a platter to her.

"Fried chicken cutlets," I said. "They're easier to cut than chicken on the bone. And, look, there's rice and gravy and lima beans and fresh squash."

"I like me a thigh," she muttered, picking through the cutlets with a fork.

"It's all white meat, Trixie. Take a piece and pass it on." My eyes rolled heavenward as she finally stabbed a piece and dumped it on her plate. Then she picked it up with her fingers and commenced to eat.

"Trixie," I said as gently as I could manage and with a forgive-me glance at Lloyd, "the reason we have cutlets is so Lloyd can become adept at using a knife and fork without ending up with a piece of chicken in his lap. We'll advance to chicken on the bone as soon as he's ready. I'll tell you both, though, that it is perfectly acceptable to eat chicken with one's fingers when it's served at a picnic or some other casual event."

She looked at me with a cold stare, then let the cutlet drop to her plate. Licking her greasy fingers, she finally noticed the napkin still folded on the table and proceeded to use it.

"You know what I think," Sam said jovially and just in time to divert and cool Trixie's anger at being corrected. "I think we need to invite some people in to meet Trixie. The problem is, however," he went on, directing the remark to Trixie as if he were imparting a secret, "we don't know any folks that you'd like to meet. So I'm wondering if you've met anyone you'd like to invite to dinner. I'd enjoy having a few new faces at the table with new things to talk about. What do you think, Trixie? I know you haven't been here very long, but have you met anybody you want to have over?"

Well, I thought to myself, *Sam is much more tactful than I.* My plan had been to flat-out tell Trixie that any person with whom she intended to spend time had to first be appraised and approved by us.

Trixie gave Sam that flat stare for which she was becoming noted, while I wondered if perhaps a certain amount of time was needed for her to absorb and understand what was said. Finally, she said, "You mean that?"

"Of course," Sam assured her. "We enjoy having guests."

Trixie's eyes slid over to me, then quickly away. She knew, I thought, that I didn't enjoy the guest I already had. A stab of shame shot through me, but it wasn't sharp enough to turn me into a hypocrite.

"I might know somebody," Trixie mumbled over her plate as her hair fell around her face.

"Good deal!" Sam said, sounding excessively pleased. "Whenever you want, Trixie. Just let Lillian know so she can plan something special for your friend. Could you tell us a little about him—or her—so we'll have something to look forward to?"

A small smile played around Trixie's mouth. "It's a him, and he has a job that all that economic stuff can't hurt. Meemaw told me to look for somebody like that."

"How did you meet him?" I asked and got drowned out as Lloyd jumped in, waving his hand under the table at me to stay off that subject.

"I'd sure like to meet him," he said a little louder than he usually spoke. "Anybody with a safe job these days is worth knowing."

Trixie nodded at him, pleased, I thought, with his enthusiasm. "He says he never has to look for customers 'cause everybody in the world works for him. They just keep a-comin', and all he has to do is set and wait for 'em. They's a never-endin' stream comin' through the door."

"My goodness," I said, trying to equal Lloyd's interest. "I'm impressed. What kind of job does he have?"

"He's a trainee, just like I'm gonna be." Trixie pushed her hair out of her face, sat up a little straighter, and announced with pride, "But he's not just startin' out like me. He's in his second year, and after one more, he'll have his license and can go out on his own or get promoted." Then, with some smugness, she went on, "And he's got another business on the side, workin' for hisself, not somebody else."

"Sounds like he's a real go-getter," Sam said.

"He is!" Trixie nodded vigorously. "An' that's just what Meemaw wants."

I wanted to ask, *But what do you want, Trixie?* but I didn't. We were getting more conversation out of her than ever before, and I didn't want to spoil it by undercutting that grandmother of hers. Time enough for that later on after we'd met this paragon of diligence.

"I wonder if we already know him," Sam said. "I like to keep up with the industrious young men around town. What's his name?"

"Rodney," Trixie said, looking expectantly at Sam as if he couldn't possibly know more than one Rodney.

"Rodney who?"

"Pace or Peace or something like that," Trixie said, as if his family name had no importance. I had to fight to keep my eyes from rolling back in my head.

"I know a lot of Paces," Sam said, seemingly unperturbed at

Trixie's ignorance of her gentleman friend's familial ties. "It'll be interesting to discuss it with him. You know how we Southerners like to talk about kinships and who knows who. We can sometimes find that we're related on one side or the other." Sam smiled playfully at her. "Kissin' cousins, even."

A distressed look passed across Trixie's face. "Better *not* be! Meemaw don't hold with such as that."

"Sam's teasing you, Trixie," I said. "He's just making conversation. I can't imagine that any of us are related in any way at all."

"Mama might be," Lloyd put in. "Seems like she's kin to half the people in the county."

Trixie frowned, studying the matter. "That might be all right."

"I'm sure it will be," I said firmly, anxious to steer the conversation away from a discussion of illegal cohabitation, which I assumed was what troubled Trixie and her Meemaw. "And, look, here's Lillian with dessert. What do we have tonight, Lillian?"

"Pecan pie," Lillian said proudly, setting the pie and the dessert plates before me. "If anybody want ice cream on top, let me know."

"I don't," Trixie said. "Miss Odell told me to cut down on sweets, so I'll just have pie."

"Coming right up," I said, wielding the pie server to slide a slice onto a plate and passing it to her. I was pleased to hear that Trixie seemed to be taking her new job seriously. "Lillian," I said, stopping her as she started back to the kitchen, "Trixie will be inviting a young man for dinner soon. She'll let you know when as soon as she discusses it with him. So, Trixie, when you know the date, why don't you talk over the menu with Lillian? We'll want to have something that he'll enjoy."

She cut her eyes at Lillian, then gave me that flat look again. "Okay, but he's awful busy. He's on call a lot."

"Is he a doctor?" Lloyd asked.

Trixie thought that over, then found an answer. "Pretty close to it. But he don't make that kinda money yet."

"What is he then?" Lloyd asked, posing just the question I wanted to ask. "What does he do?"

"He works at McCrory's down on East Avenue." Trixie looked around the table with proud defiance, as if she just knew that we'd expected some low-class employment like changing tires or picking up recycling bins.

I frowned in thought, trying to picture the businesses on East Avenue, even as Trixie kept on singing his praises. "He's already been to college an' everything," she said, "an' now he's just before being a full-fledged mortician."

I swallowed hard. "How interesting," I said, perfectly balancing my tone with both indifference and curiosity.

Chapter 18

Sam's eyebrows went up at this announcement, and Lillian, her face a mixture of wonder and fear, stood stock-still listening to Trixie.

Lloyd, undeterred, asked, "Where'd he go to college? Is he a Tarheel?"

Being from Georgia, Trixie didn't know what to make of the last question, so she ignored it. "He made all As, and graduated from the Forsyth County Technical Institution."

My eyes widened, hoping that she meant *institute,* not *institution,* which evoked a mental asylum in my mind. But who knew?

Sam, smooth as ever, nodded and said, "He is certainly right that he's in a recession-proof industry."

Lloyd was fascinated. "Does he actually *embalm* people?"

"He does everything," Trixie said. "Just wait till you hear. He'll tell you all about it."

Putting down my fork with my pie half eaten, I murmured, "I can hardly wait."

After dinner and after Trixie had again left the house with not one word to us, Sam and I sat in the library while Lillian finished up in the kitchen and Lloyd ran over to his mother's house to play with his sisters. I had lingered in the kitchen to ease some of Lillian's concerns before going to the library.

"Miss Julia," she'd said, "is she gonna bring a *undertaker* in our house? Somebody that work on *dead* people? What if he don't wash his hands an' he reach under the napkin for a biscuit an' touch all of 'em?"

"I don't think we need worry about that," I'd assured her. "In

my experience, undertakers are very careful about their hygiene."
My experience, however, was quite limited, and I, too, couldn't
help but wonder where certain hands had been and what they'd
done. "Let's just hope he's suitable for Trixie and put the rest out
of mind."

"Well," I said to Sam when I joined him in the library and as soon
as the nightly news was over, "I guess we're in for it now. A mortician, of all things."

Sam muted the television and turned to me with a smile.
"Funeral directors do quite well, Julia, and they're generally a
respectable group of professionals. Believe me, Trixie could do a
lot worse."

"I know. I keep telling myself that. At least he—whoever he
is—has a job with prospects. But I keep thinking of how she
must've met him. *Online*, Sam. Now, just what does that say about
him? Because obviously he was looking to meet somebody the
same way. So does that mean he can't get a date on his own? I
mean, that's Trixie's reason, but is it his, too?"

"Could be," Sam agreed, "but it could mean that they have
something in common. Maybe they're both shy and uncomfortable
in social situations."

"Well, that's the thing, Sam. At first I thought Trixie's problem
was shyness, but now she's acting headstrong and willful and won't
listen to anybody. I'd hoped that Hazel Marie would be able to
reach her, but now Trixie's mad at her for not letting her buy completely inappropriate outfits. She's just determined to have her own
way in everything."

"Let's wait and see who she brings home, and if it's this Rodney
she mentioned, I expect we'll be pleased. McCrory's is not going
to train anybody who's unsuited for the field."

"I guess so, unless he's low man on the totem pole and training
to be a gravedigger." I was unconvinced that Trixie could aim much

higher. "Well," I sighed, "be that as it may. How's the campaign going?"

"Funny you should ask," Sam said, smiling. "If you wouldn't mind driving me, I'd like to make a few stops tomorrow. Now wait," he said, holding up his hand as I started to protest. "All I want to do is shake some hands when folks go in to work and again when they get off—maybe stop at some diners around lunchtime. Could you do that for me?"

"Of course I'll drive you, but just for hand-shaking, Sam. You don't need to be doing anything else until you've fully recovered."

"Okay," he said, "I promise. But, I warn you now, I have a full day planned for Saturday. Lloyd's already agreed to go with me to tack up posters on telephone poles and put out yard signs wherever we can. We're going to headquarters early that morning and load the truck, then we'll cover as much of the county as we can. Millard and some volunteers will be working the other two counties."

"That's too much, Sam. You shouldn't be doing all that so soon after surgery."

"I'm only going to drive the pickup. I won't be getting in and out, and certainly not bending over, which I still can't do very well. But those signs and posters have to go up. And," he went on, "I'm thinking of asking Trixie to go with us."

"Why don't you tell her that getting in and out of the pickup is good training for her job—it'll be like one of those stairstep machines."

"Good idea," Sam said, laughing. "And, listen, I have something for you to do."

Uh-oh, I thought, having just felt relieved that he'd not asked me to cram myself onto the bench seat of his old truck.

"Whatever you need," I said, crossing my fingers.

"I'd like you to watch as much television as you can stand all day Saturday. Word is that Jimmy Ray will begin running his ads then, and I want to know what he says."

"Oh, I can do that," I said eagerly. "I mean, I can't watch twelve straight hours of it, but I can keep the set on and check every ten minutes when they interrupt the programs for commercials. And Lillian can watch the set in the kitchen, too."

"Thanks, sweetheart, that'll help a lot. Write down as much of what he says as you can, and keep track of how often the ads run. That'll give me some idea of how much money he's spending on them. Oh, and one more thing," he said. "There'll be big doin's on the Fourth—a picnic in Transylvania County, a pig-pickin' and square dance in Polk County, and that night, the big fireworks show out at the park. We're going to try to show up at all of them— a whole group of us, as many as I can get. Sort of a get-out-the-vote campaign with lots of Murdoch signs and banners."

"Goodness, is the Fourth of July already here?" I asked, seeing a brighter future ahead. "That means the summer's half over, doesn't it?"

Sam laughed and patted my knee. "Not quite. I don't think Elsie will consider the Fourth as the halfway point of Trixie's visit. She's hardly been here any time."

"Seems longer than that to me." I sighed and took his hand in mine.

Chapter 19

Sam and I were up before daylight the following morning, getting dressed to go shake hands with people who rose from their beds at that time every morning. I watched Sam carefully, searching for any signs of discomfort that he might show, still fearful that he was pushing himself too hard. It was somewhat disconcerting, though, to realize that he was moving faster and easier than I was, and I hadn't had surgery.

In fact, he had a cup of coffee waiting for me when I finally got down to the kitchen. "Just enough to get us started," he said. "We can stop at a drive-thru and get a biscuit and more coffee. I want to be at that hubcap plant on Airport Road by six-thirty."

And so we were. I parked near the gate to the yard surrounding the large Morton building and sat in the car while Sam stood greeting workers as they arrived. I watched as he shook hands, gave out pamphlets, and spoke briefly to each person. I marveled at how easily he laughed and conversed with perfect strangers, and it struck me that the reason was because he truly enjoyed meeting them. I couldn't have done it that comfortably in a million years— too self-conscious for one thing, and too aware of feeling like an idiot to be accosting people before the sun was halfway up.

"That was good," Sam said as he slid into the car. "Must've shook twenty-five hands, which I hope will turn into twenty-five votes."

"How're you feeling?" I asked, turning the ignition.

"I'm feeling fine." And he looked it, too. Maybe this was exactly what he needed, if he wouldn't overdo it.

"Where to now?" I asked as I pulled onto the highway.

"Well," Sam said, studying his notes, "the problem is that most plant workers go to work and get off at the same time, and I can only be at one place. Let's save that big ceramic company on the south side for this afternoon. We'll get there about three when they get off. But for now, drive out Ridge Road and let's see what's going on at some of the packing houses. It's too early in the season for many folks to be working, but probably a few will be hanging around."

So I went back through Abbotsville and took the two-lane road which wound for miles around orchards and fields where the large open-sided packing houses were located. After a number of miles, I turned in at the largest and parked on the side of the hard-packed dirt yard. As Sam got out of the car and walked toward the dock, I opened all the windows, for the sun was high and the heat was building up. There was no shade in sight. I watched as Sam wandered around, speaking to a few people who seemed to be doing little but counting and stacking empty crates. The place would be a hive of activity in a few weeks when big trucks would come roaring in to be loaded with apples and beans and other produce, then pull out to head for grocery stores all over the country.

"We need to come back in August," Sam said as he got back in the car. "September, too. But no visit is wasted, and I have to get votes where I can. The owner promised a campaign contribution, so it was worth the trip. Hurry, honey, and get the air-conditioning going. I'm about to melt."

I turned the car to get us headed back toward town, and soon we were cruising along in the cooling car at about thirty-five miles an hour, which was the limit on the narrow, curving road. We passed a dusty, hard-used car parked on the shoulder of the road, all its windows down, except for the cardboard in the passenger's window.

A half mile or so farther on the empty road, I spotted a small, scrawny-looking man with a gas can trudging along in the weeds on the side of the road. He looked as used up and out of gas as the car I presumed he'd just left.

"Pull over, honey," Sam said. "Let's give him a ride."

I lifted my foot from the accelerator, slowing the car, and looked at him in surprise. "You want to pick up a stranger? Sam, it's not safe."

"Not for you alone, but we saw his car and obviously he's going for gas. It's a good five miles to the nearest station and too hot to be walking."

"Well, my goodness," I said, bringing the car to a stop alongside the man. "One might think you're hard up for votes."

Sam laughed and I did, too, but I was uneasy about inviting a stranger into our backseat. But not Sam, for he rolled down the window and offered the man a ride. The man, who was hardly larger than Lloyd, accepted with alacrity. He crawled into the backseat bringing fumes from the gas can with him. He was wearing a thin cotton shirt and blue jeans so long that they were rolled up on his sockless ankles. His belt—I had to look twice to be sure—was two plastic grocery sacks tied together and run through the belt loops to end in a knot in front.

"Sam Murdoch," Sam said, offering his hand over the seat. "And my wife." I nodded, and made a mental note to keep some hand sanitizers in the car from now on. No telling what Sam would pick up from all the hands he was shaking.

"Much obliged," the man said, grinning broadly and settling into the leather seat. "Name's Lamar, Lamar Owens from Mills Gap. I sure 'preciate this, but I figgered if I took it easy an' didn't push myself, somebody or other'd come along an' gimme a lift. Them sheriff's deputies don't let this road go too long 'fore givin' it a pass, an' they pretty good 'bout lendin' a hand. 'Course," he went on, with some complacency, "they all know me."

I cut my eyes at Sam, fearing that Mr. Owens was telling us something I didn't want to hear, namely, that he had been arrested numerous times.

"You run out of gas often?" Sam asked.

"Naw, sir, but that ole car breaks down ever' other day, seems like. You know how it goes, if it's not one thing, it's two more. But them deputies, they're pretty good guys. Most of 'em, anyway. 'Course it takes one to know one, an' they know I'm in the same line of work as them."

Sam's eyebrows shot up as he turned sideways—as much as the seat belt would allow—to look at our passenger. "You're in law enforcement?"

"Sure am," Mr. Owens assured him. " 'Course I don't have no badge or nothin', but I take care of things them deputies don't get to know about, kinda 'round behind the law, if you get my drift. Take, for instant, the other night when I heard about this sorry piece a work—I happened to know him and I knowed he wadn't no good an' never has been. Anyway, I heard he beat the livin' . . . uh, daylights, I guess . . . sorry, ma'am, my manners ain't too good. But, anyway, he beat up real bad on his ole lady, an' I don't hold with that atall. So I looked him up and beat the you-know-what outta him. He won't raise a hand to her again anytime soon, I tell you that. No, siree, he won't."

"Well," Sam said, somewhat at a loss for words. "I expect she appreciated it."

"Naw, she didn't, but she will next time he gets drunk. An' he'll know what he's in for if he whups up on her again. And that," he said, hunching forward to make his point, "is what you call Outlaw Justice, an' she might not 'preciate it, but them deputies sure do. See, I handle a lot a cases like that an', you know, kinda give them boys a helpin' hand."

"I declare," I murmured.

And Sam said, "Well, Mr. Owens, it's a pleasure to meet a man who is so supportive of local law enforcement. I hope I can count on your vote in November."

"What?" Mr. Owens's face lit up. "You runnin' for sheriff?"

"No, I'm running for the state senate."

"Well, sure, I'll vote for you. Two or three times if you want me to. But I'd sure like to see somebody else be sheriff. The one we got, he holds to the law too much to suit me."

Sam had a sudden coughing fit just as I saw the first gas station. I gratefully pulled in and parked by the gas pumps.

Mr. Owens hopped out with his gas can, thanking us profusely, and I, with a sidewise glance at Sam, said, "Fill up your can, Mr. Owens, and we'll drive you back to your car. It's too hot to be walking."

When he closed the door and headed for the pump, Sam said, "I'd just as soon let him walk. Did you hear him say he'd vote two or three times?"

"Well," I said, making an effort to keep a straight face, "you did say you had to get votes where you could."

Chapter 20

Lillian looked up from the counter where she was working as we walked in late that afternoon. "Glad y'all home," she said, drying her hands. "If you need to rest 'fore supper, you better get to it. Miss Trixie, she invite her gentleman friend to eat with us tonight."

"Already?" I asked, surprised at how quickly Trixie had asked and her friend had accepted. Although how much of a friend he could be was an open question—they couldn't have known each other more than a day or two. I wasn't going to quibble over it, though, for Hazel Marie's suggestion was proving effective. So far. "What're we having? Did Trixie help you with the menu?"

"Yes'm, she tell me he like hot dogs and spaghetti, an' I say 'tween the two, I fix spaghetti. But it don't feel right to serve something that don't have no rice an' gravy to go with it."

I knew what she meant. She was referring to a normal Southern company meal complete with two or three vegetables and a roast along with rice or potatoes with gravy. "You made the right choice, given the choices. I say, hot dogs!" I shook my head at the thought of serving a guest such casual fare. "Well, a nice big salad will help fill out a one-dish meal."

"Yes'm, I got all the fixin's for a salat, an' I talk to Miss Hazel Marie an' she tole me how to make a anti-somethin'-or-other platter. Which I already got in the 'frigerator."

"You asked Hazel Marie?" I said, stunned that Lillian would discuss food preparation with the most inept cook in town.

"Yes'm, Mr. Pickens an' her like to go to that spaghetti place over in Asheville, an' what she tole me was real easy to fix. You jus' buy what you want an' lay it out on a plate so it look nice, an' that's all there is to it."

"Then I'm sure it'll be fine. Sam," I said, turning to him as he stood looking bemused at our conversation, "you'll have time to rest before our guest arrives. Why don't you lie down for a while?"

"I'll take a shower, then do that," he said, heading toward the stairs. "I'm looking forward to meeting Trixie's undertaker-in-training."

Addressing Lillian, I asked, "Where is Trixie, anyway?"

"She over to Miss Hazel Marie's gettin' her makeup put on."

"Well, that's an encouraging sign," I said, pulling out a chair from the table and sitting down. "At least she recognizes a special occasion when she sees one. Oh, me, Lillian," I said, leaning my head on my hand. "It's been a long day, and I could do without this tonight. But we asked for it, so I can't complain. I just hope he's better at conversing than Trixie is. It'll be a long evening if he's not."

"Yes'm, but I as soon not hear 'bout no dead folks while I'm servin'."

About that time, Trixie eased through the door, glancing around as she came to see who was in the kitchen. I sat up and took notice.

"Why, Trixie!" I said. "You look beautiful." Which was not entirely true, but I believe in giving credit where credit is due. At least an effort had been made, for Hazel Marie had done a remarkable job on Trixie's face. The rest of her was another matter.

"I got to fix my hair," Trixie said, pushing a hank of it from her face. "The babies started cryin', an' Hazel Marie didn't have time to do it. But she loaned me her curlin' arn an' I'm gonna do it."

"You need any help?" I asked, hoping she didn't because fixing hair was not my strong suit.

"I can do it." And off she went without one word of thanks or an offer to help with preparations for her guest.

Lloyd came in just then, forestalling any further comments, although I still had many to make. He was looking a little worse for the wear—his shorts and T-shirt rumpled from the heat, his hair standing on end, and his face sunburned from a few hours in the swimming pool at the club.

"I was going to eat at Mama's," he said, "but she told me that Trixie's undertaker friend is coming over. Is it all right if I eat here? You have enough for me, Miss Lillian?"

"I always got enough for you," Lillian said, smiling at him.

"I need to take a shower if I have time." He looked at me, his eyebrows raised in a question. "What should I wear?"

"Oh," I said, "we want this to be a casual family dinner, so just wear some khakis and a nice shirt. A tie isn't necessary."

"Okay," he said, heading out of the kitchen. I followed to take care of my own ablutions and preparations for observing the progress of a match made not in heaven, but on an online dating service.

Sam was waiting in the library when I came down, both of us prepared to welcome a stranger into our midst. Sam, as usual, was dressed appropriately for the occasion in summer-weight trousers and a tie and a light blue shirt, the color of which was his bow to a casual evening. His more formal wear would have been a white shirt and silk tie under a suit coat.

That man pleased me in more ways than I could count and always being dressed in a fitting manner was close to the top of my list. That was not often the case with men as they aged. I had noticed among those I knew around town and in church that many of them became less and less careful of their personal hygiene and of their outward appearance as the years passed. Some allowed themselves to become downright sloppy, feeling, I supposed, that they'd spent a lifetime dressing for work and, now that they were retired, no further effort was required. So they made none.

I smiled at Sam, but before I could speak, Lloyd walked in looking neat and clean in khakis and a plaid shirt. And before I could speak to him, Trixie appeared, and I kept my mouth closed. Lord, the girl—or, now that I knew her age, the woman—had no idea of how to prepare herself for a special occasion. She had curled her hair with Hazel Marie's curling iron, but she had been able to reach only the hair around her face. She'd made an effort to curl the back of her head, but it had been a failure. I sympathized because I'd never been able to wield one of those devices without burning myself in half a dozen places.

But I gave her credit, for she was wearing an outfit that I assumed Hazel Marie had helped her select—a sleeveless blouse and a floral skirt. Unfortunately, though, she had on high heels or, rather, a pair of those high wedge-heeled sandals that caused her to mince instead of walk. The worst, though, was the pair of earrings that dangled to her shoulders. No, the absolute worst was the additions she'd made to Hazel Marie's application of makeup—gold eye shadow and another layer of rouge.

Sam immediately complimented her, saying how lovely she looked. She ducked her head, smiled, and blushed, making me realize how important this evening must be to her. I determined to do whatever I could to make it a success.

"Can we sit in the living room?" Trixie asked. "So I can watch for him?"

"Of course," I said, and we all adjourned to the front room where Trixie could watch from the windows. I wanted to tell her that, when wanting to impress a young man, it wasn't good policy to appear too eager, but I refrained. This was her evening, and I didn't intend to spoil it for her.

Trixie went immediately to a front window, looked out, then hurried to the door. "He's here!"

She had the door open before he could ring the bell. I heard him tell her how nice she looked, making me wonder even more about him. But I clamped down on my usual critical attitude and hoped that his compliment reflected proper raising.

They walked into the living room, Trixie beaming with pride and her friend seeming perfectly at ease to be withstanding an appraisal by her family. I don't know what I expected, but it wasn't his smooth manner and polished exterior.

Trixie said, "This is Rodney."

"Rodney Pace," Rodney said, striding over to meet Sam in the middle of the room and offering his hand.

"Welcome," Sam said. "Good to meet you. Are you an Abbot County Pace?"

"Lived here all my life except for my years in college. And, yes, sir, I'm kin to all the Paces."

Sam introduced him to me and to Lloyd, then, as we all seated ourselves, said, "Well, I expect they call you Rod?"

"No, sir. I go by Rodney. In my line of work, it's important to avoid nicknames and abbreviations. Formality is the desired image we like to project."

Sam nodded sagely. "Understandable, I'm sure."

They chatted amiably about Rodney's family, many of whom, as it turned out, Sam knew. Trixie, who couldn't move her eyes from Rodney, and Lloyd, who was eager to ask a few questions, listened in, giving me the opportunity to assess our guest. He was tall and lanky, closer to thin than merely slender, with dark, well-cut hair, except for his sideburns, which were just a tad long. He was wearing a dark gray suit, a white shirt, and a somber tie. He looked ready to conduct a funeral.

As for his age, if I had to guess, I'd guess somewhere in his thirties, and I wondered at his unmarried state. Most local young men were married by that age, but maybe that was why he'd taken to advertising on a dating service, which was the way I assumed he'd met Trixie. He had a mature air about him, but as the evening drew on, it seemed to me to be an assumed manner, something learned rather than a natural progression toward maturity. And all the while, in spite of my determination to squelch any critical assessment, I wondered what he could possibly see in Trixie.

Lillian came to the door of the living room. "Dinner is served," she said, and we all rose to go to the table.

Chapter 21

I placed Trixie and Rodney together on one side of the table, Lloyd opposite them, with Sam and myself at the head and the foot. It was the best I could do, although I do like a balanced table. Trixie allowed Rodney to seat her without flinching, so that was a good start. I wracked my brain for a suitable table topic to put the two of them at ease.

Thank goodness for Sam. He both started and kept the conversation going, drawing out Rodney and Lloyd, but failing with Trixie. As that was not unusual, the discussion of the weather, the economy, and plans for the summer went on apace without any additions from her. And I must admit from me, either. I was entranced by Rodney's request to Lillian for a tablespoon, with which he proceeded to twirl his spaghetti like he'd been born in Italy. I'd have been surprised, though, if any of the Abbot County Paces had ever been farther from home than Myrtle Beach.

Lloyd watched the spaghetti twirling with intense interest, then asked Lillian for a tablespoon of his own. Sam did, too, and their efforts, guided by instructions from Rodney, proved mildly entertaining and occasionally messy. Trixie didn't attempt to twirl, just kept struggling to get a forkful to her mouth before it fell back to the plate. I, of course, continued to use the edge of my fork to facilitate noodle management.

After we'd finished the strawberry shortcake that Lillian served, I suggested we return to the living room. As we began to leave the table, Rodney complimented Lillian, raising him a degree or so in my estimation.

Trixie, who'd hardly said a word throughout dinner, said, "We're going to a movie, so we can't stay long."

Rodney gave her a distant smile. "We have time to talk awhile. Can't just eat and run, you know."

"Oh, good," Lloyd said, settling into a corner of the Chippendale sofa. "I want to hear all about your job. Tell us what you do with dead people. What if somebody dies at night? Do you have to go out in the dark and pick them up? And who gets to drive the hearse? Oh, and how did you get into the business?"

"Lloyd," I murmured, cautioning him against asking too many specific questions, the answers to which I wasn't sure were suitable for Rodney to give or for Lloyd to hear.

I hadn't needed to concern myself about Rodney. He sat up straight in one of the wing chairs and commenced to talk about what was clearly his favorite subject.

"Mortuary science is a wide-open field, Lloyd, and you'd do well to look into it yourself. If you're the right kind of person, it's both gratifying and profitable. For one thing, it's recession-proof, so more and more people get into it during tough financial times. The thing about it is," he said, scooting up to sit on the edge of his chair, his hands dangling between his knees, "there's more to running a mortuary than just burials. You have to have a good selection of caskets and somebody knowledgeable enough to guide families in the selection process. You'll be real interested to know this—everybody is—we can now get caskets that feature special interests of the deceased—you know, like a favorite football team or Harley-Davidson or a college logo. One family wanted a NASCAR casket and we were able to get it for them. 'Course a lot of people are leaning toward cremation these days—it's cheaper than your regular interment because you don't have to buy a casket or a vault or a plot in a cemetery. We offer personalized services for every need or desire a family can come up with."

"I declare," I said, noting Trixie's rapt face as she listened to Rodney. I tried to think of some way to change the subject, because Lloyd was entirely too interested.

"But," Lloyd said, "what about fixing up a dead person? I mean, what if somebody gets run over and they come in all dirty and messed up?"

"Under those circumstances," Rodney said, with an air of importance, "we ask for a picture from the family so the body can be prepared as close to the living state as possible. And of course the family brings in the clothes they want their loved one to wear. You'd be surprised at the problems that can create sometimes. I remember two sisters who were in charge of the arrangements for their father and they couldn't agree on what they wanted us to put on him. One wanted him to wear what he always wore, which was just a shirt and tie. The other sister insisted on the suit that he'd had hanging in a closet—the only one he had from the sound of it. Problem was, though, he'd outgrown it. The first sister said she wasn't gonna have people know they'd sent their papa into eternal rest wearing high-water pants and a jacket that wouldn't button. They almost had a fight over it right there in the consultation room, but I came up with a solution. See, Lloyd, that's part of what makes a good mortician—being able to help with clothes selection and the like, as well as being aware of the emotional stress the bereaved are under. You have to be able to think on your feet." Rodney paused as if to acknowledge with a moment of silence a family's grief or his ability to deal with it. Then he continued on. "I pointed out to the sisters that the casket would only be open to the waist, so nobody would see the length of his pants. And I told 'em that we'd just split the back of the jacket and it would button fine in the front. Their daddy looked just like he was ready to get up and go somewhere when I got through with him." Rodney sat back, looking pleased and proud.

"Extraordinary," Sam said. "I can see that you have to have a lot of tact and understanding."

"That's exactly right," Rodney said, hunching forward again. "We have to have good communication skills and be able to show the proper respect and compassion toward the bereaved. And, of course, guide them into making good decisions during such an emotional time as the loss of a loved one. And speaking of that, Mr. Murdoch, you and Mrs. Murdoch should consider doing some advance planning. When you have your own funeral already planned and paid for, it takes the burden off those who're left behind. I'd be happy to work with either or both of you. People tell us all the time what a relief it is to know that their funerals will be carried out exactly the way they want them to be. No surprises at all." He looked expectantly from Sam to me, waiting for our response.

"I hope there's no hurry," I murmured.

And Sam said, "Something to consider, all right."

"Well," Lloyd said, "but what exactly do *you* do?"

"Everything," Rodney replied, with a wave of his arm. "A well-rounded mortician is trained for it all. Some days I work in the embalming room where I—"

"If it's all the same to you, Rodney," I said, "I'd as soon not hear the details."

He gave me a quick glance, nodded his head, and went on with the same intensity he'd been exhibiting. "Perfectly understandable. I do plenty of other things, like working with families, as I've just said, and then there's flowers to see to, making sure the family's minister is informed, and the church is scheduled. There're notices and obituaries that go to the newspaper. Death notices have to be filled out and sent in to the state. Then there's the chair arrangement in the viewing rooms, which we have to be careful about if there're any family squabbles, and we take care of transport of the body if it's to be buried elsewhere. Oh, and we keep a constant check on our refrigeration facility if there's any delay. Another thing we do is make sure the family has chosen and informed the pallbearers they want, and another big job is washing our hearses and the cars we use to transport the families. We're always conscious of our public appearance. Oh, there's a lot that goes into dealing with the dead, but to us, it's all in a day's work."

During all of this, Trixie had said nothing, but she'd listened intently, nodding agreement occasionally as if she'd heard it all before and was checking to see that he left nothing out. If I hadn't known better, I'd have thought that she was anxious for Rodney to make a good impression on us. As it was, though, I wasn't sure that Trixie cared one way or another what we thought of him or of anything else.

"We better go," she finally said. "We'll be late."

"Okay," Rodney said, standing. "Mrs. Murdoch, I want to thank you for inviting me. Dinner was delicious, and I'm glad to get to know Trixie's family." He turned to Sam. "Mr. Murdoch, I'd like to give you my card in case you're interested in relieving Mrs. Murdoch of the burden of your final expenses. But I'm not speaking for McCrory's Funeral Home now. This is a business I have on the side—I'm a freelance representative—so you can choose any mortuary you want."

"Well," Sam said, always polite as he accepted the card, "I'm not—"

"No need to decide now," Rodney assured him. "Just think about it. You're guaranteed acceptance, because physical exams aren't required. In fact, you can't be turned down for health reasons of any kind—you could be on your deathbed and you would still qualify. And the beauty part of it is how affordable it is. The rates never increase and the coverage never decreases. Premiums are only nine ninety-five a month for each unit, and you can get as many units as you want. It's real personalized and it'll give you peace of mind like you wouldn't believe."

"I'll certainly consider it," Sam said, while my eyes rolled back in my head.

"Oh, and Lloyd," Rodney said, turning to him. "If you're interested in going into mortuary science, you should know that there're a lot of sideline opportunities in the business. Like, for instance, perpetual care cemeteries, cosmetic services, monuments both granite and bronze, accessories like urns and plaques and miniature personalized caskets, selling family plots, although we call them family estates because they have prearranged slots for each family member, and there's a new idea out there that I'm interested in. In fact, I'm looking out for some acreage to buy so it can be landscaped as a scattering garden." Rodney stopped to take a breath, but it was a quick one. "I tell you, it's a wide-open field, and if you want to know how to get into it, I can give you all the ins and outs."

"Not now, Rodney," Trixie said, taking his arm, and for once I was glad for her interruption. "We got to go."

Lloyd said, "Tell me next time. I need time to think about it."

"Oh, Trixie, before you leave," Sam said, "I wanted to ask if you'd go with Lloyd and me tomorrow to distribute campaign posters. We'll be nailing them up on every telephone pole we see and putting out yard signs wherever we can. I could sure use your help."

Trixie's eyes narrowed and her face reddened. She was just before either ungraciously agreeing or flat-out refusing, but Rodney jumped in.

"That sounds like fun," he said. "Could you use another volunteer? I'd like to help, if Trixie wouldn't mind me tagging along."

Trixie didn't mind at all. In fact, under those circumstances, she didn't seem to mind going herself. Her face lit up and she nodded her head vigorously.

"Good man, Rodney," Sam said. "I'm more than glad to have you. Meet us here at eight o'clock in the morning, and we'll get as many signs up as we can. By tomorrow night, everybody'll know who's running for the senate."

Chapter 22

We stood in the door a few seconds watching as the dating couple walked toward Rodney's shiny black car parked at the curb.

"Man," Lloyd said, admiration in his voice, "Rodney must be getting rich working at McCrory's. That's a Cadillac SUV—an Escalade—and they cost a *mint*."

Sam put his hand on the boy's shoulder as we turned from the door. "They certainly do, but remember, Lloyd, that some people stretch themselves financially just to make a good impression. They end up house-poor or car-poor or whatever. I expect that SUV has Rodney stretched pretty thin."

Listening to this, I smiled. Sam, who could afford a new car every year if he wanted one, drove a four-year-old Lincoln and an ancient Ford pickup. When I'd once questioned him about it, he'd said, "They're still running fine. I don't see any reason to get rid of something just because it's old."

He laughed when I replied, "I hope you feel the same way about wives."

I turned to Sam as we walked back into the living room, still trying to make up my mind about that forward young man. "Was Rodney trying to sell you some insurance?"

Sam chuckled. "Yep, he sure was."

"I figured as much," I said, my mouth tightening, righteously offended at a guest who used a social occasion to drum up business from his host.

"What kind of insurance?" Lloyd asked. "I thought you just had to have that when you went to the hospital."

"Oh, sugar," I said. "You wouldn't believe all the different kinds of insurance there are, most of which you have to have."

"That's right, Lloyd," Sam said. "Besides health insurance, there's insurance on your house, homeowner's insurance, car insurance—plus more if you have a boat or motorcycle—flood insurance, liability insurance, term insurance, life insurance, and probably a dozen more. But what Rodney was selling is called burial insurance. It helps you buy a casket and a cemetery plot and whatever else you need when you bury somebody."

Lloyd thought about that for a minute. "Sounds like it would all go to pay the funeral home."

Sam laughed and put his arm around the boy's shoulders. "You got that right. That's exactly what it does. Rodney is working both ends—selling insurance while you're alive, then collecting the payout when you die." Sam shook his head. "You have to give him credit. He's a go-getter, all right."

"Well," Lloyd said, still studying the matter, "why would anybody want to buy that kind of insurance? I mean, if the money's just for your funeral, you wouldn't be around to care what kind you have."

Sam sat down and looked up at the boy. "But it is important to a lot of people, especially to those who live from paycheck to paycheck without any savings to cover, say, a sudden death. And there are people who think a big, expensive funeral is an indication of how much the deceased person was loved." Sam turned to me. "You remember, Julia, when the insurance man used to go around certain neighborhoods every Friday and collect a quarter or so from the families who'd bought burial insurance? He'd go around on Fridays, Lloyd, because that was payday, and his clients would have enough on hand to pay the premiums."

"I do remember that," I said, "and it wouldn't surprise me if they aren't still doing it." I made a mental note to ask Lillian if she had burial insurance, and if she did, to tell her to stop wasting her money. I'd bury her, if need be, and I'd make it as lavish as she'd want if she were there to enjoy it.

Sam was up early the next morning, eager to begin papering the town with VOTE FOR MURDOCH signs and posters. By the time I got downstairs and headed for the coffeepot, he was already on the phone making arrangements to borrow a truck from Deputy Sergeant Coleman Bates.

"Hey, Miss Lady," a high-pitched little voice pierced through the fog of sleep I was still in.

"Why, Latisha," I said, looking down at Lillian's great-grandchild, who was holding an almost naked Barbie doll. Latisha's hair was in cornrows with clacking beads on the ends of the braids, and she was wearing a white T-shirt, yellow pedal pushers, and orange polka-dot sneakers. "I haven't seen you in forever. How are you?"

"I'm doin' good 'cause today's Sar'day, an' I don't have to go to school an' eat that mess they give me on a tray. I tole Great-Granny she ought to go over there and show them ladies how to cook. All they know how to do is put hairnets on their heads, but they could just let them ole gray hairs fall whichever place they want to, for all the eatin' that gets done."

"Law, Latisha," Lillian said. "Miss Julia don't want to hear that."

Before I could assure her that I found the perils of the school lunchroom fascinating, Latisha changed the subject. "Guess what, Miss Lady? I'm gonna go with Lloyd an' Mr. Sam to do some hammerin' on telephone poles."

"You are?" I looked to Lillian for confirmation.

She shrugged, resigned apparently to letting her go. "I tole Mr. Sam she gonna talk him to death, but he say she entertain him an' he wants her to go." Lillian rolled her eyes just a little. "I hope he know what he doin', 'cause she about to talk my head off."

Sam hung up the phone and turned to us, a pleased smile on his face. "Got us a big, roomy truck that will carry us all."

"I thought you were going to use yours," I said, thinking of the old, wired-together pickup that came with Sam when we married and which was still taking up space in the garage.

"Coleman has a double cab," Sam told me, "which, if we all go together, we'll need so everybody'll have a place to sit. If we took mine, somebody would have to sit on somebody's lap."

Lloyd looked up from the piece of toast he was smearing with peach preserves. "I'd probably have to hold Trixie and get smushed flat."

"Lloyd," I warned softly, but I couldn't help but smile at the image of Trixie on his lap.

"No, you won't, Lloyd," Latisha said. "I'd jump on your lap 'fore she can get there. Won't be no smushin' goin' on with me around."

"Thanks, Latisha," Lloyd said, grinning. "I'll count on that."

"We're in good shape now," Sam said, rubbing his hands together, as I realized how excited he was to be out on the campaign trail again. "Coleman wanted to go with us, but he's on duty. Hurry up, Lloyd, as soon as Rodney gets here, we'll be off. Where's Trixie?"

"I heard her in her room," I said, "so she's up. Sam, please for my sake, take it easy today. It takes time for your internal organs to adjust to having something removed, so you ought not to jiggle around too much."

Lloyd looked over at me, his mouth open. Then he started laughing. "You mean there's an empty place inside Mr. Sam and all his other organs have to scramble to fill it up?"

Sam and Lillian laughed, and Lillian said, "I can jus' see that now."

"Well, it stands to reason," I said. "But whether they're in there scrambling around, I don't know."

Just as the front doorbell rang, we heard Trixie bounding down the stairs to answer it. She was beaming as she ushered Rodney into the kitchen, but my smile of welcome dried up fast. Rodney was in pressed blue jeans with a polo shirt and looked neat and ready for action. But it was Trixie who took my breath away. She was wearing a pair of those skintight spandex athletic shorts, which weren't too short as they came almost to her knees, but they were molded to every roll and bulge the poor girl had. She also had on a halter of sorts, something that looked like a sports brassiere that I'd seen in a Title Nine catalogue which had appeared unsolicited in our mailbox.

"This is my work uniform," she proudly explained to Rodney. "It's what I have to wear at the fitness center. I think we're going to get a lot of exercise today."

"Perfect," Rodney said, manning up to what was probably more than he'd expected to have to deal with.

"Well, folks, let's be off," Sam said, picking up a toolkit full of nails and hammers. "Rodney, you and Trixie can pile in with us or you can follow us to Coleman's to get his truck."

"We'll follow you," Rodney said. Then to Trixie's obvious dismay, he added, "Anybody want to ride with us?"

"We better go with Mr. Sam," Lloyd said. "Come on, Latisha, let's go."

"Lloyd," Latisha said, as loud as if he were two blocks away. "How 'bout me an' you ridin' in the back of that truck?"

Lloyd shook his head. "Can't, Latisha. It's against the law."

"Well, shoot," Latisha said. "I was countin' on everybody gettin' to see us."

"Honey," Sam said to me as he started for the door, "remember to watch for Jimmy Ray's ads today. You and Lillian both, if you will."

"We will," I assured him. "And we'll give you a complete rundown when you get home. But, Sam, please don't do too much. If you get tired, come on home."

"I will, but I'll be fine." And with that, the whole crew of them left for Coleman's so they could go politicking in his double-cab pickup with a long bed full of posters and yard signs.

Chapter 23

"Lillian," I said, as soon as the door closed behind them. "What're you doing here this morning? I didn't think you were coming in today."

"Well, I wadn't till Latisha say she had to see what Lloyd was up to, an' she wanted to see Miss Trixie, too. So we come in, an' now off she go with 'em."

"Then why don't you go on home? You'll have the whole day to yourself for a change. But if you don't mind, keep your television on and watch for Jimmy Ray Mooney's ads. Make some notes so Sam will know what they say."

"I think I'll go on then. You want me to come back an' fix some supper? They all be comin' in starvin' to death."

"No, you don't need to come in. I'll have supper ready for them."

Lillian didn't say a word, but she stopped what she was doing and stared at me.

"Don't look at me like that," I said, laughing. "I hope to goodness I'm capable of boiling some hot dogs and putting out ketchup and mustard."

"*That* what you gonna serve?"

"I sure am. It's Rodney's second favorite dish and I hope Trixie will notice my effort to please. I'll run to the store a little later and get what we need."

"I'll make you a list so you won't forget something. An' I'm gonna put down some baked beans and some slaw and such like that. You can get it all at one of them deli counters at the store. You might not even think of filling up a plate till you see they's nothin' on it but a hot dog all by its lonesome."

"I'm sure you're right, so thank you. If Latisha wants to eat with us, I'll let you know. We'll get her home after supper."

After Lillian left, I wandered somewhat aimlessly into the library, wondering what I should do with a long, quiet day all to myself. But not so quiet after all, because I had to nerve myself to turning the television set on, assuming that Jimmy Ray would use the local channel beaming from Asheville for his ads.

So with the constant din of children's shows and commercials for cereals and juices and toys, all aimed at the Saturday morning audience, running in the background, I tried to catch up on some piddling work I'd been putting off. Well, not work, exactly, but an attempt to weed out my address book by transferring current addresses and phone numbers into a new book. My old book was half covered with strike-throughs and erasures of names of those who had moved away or passed on. It was slow work because I had to stop every time the shows broke for commercials—which seemed to be every five minutes—so I could see if Jimmy Ray was on.

By the time I got to the Cs, I put down my pen and sat back in the chair. This was mindless work, and my mind had been going its own way, thinking over what was happening in our lives. Here Sam had survived a major operation and I had survived public speaking, and we were both trying to survive Trixie. It was time to take stock again and see where we were headed. It could be to Raleigh, which would mean a real change in our lives, even if it were for only two years. On the other hand, it could be that we'd be staying right here after a loss to Jimmy Ray.

As a rule, whenever I took time to take stock, I ended up feeling grateful and reassured that things were as they should be, but not this time. Sam seemed to think that there was a real possibility that he could lose the election, and, I now realized, he had steeled himself against disappointment by saying from the first that he could take it or leave it.

I no longer believed that. Seeing his excitement and enthusiasm for nailing posters on telephone poles, recalling his anxiety about meeting his commitments while he was in the hospital, I realized that he really wanted to win.

When the outcome of something doesn't matter to me, I just turn it over to the Lord, telling Him that whatever He decides will be fine with me. And I'll be honest about it—it didn't much matter to me which way this senatorial race turned out. If Sam won or if he lost, I could accept either one with equanimity. Maybe because I had so little invested in it, the outcome was of little consequence to me. But, as I now knew, that wasn't true of Sam.

However it turned out, though, I would have to be prepared to be a support to him. And I'll just be honest and admit that so far supporting Sam in his campaign had become more and more of a burden for me. It wasn't that I wanted him to lose; it was just that I kept wishing he hadn't gotten into it in the first place. I wanted to be—and intended to be—supportive, but my heart wasn't truly in it. Given the choice, however, between beating the bushes for votes and sailing on the high seas, I had resigned myself to beating the bushes. At least we were sleeping in our own bed at night.

I sat up straight and reached for the remote to turn up the sound—the ad I'd been waiting for was on. There they were—Jimmy Ray and his daughter, Jimmie Mae, and her three stairstep children, pictured on a front porch swing. The camera zoomed in on Jimmy Ray and, as I scribbled as fast as I could, he said, "I'm Jimmy Ray Mooney, and I'm asking you to send me back to the North Carolina senate so I can continue to support education for my grandchildren and all the children in the district. Children are our future, and I know you want the best for yours as I do for mine. *No one* will support education like I will." Then the camera moved to the faces of his smiling grandchildren, and as the scene faded away, a voice-over said, "A vote for Jimmy Ray is a vote for our children."

I threw down my pen, just so aggrieved I didn't know what to do. The nerve of the man! I knew for a fact that Jimmy Ray had voted to cut the number of teachers' assistants and had also been quoted as saying, "We don't need to be spending money on art classes. Kids can watch public television and get all the culture they need." Now here he was advertising himself as the great supporter of education, and doing it as if no one else would.

It was hard to go back to copying addresses after that, my mind was so full of responses I wanted to throw at the Mooney campaign. What did Jimmy Ray know about education, anyway? He didn't have any himself, being a high school graduate back when it took only eleven grades to be one. And since then he'd lived off taxpayers in one local bureaucratic job after another.

Well, I thought with a sigh, *maybe he realizes his lack and wants better for his grandchildren.* Of course, he hadn't done so well by his daughter. Jimmie Mae had left school early because back then they didn't allow girls in the family way to graduate.

Still, I thought, trying to give him the benefit of the doubt, as I leaned my head on my hand, *it's commendable to want the best for children,* and I tried to come to terms with that. But behind Jimmy Ray's ad was the implication that *he* could better provide for the educational needs of our children than Sam could. And I didn't like that one bit.

Finally, I realized that the ad could've been worse. In fact, as these things go, it hadn't been so bad. Half the people who saw it wouldn't even know who he was running against. And everybody who was running for any office—local, state, or federal—ran on an education platform. Jimmy Ray was doing no more nor less than every other candidate, and with that, I decided that it wouldn't hurt Sam's chances at all and I went back to copying addresses.

About noon I went to the kitchen to make a sandwich, switching on the set there to keep up with Jimmy Ray's ad campaign. Just as I opened the refrigerator, a new ad came on. There he was, dressed in a plaid shirt and a pair of jeans, leaning casually against a white fence with a horse pasture in the background. Beside him on the fence was a large sign reading: JIMMY RAY, YOUR MAN FOR THE NC SENATE. Jimmy Ray looked straight into the camera and, in a sonorous voice, said, "A vote for Jimmy Ray is a vote for experience. I've served three terms in the North Carolina senate, while my opponent has served none. All he's done is retire from practicing law and go fishin'. There's already too many lawyers in the Assembly now, so let's let him stick to his fishin' while the rest of us get the things done that need to be done." Stirring music swelled around him as he smiled and said, "I'm Senator Jimmy Ray Mooney, and I paid for this message."

I couldn't believe it! That was a direct slap at Sam, and it made me so mad I couldn't see straight. I grabbed a pad and pen and wrote down as much as I could remember so Sam would know the low blows that were coming his way. Actually, I hadn't needed to do that, because the ad ran three more times during the afternoon, and by that time every word said was stuck in my memory.

I forced myself to eat the sandwich I'd made but I hardly tasted it, so fired up that I could do nothing but think of ways to counter Jimmy Ray's negative advertising. And the more I thought about it, the more I wanted Sam to win—if for no other reason than to keep Jimmy Ray out of that seat.

I'd started out the morning realizing that Sam wanted to win much more than I'd thought, so on that basis alone, I'd wanted him to win, too—although with much less enthusiasm. Now, though, after Jimmy Ray's personal attack ad, I *really* wanted him to win. No longer could I be content to leave the outcome up to the Lord, I had to set myself to petitioning Him without ceasing. And maybe doing a few other things, as well.

I knew, of course, that Jimmy Ray, and Jimmie Mae, too, would be praying just as hard for Sam to lose. So in the long run, it would still be the Lord's will that would be done, but at least He was going to know whose side I was on.

Chapter 24

The thing to do was to stop sitting around mooning over stock-taking, which never resulted in my doing anything anyway, and take myself in hand and get something done. Sam needed some fire in his campaign, and he was too much of a gentleman to do any active stoking. That's where I could come in, because when pushed far enough, even a lady, especially a lady of age with years of correct deportment behind her, could get away with a few unladylike words and actions. About the only good thing I could say about old age was that you were allowed much more leeway to say and do whatever you wanted. And I intended to take advantage of it on behalf of such a good cause. If it took a complete makeover of my normally retiring personality, why then, so be it. I was going to become politically active!

The first thing I'd do—as soon as Sam got home—would be to make another monetary contribution to his campaign. To do so had not occurred to me before this, because Sam and I had designated a certain amount when he first announced for the seat. So I had assumed that if he'd needed more, he would've asked for more. But, I told myself, needing campaign funds wasn't the point. The point was that I demonstrate my commitment by making a voluntary contribution.

So that was the first thing. The next thing was to become one of those modern solicitors who baled, bundled, bagged, or somehow collected funds for political purposes so that Sam could match Jimmy Ray ad for ad. Money talks, especially on television, and I was going to see that Sam became a political star. I visualized an ad that featured Sam in his boat out on a lake, his old hat on his head while he holds a fishing rod. He could say something like, "Fishing settles a man, puts things in perspective, and sharpens the mind. I'm recommending it to someone who's been in the North Carolina senate for several terms—a restful vacation would be good for him. And for us."

Well, maybe not. But Sam could think of something better to say, something not quite so subtle.

So far, I had been reticent to speak of Sam's campaign to friends for fear that they'd think me forward. If I'd even mentioned it, I knew that LuAnne Conover, for one, would immediately accuse me of putting on airs, and there was always the possibility that some of them were so unenlightened that they planned to vote for Jimmy Ray. So I'd kept Sam's involvement quiet, not wanting to embarrass anyone by putting them on the spot.

But I could now see that there was no reason in the world why I shouldn't suggest, ask, cajole, and beg contributions from everyone I knew. There comes a time when reticence is not only unnecessary but ill-advised, and that time had come. Sam needed every vote he could get, and it's a settled fact that where your money is, there also is your vote. So I would go after the money.

To that end, I began to plan my own campaign, then remembered that I had to go to the store and prepare supper for a truckload of ragtag volunteers. If Sam hadn't been worn to a frazzle by Rodney and Latisha trying to out-talk each other, I'd be surprised, so I needed to have food on the table.

I *was* surprised, for by the time they all came in, Sam, far from being worn to a nub, seemed to be rejuvenated. "We must've nailed up five hundred posters, Julia," he told me, happily exaggerating. "And when we parked out at the mall, we couldn't give away yard signs fast enough. You should've seen Latisha handing them out right and left. That little girl is a worker."

There was a din of talking and laughing as they gathered around the kitchen table, fixing their hot dogs from the array that I'd laid out. Even Trixie joined in occasionally, which was enough to make me think that there were possibly more makeovers going on than my own. Maybe she was coming out of her shell, although Rodney didn't seem to notice. He was, however, noticeably attentive to Sam, listening respectfully when he spoke, making sure Sam's glass stayed full of tea, and sliding a few words now and then into the conversation about the wisdom of being prepared for the inevitable.

It was a relief when Sam took Latisha home, when Lloyd helped me straighten the kitchen then went upstairs to bed, when Trixie huffed off to her room because Rodney, pleading fatigue, said he had to check on the funeral scheduled for the following day and took himself off without her.

As Sam and I prepared for bed, I handed him a sizable check made out to the Sam Murdoch Campaign Fund.

"What's this?" he asked.

"It's a tangible indication of where my heart is."

"Julia," he said, laughing, "I know where your heart is. And the two of us set up a fund when I announced, so you don't need to contribute any more."

"Why? Is there a limit?"

"No, not for a spouse."

"Well, then take it, because I want to give it."

"In that case, thank you," Sam said, accepting the check. "But I'd rather get small contributions from a lot of voters than big ones from a few."

"But you wouldn't mind if a few big ones came in, would you?"

"Not one bit," he said. We both laughed, then went to bed. Instead of going to sleep, though, Sam still wanted to talk. He asked me about Jimmy Ray's ads—something I'd planned to discuss the next day when he was rested. Nothing would do, though, but that I recite every word and describe every visual of his opponent's ad campaign.

"So, Sam," I wound up, "you have to get on television, too. I hope you know some capable people who can put together attractive and informative ads. You're so much more photogenic than Jimmy Ray that people will vote for you on that basis alone."

Far from upset over being upstaged by Jimmy Ray, Sam laughed
and hugged me, assuring me that his ads would be things of wonder and for me not to give Mooney another thought.

Easy to say, but hard to do. Jimmy Ray was far ahead of Sam
in getting his name out over the airwaves, and as far as I knew, far
ahead of him in committed voters. I didn't mention my fears or my
intention of increasing the size of his campaign chest—just listened to him as he spoke warmly of Rodney, who had eagerly
pointed out tackable places for Sam's posters and who had apparently done most of the day's work.

"I'm impressed with that young man, Julia," Sam said. "And so
is Trixie, as I'm sure you've noticed. I couldn't decide on his feelings
for her—he was solicitous of her, but not overtly affectionate.
Which is too bad, because he's just what her grandmother ordered."

"Yes, well, be careful, Sam. There's no need to buy burial insurance just because you like the salesman."

He laughed again. "He didn't let me forget that sooner or later
you and I would have need of it."

"So will everybody else, but count me out. I'll take care of my
own funeral."

We finally went to sleep, but my own plans for vote getting
continued to run through my head.

Sunday morning dawned hot and still, the sky as clear as a bell.
When I came downstairs, I found Lloyd dressed and ready for
church, announcing that he would have lunch at his mother's
house afterward. Trixie, too, was already in the kitchen, eating
cold cereal, but in no way prepared for a church service. She was
wearing either another workout outfit or the same one she'd worn
the day before.

Before I could say anything, she gave me a squinched-eyed
stare and said, "I have to work this morning. Not everybody goes
to church, you know. A lot of people only have Sunday mornings
to exercise."

I just nodded, because what do you say to that? I wanted her working, so I could hardly object to the hours assigned to her. But, my goodness, spandex, or whatever it was, did not lend itself to Trixie's frame, especially on a day normally devoted to one's best.

Which reminded me that I should talk more with Hazel Marie about Trixie's makeover. She had started out enthusiastically with Hazel Marie, but then had seemed to ignore any suggestions for betterment and had gone her own headstrong way. Now that she was seeing a young man, though, she might be more amenable to taking advice.

So it was only Sam, Lloyd, and me sitting after Sunday school in our regular pew for the service. I declare, I can't tell you what Pastor Ledbetter preached on—my mind was too busy making plans and rehearsing what I should say to each person I planned to approach. I had almost made my pitch to the members of the Lila Mae Harding Sunday school class, since most of my friends were there and I could've reached them all in one fell swoop. At the last minute, though, I'd thought better of it—some would've been offended if I'd brought up politics either before or after the lesson, and if the shoe had been on the other foot I would've been, too. Besides, the lesson had been on giving to the poor, and Sam hardly qualified.

When the service was over and Lloyd had scampered off to his mother's, Sam suggested that we go out for lunch. That suited me, so we joined the long line of churchgoers at the S&W cafeteria, speaking to people we knew and slowly shuffling along to the serving tables. It had once occurred to me to suggest to Pastor Ledbetter that he shorten the Sunday morning service by about ten minutes, so we could get to the cafeteria before the Baptist and Methodist churches let out. He'd just stared at me a few seconds, then said, "It'd work just as well if I lengthened the service by ten minutes. That way, the line would be cleared out by the time you got there." I'd stared back and said, "Given the choice, let's keep it the way it is."

On our way home after a nice Sunday dinner, Sam drove by the erstwhile gas station at the end of Main Street where Susan Odell had her fitness center. FIT, ABLE, & HEALTHY, which sounded like a law firm, was printed on a large banner strung across the front of the station. Long-emptied gas pumps testified to the station's former purpose, but several cars parked along the edge of the paved lot confirmed Trixie's expectation of Sunday morning exercisers.

But the overall appearance was not what took my attention, for out in the lot were the exercisers themselves—young women in the same skimpy attire as Trixie—and you wouldn't believe what they were doing. Several of them—including Trixie, wet with sweat—were squatting down, knees aspraddle to get enough leverage to lift upright, then push over these monstrous tractor tires. The tires stood upright for a second then fell over with a crash, after which the women squatted and struggled to lift them upright again. Others, all in a line, pranced around the lot carrying in both hands some kind of heavy weight while they *skipped* along, highly conscious of being the center of attention to every passing car.

"They Lord," I said to Sam, "have you ever seen such a spectacle?" I couldn't for the life of me see why young women would want to parade around in public exerting themselves in such an outlandish fashion. The whole scene reminded me of Latisha wanting to ride in the bed of the pickup just so she could be seen.

Sam chuckled as he drove on past. "Let's just hope Trixie enjoys it enough to stick with it."

I nodded agreement. "That's on my prayer list."

Chapter 25

Later that afternoon, Trixie came home, quickly showered, dressed, and parked herself by the front window to watch for Rodney's arrival.

"Trixie," I ventured, careful to keep the least hint of criticism out of my voice, "it might be better to wait upstairs and let us call you when Rodney gets here."

She frowned, cutting her eyes at me, then turned back to the window. "Why?"

"Well, it doesn't do to appear too eager. Young men expect to wait, and waiting increases the suspense of getting to see you again. And, well, I don't know. It's just always been the way things are done."

She mulled that over, then said, "How long?"

"Oh, just a minute or two. I'll answer the door and invite him in, then usher him into the living room where he can visit with Sam while I run up and get you. And see," I went on, "that way you can come down the stairs and appear suddenly in the doorway. Rodney will immediately get to his feet and give you a big smile."

Trixie frowned again, thinking about it, then said, "Okay." And up the stairs she went.

And it happened just that way, although as soon as Rodney rang the doorbell I glanced upstairs to see Trixie's bedroom door already open—her way of getting ready to dash down the stairs as soon as she was called.

I delayed calling her for a few minutes, because as soon as Rodney was seated, he began talking to Sam. Explaining his sedate dress—a dark gray suit with a light gray tie—Rodney made sure that we knew he'd just conducted a funeral. He was a somber picture of a mortician, but that didn't curb his enthusiasm for discussing his newest venture with Sam.

"I'm thinking," Rodney said, as he leaned forward in his chair, intent on gaining Sam's interest, "that Abbot County could use another funeral home, located maybe out toward Delmont. McCrory's gets all their business now and I tell you it's booming—the demographic out that way tends toward the elderly. So I'm thinking of organizing a consortium of investors to purchase some land out there and putting up a nice Colonial-type house that looks nothing like a funeral home. We wouldn't want any kind of commercial or modern-looking building. The bereaved feel better in a homey, family kind of setting."

Sam just nodded, but Rodney needed no further encouragement. "Yes, I'd like enough land to have a scattering garden with a few appropriate statues and benches for the bereaved to rest on while they commune with their departed. And with enough land, we could have our own cemetery—with perpetual care offered, of course. I've been looking around and I've found the perfect place out on Springer Road. It's level and I think it's big enough. I guess you know you have to have not less than thirty acres to get a license from the state cemetery commission. And they're firm about that." Rodney grimaced at the picky requirements of government bureaucracy. "Anyway, it's close to the highway for easy access, and we wouldn't have to tear down anything—just move out some mobile homes and we'd be in business."

Sam's eyes slid toward me, and I knew he was about to laugh. I jumped up and said, "Excuse me. I'll get Trixie."

She was waiting at the top of the stairs and as soon as she saw me in the hall, down she came. "You look very nice," I whispered, only half truthfully. "There's no need to sit and visit any longer. You and Rodney can go right on with your plans."

And so they did, but as I returned from seeing them off and Sam had retaken his chair, I was fuming.

"You know what he was talking about, don't you?" I demanded. "He had to be talking about the Hillandale Trailer Park—*my* trailer park where Etta Mae and a dozen other people live!"

Sam grinned. "I know, but I don't think he did."

"I'm not so sure. He's probably been to the county clerk's office and looked up the owner, the taxes I've paid, and everything else about it."

"Oh, I don't know. I think he was trying to get me interested in investing in his project, and just threw out that land as an enticement."

"Well, he can just throw it back in. I'm not selling, so if you do get involved you can nip that in the bud. I wouldn't any more evict Etta Mae than I would fly. And you know how I feel about flying."

"Don't worry about it," Sam said, still amused. "I'm not getting involved in anything. I have enough on my plate as it is."

"I know," I said, sitting down and calming myself, "but Rodney has certainly latched on to you, and he's likely to pester you to death about investing in his project."

"Well, let him pester. It just rolls on past me. Besides, the senate race is all I can handle."

"But, Sam," I said, "have you noticed that he seems more interested in you than in Trixie? You don't suppose he's calling on her just to get to you, do you?"

"Oh, I doubt that. Although," Sam went on in a musing way, "I can't help but wonder what he sees in her—they don't appear to have much in common."

"My sentiments exactly. They're as mismatched as, well, as I thought you and I were."

Sam's eyes twinkled as a smile spread across his face. "Just goes to show, doesn't it?"

About nine-thirty that evening, while Sam and I sat in the library, the television set almost muted as he read and I worked on a needlepoint piece, we heard the front door open. Rodney had brought Trixie home, then lingered in the hall while they whispered for a few minutes. I stuck my needle into the canvas and waited, assuming that Rodney would soon come in and pick up where he'd left off with Sam.

Instead, only Trixie appeared, surprising me, as she usually went straight upstairs, never bothering to speak or to wish us a good night.

"Come in, Trixie," Sam said, putting aside his book. "Did you have a good time?"

She half sidled into the room, giving me a brief glance, but obviously intent on Sam.

"Rodney said I ought to be looking for more opportunities," she said, easing onto a chair beside Sam. "He said to talk it over with you."

"I'll be glad to help if I can, Trixie. What do you have in mind?"

The better question is what does Rodney have in mind? I thought and took another stitch.

"Well," Trixie said, squirming in her chair, "Rodney thinks the fitness business is gonna run its course pretty soon if something's not done to perk it up. So he thinks I ought to think about opening a hot yoga room somewhere—kinda as a sideline. I could keep working for Susan Odell and get some of her customers."

"Hot yoga?" Sam asked, his eyebrows practically up to his hairline.

"Yeah, what it is, see, is a place where you do regular yoga, but you turn the heat up high. That way you sweat out all the poisons, and it leaves you clean in mind and body."

And limp as a dishrag, I thought.

"I guess that's something new," Sam said. "What would you need—a rented place with a good heating system?"

"I guess, and some yoga mats. Maybe a water fountain and a drinks machine—you're supposed to keep the heat up real high."

"How high?"

"I don't know," Trixie said, shrugging. "Eighty or ninety degrees, I guess. Maybe more. I'd have to find out."

It was ninety-two degrees this very day. Trixie could've yogaed to her heart's content in the backyard.

"Well, here's the thing, Trixie," Sam said, seemingly giving her business plan serious consideration. "What's your background in yoga? Do you know it well enough to teach it?"

"Uh-uh, I never done it before."

"Oh," Sam said, his eyebrows on their way up again. "Well, I think you have to have a lot of experience before you can offer instruction to other people. Don't you think?"

"I guess." She lowered her head, then said, "Rodney thinks I could learn real quick, but I don't know as I want to."

"Well, my advice, if you want it, is not to go into a business until you know it backward and forward. And you have to really want to make it work. I think, if I were you, I'd find something I wanted to do, train myself in it, and then open up for business."

"I'll tell him."

"But, Trixie," Sam went on, "I'm glad you're thinking of your future and what you'd like to do. Is there anything you're really interested in?"

Her head came up and, if I wasn't mistaken, her eyes began to shine. "Yeah, I been thinking about it and I want to be a cosmetician or a beautician or whatever you call 'em and work with Rodney. He says it's a wide-open field, 'cause not many beauticians want to work on dead people. But I could do it. It wouldn't bother me at all, and Rodney would be there to keep me comp'ny, so even if I had to do it at night I wouldn't be afraid."

They Lord, I thought, jabbing my needle into the canvas.

Sam, ever considerate of her feelings, said kindly, "I think you have to have a license to be a cosmetician, Trixie. Which means going to beauty school. Are you willing to do that?"

"You got one around here? I don't want to go off somewhere."

"There might be one. We could find out if you're really interested."

"Oh, I am, and I could have business cards with my name on 'em, something like Beautician for the Bereaved or something. And I could pass 'em out at funerals. You know, so people in the right frame of mind would have 'em for future reference. Rodney says you have to advertise yourself."

"Well," Sam said, clearing his throat, "the first thing to do is look into getting yourself trained. Why don't you check the yellow pages for beauty schools, then go from there."

"Okay," she said and hopped up from her chair. "But Rodney already said I could have a job at his funeral home when he gets it. I oughta be trained by the time he opens for business, and if I'm not, he could show me how to do it." She stood for a few seconds, apparently thinking it over while one hand scratched her other arm. "And if I'm not too good at it at first, it won't matter. It's not like a dead person would be a return customer anyway."

And off she went to bed, while Sam and I just sat and looked at each other, too stunned to say a word.

Chapter 26

The next morning, as soon as Sam was off to plan his ad campaign and Lloyd, who'd spent the night at his mother's, had called to say he was meeting friends at the tennis courts, I picked up the phone to start my own campaign.

"LuAnne?" I said when she answered her phone. "I've been thinking about you and thought I might run up for a visit this morning if you're not busy."

"Well, how nice, Julia, but I'm on my way out the door right now. I've got to get to the post office and the bank, then pick up at the dry cleaner's. It's one of those days, don't you know. But I tell you what. Why don't I drop by your house when I get through, maybe in a couple of hours?"

"That'd be lovely," I said, delighted that I wouldn't have to make the drive up the mountain to her condo. "Why don't you plan to have lunch with me? We'll have something light and have time to catch up with each other."

So it was settled and I went into the kitchen to ask Lillian to plan for a luncheon guest. But with plenty of empty time before LuAnne appeared, I didn't want to lose momentum. So I went back to the library and dialed Miss Mattie Freeman's number, preparing myself to be frustrated. Miss Mattie was either hard of hearing or intentionally dense so she could get out of doing something she didn't want to do.

"Miss Mattie? It's Julia. How are you?" I began when she answered. "No, Julia Murdoch. We talked yesterday at Sunday school, remember?"

"Oh," she said, "of course. Sorry, but I always think of you as Julia Springer. If you're having a party, I'd love to come. When is it? I'll get my calendar."

Miss Mattie lived for parties, and no one would dare have anything without inviting her. This time, though, she was going to be disappointed. I didn't have time to plan a party . . . although, I mused while waiting for her to return to the phone, maybe I should have something for Sam. And if I did, I told myself, I'd be up front about its purpose. I'd never invite people to a social affair, then spring a political harangue on them as some people had been known to do.

"No, Miss Mattie," I said when she picked up the phone again. "I'm *thinking* of having a party, but I'm just in the planning stage. Right now, though, I'm contacting people I know we can count on to tell them that Sam is running for the North Carolina senate and, as much as I hate doing it, asking them for a donation to his campaign. Would you be interested in contributing to his senate race?"

"Race? What are you talking about? Like a Walk for Hunger thing?"

"No, no. It's to support Sam so he can represent us and do some good for the people of the district. There're an awful lot of people who need help and they're not getting it. It's up to us to see that they do."

"What? What? I'm already tithing, Julia, yet every time I turn around, the church is asking for more. I'm about tired of it."

"It's not for the church, Miss Mattie. It's for Sam."

"Sam? Why? Is he broke? I told him years ago to stay out of the stock market. But, Julia, you have a nerve asking for money for him. He's your husband, not mine."

By the time I got off the phone with her, I still wasn't sure that she'd fully understood. Nonetheless, she'd finally promised to send a small check to Sam's campaign. It was, however, one of the most unsatisfactory calls I'd ever made, and I wondered if I was cut out for this kind of solicitation.

Taking a determined breath, though, I dialed Mr. Pickens's office number, expecting to get his answering service.

I got him instead. "Pickens Investigations, Pickens speaking," he said, sounding abrupt and professional.

"Mr. Pickens, it's Julia Murdoch. How are you?"

"Ah, Miss Julia," he said, and I could picture him leaning back in his creaky chair. "What can I do for you? You having trouble?"

"Oh, no. No trouble, it's just . . . well, maybe I am." And I went on to explain that Sam was far behind Jimmy Ray in his race for the senate and that I was asking, though I hated to do it, for campaign contributions.

"Why, sure," Mr. Pickens said, lightening my heart, "we've already sent something in, but I think we can manage a little more. I tell you what's a fact, Miss Julia, we need somebody down there who knows what he's doing."

I heartily agreed and hung up, feeling reassured that I was on the right track.

When LuAnne arrived a little after eleven-thirty, she came in wiping her face with a Kleenex. "I'm about to melt," she announced and, heaving a big sigh, sat down on the sofa. "It's good to sit for a minute and catch my breath. I just hate these days when it's one chore after another, don't you? But I'm glad to get them done. How are you, Julia, I never see you anymore except at church when we don't have time to talk. Have you heard about Thurlow?" She leaned forward and, without giving me time to respond, went right on. "I heard that he's about to make a big contribution to the town—some kind of park or something, maybe for skateboarders or for bicycle or walking trails, I don't know. Maybe he wants a place for Ronnie to run, something weird like that."

"Why, no," I said, picturing Ronnie, Thurlow's Great Dane, bounding around a racetrack. "I haven't heard anything. But why in the world would he do something like that? I mean, he's strange, but that's a little much even for him. Especially as tight as he is with money."

"Well, don't quote me, because I really don't know. All I've heard is that he's about to make a big contribution for the good of the town. And name it in honor of somebody—like a public servant or something—but nobody knows who."

That struck fear in my heart, because Sam had said that Thurlow was a Mooney supporter, and in the midst of a senate race, who else but Mooney would benefit from a big contribution for the good of the town? And if it was built in his honor, why, Sam might as well go back to fishing. I could just see the bronze plaque:

THE JIMMY RAY MOONEY DOG-WALKING PARK

IN HONOR OF HIS MANY YEARS OF
SERVICE TO THE DISTRICT

With great effort, I managed to keep my anxiety under control. It wouldn't do to let LuAnne know how disturbing her news was— it'd be all over Abbotsville by nightfall that I was worried sick about Sam's chances.

As we sat at the table eating the chicken salad that Lillian had served, I kept wondering how to approach LuAnne about making a campaign contribution to someone who was a long and dear friend and who was also the husband of a long and dear friend. She would, I knew, not respond well to that kind of approach, and would immediately accuse me of imposing on our friendship.

But finally I steeled myself to bringing up the subject, straight out asking for her support in the form of a sizable contribution.

"Oh," she said, putting down her fork, "well, Julia, I'll have to think about it. And talk to Leonard, although he's the least political of anyone I know. But you know Jimmy Ray's doing a good job—at least he's not being investigated. And I'll tell you frankly that I've voted for him every time, so I'll have to give this some thought." She picked up her fork again and moved some salad greens around on her plate, not wanting to look at me. Then she laughed. "Oh, now I get it. Sam's just doing it for the experience, isn't he? I bet he's going to write about it in his book. He doesn't really want the job, does he?"

I had to hold on to the sharp retort that almost got away from me. Instead, I responded as forcefully as I dared, saying, "Why else would he run, LuAnne? Of course he wants the job, and both of us expect our friends to support him, if not with a contribution, at least with their votes."

The visit went downhill after that although the subject changed several times. When she left, the atmosphere was a little huffy, but friendly enough. The only good thing, I told myself as she drove away, was that I had not actually lost Sam a vote, it had just never been there in the first place.

I was about half discouraged by this time, but decided to make one more phone call, then call it quits for the day. And if that didn't work out, I'd have to rethink my bundling efforts.

I dialed Emma Sue Ledbetter's number, hoping to catch her at home. Our preacher's wife was forever on the go doing one good deed after another, then worrying herself to death for not doing enough.

"Emma Sue?" I asked when she answered, although I knew good and well who it was. *Why do we do that?* I wondered. "It's Julia. How're you feeling? We missed you at Sunday school."

"Oh, I'm much better, thanks for asking. I hated missing Sunday school, but when a migraine hits it's just better to give in and let it run its course. Although of course I never like missing a church service. It's the least we can do."

"I know, and you are the most faithful of us all."

"Well, I have to be, don't I?" she said, sighing. "If the minister's wife doesn't go, how could we expect anybody else to? Be that as it may, though, how are you, Julia?"

"Oh, I'm fine, but the reason I'm calling is to ask if you feel you could support Sam in his race for the state senate, and if so," I said, hurrying on to get it all out at once, "would you care to make a contribution to his campaign. It's tax deductible, I think."

"Oh," Emma Sue said, pausing to ponder her response. "Is Sam running? I didn't know that. Well, I tell you, Julia, I try not to mix politics with my faith. Render unto Caesar, you know."

Can you believe that? She was turning me down and doing it on the basis of her faith! And after all Sam and I had done for her and the pastor.

It was all I could do to hold on to my temper, but I managed a cool head and a moderate response. "Yes, I understand, but that's what I'm asking for—Caesar's portion for Sam."

That didn't go over too well and certainly didn't change her mind. She put me off, saying she'd have to talk to Larry and pray about it, then she'd let me know. Which meant it'd probably be the last I heard about it from her.

I put down the phone, completely disheartened, wondering if it had been my methodology that put people off or if the people I thought were our friends really weren't. Whatever it was, I had not done well, either by the bundle or by one small bill after another.

It was time to go see Mildred Allen.

Chapter 27

It was too late in the day to be visiting anybody, so I put off seeing Mildred until the morrow. Supper was a hurried affair that evening since Sam had a meeting to go to, and Lloyd seemed to have something on his mind, and Trixie was even more sullen than usual. Rodney must've been busy with an inconvenient funeral.

When both Sam and Lillian left, I sat alone in the library trying to plan my approach to Mildred. If she turned me down, I didn't know what I would do—decide that Sam and I didn't have a friend in the world, I guessed. All I could think of was *just wait until they want something from me.*

"Miss Julia?" Lloyd came into the library, walked over to my chair, and said, "I need some advice."

"Well," I said with a smile, "you've come to the right place. What can I do for you?"

"It's like this," he said, sitting on the ottoman next to my chair. He looked so serious that I regretted my first flippant response to him. "I don't think I'm ever going to grow. I'm just always going to be smaller and shorter and skinnier than everybody else, and I don't like it. It looks like I'm going to be like this for the rest of my life."

"Oh, I hardly think that. You just haven't reached your growth yet. But don't worry—you will. Boys seem to lag behind girls in that respect, but about the time you're fifteen or sixteen, you're going to have a growth spurt. I've seen it happen a million times."

"That's a long time to wait while everybody else is growing. You know what the tennis coach told me? He said my form was good, but I don't have enough power behind my strokes, and, Miss Julia, I hit that ball as hard as I can. And sometimes it just dinks across the net. It's pretty discouraging."

"I expect it would be. But surely with all your practicing, you'll get better and better." I stopped, almost patting his shoulder until I realized that would be patronizing his feelings. I thought of reminding him that his father had been a small man who had made some unfortunate compensations which Lloyd should avoid, then realized that bringing up hereditary characteristics would offer no comfort. He knew that his mother was a tiny woman, which had probably already convinced him that he had no hope of increasing his stature or his strength. "But, Lloyd," I went on, "the people who do the best in life are those with great moral character and excellent minds, and you have an abundance of both. You don't need to take a backseat to any big, brawny specimens who tower over you."

"I don't 'specially want to be big and brawny. I'd be happy with just half the muscles that Trixie has."

"I expect she'd trade with you. But, seriously, Lloyd, she's in the fitness business, so she might be able to help you build up your muscles."

He ducked his head and grinned. "I don't know about that. I'd be afraid she'd outdo me. But, Miss Julia, here's what I was thinking. I'm thinking of asking Miss Lillian to get me some of those protein drinks. See, they're supposed to build muscles, though I don't guess they'll add anything to my height. But do you think that'd be all right?"

I thought about it. I thought about all those growth hormones they give chickens and cows and bicycle racers, and shivered at the thought of Lloyd being pumped full of who-knew-what just to make over his physique. "I don't know, Lloyd. That could be dangerous to your health."

"No, ma'am, they're not. They're just protein with nothing else added. I wouldn't drink any kind of drugs or anything."

"Then I'll tell you what you should do. Talk to Mr. Pickens, I mean, your father." I had to correct myself, for Mr. Pickens had adopted Lloyd, and it was to him that the child should look, without any reference to the scrawny excuse for a man who'd engendered him. "He's a big man and he was an athlete of some kind when he was young. I expect he'll know exactly what's safe and healthy for you to do."

"You know," Lloyd said, looking up almost in surprise that he'd overlooked the fact that he now had a father to whom he could turn, "I think I will. Thanks, Miss Julia, that's what I'll do. I'm going over there right now. He's home, and all he's doing is reading the paper."

And off he went, confident now that he had a source for masculine advice, and I, too, was confident of the same. If Mr. Pickens didn't know about manly matters, I didn't know who would.

After Lloyd left for his mother's house, I glanced at my watch wondering how late Sam would be. The afternoon had lengthened into twilight, one of those long, soft summer evenings that made me think I should be outside walking and enjoying it. Instead, I sat in the library and gave some thought to adding a back porch to the house, a place to be outside without really being out. Maybe a patio even, where we could eat occasionally, something that would engage Sam in its planning and construction in case he lost the election.

I shook myself for such negative thinking, but I knew I had to be realistic and be prepared for every contingency.

"Hey."

The abrupt greeting startled me. I looked over my shoulder to see Trixie edging around the sofa as she slid into the room.

"Why, Trixie," I said, hiding my surprise. "Come join me. I was getting lonesome down here by myself."

"Me, too."

"It's a lonely evening, isn't it, with everybody gone. Sit down and let's talk. Or would you rather watch television?"

"It's all reruns." But she sat, surprising me again, for she had up to this point avoided my company whenever she could.

Wracking my brain for a comfortable subject on which to converse, I made a stab at one that I knew she was interested in. "Tell me about Rodney. How did you two meet?"

"We matched up."

"Matched up? How did that happen?"

"Just . . . ," she said, shrugging. "I don't know, just matched. You know, our profiles. Rodney said that was because it was meant to be."

So, I thought, the match had been made in cyberspace just as Lloyd suspected.

"Well, that sounds serious," I said lightly, not wanting to put her off since she was so easily put. Yet at the same time, I felt she was heading for a great disppointment and wanted to prepare her for it.

Trixie gave me a glowering look, and I feared she was about to walk out. Almost anything I said to her was taken in the wrong way—she kept me so on edge that I hardly wanted to open my mouth around her.

But she lifted her shoulders and said, "We're serious, all right."

"Well, Trixie, I don't want to throw cold water, but it's awfully fast to be that serious. I'm thinking of your grandmother now, and I know she'd remind you that you and Rodney barely know each other."

"I know all I need to know, and Meemaw would tell me the same thing. We're going into business together just as soon as Rodney builds his funeral home. And he's already found the land he wants, so it won't be long now. And Rodney said he'd hire Meemaw to keep the casket room stocked and Pawpaw to look after the grounds, so we'd all be together."

I was struck dumb, almost. "Here? In Abbotsville?"

She nodded as if having Elsie and Troy Bingham in the same town in which I lived was the most normal thing in the world. But not for me, it wasn't.

"Rodney said," Trixie went on, quoting the oracle again, "that the land he wants is not on the market yet, but he knows how to make a deal. You just offer enough money and you can buy anything you want.

"Anyway," Trixie went on, as she sat slumped over, not looking at me even as she spoke, "none of it can come about 'til he gets that property. That's all that's holdin' him up."

"I imagine so," I said indifferently, because that wasn't all that was holding him up—there was the matter of getting investors willing to risk their money. "People are generally leery about committing financially to an enterprise that's only in the dreaming stage."

"It's more'n just dreamin'," Trixie assured me. "Rodney's already lined up somebody to back him. All he has to do now is go out there and walk the property. You know, measure it and such to make sure it's big enough for what he wants."

"Oh, really?" I asked, raising my eyebrows as I wondered who in the world could be Rodney's silent partner. "All that and it's not even for sale?"

"He'll get it. One way or the other, 'cause he says if you want something bad enough, you'll get it."

"Well," I said, my mouth tightening, "just wanting is not always enough. And you might remind Rodney that taking such liberties with someone else's property could be misinterpreted."

She cut her eyes quickly at me, then just as quickly looked away. Then she suddenly stood up. "I got to go to bed." And off she went without a good night or a kiss my foot.

What was that all about? I wondered, unless it was to let me know that Rodney intended to present me with an offer to purchase. Yet neither she nor Rodney seemed to know who owned the property, and maybe, I suddenly realized, Rodney was looking at an entirely different plot of land—one that had nothing to do with me.

But regardless of where the property was located or who owned it, the thought of the Binghams moving to Abbotsville was enough to make me ill. If they were a part of Rodney's plans, I wouldn't sell even if my property was on the market, which it wasn't.

Maybe, I thought, sitting up straight, I should find out exactly which property Rodney was interested in and, if it wasn't mine, buy it out from under him just to keep the Binghams in Florida.

Of course, he'd just look for another location, so I'd have to keep going behind him, which meant I'd be buying up property piece-meal all over the county.

Maybe I'd eventually run him—and them—out of the state.

The telephone rang then, loud enough in the quiet house to jangle my nerves. Hoping that it wasn't Sam saying he'd be later than expected, I answered it.

"Miss Julia? It's Etta Mae," Etta Mae Wiggins said, her voice stretched tight and thin.

"Why, Etta Mae, how are you?"

"Not so good. Miss Julia, I didn't know you were going to sell the trailer park, and we're all worried sick about where we'll go."

"Sell the trailer park?" My hand tightened on the receiver as I held it. "No, Etta Mae, no, I'm not selling it. Where did you hear such a thing?"

"Well, there was a man out here today with a tape measure. He drove up in a fancy black SUV and walked all over the place, looking at everything and measuring it, and he told us we ought to be looking for a new place for our trailers because he was buying it to put a cemetery on it. Or in it."

That confirmation just flew all over me, and it was all I could do to hold myself together. "I know exactly who that was, Etta Mae, and he has no right to even be on the property, much less to tell you you'll have to move. That land is not for sale, and I have no plans to put it up for sale—not as long as you are there, anyway."

And I meant that. Etta Mae Wiggins had proved over and over to be a stalwart friend. We were nowhere near the same age, nor were we of the same background, yet we thought alike and we were both willing to risk life and limb for the other. She had demonstrated that over and over in our several escapades of the past—often, I admit, at my urging, but still, she was always willing. She and I had gotten off to a poor start, mainly because she had a reputation for a certain amount of looseness in her dealings with men, some of whom she'd married and some she hadn't. I'd had little use for her at the time, especially because she seemed to have eyes for Sam, but that had been before I'd gotten to know her kind and needy heart. All she wanted from life was to be somebody, somebody respected for her innate decency and intrepid spirit—and she had found it in me. Why, what would I have done without her help in chasing jewel thieves or detaching the statue from the courthouse dome or rescuing Mr. Pickens from the clutches of a misinformed sheriff?

I could count on Etta Mae Wiggins, and had, in fact, made her the manager of the trailer park, reducing her rent, and paying her a minimal wage to keep the place up, and she was doing an excellent job. She'd gotten rid of the riffraff, kept the area free of litter, and markedly cut down on the number of domestic complaint calls to the Abbot County Sheriff's Department. As long as Etta Mae wanted to live at the Hillandale Trailer Park, it was going to be there for her.

So, if Rodney Pace expected to buy that land just because he wanted it, he was going to have to lower his expectations. And deal with me while doing so.

"Etta Mae," I said, picking up our conversation, "you don't have anything to worry about, and you can tell all the other residents out there that *I* said so. Just go on about your business, and let me handle this. I'll put a stop to it in short order, but if you see that man out there again, let me know. I'll have him arrested for trespassing."

"Whew," she said, "I'm sure glad to hear that. I didn't know how I could afford to hire somebody to move my single-wide—it takes a *mint* to do that. Plus find another place as nice as this and lose my manager's job, too. Thanks, Miss Julia, I'll sleep better tonight knowing you'll take care of it."

Assuring her that indeed I would, I hung up the phone and studied the best way of going about taking care of it. My first impulse was to call Rodney and straighten him out in no uncertain terms. But then I reconsidered, realizing that any interference on my part could put a big kink in his relationship with Trixie, and do it just as Sam and I had determined to welcome Trixie's friends into our home. So my next thought was to bide my time and let him commit himself one way or another to my face. Then I would politely but firmly tell him the property wasn't for sale, and that would be that.

Maybe in the meantime, he would have learned, if he didn't already know, who owned the property. Learning who owned it could put a damper on his whole enterprise, unless . . . unless that had been the driving force behind his interest in Trixie all along. That very thought made me ill for her sake, but I had to consider the possibility.

During all of this deep and troubling thinking, I had held myself together well enough, but I made one great determination right then and there: if Rodney thought he was going to put a mortuary, scattering garden, crematorium, cemetery, or anything else on *my* property, he was sadly and eternally mistaken. Mr. Rodney Pace had just about gotten too big for his britches.

Chapter 28

By the time Sam came in from his meeting, I was already upstairs grimly preparing for bed. "Thank goodness you're home," I said, tightening my robe as he entered the bedroom. Then I launched into a litany of outrage.

"You won't believe this, Sam, but I just had a call from Etta Mae telling me that Rodney's been out there measuring my property and"—I stopped and took a deep breath—"*and* he had the nerve to tell her to get ready to move, and not only her but all the other residents. And, even worse than that, Trixie told me that Rodney's going to hire Elsie and Troy to work at his mortuary, and that means they'll be moving here, and the very thought of it makes my head hurt. And LuAnne told me that Thurlow is donating some kind of park to the city and I think he's planning to name it for Jimmy Ray in honor of his service to the district, and, futhermore, it would be just like Thurlow to announce it right before the election." I stopped and tried to think if anything else had happened. "And, well, I guess that's all. How was your meeting?"

"Fine," he said, loosening his tie, "very good, in fact. We'll have a television ad on the air in a week or so. And some radio ads, too. But it sounds as if you've had a busy evening."

"I have," I agreed. "I doubt I'll ever get to sleep. There's so much going on that I don't know which one to worry about the most."

"Well, hop in bed and let me brush my teeth. Then we'll talk about it." Sam headed for the bathroom as I hung up his jacket.

When we were both in bed, propped up on pillows side by side—our favorite place to talk over any problems—I thought again of how special such times were, even when the problems we dealt with were dire and unsettling. A brief memory of my first marriage flashed through my mind—Wesley Lloyd Springer believed that you went to bed to sleep, not to talk or to read or to do anything else except on infrequent occasions, and even then he hadn't had much to say.

"Okay," Sam said, taking my hand, "tell me all about it."

"I hardly know where to start, but let me ask you. Have you noticed how Trixie has gone from one thing to another? First she wanted to be a fitness trainee, then she wanted to switch to some hot box yoga business, now she wants to be a beautician to the dead. What in the world is she thinking? She's not trained for anything, and she doesn't light on anything long enough to get trained. I think that any time Rodney mentions something, she just latches on to it."

Sam nodded. "Probably. And we don't know if he's just talking in general or if he's actively encouraging her. One thing's for sure, though, she is entirely too dependent on what he says. And did he really promise to hire her grandparents?"

"That's what she told me. Oh, Sam, I couldn't stand having them around. You better win this election or I'll have to move to Raleigh without you."

He laughed. "Without me? Not a chance. Now, listen, put the Binghams on the back burner. That's a long way off, if it ever happens. I have a feeling that Rodney just talks a lot about his plans and all the possibilities he can dream up, and Trixie hears what she wants to hear. She's headed for a great disappointment, I'm afraid."

"So is he, because if all his plans hinge on getting the Springer Road property, he might as well pack it in. Sam, how much land is out there, anyway?"

"I'll have to look at the plat, but probably close to thirty acres or so. Maybe a little more."

I looked at him in surprise, as well as some dismay, because I'd hoped it wouldn't meet Rodney's criteria. "That much? Surely the trailer park isn't that big."

"No, most of it's woods. Actually, I did a little research on the state requirements for a cemetery, and Rodney's going to need a lot more than thirty acres—that's the minimum for a cemetery itself. It wouldn't include room for a mortuary, crematorium, scattering garden, parking area, and all the other big dreams he has. Unless, of course, he plans to locate that part of the business elsewhere, which is what a lot of mortuary owners do. Your property would probably be workable if he wants it just for grave sites, but not for anything else."

I pictured the location on Springer Road—the clearing where the mobile homes were located was densely surrounded by pine trees, cedars, and hemlocks with a scattering of dogwoods that bloomed in the spring—a lovely pastoral setting marred only by single- and double-wide trailers and their hook-ups. I'd had the woods underbrushed several years before and now hoped that the blackberry bushes and briars had grown back thick enough to discourage Rodney.

"I think," Sam went on, "there's an old homestead back in there somewhere, maybe just a chimney still standing. And there may be some hardwood, too, in case you ever wanted to clear it for timber."

"I don't."

Sam grinned at me. "Well, I'll tell you, it would take an awful lot of effort and money to turn that place into a grassy cemetery. Think of all the stumps that would have to come up."

That thought cheered me considerably, and I finally got to sleep, picturing Rodney, hot and sweaty, swinging a pickax.

Knowing that Mildred was not an early riser, I called her late on the following morning to see when would be a convenient time for me to visit.

"Come right now," she said brightly. "I've just finished breakfast, and if we wait too long it'll run into your lunchtime." She laughed. "We seem to operate on different schedules, Julia."

I knew that, which was one reason I never visited Mildred without calling. Another reason was that I never visited *anyone* without a call first. Drop-in guests, and I'm including LuAnne, are never quite as welcome as ones who are expected.

"Good morning, Ida Lee," I said when Mildred's housekeeper opened the door. "How are you?"

"Quite well, thank you," the lovely and efficient Ida Lee greeted me. "Mrs. Allen is looking forward to seeing you—she's in the morning room."

I followed Ida Lee across the spacious foyer to the small room beyond the curving staircase. Mildred was sitting in a cushioned wicker chair, a tea service on a table beside her. A row of windows behind her revealed the well-kept grounds surrounded by a box-wood hedge with flowering shrubs and ornamental trees strategically placed.

Mildred smiled as I entered, saying, "I would get up if it wasn't so much trouble and you weren't such a close friend."

"Stay right where you are," I said, taking a chair beside her. "No need to get up for me." Mildred was a heavyset woman who hated to move once she was settled, so she stayed settled most of the day.

"Mildred, your yard is lovely," I went on. "If I were you I'd sit here all day and admire it."

"I just about do," she said, laughing as she reached for the teapot. "I thought tea would be nice for a change. Around this time every summer, I've about had my fill of lemonade."

"So," I said as we sipped from Mildred's porcelain cups, my hands shaking just a tiny bit. The worst thing, to my mind, was being in a position of having to ask for money. "I expect you know I've come for a special reason. And I hope I'm not imposing, but, Mildred, I'm afraid Sam's running behind in the senate race, and I'm worried about it."

"How much do you need?"

"Oh," I said, taken aback, "am I that obvious?"

"Elections take money, Julia. No one knows that better than I do. I've already contributed to his campaign, but I don't think I've reached the limit. If I have, then I'll send more from Horace and Tonya."

"Oh, Mildred," I said, a wave of gratitude washing over me. "You don't know how much I hate asking for financial help, or how much I appreciate your generosity. I want to assure you that Sam does not know I'm doing this, but I'm sure he'll know who his contributors are and he'll be ever so grateful."

Mildred gave a languid wave of her hand. "Just tell him I expect to be invited to the Inaugural Ball, regardless of who wins the governorship. And there might be a few more favors along the way. I'll let him know as I think of them."

I was really getting a lesson in the art of politics, because even though Mildred was smiling, I knew she meant what she said. She would expect to have a state senator at her beck and call, and I wondered if she'd covered all the bases by contributing equally to the Mooney campaign.

I thought about that on my way home—which was just down Mildred's drive to the sidewalk, then a few yards to my house— but it was long enough to give me an idea of how to approach Thurlow Jones. With that idea in mind, as well as with the elation of having gotten a sizable contribution just by asking, I walked past my house, turned the corner, then another, and went straight to Thurlow's house before I lost my nerve.

For the first time ever, I found him puttering around in his large yard with pruning shears in his hand. It was about time that somebody did something about the overgrown place. I had to untangle an out-of-control wisteria vine from my hair when I opened the front gate.

Thurlow looked up as the gate squealed in protest as I entered. "Well, well, the Lady Murdoch draws nigh," he announced with his usual mockery. "To what do I owe this unusual visit? I don't normally receive unexpected visitors, but I'll make an exception for you."

He dropped the pruning shears where he stood, then came over to the brick walk, studded with weeds, where I waited. I was a little discomposed, since I had only recently prided myself on my courteous habit of calling before a visit. But, I assured myself, Thurlow wouldn't know a courtesy if it bit him.

"Thurlow," I started strongly, "I'm well aware that you are a Mooney supporter, but I think you should give some thought to supporting Sam's campaign, too. That's what big corporations do: give to both sides so they'll have access regardless of the winner. Besides, you know Sam, and you know he'd make a better senator than Jimmy Ray any day of the week."

"Oh, so that's what you're here for. I shoulda known you wouldn't give me the time of day 'less you wanted something. Well, dear lady, I always put my money on the winning horse, and that ain't Sam Murdoch."

That *dear lady* put my back straight up, and his effrontery in presuming that Sam would lose just flew all over me.

"You don't know that, and, furthermore, it would be a fair race if you'd stay out of it. I heard about that park you're planning, and I know that Jimmy Ray wouldn't stand a chance without your backing, and I think it's a crying shame that you have more say-so in an election than all the voters in the district. And, and, well, that's what I think."

He threw back his head and cackled, loud and long, and if those pruning shears had been at hand I might've been tempted to use them. Instead, I turned and walked off, my head held high, even though humiliated as usual after any run-in with him.

"I'll think about it," he yelled behind me, but I knew better than to count on any help from him.

Chapter 29

"I'm glad you fin'lly home," Lillian said, looking up from the sink as I walked into the kitchen.

"Why? What's going on?"

"Let me get this mess cleaned up," she said, as she gathered a pile of husks from the corn ears she'd just shucked and dumped them into a waste can.

Wiping her hands with a towel, Lillian said, "Miss Trixie jus' come home cryin'."

"Oh, my, I was afraid that was coming sooner or later. What did she say?"

"She don't say nothin' to me. I jus' see her come flyin' through here, her face all red and drippy. She run upstairs an' I hear the door slam. That's all I know."

I plopped down in a chair by the table, wondering if I had the energy to deal with Trixie so soon after my confrontation with Thurlow.

"You want some lunch?" Lillian asked. "I don't know where you been, but it past time for it."

"Yes, I guess I do. Just a bite, though, enough to see me through whatever's going on with Trixie. But if I had to guess, it'll be something to do with Rodney. Oh, me, Lillian," I said mournfully, "I'm not cut out for this, or for electioneering, either."

"What you mean?" Lillian said, glancing at me as she prepared a sandwich.

"I mean giving advice to the lovelorn, for one, and for another, trying to talk friends—longtime *good* friends, too—into supporting Sam for the senate. You'd think they'd be eager to have him represent them, but, no, they have to think about it or talk to their husbands about it or pray about it. All except," I said with a heaving breath, "Mildred, bless her heart. She just asked how much I wanted and wrote a check."

"Miz Allen, she a good lady. But you don't need to worry 'bout Mr. Sam, everybody I know gonna vote for him. I tell 'em they better."

"Well, that's reassuring," I said, leaving half the sandwich as I stood up. "Thank you, Lillian, more than I can say. Now, I better get up there and see about Trixie."

After trudging up the stairs, I tapped on Trixie's door, softly calling her name. When no answer was forthcoming, I opened the door and walked in. She was on the bed, turned toward the wall, her shoulders heaving with shuddering and, as I approached, increasingly loud sobs.

"Trixie? Honey?" I murmured as I leaned over her. "What's wrong?"

No answer, just more sobbing. I sat on the side of the bed and put my hand on her shoulder. "Can you tell me what the matter is? Maybe I can help."

"*Nobody* can help! Not you, anyway. You don't even care what happens to me."

"Well, but I do. I don't like seeing you so unhappy. Tell me and let's see what we can do."

"Susan Odell *fired* me!" Trixie screamed. "They's nothing you can do about *that*!"

I was taken aback, not expecting such news. From what I'd seen, Trixie could lift and turn tractor tires as well or better than any of the other exercisers. "I don't understand," I said with true sympathy, "you've been doing so well there. What reason did she give?"

Trixie half turned toward me, revealing her red, mottled face with no embarrassment. If it'd been me, I'd have covered up. "She said," Trixie said, sniffing as she stumbled on the words, "she said I wasn't responding like I ought to."

"I don't know what that means."

"It *means*," Trixie practically shouted in my face, "I didn't get thin like I was s'pposed to! And it means I'm too ugly to work for her!"

"Oh, no," I said, drawing back, shocked. "She couldn't have meant that. No one would be that cruel. Besides, it's not true."

"Yes, it is," she said, lying back, seemingly resigned to Susan Odell's verdict. " 'Course she don't know it, but I was gonna quit anyway and go work for Rodney."

"Ah, Rodney." I sighed, wondering what was to come next. "I would think he'd reassure you. He's been so helpful and interested in you and your future."

"Not no more, he's not. He thinks the same thing she does."

"I find that hard to believe, as attentive as he's been to you. What does he say about your losing your job?"

"Nothin'. He don't know." Her fingers picked at the picot edging of the sheet, and I heard for the first time real pain in her words. "He said . . ." She stopped as tears flooded her streaked face. "He told me we ought to see other people." She took a long, wracking breath that moved me. "And I don't have nobody else to see."

"I'm so sorry," I said, and tried to think of something encouraging to say, even as I had a surge of joy that the Binghams would stay where they were. "Well, Trixie, I've found that young men often get cold feet just as they're about to commit themselves to someone. Maybe that's what's happening with him. Maybe he thinks things were moving too fast, and he needs to step back a bit to be sure of his feelings, and yours."

"He knows mine."

"I'm sure he does, but marriage—if that's what you're thinking of—is a big step for a young man with so many irons in the fire. He has such big plans that maybe he's afraid to take on anything else for a while."

She gave me a speculative glance that I couldn't interpret, but I could see that the tears on her face were beginning to dry up. "You reckon?" she asked, frowning. Then, right before my eyes, her face began to clear. "I bet that's what it is. I bet he's got too much on his mind right now. He probably wants to get his ducks in a row before taking on anything else."

I nodded. That's what I'd just said.

"So I'll just wait till he's ready." Trixie's eyes lit up at the thought. "And as soon as he straightens things out, he'll have time for me—he'll need me then. Besides, it don't matter what he said, I'm still gonna help him. He won't be scared to take me on then."

"I'm glad to hear it. The thing to do is to make your own plans, work on yourself and your feelings, and try, as best you can, not to let him know how devastated you are. Nothing intrigues a young man more than to have his former girlfriend appear to do well without him."

"Yeah," she said with some strength as she pushed herself into a sitting position, "he'll be sorry when he hears about it. Then he'll want me back, see if he don't."

There was no telling what she had in mind, and I didn't care to ask. Instead, I suggested she talk again with Hazel Marie. "I know you weren't enthusiastic about the changes she suggested at first, but it might be worth a try."

"I wadn't, 'cause Meemaw always said natural's better'n unnatural. She don't like a whole lot of primping and putting on, either, but, like you said, that's what she sent me up here for. And if she finds out I let Rodney get away, she'll be mad as fire, so I better do something whether she likes it or not."

"I couldn't agree more," I said, hoping I'd heard the last of what Meemaw wanted. "Let's ask Hazel Marie to give you a complete makeover. It might not bring Rodney back, but it'll make him think twice when he sees you. And it'll give you something to do, and make you feel a whole lot better."

"Okay. Can we go now?"

"Well, no, it's too late in the day to start something like that. I'll call Hazel Marie, though, and maybe she can see you first thing in the morning."

"Tell her I want the works—whatever she wants to do, I want it. And when I get all fixed up, I'm gonna go show ole lady Odell what I look like so she can eat dirt." Her face grew hard, and I heard the screech of teeth against teeth. "Then," she ground out, "I'm gonna let Rodney know what he almost throwed away and watch him come crawlin' back."

My word, I thought, as I made haste to withdraw with the excuse of calling Hazel Marie. I hadn't been wrong to think that Trixie had a lot of anger stockpiled inside her, started by her grandmother, and apparently added to by whomever else crossed her. It gave me pause to realize that I'd probably been one of them.

"Lord, Sam," I said as I came downstairs to find him home. "Trixie's about to go on the warpath, and I don't know whether to rejoice or get out of her way."

Sam put aside the papers he was working on—something to do with the campaign, I assumed. "Oh? What's going on?"

"Well, first thing is she was fired. Or else she quit, which she said she was about to do anyway. And the next thing is that Rodney told her they should see other people, and that seemed the worst. Although if what she said your friend, Susan Odell, told her is true, that would be the worst in my book. I'm not sure I believe that she flat-out told Trixie she's too ugly to flip tractor tires. But it all culminated in her resolving to make them both sorry, and that's when I left." I sat down in a wing chair across from him. "Oh, and now she wants, and I think *expects,* Hazel Marie to work some makeover magic to help her get even."

"That's some pretty heavy blows to hit her all at once," Sam said, stacking his papers and putting them aside. "Should I talk to Ms. Odell?"

"No, I think not. We should stay out of it. Even though I can't imagine that anyone would say such a thing, Trixie feels that's what Ms. Odell meant, so I doubt she'd go back anyway. No, if she's now willing to give Hazel Marie a free hand, let's let that play out and see if it improves not only her looks, but her attitude."

I sighed and went on. "As for Rodney's wanting to see other

people, there's nothing we can do about that, either. Actually, the surprise for me was his interest in her in the first place."

"I'm sorry to say it," Sam said, "but I've wondered about that, too. A mismatch, if there ever was one."

"I believe we've had this conversation before," I said with a smile. "But of course, I agree with you. Well," I went on, rising, "let me call Hazel Marie and see if she's up for it. I couldn't blame her if she's had her fill of Trixie's headstrong ways. And all that sulling up when anybody suggests something for her own good, too."

"By the way," Sam said before I left the room, "you remember Lamar Owens? We picked him up the other day when he'd run out of gas."

I smiled. "You mean the man who offered to vote for you several times?"

"That's the one. He showed up at headquarters today wanting to volunteer. The ladies who were there didn't know what to do with him, even though he told them he could do anything—take out trash, lick envelopes, whatever we needed." Sam laughed. "But they were really done in when he said if we'd put gas in his car he'd bring in voters by the dozen on election day. And make 'em vote right, too."

"How in the world could he do that?"

"That's what they asked him, and he said he just wouldn't drive anybody to the polls until they swore up and down and sideways that they'd vote for me. He said that anybody who'd give a man a round-trip ride for gas was worth electing. And it was you, Julia, who made the round trip that got him on board, so," Sam said, enjoying my dismayed expression, "thank you."

"You're welcome," I said. "I think." Then I did a little teasing of my own. "I'll visit you both when you're in the Atlanta Pen for voter fraud."

Chapter 30

Trixie hadn't come down for supper so, giving her a pass because of her understandable misery, I took a tray up to her.

"I can't eat that," she said as I put the tray on the bedside table. "I'm goin' on a liquid diet."

"Liquid diet? Why?"

" 'Cause it makes you pee a lot, and that makes you lose weight."

I blinked. Lloyd wanted to gain weight, and she wanted to lose it. And both of them were turning to some kind of liquid to accomplish their goals. I wasn't sure it made sense, but what did I know? One thing I did know, however: the word she used was another of those cringe-producing words about which I've already spoken. How much more refined and soothing to the auditory nerves to say *use the ladies'* or simply ask to be excused. I mean, if it has to be mentioned at all.

"Well," I said, not wanting to argue with her, "I brought a glass of tea, so you can start with that. And I talked to Hazel Marie, and she's excited about what you want to do. In fact, she suggested that you move over there for a few days so you can have what she called twenty-four-hour instruction. Would you like to do that?"

"I don't mind. I just as soon live over there as here, anyway."

I did my best to ignore the insult, just rolled my eyes and said, "Well, but let me caution you, Trixie, I emphasized to her that you're serious about this, and she's taking you at your word. She intends to cover everything, not just cosmetic applications and appropriate dress, but posture, table manners, social interactions, elocution, you-name-it, she expects you to be willing to do it all. So I hope you're ready to put yourself totally in her hands. No more wishy-washy, back and forth about it, and no more quitting because you don't like something, or because you think Meemaw won't approve."

"I'm ready, all right, and more'n willing," Trixie said, sounding as if she meant it. "I just hope she knows enough to help me."

"Believe me," I said firmly, "if anybody knows enough, it's Hazel Marie." I thought of the overly made up, gum-chewing woman who had first appeared on my front porch that day when my life turned upside down. I recalled the brassy hair—teased within an inch of its life—the tight, thigh-revealing dress with cleavage that had made my eyes pop, the long painted nails on her hands and the same peeking out of the open-toed shoes she teetered on.

Oh, yes, Hazel Marie knew about makeovers. She'd made herself over from the inside out, and she hadn't needed an instructor to do it for her, either. She'd watched, listened, read, and, I must admit, conformed to my example and heeded my carefully worded advice. Now she was a model of gracious beauty, carriage, and conduct. Not, I hasten to add, that she'd given up dyed hair, cosmetics, and tight-fitting clothing—far from it. But she now knew the difference between the decorous presentation of oneself and making an in-your-face, inappropriate impression by what she wore, did, and said.

Early the next morning, I helped, or rather watched, Trixie pack to move temporarily to the Pickens house. It crossed my mind to recall all the times I'd dreamed of packing Trixie's things up right before packing Trixie herself off. This wasn't exactly what I'd hoped for, but it would do for the present.

The only thing that concerned me was how Trixie would fit in with an active family like Hazel Marie's. There were the twin baby girls, just toddling around, and Granny Wiggins, Etta Mae's grandmother, who helped with them and who didn't mind adding her two cents' worth to anything that came up. And, of course, there was James, who did the cooking, and Mr. Pickens, who did whatever he wanted. Trixie's joining them made for a potentially volatile situation. But, I reminded myself, it had been Hazel Marie who'd suggested the move, so who was I to demur? Maybe it would work.

And maybe Hazel Marie could work some transforming magic on Trixie, especially now that Trixie had set her eyes on the prize. But what kind of prize? Revenge was what it had sounded like—getting back at both Susan Odell and Rodney.

I could understand wanting to make them regret that they'd treated her so dismissively, but how much more admirable it would've been if Trixie had wanted to improve herself for herself alone. As it was, she seemed to have only one goal in mind, and that was getting even. For that reason, she was putting all her eggs into Hazel Marie's basket, expecting not only to be made over, but made *into* something else entirely.

Hazel Marie, however, was not a miracle worker, and there was only so much she could accomplish, considering what she had to work with. One had to take into account, I mused, the raw material before projecting such an unrealistic result. And, as far as I knew, every effort to transmute base metal into gold had proven to be not only an unsatisfactory pursuit, but entirely futile in the end.

"I'm ready," Trixie said, snapping her hard Samsonite suitcase closed and turning to me, the bulging shopping bag she'd arrived with in her hand. She stood there, waiting, it seemed, to be told what to do next.

"That's pretty much of a load to be carrying," I said. "Don't you want to leave some of it here?"

She shook her head. "I might stay over there."

"Well, now, I wouldn't count on that, Trixie. You'd have to be *invited* to stay." Not, I thought, that she or her grandmother put much stock in invitations. "Remember that Hazel Marie already has a full house, and she's doing you an extraordinary favor by having you for a few days. Let's not expect more than she's able to give."

"I won't be no trouble," Trixie said. "I aim to help out."

"Good, I hope you will. A guest does have responsibilities to her hostess," I said, picturing a table full of dirty dishes and won-dering why she hadn't helped out in my house. "Well, come on and I'll drive you over."

"I'll walk."

"But you have so much to carry."

"Yeah, but it'll make me sweat off some weight."

"Oh, well, maybe it will." Since the day was edging up into the nineties, I had little doubt of it. And, on reflection, I decided that her decision to walk four blocks with her hands full was a hopeful sign of her determination to make some deep changes.

"Off you go then," I said, waving her toward the stairs.

As she bumped the huge suitcase down the stairs, I followed, then opened the front door for her. Mentally biting my tongue, but wanting to set an example of graciousness, I said, "I hope you have a good time, Trixie, but we'll miss you."

"Yeah, okay," she said, then stopped on the porch to look back. "You can come see me over there."

"I'll do that, but I'll call first in case you're busy."

She nodded, then bumped the suitcase down the front steps, gave it a hefty swing, and strode off down the sidewalk.

"Well, Lillian," I said, entering the kitchen and pulling out a chair from the table, "she's gone. Unfortunately, though, not far or long enough. Oh, me," I went on with a sigh, "I hate feeling that way, but Trixie's been the most unsatisfactory houseguest we've ever had."

"She not so bad," Lillian said, setting down two glasses of tea on the table, and taking a chair herself. "She jus' don't know all the ins and outs, an' I tell you something else, she *know* she don't know 'em. So she don't know what she oughta be doin', an' that make her be a little on the snippy side."

"I declare, Lillian, you are the most compassionate and forgiv-ing person I know. Trixie has been ruder to you than to anyone else, and she's been plenty rude to the rest of us."

Lillian tasted her tea, then reached for the sugar bowl. "It don't bother me none, 'cause if people don't know any better, I know they can't help theyselves."

"Well, let us hope that Hazel Marie can teach her something. But, I declare, I hope she hasn't bitten off more than she can chew." I paused, recalling Trixie's sullen responses to any advice or correction by me. Then I thought of something else. "Oh, and let me tell you what else is going on." And I proceeded to relate what Trixie had told me about Rodney's plans for my property, his promise to hire the Binghams, and her intent by way of Hazel Marie's ministrations to help Rodney make it all come about.

"Sound like they countin' they chickens 'fore they hatched," Lillian said.

"They certainly are—both in their own way, too. And when Trixie realizes that Hazel Marie can't work miracles, she'll be even harder to live with."

"I 'spect Miss Hazel Marie send her back if she can't handle her, an' if she don't, Mr. Pickens will."

I laughed, as much as I could manage given the circumstances. "You're right, for one thing he won't put up with any rudeness to Hazel Marie. Law, Lillian," I went on as I pictured what his reaction would be to some of Trixie's more disagreeable moments. "Maybe Mr. Pickens ought to be the one to renovate Trixie. He'd have her straightened out in no time."

"I don't know 'bout that," Lillian said, a smile curling around her mouth as she thought about it. "He prob'bly not too handy with something like lipstick, 'cept when he smearin' Miss Hazel Marie's."

Chapter 31

"Well, let me get up from here," I said, rising and moving from the table. "I need to be doing something, now that Trixie's gone. You know, Lillian, when you get down to it, she really didn't demand a whole lot of time and attention, yet the very fact of her presence in the house weighed on me. I feel as if a burden's been lifted. Although," I went on with a wry smile, "there's no telling when it'll be right back upstairs hanging over my head again."

"You ought not be worryin' 'bout what happen tomorrow or the next day," Lillian said, picking up our glasses. "We jus' got today, an' we oughta 'preciate our enjoys when we get 'em."

"Truer words . . . ," I started, then stopped at the sound of the front doorbell. "Who could that be? It's too early for a visitor, even for a Jehovah's Witness. Oh, my goodness," I said, suddenly thinking of another possibility. "If it's Rodney, I'm not at home. You know what he wants, don't you? He wants me to sell him that property where Etta Mae lives, and I'm not going to do it. But I'm not ready to tell him so—that would really run him off from Trixie."

"Yes'm, you tole me. I find out who it is," Lillian said, moving toward the door to the dining room.

"If they're collecting money for something," I called after her, "we've already given, and if they're selling something, we don't want any."

"Uh-huh," Lillian said as she left the kitchen.

I sat back down at the table, waiting for Lillian to get rid of whoever it was. I wasn't in the mood for company, actually not in the mood for anybody or anything that would disrupt the day that spread out, almost free and clear, before me.

The only thing on my calendar was a meeting with Sam at campaign headquarters at four o'clock to preview his television ad. After that, I thought, if Lloyd was planning to eat at his mother's, and if we had a mind to, Sam and I could go out for dinner. Trixie's absence was proving beneficial in a number of ways.

"Miss Julia?" Lillian said as she came back into the kitchen. "Somebody callin' on you."

"Somebody who?"

"Somebody name of Miss Etta Mae," she said, giving me a pleased smile. Lillian liked Etta Mae. "She in the livin' room."

"Well, for goodness sakes, why didn't she come on back here?"

"She say she got business to talk about, so I tole her I get you." Lillian was better than I when it came to deciding on what was appropriate and what was not. From her viewpoint, business should be conducted in a more formal setting than the kitchen.

I smiled and went through to the living room. "Etta Mae," I said, as she stopped pacing and turned toward me. She was wearing one of those modern nurse's uniforms, consisting of a light blue V-necked tunic over a pair of drawstring pants, along with white sneakers. "It's so nice to see you. How have you been?"

"Miss Julia," she started, her face drawn with anxiety, "I'm sorry for dropping in on you like this. I know it's early, but I had to be over this way to see a new patient, and I thought, well, it might be the only chance I had to talk to you." Etta Mae was a licensed practical nurse who worked for the Handy Home Helpers out of Delmont. Her work consisted of making home visits to the elderly and other shut-ins, assisting with baths, minor medical procedures, and light housekeeping.

"Sit down, Etta Mae. I'm glad to see you. You know you're welcome to come by anytime you want, no matter the time. Come sit on the sofa with me and tell me how you've been."

She hesitated, but sat when I did. "I hate to bother you with this, but you did say to let you know when that man came around again. And, Miss Julia, he's there now, with two other men. I mean, they were there when I left, and I wouldn't have left but I had to. I had patients I had to get to early this morning, and, well, I couldn't just hang around all day just watching them."

"Of course you couldn't," I assured her.

"I thought of just calling you, but when two of them got these long-handled instrument-looking thingys out of their van and took off through the woods, I thought it'd be better to come tell you directly. If that's all right."

"It's always all right, Etta Mae. But what're they doing out there? Was one of them the same man you saw before?"

She nodded. "He didn't go with the others, just wandered around, looking at our trailers. I couldn't see too much. I had to go from one window to the next to keep an eye on him. So when I had to leave, I just went up to him and asked him what he wanted."

"Good. You had every right to. What did he say?"

"Said his name was Mr. Pace, and that he knew the owners, and they wouldn't mind him looking things over."

"He was wrong about that," I said, feeling more and more outraged at Rodney's arrogance.

She nodded again. "I told him I was the manager and that there was a NO SOLICITING sign at the entrance—pretending, you know, that I thought he was selling something door-to-door."

"What'd he say to that?"

"He just sorta smiled and said he wasn't soliciting, he was counting the trailers and figuring how long it'd take to move them. Then he said not to worry, that he'd give us thirty days' notice when we had to move, but that'd be all we'd have, so we'd better be looking around for another park."

The slow burn that had been simmering below the surface suddenly burst into flame, and I almost blew my stack. "That beats all I've ever heard! He had no more right to say such a thing to you than he'd have to say it to me in my own house. Who does he think he is, anyway!"

"Well, I didn't know what to think, especially when he said he

knew who owned it. But then I didn't much believe him because
he said *owners,* and I knew there was only one owner. Unless," she
said, looking anxiously at me, "you've made some changes."

"No changes, Etta Mae—none that I've made or that he's going
to make. And," I said, as the thought of Rodney's nerve flared up
again in my mind, "I am going to put a stop to this presumption.
You know, he has not said one word to me about even being interested in that property. All that walking and looking and measuring, and whatever else he's done, has all been on his own. If it
hadn't been for you and Trixie, I wouldn't know anything about it."
So then I had to tell Etta Mae about Trixie and the problems I'd
had with her, as well as the problems Trixie was having with
Rodney.

"So it's all tangled together," I summed up. "Which is the reason
I've not come down on Rodney before this. I've been waiting to see
how he'd approach me, thinking for one thing that he wouldn't have
the money to make an offer, and thinking for another that he'd
lose interest and find another piece of property. Instead, it's Trixie
that he's lost interest in, and he's still after the trailer park." I sat
for a few seconds, thinking over what I should do. "Listen, Etta
Mae, here's the thing. I put off confronting Rodney when I first
heard about his interest in the property, hoping, as I said, that he'd
get over it, and I didn't want to create any friction between him and
Trixie. But the friction is already there, and it no longer matters if
I create a little more. Which is what I aim to do.

"Etta Mae," I said, standing up, "when do you get off work
today?"

"I don't know. It'll probably take another hour for this patient
I have to see. Then I'm supposed to go to the office and do some
paperwork."

"Can you·put off the paperwork?"

"Sure, I can go in later and do it."

"Then," I said, consulting my watch, "you go on and see your
patient. Then, if you're up for it, I'll meet you at your trailer in an
hour and a half, give or take."

"Okay," she said, standing with an eager look on her face. "What're we going to do?"

"What I should've done already. I'm going to the hardware store and get some NO TRESPASSING signs. Then you and I are going to put them up all over that property. And the next time Mr. Pace sets foot out there, you're going to call the sheriff."

A familiar, ready-for-action grin spread across her face. "Don't forget the nails. I've got a hammer."

Chapter 32

As soon as Etta Mae left, I headed for our new library and began pulling out the built-in file drawers. With a vague memory of having seen some copies of the plats of several properties that had come to me upon Wesley Lloyd Springer's demise, I hoped to find the one I was looking for.

Of course they were all in the lowest drawer, so I got on my knees—knowing full well I'd have trouble getting up—to flip through the folders. Finally finding the one showing the Springer Road property, I struggled to my feet and began to study it. Most useful for my purpose was the drawn outline of the property—I could understand it. It was shaped like a lopsided rectangle, which probably had a specific mathematical name unknown to me, and was bordered by Springer Road on the east and Longview Road on the west. As for the north and the south boundaries, I suspected we'd find nothing but undeveloped, thickly wooded areas which I feared we'd have to traverse on foot. Except, from marks made by the surveyor across both Springer Road and Longview and pretty much following the south border of my property, there had at one time been a railroad track.

That was interesting, because I knew there were no railroad crossings on those roads. Maybe, I thought, we'd find an old railroad bed once used by loggers, but now abandoned.

Peering closely at the plat, I tried to interpret the numerous jottings on it, wishing for Sam, who would know in a minute what each one meant. I mean, there were latitudes and longitudes, and apostrophes and commas indicating I-knew-not-what, but most likely had something to do with the size and location of the area. Then I saw *29.9 acres* written in blurred ink, apparently by the surveyor, in the upper-right-hand corner of the page. I looked up and smiled. *Ha! Not big enough, Rodney.*

His plans for the Hillandale Trailer Park had just been put permanently on hold, and I couldn't wait to tell him.

Then I looked closer, trying to make out what looked like a smudge. But, no, it was a faint ink mark that the copying machine had barely picked up. Then it became clear: +/-.

Plus or minus, that's what it was, meaning that there could be a little less or—have mercy—a little more than thirty acres. No wonder Rodney had people out there looking around, but with what? They couldn't have had surveying equipment. No licensed professional surveyor would do so much as set up a tripod without the owner's permission. So what kind of long-handled instrument-looking thingys could they have had?

I shrugged it off because it didn't matter what they were lugging around or whether the acreage was plus or minus thirty, the title was staying right where it was. But I had wanted the property to prove unsuitable, thereby avoiding an uproar when I had to tell Trixie's beau that I wouldn't sell if it'd been a hundred acres. I could just see her start sulling up, a slow burn flaming her face, at my selfishly standing between Rodney and his dream of a scattering garden, even though by now it seemed he'd fired her before he'd fully hired her.

Did I care what Trixie thought? Not really, but on further thought, maybe I did.

So absorbed in interpreting the surveyor's marks on the plat, I jumped when Lillian called me to lunch. "Be there in a minute," I called back. Quickly folding the plat, I put it in my pocketbook and hurried not to the kitchen, but upstairs.

Not having strolled through any woods recently, I wasn't sure of the appropriate attire and didn't have time to give it much thought. I quickly exchanged my Ferragamos for a pair of clunky rubber-soled walking shoes, then grabbed a hat to ward off sunburn.

Hurrying back down to the kitchen where Lillian was waiting with a ham and tomato sandwich, I started to eat standing up.

"You better set down an' eat right," she scolded. "You make yourself sick, eatin' like that."

"I know, but I've got to get to the hardware store, then out to Delmont. Etta Mae will be waiting for me." Then I had to tell her what we were planning to do.

She just shook her head. "Why don't you hire somebody to do that? You and Miss Etta Mae don't need to be trompin' through no woods. You gonna get eat up with chiggers an' redbugs."

"I don't have time to find somebody else. I have to get the signs up before Sam thinks he has to do it, and he certainly doesn't need to be tromping through the woods. And I want them up so Rodney will take his business elsewhere and stop scaring the residents half to death. For all I know, some of them may already be planning to move." I swallowed the last bite of sandwich, washed it down with iced tea, then said, "My garden gloves are out in the garage, aren't they? And didn't Sam have some nails left over?"

Rolling her eyes because I was blatantly ignoring her advice, she went to the pantry. "Nails in here where Mr. Sam left 'em after puttin' up his signs. An' where you left them gloves las' time you cut some roses."

She handed me a pair of green gardening gloves and a box of nails, shaking her head as she did so. Picking up my sun hat and pocketbook, ready to leave, I said, "Lillian, don't worry. It won't take us thirty minutes to get those things up, and I'll be back before you know it."

Frowning, she put her hands on her hips. "Uh-huh, but I don't know why ever'body 'round here got to be puttin' up signs all over the place. Ever'time I turn around somebody pickin' up a hammer an' nailin' something."

I drove as fast as I dared to the Ace Hardware store, not even considering Walmart's, which would've taken me half an hour just to walk to the entrance and another half hour to find what I wanted, much less anybody to help me.

As soon as I walked into the hardware store, I was met by a clerk who took me straight to the counter where all kinds of signs—FOR LEASE, FOR RENT, FOR SALE, and, finally, NO TRESPASS-ING and POSTED KEEP OUT—were stacked waiting to be purchased.

"I'll take eight of those," I said, pointing at the last named. "No, let's do ten—five each of these two. On second thought, maybe I'd better have six of each." Actually, I had no idea how many signs we'd need. A couple nailed up at the entrance, I thought, then certainly one at each corner of the property, if we could find the stakes. At the thought of searching for stakes on twenty-nine-point-nine acres, plus or minus, I had a sneaking suspicion that keeping Rodney out might take longer and more effort than I'd originally counted on.

As soon as I pulled up beside Etta Mae's single-wide, out she came, hammer in hand. She'd changed from her uniform and was now wearing a pair of jeans, a long-sleeved shirt, a baseball cap, and, of course, her pointy-toed cowboy boots.

"Hey, Miss Julia," she said cheerily, as she crawled onto the front seat beside me. "This is a great idea. He'll think twice from now on when he sees our signs."

Putting the car in reverse, I backed out onto the drive that ran through the park and headed toward the entrance. "I hope so. Is he still wandering around? What about the men who walked off into the woods?"

"Haven't seen hide nor hair of any of 'em since I got home. They're either way back in the woods or they've left."

"Doesn't matter," I said. "These signs are going up, and they'd better pay attention to them."

I parked where the entrance drive to the park fed onto Springer Road, put on my hat, gathered a couple of signs, the box of nails, and stepped out. "I'll hold the sign, if you'll nail it in. We can take turns with the hammer."

And that's what we did, but first we had to struggle through a weed-filled ditch to get to a suitable tree, then do it again on the other side of the entrance.

By the time we were back in the car, I was hot, sweaty, and complaining. "I don't know if it's the county or the state that's supposed to mow the roadsides, but whoever it is, they're not doing the job." Pushing back my hair, I said, "My goodness, it's warm today."

Turning to the right on Springer Road, I handed the plat to Etta Mae. "We have to find the corner stake, Etta Mae. See if you can figure out how far we have to go before I slow down to look for it."

She studied the plat for a few seconds, then said, "It's a pretty far ways. Maybe we ought to put a couple here and there between the corners."

She was right, so I stopped on the roadside twice, while we scrambled into and out of ditches—once sinking into a damp spot—and pushed aside weeds and laurel bushes to reach the trees, where we nailed up two more NO TRESPASSING signs and a POSTED sign.

On the road again, and thankful that we were on a county road with little traffic, I drove slowly, glancing now and then to the right to find a corner stake. "Etta Mae, how in the world are we going to find those stakes?"

"I was wondering that myself." She was looking to the right, too. "They usually just stick up a few inches out of the ground, and they could be covered with leaves and vines and I don't know what-all. We may have to get out and beat the bushes to find them."

"My goodness," I said, leaning down to look out her window. "There's nothing but trees and clumps of laurel and rhododendron. And vines and briars, and no telling what else. This might not've been such a good idea—there's no way we're going to find little tiny stakes in all that. And on all four corners, too."

"Not from the car, we're not," Etta Mae said glumly. "I guess we'll have to beat the bushes after all."

"Well," I said, letting the car coast along the road, "I should've listened to Lillian and hired—"

"*Oh! Oh!*" Etta Mae suddenly cried, bouncing up and down on the seat. "I know, I know!"

"What? Know what?" I came to a stop right in the middle of the road.

"*Metal detectors!* That's what those men had. I *knew* I'd seen those long-handled thingys before. I'll bet you anything they've already found the stakes, and all we have to do is look for whatever they tagged them with. And it'll be something that can be *seen*, 'cause they'll want to be able to find 'em again.

"And look!" she cried, pointing. "See that? Right there across the ditch at the top of the bank. See that little orange tie, or whatever it is?"

I looked, and sure enough, there was something bright orange and low to the ground, easy to see among all the green leaves, branches, and weeds—some of which had been trampled down around it. "It could be a sock or something thrown from a car."

Etta Mae laughed, her good mood restored. "That's a plastic tag tied to a stake. Miss Julia, we've just found the first corner. *And*," she went on brightly, "it just may be that the other three corners will be just as easy to find."

"You mean," I said, brightening a little myself, "Rodney's done all the work, and all we have to do is look for something orange?" I braked and pulled to the side of the road. "I'll remember to thank him when I tell him to stay away."

The ditch was deeper here than at the entrance, and the climb up the other side steeper. I had to use hands and knees to get up it. As I scrambled to the top, a hemlock branch knocked my hat off, sending it to the bottom of the ditch. I just left it, while Etta Mae, even carrying the hammer and two signs, clambered up with little effort. "Why don't you wait in the car?" she said, noticing my heavy breathing.

"No, I'm all right," I said, pulling a briar tendril off my skirt tail. "Let's get this done."

As she finished hammering a sign onto a tree, I looked through the trees along where I assumed the property line would run to the west. "While we're up here, why don't we go a little farther in and put up another sign? It's clear enough here for two to be seen from the road. See that huge oak? Let's put one on it."

We started for the tree, but it wasn't long before the underbrush got thicker, and I stopped for a quick survey. "Hold on, Etta Mae, we better go around this laurel thicket."

I attempted to detour, but kept being pulled by briars reaching out and snagging my dress, my stockings, my arms, and my legs. Trying to push on by through thick weeds, I began to think that the bush was alive and determined to ensnare me.

"Wait, Miss Julia!" Etta Mae said, backing out. "Don't go any farther. Come on back outta there."

I started backing out, but more briar tentacles tugged at me and scraped along my skin. I thought of Brer Rabbit—he'd been happy in a briar patch, but I was fairly close to panicking.

Etta Mae gingerly pulled briar limbs off my dress, then took my arm as I carefully backtracked. Scraped and bleeding a little, I finally got free, but she kept urging me to hurry.

After manuevering down and across the steep-sided ditch, grabbing my hat as I went, and climbing into the car, I looked over the damage. "My stockings are ruined. Look at that, Etta Mae, they're in shreds. And look at this! There's a rip in my dress." I flung the hat in the backseat and began to mop the sweat from my hairline.

"Well," Etta Mae said drily, "you didn't exactly dress for a hike in the woods."

"True," I acknowledged with a shrug. "But I wanted another sign on that big tree—Rodney couldn't fail to see that. I should've pushed on through and gotten it up. I mean, how much more damage could it have done?" I smoothed back the damp hair from my forehead, then used a dab of saliva on a Kleenex to clean a bloody scrape on my arm.

"A lot more," Etta Mae said. "That was a *blackberry* patch, which I didn't realize till we were in it. And where there's black-berries, you can pretty much count on snakes, too."

"Oh," I said, wondering if any of the scratches on my legs could be fang marks. I shivered, cranked the car, and headed south to the turnoff to Longview Road, which would take us up the other side of the property. It was a fairly long way to the turnoff, maybe half a mile or so, and I wondered who owned the thickly wooded area that bordered my property. Rodney might even now be nego-tiating to buy enough to fill out what was lacking in mine.

Or, I suddenly thought, negotiating for an acre or two on the north side—he could make up his thirty acres from either direc-tion. There was a small farm on the north side, mostly pasture land with a few cows sleeping in the shade of clumps of trees. A thickly wooded area separated the pasture from the trailer park, in which I assumed we'd find the boundary line. If the kudzu-covered barbed-wire fence that enclosed the cows was any indica-tion, the farm extended on the north to the back of a line of stores that faced the Delmont highway. And from the looks of the place, the farmer would probably jump at the chance to sell off any or all of it. Something else to worry about, except, as I kept telling my-self, I wasn't going to sell, so why worry about any of it. It would be so much easier, though, if Rodney would just turn his sights elsewhere.

Easing the car along the road, I kept slowing to search for a streak of orange plastic on the sidelines. "My goodness, Etta Mae," I said, as the car went over a couple of bumps in the road, "I didn't know there was a railroad out here."

"Been here forever," she said, "but I don't guess a train's run this way for years—not since I've been around, anyway."

"Well," I said, straining to see out her window, "looks like it runs through that tract next to mine. No wonder nobody's done anything there. Who'd want the possibility of a train running through the front yard?"

Finally, we found the orange-tagged stakes at the other three corners, although we had to get out of the car a couple of times to search through the tall weeds. In fact, though, after climbing a steep bank at two corners, we found that the weeds and bushes had been trampled down by those who had come before us, so we were able to quickly nail up our signs and move on. I had a number of signs left over, so, unwilling to venture again into the wilderness, I asked Etta Mae to put them up all around the mobile homes when she had time.

When we got back to her trailer, she urged me to come in and let her put something on my scrapes and scratches. They were stinging by this time, and I was tempted. But it was nearing four o'clock, when I was to meet Sam, so I thanked her profusely for her help, assured her that I'd tend to my wounds when I got home, and anxiously headed toward Abbotsville.

Chapter 33

But wouldn't you know it? The Highway Patrol had chosen just that time to conduct a driver's license check, so there I sat only two miles from Abbotsville with the car idling in line as time ticked on. My plan had been to hurry home, quickly shower, change clothes, do something with my leaf-filled hair, and get to campaign headquarters to meet Sam. Yet there I was, inching slowly forward as one car after another was checked, and each time I moved my foot from accelerator to brake and back again, I felt another run slide down my leg. With all the snags in my stockings, they'd be in shreds by the time I got anywhere.

On top of that, I suddenly realized that the skirt tail of my dress, along with my stockings, was covered with beggar lice. It would take hours, which I didn't have, to pick each one off. Maybe, I thought, they'd blend in with the floral design of my dress.

Tapping my fingers against the wheel, I fretted over the delay. Sam would worry or, worse, be disappointed, if I didn't show up, and as usual, I didn't have a cell phone with me. I declare, I couldn't get used to taking the thing with me every time I left the house, but this was one time I sorely regretted it.

When my turn came for a huge trooper to lean down to my window, I held up my license. He glanced at it, frowned when he took a look at me, then nodded, wished me a good day, and turned to the next car in line. I had to restrain myself from speeding away.

By the time I got to Main Street, I'd given up hope of making it in time. Four o'clock on the dot. I could either disappoint Sam and go on home, or I could give him and those with him the shock of their lives by going to preview his television ad just as I was.

I went straight to campaign headquarters. Deciding as I parked that I would not confirm the state I was in by consulting a mirror, I went inside. Campaign central, as they called it, was located in an empty store, rented for the duration, and consisted of one large room filled with desks with telephones on them and a large table covered with Murdoch posters, yard signs, and pamphlets. In the back were a couple of smaller rooms, one of which was being entered by several people.

Speaking quickly to a suddenly wide-eyed woman manning the front desk, I hurried back to the room, relieved to find as I entered that it was dark—well, somewhat dim. Sam stood at the front of two short rows of folding chairs, while Millard Wilkes, his campaign manager, checked a large television set. Six or so volunteers had taken chairs, waiting to see and critique the ad.

I slipped into a chair in the back corner, gave a wave to Sam, who smiled back, and hoped no one would notice how unkempt I was. Millard fiddled with the television set, finally inserting a disk or a cassette or whatever it was into the slot, and we all sat back to await the showing.

"We only have the one," Millard said. "Two others are in the works, but we wanted your opinion on this one before proceeding. Let us know what you think."

The screen lit up and there was Sam's image standing before a large wall map with our district oulined in black. He began to speak—the same words I'd heard a hundred times or more from other candidates—but with an ease and a directness that were his alone. At the end of the thirty-second ad, he smiled, not at the camera, but seemingly at each viewer. Sitting there in the dark, I glowed with pride, or maybe sunburn. I could've fallen in love again if I hadn't already been in as far as I could go.

When the ad ended, everybody clapped and began to express their approval. Just as the lights came on, I stood up, hoping to ease out before anybody could get a good look at my disheveled state. I slipped out into the hall, ready to make tracks, but Sam was right behind me.

"Julia, what in the world happened to you?"

"Don't ask," I said, patting his arm as if nothing was amiss. "I'm on my way home to repair the damage."

That didn't allay his concern, which was all over his face. "Did you have an accident? Are you hurt? Honey, what happened?"

The volunteers began to edge out around us, eager to get back to the telephones, but not before they gave me a good going-over with their eyes.

"I'm all right, Sam," I assured him. "There wasn't an accident. I just took a stroll in the woods with Etta Mae, and, well, it was a little more strenuous than I'd imagined." I brushed a trickle of sweat from the side of my face. "Really, I'm all right. And, Sam, the ad was perfect." Trying to change the subject so I could get out of there. "You did such a good job, and the map showing our district was an inspired touch. I'm so glad you didn't stand in front of an American flag—not that I'm not proud of it, but it's so overused by candidates. I mean, voters generally know what country they're in, but they don't always know which district."

I was at the door by that time, still talking fast to ease Sam's concern. It didn't seem to be working.

"Thanks," Sam said, holding on to my arm even as I, wanting to make a hasty retreat, opened the door. "I appreciate that, but, Julia, what were you doing in the woods?"

I released his hand from my arm and said, "Keeping Rodney out of them." I slipped through the door, giving him a carefree smile on my way. "Hurry on home. I'll tell you all about it."

Restored to some semblance of my usual appearance by suppertime, I told Sam of our trek through the woods off Springer Road. With both Trixie and Lloyd eating at Hazel Marie's, we had a quiet meal, then retired to the new library. I'd hoped by that time to have put his concerns to rest, but in spite of my attempts to focus our discussion on his spectacular venture into television advertising, Sam kept returning to my risky afternoon of putting up NO TRESPASSING signs.

"Whatever possessed you, Julia," he asked, "to take that on yourself?"

"I didn't. Etta Mae was with me."

"But that's a huge parcel of land to be walking around."

"Oh, we drove it, mostly. Sam, I had to get those signs up. Rodney was out there this morning with *metal detectors*. He undoubtedly knows about that plus or minus mark, and he was making sure of the exact acreage. Something had to be done."

"But, honey," Sam said, "you've said you aren't selling it, so what did it matter?"

"I don't know, Sam," I said, leaning my head on the back of the chair. "I've been asking myself that all day—especially since I'm eaten up with redbugs." I reached down and scratched my ankle. "Anyway, I just don't want that property to come between Trixie and Rodney, because it will when I refuse to sell it—as I most certainly will continue to do. I know, I know," I went on as he started to speak, "he's told her they should see other people, which is as good as dropping her, but she's still holding out hope. She thinks if his mortuary dream works out, he'll need her and want her back. I don't want to be the one who's blamed when he doesn't get the property and she doesn't get him."

Sam smiled. "You have a soft spot for her, don't you?"

"Oh, Sam, I just feel sorry for her. I can't help but think that Rodney has known all along who the owner is, and he picked Trixie out of the other Internet applicants because of it. She's been beaten down for so long that I don't want to add to it. How much better it would be if Rodney got over his untenable attachment to that land on his own, and it's my intent that he, himself, decides that it won't do for his purposes. Oh, and by the way," I said, looking up expectantly, "I use that word specifically, because I looked it up. Do you know what *untenable* means?"

A dictionary was rarely far from Sam's side, so he smiled. "Legally speaking—not defendable?"

"Well, yes, but it also means, and I'm quoting, 'not suitable for occupation.' It's a perfect fit for this situation, and the sooner Rodney figures that out, the better."

Sam laughed, then, at the slam of the back door and the hurried squeak of tennis shoes on the floor, we both sat up straight and looked around.

"Mr. Sam!" Lloyd yelled. "Mr. Sam! Where are you?"

Sam stood and started for the hall door. "In here, Lloyd. What's the matter?"

Lloyd skidded into the room, grabbed the door to stop himself, then leaned over panting. "I rode all over town . . . as far as I could . . . ever since supper . . . on my bike. And, and . . ."

I was up by this time, hurrying to him. "Slow down, honey, and catch your breath. Is anything wrong at home? Your mother all right? The babies?"

He shook his head, tried to speak, then took a deep breath. "They're okay, but, Mr. Sam, they're all gone. Every last one of 'em!"

Chapter 34

"What!" My heart almost stopped. *"Everybody?"*

"Wait, now," Sam said, putting his hand on my arm as he tried to make sense of what we'd heard. "Who's gone?"

"Not who, but *what!*" Lloyd cried, flinging out his arms. *"Your campaign posters!* There's not a one anywhere! See, I rode my bike home from the tennis courts, and I noticed there weren't any along Park Road—and I *know* we put some there—and I thought, well, maybe the rain or something got them. But I got to thinking about it, so after supper, I went riding around again, and *all* your posters on this side of Main Street are gone. And, for all I know, in the whole county, too! And, Mr. Sam, it was like whoever did it knew exactly where they were. It was like somebody came along and, and just *stole* every last one of 'em!"

"No," Sam said, putting his arm around the boy's shoulders and leading him to a chair. "Nobody stole them. Somebody took them down deliberately."

"That's right!" Lloyd said, as if the entire situation had suddenly become clear. "Because the posters for all the other candidates are still up. Who would do such a thing?"

"Jimmy Ray Mooney," I answered, as sure as I could be.

"No," Sam said, shaking his head, "not Jimmy Ray. He knows better than to get into that kind of trouble. But it had to be some of his supporters—thinking they were being helpful. Or it was somebody who really dislikes me."

"I can't believe that," I said.

Lloyd straightened his shoulders. "There's only one thing to do—put 'em all back up again. We still have a lot left over, so anytime you want to, Mr. Sam, I'll help, or I'll go by myself and do it. I know the exact places we put them the first time, so it won't be a problem."

"Thank you, Lloyd," Sam said. "I'll take you up on that, but not by yourself. I'll go with you and maybe we can find some more help, as well."

"I bet Rodney'll help again," Lloyd said, eager to organize another poster-hanging outing.

Hm-m, I thought, given Rodney's sudden loss of interest in Trixie and the sudden appearance of NO TRESPASSING signs on his chosen property, I somehow doubted he'd be eager to volunteer again.

After assuring Lloyd that such dirty electioneering tactics were both illegal and deplorable, but not entirely unexpected, Sam sent him home with the promise of another outing on Saturday. "We'll get 'em back up," Sam assured him, "and it might all turn out for the best. It could be just the thing to get our volunteers fired up."

When the boy left for his mother's house, I sank down on the leather sofa and leaned my head back. "Oh, me, Sam," I said, "who could've done such a thing? It feels so personal, so deliberate and malicious. I hate thinking that anybody could dislike us so much."

Sam sat down beside me and took my hand. "You can't take it personally, Julia. It would've been the posters of whoever was running against Jimmy Ray. I'll talk to him tomorrow, let him know what's happened, and he'll give his volunteers a dressing down."

"I don't think that's enough—they could do it again. I think you ought to tell the sheriff."

"I will, and the newspaper, too. A little publicity will do wonders to keep it from happening again. Everybody will think just what you thought—that it was Jimmy Ray's doing, or at least with his approval. Jimmy Ray will know that, so he'll do what he can to put a stop to it."

"Well, the whole thing has given me a moderate to severe

headache." I rubbed my head to ease the pain, then scratched my shin to ease an itch. "I know it's early, but I'm going to bed."

Sam stood, then held out his hand to me. "I'm right behind you."

Walking along the sidewalk on my way to Hazel Marie's house the next morning, I tried to put the missing posters out of my mind. Sam was taking it so well—not happy about it, of course, but accepting it as part of local politics—but I was still angry for his sake. He'd been singled out and deliberately targeted. Well, I mean his posters had been, and though I wished no harm to anybody else, I'd have felt better if the posters of a few other candidates had suffered the same fate.

As I stepped up onto the walk leading to the front porch of Sam's beautiful old house, which the Pickens family now called home, I steeled myself to deal with Trixie again. Hazel Marie had called while Sam and I were having breakfast, asking me to come over to see how the makeover was progressing.

When I rang the doorbell, Trixie opened the door. She stepped back, giving me room to enter. "Good morning, Miss Julia," she said, her eyes slightly glazed as if she were studying a script. Then, with a practiced smile, she went on. "Please come in. It's so nice to see you."

"Well, it's nice to see you, too, Trixie, and to see you looking so well." And she did. No miraculous makeover, of course, but an improvement nonetheless. Her hair had been expertly cut much shorter and in layers, removing the brassy pink-dyed ends. Hazel Marie had undoubtedly gotten Trixie to Velma, and done it without Trixie throwing a fit—a miracle in itself.

Trixie's face was lightly made up—perfectly appropriate for daytime, especially since the bronze eye shadow she'd been so partial to had been left off. A little gloss on her lips and a soft glow on her cheeks were evidence of Hazel Marie's deft hand with cosmetic brushes.

Most impressive, though, was the fact that she'd looked in my direction as she'd spoken—not directly *at* me, yet what a difference even that made! Well, the barely noticeable fine line of eyeliner around her eyes made a difference, too—maybe the most difference, for now her eyes were no longer lurking deep in her head, nor were they hidden beneath lowered lids. I must admit that at one time, I had assumed that the presence of black lines around a pair of eyes were an indication that the woman who'd drawn them was slightly on the fast side. My judgmental attitude, however, had slowly evolved over the years—perhaps I had become inured by the enhanced eyes of both Hazel Marie and Etta Mae.

Following Trixie into the living room, I noted that the few days under instruction had not done much for Trixie's figure. Bless her heart, she was born short and stocky, and remained that way. Still, the tailored Bermuda shorts and soft linen blouse—tucked into the waist—that she wore streamlined the bulky muscles underneath. But it was her erect posture and practiced carriage that did the most to disguise her unfortunate frame.

"Hazel Marie," Trixie said, speaking clearly but as if from memory, "Miss Julia has come to call."

Hazel Marie jumped up from the sofa and hurried over to clasp me in her arms. She couldn't help it, she just had to fling herself on anyone she cared for, so I had about become resigned to enduring a hug whenever we met.

"I'm so glad to see you," Hazel Marie cried, and I knew she meant it—she always did. And as always, Hazel Marie was neatly dressed and carefully made up—an ideal model for Trixie to emulate. "What do you think of Trixie?" Hazel Marie asked. "Isn't she lovely? Velma did such a good job on her hair, and Trixie has just about mastered a curling iron. Sit down, Miss Julia, sit down. The little girls are napping, and James is fixing us some lemonade. We can have a nice visit."

As we seated ourselves, I noticed Trixie run her hand under her bottom as if she were smoothing a skirt before sitting. I mentally nodded, approving also of Trixie's straight back as she sat, ignoring the soft cushion at the back of her chair. She crossed her ankles, turned her body to the side, and rested her hands in her lap—a perfect and attractive pose, perfected no doubt by balancing a book on her head. I wondered how long she would hold it.

"Well, I must say, Hazel Marie," I began, "that the two of you have really been working. Trixie, you are looking exceptionally well, and I can see that self-confident glow which we always have when we know we're looking our best. That makes striving to look our best worth the effort. I hope you never listen to those who push you to look *natural*—that's what we look like when we first get up in the morning. Just keep on doing whatever you're doing, because you are lovely. Just remember," I couldn't help but add, "that pretty is as pretty does."

Trixie blushed, ducked her head, and murmured, "Thank you." Not quite in the mumbling way she used to respond, yet quite appropriately for a compliment.

"Here we go, ladies," Granny Wiggins called out as she carried in a tray loaded with glasses, a pitcher of lemonade, and a plate of cookies. "James has got his hands in a mess of collard greens, so he give me this job. Mrs. Murdoch, how's the world treatin' you? Real nice to see you again." Granny set the tray on the coffee table, then peered closely at me. "You're lookin' a mite peaked. You're not sick, are you?"

Don't you just hate it when people draw attention to your looks? I couldn't help it if I had a lot on my mind, worrying me half to death day and night.

"No," I said, as serenely as I could manage, "I'm not ill. But you're looking well, Mrs. Wiggins."

Granny Wiggins was Etta Mae's grandmother, a widow lady who lived on a no-longer-working farm out in the country. During Hazel Marie's weeks of distress when her twins were teething and James was laid up and she was run ragged trying to care for them all, Granny had come to help and stayed. I had fretted that she was too old, too thin, and too weak to be much use, but Granny could outwork us all. In a housedress that looked recycled from a flour sack, a practical apron, stockings that were rolled down her pencil-thin legs to her high-top tennis shoes, she flitted around the house, dusting, vacuuming, crooning to the babies, and endearing herself to both Hazel Marie and Mr. Pickens. In fact, Mr. Pickens had occasionally teased Hazel Marie by saying that he had a mind to trade her in for Granny Wiggins. Granny Wiggins could do it all with—as she said—one hand tied behind her back.

"Sit down, Granny," Hazel Marie said as she reached for the pitcher. "Have some lemonade with us."

"Well, I got lots to do," Granny said, her hands on her hips. "Them bathrooms upstairs need a good scrubbin', but I reckon I can set for a minute." And so she did, accepted a glass from Hazel Marie, then commenced to give us her assessment of whatever entered her head.

"Well, I tell you," Granny began, "I been watchin' Little Miss Trixie get all gussied up, and, honey, you're lookin' good, no two ways about it. But let ole Granny tell you what'll really do the trick if it's a man you're a-lookin' for. Learn to cook, and I don't mean all this fancy stuff that'll give you heartburn and dyspepsy. You jus' ask the man you got your eye on over for supper, an' give 'em fried chicken from a young and tender pullet you raised yourself. Give him beans and corn and 'maters and cukes and whatever else you got outta your own garden, and he won't care what you look like. Top it off with a caramel cake you made from scratch, and all he'll say is, 'What time's supper tomorrow?'"

Granny nodded her head sharply, as if she'd just given the last word on the subject. But she had a few more. "Now that's for summertime cookin'. If it's winter, just go out and get a fat hen that's too old and tough for fryin', and you just boil her down, and drop some dumplin's in it, and, honey, I tell you, he'll be a-knockin' on your door ever' night."

She stopped, took a long swallow of lemonade, then went on. "'Course it don't hurt none to look as pretty as you can when you're dippin' all that up for him. But it's the cookin' that'll get 'em ever'time. An' I oughta know. I kept a husband for fifty-some-odd years, an' been a widder ever since 'cause I don't want another'n. I already turned down three offers, an' they sure didn't come sniffin' around on the basis of my looks." She stood up, put her empty glass on the tray, and began to take her leave. "Well, this ain't gettin' it done. Whoops!" she said, whirling around as the telephone rang. "Y'all just keep on a-settin', I'll get it. You ladies have a nice visit now, an', Miss Trixie, you want any more man-gettin' advice, you just come to me."

We were left staring at one another, not knowing whether to laugh or to take her advice seriously.

"Well," I said, "that was interesting, but, Trixie, I don't think you need worry about keeping chickens and working a garden. You just keep doing what Hazel Marie tells you, and you'll be fine."

Trixie had, by this time, lost her model's pose and was now slumped back in the chair. "I guess," she mumbled. " 'Cept I like raisin' chickens, but Rodney don't. He don't even like chicken, period. He says he could go the rest of his life without ever seein' another pulley bone."

Chapter 35

Fairly content that Trixie was following instructions when she remembered them and giving Hazel Marie no trouble, I walked home, turning my mind to other problems such as Sam's senate campaign and Rodney's campaign for my property.

As for Rodney, I decided, he could just knock himself out running around in my woods, metal detecting and tying orange plastic strips on stakes, and whatever else he was doing—it would do him no good. Well, actually it might do him some good in another way. Maybe he'd get so tired of dealing with briars, chiggers, redbugs, and snakes that he give up his dream of building a mortuary and turn his mind to something else—maybe a hot yoga business. I had a building I'd be happy to rent to him.

When Hazel Marie had walked me to the door, she'd whispered that Trixie had not heard from Rodney, but that she was still convinced she'd win him back.

"How's she going to do that?" I'd said, whispering, too.

"I don't know," Hazel Marie said with a frown, "but she seems to have some idea up her sleeve. She's, well, just real confident that she can bring him around."

I thought about that as I walked, wondering what in the world Trixie could have in mind. It was a settled fact that, in spite of Hazel Marie's ministrations, the girl would never be what one would call a raving beauty. Markedly and impressively improved, I was happy to concede, but never strikingly beautiful. More's the pity, but how many of us actually are? We all have to work with what we're given and try to make the best of it.

And then there was Sam. I had a bad feeling about his chances for winning the senate race, and the thought of him being disappointed hurt me deep inside. I had gone with him to a few dinners and rallies, but the crowds had been sparse. The small numbers hadn't seemed to discourage him, though. He kept assuring me that the word was getting around and that things were looking up.

"All of a sudden," he'd said with a pleased smile, "we've had an influx of donations—a couple of big ones, too. That means people want to get in on the winning side."

"Who were the big donors?" I asked, wondering if my bundling efforts were paying off after all.

"Right now, I just look at the bottom line." Sam glanced at me, his eyes twinkling. "I don't want to be influenced by knowing how much or how little anybody's contributed. And I'll tell you, it's come in at just the right time—we were scraping the bottom of our campaign barrel. So now we'll be able to flood the local airwaves with radio and television ads. I think we're going to see an uptick in the polls, too."

Sam was also enthusiastically planning an all-out effort on the Fourth of July when people would be out celebrating. The holiday was fast approaching, and the day would be filled with barbecues, hot dogs, watermelon cuttings, bluegrass bands, a little beach music, parades, and speeches from one end of the district to the other, lasting long into a fireworks-filled night. He was looking forward to it and I was trying to.

"You don't have to go to everything, honey," Sam had said, considerate as always. "It's going to be a long day, and Millard has a bunch of volunteers eager to make every stop. We're going to load up a van and start with a parade that morning in Polk City, then on to the next event and on and on for the rest of the day."

Just the mention of riding around all day in a van decided me. "Thank you, Sam. I'd like to see the fireworks out at the park that evening. I'll meet you there."

When I got home from my visit with Hazel Marie and Trixie, I went in the kitchen door as we were wont to do and found Lillian waiting for me. I didn't get two steps through the door before she was right up next to me, whispering.

"You got some more comp'ny," she said. "I tole him I didn't know when you be back, but he said he don't mind waitin' in the parlor, and that's what he been doin'."

"Who is it?"

"Miss Trixie's young man. That Rodney, what buries folks. I tell you, Miss Julia, I'm glad you home. I don't like bein' here by myself when he come callin'. No tellin' what he have in mind."

"Oh, I know what he has in mind, and it's about time he declared himself. Don't worry, Lillian, he'll be doing no burying around here or anywhere else, if I have anything to say about it."

As I marched into the living room, Rodney sprang from Sam's chair as soon as I appeared and greeted me with a broad smile.

"Miss Julia," he said, taking a liberty that I wasn't sure he'd been granted, "so nice to see you again. I hope you don't mind my dropping in like this, but, like I always say, when something's on your mind, better to go on and get it off than to let it simmer."

"Have a seat, Rodney," I said, having one myself as I decided to discompose him by letting whatever was on his mind simmer a little longer. "Trixie isn't here, I'm sorry to say, but I'm surprised you've come calling on her. I hear that the two of you have parted ways."

"Well, uh, no, I came to . . ."

"I think—if it matters what I think—that you were wise to slow things down a little. Trixie is still young in many ways and has a lot to learn. A sophisticated young man like you quite turned her head."

He preened just a little. "Yes, I did my best to help, but found that we had little in common—chickens, for one thing. In fact, though, when I suggested that we see other people, it was really for her own good."

"It's certainly proving to be," I agreed. "She's like a different young woman."

"Oh?" he said, betraying some dismay that Trixie might actually be better off without him.

"Yes," I said, laying it on thick, "I just saw her this morning and could hardly believe the transformation. And to think that she's only just begun. There's no telling what she'll be like when she's through. The telephone has already started ringing." That much was true.

"Well, I, uh," Rodney stumbled, "I'm glad to hear it." Then he pulled himself together, sat up straight, and plunged into business. "Miss Julia, I'm sorry that Trixie and I didn't work out, but I've come to make you an offer on some undeveloped land that's giving you hardly any return. If you'll hear me out, I think you'll be glad for such an opportunity, not only to be rid of it but to make a profit on it." He leaned forward as if to impart a secret. "I understand that county taxes are going up next year, and what you're making on it now will barely cover the increase."

"Hm-m, well, Rodney, I own several parcels around the county. Just which one are you referring to?"

"The one on Springer Road, which is mostly unused and a drain, I'm sure, on your finances."

I didn't care to discuss my finances with him, so I continued to pretend I didn't know what he wanted. "You mean where the Hillandale Trailer Park is? The income on that is quite satisfactory. But of course you must mean the remainder of the property—I'd guess some twenty or so acres?"

"No, oh no," Rodney said, shaking his head, "I mean all of it. Those trailers can be moved—trailer parks are a blight on the landscape anyway, don't you think?" When he saw my expression, he quickly corrected himself. "Well, not that one, of course. It's well kept, but I'm sure it's a constant battle with the types of people who come and go out there—you must get all kinds. I could take that worry off your hands."

Types of people stung me—I thought of Etta Mae and wanted to smack him. Before I could respond, he launched into his spiel.

"Here's the thing," he said, hunching forward. "I have a partner who, at his request, shall remain nameless for the time being. He owns the farm to the north of the trailer park, and he'll give me a long-term lease—and I mean a *long*-term—on one condition. I can't ever dig a grave and bury a body on it. You know why, don't you?"

I shook my head, although I knew a little about it.

"Once you have a grave on a site, no matter how old or even if no family is left or anything, the state gets involved. You wouldn't believe what it takes to get permission to exhume bodies and re-bury them. I mean, for all intents and purposes, the site is just about ruined for anything else unless you got the money and the time to fiddle with all the legal maneuvering you have to do. So," he said, taking a deep breath, "I'll use his land for my public buildings—the mortuary itself, the garage for the hearses, parking areas for people who come for visitations, and so on. And I'll clear your thirty acres, which is just the perfect size for the cemetery itself. It's mostly level and slightly rolling, and I've already marked some fine trees that I'm planning to leave. A lot of people want their loved ones to lie in the shade, although . . ." He stopped momentarily, frowning. "Although roots can be a problem. Any-way, when it's all planted with grass—that'll make it what's called a lawn cemetery—well, you won't find a finer cemetery anywhere. You'll be proud of it."

"No doubt, but of course it's not quite thirty acres, which, I understand, is the minimum requirement."

I wasn't sure, but I thought Rodney winced just a little. "Oh," he said, visibly recovering, "you have an old plat that was done years ago, don't you? I've seen it, too, and it's not accurate. The property's just over thirty acres—the perfect size."

"You've surveyed it? Without permission?"

"Oh, no, I wouldn't do that. Just kinda eyeballed it, and got a professional guesstimate—it's a good bit over thirty acres. I'm sure of that, else I wouldn't be interested. Have to have the state's thirty acres, you know." And he laughed as if we were in it together against the bureaucrats. "Now, Miss Julia, here's the thing. I'll give you a good price—how does three thousand an acre sound?"

"Like it wouldn't buy half of it."

"What?" Rodney leaned back, mock surprise on his face. "But, Miss Julia, you won't get a better price than that."

"Rodney," I said, leaning toward him, "you must think I'm ill-informed. First of all, that property is not for sale, and second of all, it's worth triple what you've offered, and third of all, it still wouldn't be for sale if you did triple it."

That stopped him, but only for a moment. He quickly recovered, smiled a knowing smile, and said, "I should've known that an intelligent woman like yourself would know what it's worth. But," he went on with a shrug of his shoulders, "you can't blame me for trying. Okay, let's say eight thousand an acre, which is the going price for undeveloped land in that location. That'll make you a nice chunk of change."

"I don't think you understand me. The property is not for sale."

"But, but *why*? It's not doing you any good, and I really need it. I tell you what, let me talk to my partner and we might be able to go a little higher. How does that sound?"

"It sounds as if you're not hearing me, Rodney. The property is not for sale."

He leaned back in his chair, studying me, unable apparently to understand why I'd turn down a good offer on something I wasn't using. I let him sit and study.

Finally he said, "I get it now. You're upset with me because of Trixie. Right? That's it, isn't it?"

I laughed. "Oh, Rodney, you're so far off, it isn't even funny. I simply have no intention of selling, and I'd feel that way if Trixie had never left Georgia." I made a move to rise, indicating that his visit was over, but he sat where he was. "Believe me, Trixie has nothing to do with this. My suggestion to you is to look for another location for your cemetery. Mine is unavailable and will not be available."

Until pigs fly, I wanted to add, recalling some medieval story Sam had told me. I got to my feet, looked down at him, and went on. "I know you're disappointed, but I could've saved you a lot of futile planning and unauthorized metal detecting if you'd come to me earlier. It's never been for sale and won't be in the future."

He finally bestirred himself and walked to the door, his face working as if he were grinding his teeth. I could feel the frustration steaming off him.

At the door, he turned and said, "I'm going to make you an offer you can't refuse. That property is ideal for what I want, and I'm not giving up on it."

"Rodney," I said, controlling a little frustration myself, "if it'll make you feel any better, you can have it resurveyed. When you learn that it's less than thirty acres, perhaps you'll thank me for not taking your money for an unusable tract of land."

His face lit up. "You'll go fifty-fifty on the surveying?"

"Absolutely not. You're the one who's interested in the size. You can pay for it."

He turned to leave, then stopped and said, "I saw the NO TRES- PASSING signs that nosy manager out there put up. She threatened to call the cops on me, so maybe you better tell her it's okay."

"Yes, I'll tell her you have my permission. Just go on and survey to your heart's content. She won't bother you."

"And if it's thirty acres or more, you'll sell?"

"I've already told you: the property is not for sale under any circumstances. All I'm interested in is putting your mind at rest." *So you'll go bother somebody else*, I wanted to add, but I opened the door and said instead, "Good day, Rodney."

Chapter 36

"Sam," I said as he drove us home that evening from a League of Women Voters meeting where he and Jimmy Ray had stated their platforms and answered questions. "You have any idea who Rodney's silent partner is?"

"Hm-m? Oh, no telling," he said, and I knew he still had the meeting on his mind. He'd done well, as he always did, answering every question thrown at him, even the follow-ups that demanded more detailed information—the League members were a knowledgeable group.

"Well, I wish I knew," I said. "I don't like the idea of dealing with someone behind the scenes."

Sam moved his hand from the steering wheel and laid it on my knee. "But you're not dealing with him or with Rodney, so it doesn't matter. It could even be McCrory's that's pulling his strings. Maybe they want another location and Rodney's just the front man."

"I hadn't thought of that. But, no, I don't think so. Rodney speaks too strongly about *his* cemetery and *his* mortuary and *his* plans. I think if he were just a front man, he'd have let something slip before this. Besides, he referred to his silent partner like it was an individual, not a family group like McCrory's or even a bank. Whoever it is owns that farm a little before you get to the trailer park, so we can find out easily enough. I think I'll ask Binkie to look it up at the county clerk's office and see who it is."

"If I have time tomorrow, I'll go to the courthouse and do it for you."

"Oh, no, Sam, don't do that. You're much too busy. You're speaking to the Lions Club tomorrow, aren't you? And before I forget it, I was so proud of you tonight. Jimmy Ray got befuddled trying to answer some of the questions, but they didn't stump you at all. Of course, Jimmy Ray had to defend himself on some of his votes."

Sam laughed. "That's always a problem when you're the incumbent. Anyway, I think I may have swayed a few."

"More than a few," I said, putting my hand on his. "I could tell from the looks on their faces that they were impressed with you. But, I declare, I don't know how you can eat something wherever you go. If it's not lunch, it's dinner and usually chicken of some sort, or else it's doughnuts or desserts spread out on a table. It's a wonder every candidate doesn't gain ten pounds a campaign."

"We just about do," Sam said, smiling in the dark of the car. "I've learned to just pick up a doughnut or whatever and nibble on it. And, usually, at a meal, I can start a conversation at the table, take a bite or two, and string it out until it's time for me to speak."

I laughed. "Take a tip from Lloyd. Remember how he used to stir things around on his plate so it'd look as if he'd eaten something? And remember when Lillian found some dried-up peas in a drawer in the kitchen table? He'd raked them in when nobody was looking."

"I do remember," Sam said as we smiled at each other, "and now we can't fill him up. He eats everything in sight."

"He wants to build muscles," I murmured, but my mind was still on something else. "Whoever it is has to be somebody with enough money to invest in everything Rodney wants to do. Why, it'll take millions to do what he's talking about. Who has that kind of wealth, or that kind of interest in a mortuary, of all things?"

"Well, think about it. Who do we know that would fill the bill?"

"Well, Mildred for one. She certainly has the means, but I don't know how she'd feel about owning grave sites with people buried in them. She can be squeamish about things like that. I think it has to be somebody who's just off enough to think a cemetery on my property would be a grand . . ." I stopped, jerked upright, and said, "*Thurlow!* That's who it is, it has to be! And, listen, Sam," I said, grasping his arm, "everything Rodney told me points to him. He's not *selling* that farm, he's leasing it. Long-term, but still. And that means that Thurlow will not only retain own-ership of the farm, he'll own everything Rodney builds on it. So if Rodney's business fails, Thurlow will not only get his property back, but all the improvements, too. Doesn't that sound just like something he'd do?"

"You may be right," Sam said. "He's a crafty one, that's for sure."

"I could almost feel sorry for Rodney, getting mixed up with him. But, Sam, Rodney has never mentioned the property to the south of my place, which would be as natural an extension as the farm on the north. I wonder who owns it."

"I don't know, but I seem to recall some sort of problem with it," Sam said. "But now you've got me intrigued. I'll make time to go to the courthouse tomorrow, then we'll know about both."

"Only if you have time." We rode along for a while, me thinking of my Springer Road property and him, well, I didn't know what he was thinking. "By the way," I said, "I didn't know a railroad runs through that tract on the south. Etta Mae said it's been there forever, but she's never seen a train on it."

"That's it!" Sam said. "I knew there was something that put that land out of reach. If Rodney has his eye on it, he won't get far, let me tell you. The railroad never sells anything, doesn't matter whether they're using it or not."

"But aren't some of those old rail beds used as walking trails?"

"Yep, but I think the railroad just permits the use of them. They don't sell."

"Wonder if Rodney knows that."

Sam smiled. "I would guess he does, and it's probably why he's pushing you so hard. You thinking of warning him about Thurlow?"

I thought about it for a few minutes. "No, it wouldn't do any good, and those two probably deserve each other. Besides, I'm not selling, so their plans aren't going anywhere, anyway."

When we walked into the house, the first thing I saw was the blinking message light on the telephone. As Sam went on into the hall, turning on lights as he went, I stopped by the counter, punched the Play button, and listened.

"Miss Julia? It's Hazel Marie. If you get home before ten tonight, will you give me a call? Something wonderful just happened. So, bye. No, wait, if you're later than that, call me first thing in the morning. Okay?" Then there was silence as if she were waiting for me to answer. "Well, okay, bye. Call me."

Checking the time, which was nine-thirty, I punched in the Pickenses' number and got him.

"Mr. Pickens, it's Julia Murdoch," I said after his abrupt answer. "I hope it's not too late to call, but I had a message from Hazel Marie . . ."

"Hold on," he said. "I'll get her. Big doings around here. She's beside herself, waiting for you to call."

As I waited, a number of possibilities ran through my mind. Lord, I hoped she wasn't expecting again. No, it couldn't be that—at least I didn't think so. Maybe one of the little girls did something outstanding. Hazel Marie was known to report every remarkable event—first tooth, first step, first word, first sentence, and I mean, since there were two of them, there were double the number of reports.

"Oh, Miss Julia," Hazel Marie said as she picked up the phone. "I'm so glad you called. I'd be too excited to sleep if I had to wait till morning to tell you."

I couldn't help but smile. Hazel Marie's excitement was infectious. "Well, tell me. I can't wait to hear."

"Guess who called tonight."

"I don't know, Hazel Marie. Who?"

"*Rodney,* that's who!"

Rodney didn't exactly excite me, but I asked, "What did he want?"

"Trixie! He wanted Trixie. He asked her out, and they're going to dinner and a movie tomorrow night. Isn't that wonderful?"

"Well, my goodness, I guess it is. How does Trixie feel about it?"

"Oh, she's walking on air, just thrilled, and we've been planning what she'll wear and practicing with a knife and fork . . . Oh, I didn't tell you. He's taking her to the Grove Park Inn to their fancy restaurant where each table has its own server and that's all he does, just waits on that one table. Oh, it's grand, Miss Julia. J.D. took me there on our first date after the babies were born. They treat you like royalty. Trixie's so excited she can hardly stand it."

"I hope she's not so excited that she forgets all you've taught her."

"I just wish I'd done what I've been thinking of doing before this happened," Hazel Marie said worriedly. "She really needs more practice before going public, and I've thought of having a luncheon—just a few friends so Trixie can learn by example. Do you think I should go ahead and have one, even though it'll have to be after her date?"

"I think that's an excellent idea. But, Hazel Marie, if I were you, I'd limit the guest list to our most tolerant and noncritical friends."

"Then let's do it Monday before everybody is wiped out from Fourth of July celebrations. You're invited, of course, and I think Etta Mae—she's a lot of fun and I think Trixie will enjoy her company. And Mildred Allen, who's always so kind to those of us who've never been to New York. And LuAnne, 'cause I kinda owe her. Let's see, counting me, you, and Trixie, that makes six. If I invite Mrs. Ledbetter, I'll have to think of somebody else to even up the table."

I'd already frowned at the mention of LuAnne, who never let a breach of etiquette pass without commenting on it and continuing to comment for days afterward. Emma Sue Ledbetter wouldn't do that, but she'd take every evangelistic opportunity that presented itself in the company of an unchurched person. Which Trixie, who couldn't be roused on Sunday mornings, assuredly would be in her eyes.

"I think six is the ideal number, Hazel Marie," I said. "You wouldn't want to overwhelm her with too many people she doesn't know."

"That's settled then. Let's say about noon Monday. I'll call the

216 Ann B. Ross

others this afternoon and apologize for being last-minute. But I think I'd better strike while the iron's hot, which will be right after her date. I mean, by then Trixie will surely understand the importance of being comfortable—because of knowing what to do—in any social situation, don't you think?"

"I do, indeed, and, Hazel Marie, you can pat yourself on the back. You're doing wonders with her and for her, and I hope she remembers to thank you."

"Well," Hazel Marie said, a bit wryly, "I think I'll wait and see how tomorrow night goes before looking for any thanks."

I laughed. "Good idea. But, listen, if Trixie needs a new dress, use my credit card."

After hanging up, I turned around to see Sam standing in the doorway. "Did you hear all that?" I asked. "Rodney's taking Trixie out again."

Sam's eyebrows went up, then he smiled. "That's a pretty fast about-face, isn't it?"

"It sure is, and I'm wondering why."

Chapter 37

I didn't have long to wonder. Barely forty-eight hours later, Trixie came to see me. She showed up Sunday afternoon, after her date with Rodney the evening before. Our morning had been spent at church, from which Trixie had been noticeably absent, and after lunch Sam had left for some vote mongering, taking Mr. Pickens and Lloyd with him.

Looking forward to a leisurely afternoon, I'd started on the newspaper in the library, having slipped off my shoes to rest my feet on an ottoman. I'd deliberately stayed away from Hazel Marie's the day before, knowing that the preparations for Trixie's date would be hectic, and that she'd need all the last-minute instructions in etiquette and deportment that she could get. But Hazel Marie had called, almost every hour on the hour, to let me know how the day was progressing.

"We got her a dress," she reported, barely an hour after the shops had opened. "It's just elegant and looks so good on her. She didn't really want black, until she saw it on. And when I told her I'd let her wear my pearls—the ones you gave me—why, she was as happy as she could be."

I mentally moaned at the thought of those beautiful pearls in Trixie's care, but refrained from saying anything.

Then in the early afternoon, Hazel Marie called again. "I tried to get Trixie to take a nap, but she's too excited to sleep or eat or anything. Now she's practicing how to walk in her new shoes. Really high heels, but they're all that way now."

And not an hour later, another report. "Trixie just threw up. You reckon she's getting sick?"

"Just excitement, Hazel Marie," I assured her. "But you better get her to eat a little something. She shouldn't leave on an empty stomach—she'll be ravenous at dinner. Just imagine that."

And on and on it went all afternoon, until finally Hazel Marie called a little after six. "Well, they're off, and Trixie did look nice. I think Rodney was impressed when she came downstairs, although I had a hard time getting her to wait till he got in the house. J.D. talked with him a few minutes." Hazel Marie stopped and laughed a little. "I think Rodney was happy to get Trixie and leave. You know how J.D. can be—I think he was practicing for when our girls begin to date."

I'd heard nothing more after that, not even on the morning after. Assuming that Trixie had slept late after her big night, I expected to get a complete report sometime that afternoon.

But I hadn't expected Trixie to suddenly show up in my house. She'd come in the kitchen door, walked through the house, and appeared in the library before I knew she was there. No knocking, no doorbell ringing, no phone call—she was just there. I was startled, because we usually kept the doors locked when someone was in the house alone, and I almost reprimanded her. Still, Lloyd came and went at will, and Trixie probably felt she had the run of the place as well.

"Why, Trixie," I said, putting aside the paper. "I'm glad to see you. Come tell me all about last night. Did you have a good time?"

"Real good," she said, flopping down in the wing chair opposite mine. Then, as if suddenly remembering a lesson, she sat up, put her knees together, and primly said, "It was a delightful evening, and Rodney enjoyed it just as much as me. I mean, as I did. He told me he did, and that he'd probably jumped the gun a little when he said we ought to see other people. He really missed me, so I guess we're back together."

"I'm pleased to hear it." What else could I say? I didn't trust Rodney or his intentions toward her, but I couldn't tell her that.

"Yeah," she said, her gaze wandering around the room as if her mind was somewhere else. "That place we went to was real fancy, but I could do without all that hovering the waiter did. That's what

Rodney called it, hovering. Made me nervous. I don't like some-body watching me eat, and we couldn't take a drink of water with-out him coming to pour us some more."

"Well, that's the way those places are. At least you never have to flag down a waiter to get served."

"I guess." She nodded. "But Rodney and me decided we didn't much like it. Food was good, though. Miss Julia," she went on, her eyes briefly meeting mine, then darting away, "I got something to ask you. You know that property Rodney wants for his mortuary complex?"

Mortuary *complex*? That was a new one, but I nodded. "Yes, I've been hearing a lot about it lately."

"Well, he's having it surveyed Wednesday—that's the day after the Fourth of July, I guess you know. He wanted to have it done sooner than that, like tomorrow, but they wouldn't do it. He said you gave him permission."

"I did," I agreed, "although I don't know why he's going to the expense. The property is not suitable for what he wants and I wouldn't sell it if it was."

"That's what he said. But it started me thinking, and I feel like you do. I mean, I wouldn't sell it either, if I didn't want to. Rodney says you probably want to keep it as part of your estate—you know, to pass on to whoever's in your will."

I looked at her in surprise. People don't normally bring up such personal matters as one's beneficiaries or, indeed, to remind one of the attendant matter of preparation for one's death.

"So it got me to thinking," Trixie went on, "and I know you don't have any kids and your sisters don't, either, so Meemaw has to be your next of kin. And because you don't even know my mama, and Meemaw says she don't deserve anything anyway, I figure I'm in there somewhere and it might all come to me, 'spe-cially since I know you don't think much of Meemaw. So what I want to know is why don't you go ahead and give me that land now instead of me having to wait till you die, when I'll inherit it anyway?"

If I'd ever been stunned before, it was nothing like I felt at that moment. I stared at her, simply speechless at her presumption, her boldness, and her unmitigated gall in assuming that she was in my will, much less my primary beneficiary.

Finally I was able to open my mouth. "Did Rodney put you up to this?"

"Nuh-uh," she said with a shake of her head, but it was a weak *nuh-uh*. "I thought of it all by myself. See, because I'd do just what you're doing and hold on to it. I wouldn't sell it for anything. That way, see, I'd go in with Rodney and be his partner, and we'd get married and we'd own the whole complex together. He wouldn't ever think we ought to see other people then."

If marriage vows wouldn't hold on to a man—I wanted to say, as Wesley Lloyd Springer passed through my mind—how did she expect a chunk of land to keep him in line? But that was neither here nor there at the present time.

"Well, Trixie," I said calmly, even as I marveled at my own restraint, "it seems that Hazel Marie hasn't gotten to the point of explaining to you that there are certain subjects that one does not bring up or mention in passing, or even vaguely refer to. A person's will is at the top of the list. And," I said, gathering steam, "let me just set you straight about kinship and lines of inheritance. It does not necessarily follow that just because someone is related to someone, that that someone is in line for a windfall. And furthermore, I seriously doubt that your Meemaw and I are any kin at all, and if we are, it is of the most tenuous nature and certainly not one you can count on."

She was looking at me, wide-eyed, during this, and I began to doubt that half of what I said had gotten through to her.

"Well, but," she finally said, "you don't have nobody else to leave it to. I mean, you never had no kids or nieces or nephews or anything. I'm almost the next of kin, and the most important thing is *family*—Meemaw says so. That's the way she was raised, and you were, too. So if you was to give me that land, I wouldn't ask for anything else. You could do whatever else you wanted to with whatever else you've got."

"That's very thoughtful of you," I said, but she didn't hear the sarcasm that I hadn't been able to control.

"Yeah, well, Rodney said that you're just the type to leave everything to the church or to a bunch of cats like some old ladies do. But you don't have any cats, and we need that land more'n the church does. The one you go to's got money gone to bed anyway— I could tell the first time I walked in the door."

So Rodney had discussed the dispensation of my estate with her. Why was I not surprised?

"Let me put your mind at ease," I said, getting to my feet because I'd about reached the end of my tether. "My will and my intentions for what the Lord has blessed me with are not your concern, Trixie. And I will also tell you this: family, especially far-flung family, the members of which might have no ties whatsoever to each other, is not all it's cracked up to be. There just might be people of absolutely no blood kin who are closer and more precious than anyone with a presumed family connection. In other words, there are families, and then there are *families*. So my advice to you is to look to your Meemaw for any inheritance coming to you, because the fact of the matter is: I'm neither ready to die nor am I ready to begin dispensing my assets, and I won't be for some time to come. In fact," I went on, as I fumed at Rodney's categorization of me, "I just might begin taking in a few cats."

She stared at me as if I'd lost my mind, then her face turned red as it scrunched up and a few tears squeezed out. Putting her hands over her face, she hopped up and headed for the door. When she got there, she turned back and cried, "I could have everything I ever wanted if I had that land, but you're just too *selfish* to let me have it!"

And with that, she ran out, slamming the back door as she went.

Chapter 38

They Lord, I thought, flopping down on a chair. Me, *selfish*? She'd called *me* selfish? When I'd fed her and dressed her and took her in when her own grandmother had turned her out?

To be unappreciated was the most hurtful thing, and I thought of a dozen ways with which I could've defended myself. Why, think of all the nonprofits I helped support around town, or the church which owed its new furnace to Sam and me, as well as the anonymous gifts I'd made to individuals who were in dire need or else were just those I wanted to help. And I won't even bring up the tithe because that's my reasonable sacrifice, but my over-and-above giving is worth a mention.

And of course if you want to step back and consider what I'd done for Wesley Lloyd's mistress and son, that could be thought of as going way beyond what any sane woman would've done. But, shaking my head, I refused to consider them—doing something for those you love and deeply care for probably shouldn't count when it came to qualifying as unselfish. It probably only counts when you do something you don't particularly want to do, which was the way I'd felt at first but changed my mind later on.

Finally, I lifted my head and began to think about who I'd listed in my will to benefit by my death. Should I have included Elsie and Trixie? They might indeed be of some distant kin to me, but was that enough to assure them of a mention? Not, I told myself, by any means. A will, it seemed to me, was the most personal of any document and, family notwithstanding, a place in which one could do as one wished and not have to suffer the consequences—one would be dead and buried by the time anybody got disappointed.

Sam, of course, was featured in my will, but only with a token because we'd discussed the matter and he'd told me he had plenty to last him a lifetime. Besides, he'd made it plain that he didn't want to benefit from Wesley Lloyd's money. I, myself, hadn't minded spending it because, by putting up with Wesley Lloyd for forty years, I figured I'd earned every penny, but I could see why Sam would just as soon it pass him by.

Then there was Lillian, who would never have to cook another meal or scrub another pot if she didn't want to. She'd be able to queen it at the A.M.E. Zion Church if she had a mind to and educate Latisha, too. And Hazel Marie, of course. It pleased me to think of how surprised she'd be—she'd probably cry. Wouldn't you love to be around when people learned just how much they'd meant to you? Hazel Marie had certainly been well cared for by the income from Lloyd's inheritance, but that would last only until he reached maturity. I knew that he would continue to look after his mother, but how much better it would be if she had assets of her own. Mr. Pickens flashed through my mind at that point, and I didn't know how he'd take to his wife suddenly having a few investments in her name—he'd been leery enough about marrying a woman with a wealthy child. Well, I decided, he could just learn to live with it—I *wanted* Hazel Marie to be one of my beneficiaries.

And there was the First Presbyterian Church of Abbotsville. I couldn't leave that out—that just wasn't done by a churchgoing woman—although I'd carefully specified what the money was to be used for. No need giving Pastor Ledbetter a free hand, which he already used too frequently to suit me, anyway. And there were a few more itemized charities that had a mention—Lillian's church, for instance, would come in for some unexpected benefits, not only for her sake, but because I was partial to the Reverend Abernathy, who'd once done me a kindness.

Oh, and Etta Mae, I hadn't overlooked her, and I hoped that having a nice income-producing property would give her peace of mind even if she never married again.

And just in the past year, I'd had Binkie tack on a codicil that included the Pickens twins and, much against Binkie's protestations—which I ignored—Little Gracie, Binkie and Coleman's daughter.

What was left—which would be plenty—would go to Lloyd, the precious child I'd never had and never thought I wanted, but who more than satisfactorily filled an empty place in my life. Besides, it had all come by way of his father in the first place, although I'd used my half with a great deal of pleasure and very little depletion of capital and even less thought of whence it came.

But Elsie and Trixie? No, ma'am. I'd get a whole house full of cats first.

I dozed off and on for an hour or so, waking now and then to think again of Trixie's demand, then getting irate all over again. Rodney had put her up to asking for that property, I was sure of it. But how could anyone, even Trixie, not know any better than to just walk in and ask—and *expect*—to be given something of value? It was beyond me, but still I hated to be thought selfish.

And to think that I would have to sit at the table with her on the morrow and be graciously sociable, even as I knew what she thought of me. Well, I could do that. I'd had years of practice under worse circumstances than these.

Yet I wished for Sam. I couldn't wait to tell him of Trixie's utter gall in asking and of her unfairness in calling me selfish.

I guess I wanted reassurance that I was a thoughtful, considerate, and unsparing Christian woman who was going to hold on to that property, tooth and nail, till Doomsday. Or until Etta Mae decided to move.

When the front doorbell rang, my first thought was that it was Rodney come to add his plea to Trixie's. I stomped to the door, determined to put an end to it. It wasn't Rodney.

"Well, Thurlow," I said, surprised to find him standing on my front porch. "Sam's off politicking, but he should be back soon. Do you want him to call you when he gets in?"

"No, I've come to see you, and it's just as well that Murdoch's not here. We got a business matter to discuss, you and me."

I didn't like the sound of that, suspecting as I did that he was another of Rodney's agents, but I held the door open and stepped back. "Come in then, although I don't ordinarily discuss business on a Sunday."

I led him into the living room, motioned him to a chair, and took one myself. "Well, let's hear it," I said, in no mood to be harassed about that property again. I didn't offer any refreshments.

Thurlow sat, crossed one leg over the other, and picked at the place a crease would've been on the knee of his pants, if they'd ever seen an iron. "I guess you figured out by now," he began, frowning at me, "that I'm going in with the Pace boy to turn that area out on Springer Road into a first-class mortuary and cemetery complex. And I guess you've been wondering what all we're going to do."

"No," I said serenely, "not at all. In fact, I haven't given any of it much thought."

"Then it's time you did. We've made you a good offer and there's no reason in the world for you to hold on to that land. It's not like you're using it for anything."

"Well, there's the Hillandale Trailer Park . . ."

Thurlow snorted and waved his hand as if the home of a dozen people was of no account. "That can be moved. In fact, I've got a nice hillside I'll throw in to boot. Move 'em there."

I thought of Etta Mae, and I thought of how a huge flatbed truck with a sign across the front and back fenders reading WIDE LOAD would have to be backed into the park and up against her single-wide, which would then have to be unhooked from water, electricity, and sewer lines, and how it would have to be craned up onto the truck bed, then hauled down the highway in a convoy with a car with flashing lights in front and one in back to warn other drivers. And then be dumped onto a hillside in the back of beyond somewhere—no telling where—and rehooked to the necessary utilities. And that's only if there was a sewer line out there.

They might have to put in a septic tank. Twelve times that would have to be done, to the tune of an untold amount of money that the residents, and certainly Etta Mae, didn't have.

"I'm not moving them," I said firmly, "and I'm not selling. And I really don't want to hear any more about it."

"You're just being stubborn," he said, which fired me up because I was fed up with name-calling.

I opened my mouth to tell him off, but he went right on. "Why wouldn't you want to help improve and enhance that area of the county? Delmont needs a nice business like we'd put up. Lots of job opportunities, you know. You don't want to be known as somebody who'd stand in the way of progress."

I was on my feet before I knew it. "*Progress!* I'm so tired of hearing about *progress* I can't see straight. It's just another word for change, and I've had my fill of it. Every time I turn around, somebody is wanting to tear down, cut down, and pour concrete all over everything. I keep telling Rodney, and now I'll tell you—that piece of land is not big enough for a cemetery and I wish you'd both get your minds off of it."

Thurlow didn't turn a hair, just leisurely stood up and watched as I paced and poured out what I had to say. Ignoring my outburst against progress, he centered in on the land itself. "Rodney told me you're going by an old plat, and you ought to know that the old ones always underestimate. Didn't have the equipment they have nowadays. You just wait till we get it resurveyed, then we'll talk again." He made a move toward the door, while I wondered what it would take for any of them to understand that my property was out of bounds.

"Well, think of this, Thurlow," I said, pushing down the anger in order to appeal to his business sense. "Say I lost my head and sold that land to you and Rodney. And say that you put a few million dollars into buildings and cutting down trees and digging up stumps and strewing grass seed. And let's say you had a backhoe just sitting out there on all that grassy expanse just waiting to start digging graves, and let's say that the state cemetery commission showed up and surveyed it again and told you you didn't have thirty acres and you'd have to close down. Just where would you be then? I'll tell you where—you'd be out of a lot of money and saddled with twenty-nine acres of grass—just right for an expanded mobile home park."

Thurlow hooked a thumb in the waist of his pants and smiled. "That's when having a friend in the state senate comes in handy. With all that expenditure on the line, no senator would hesitate to come to the aid of a small businessman like Rodney. There'd be a bill on the floor in no time flat making a one-time exception to the law. And there is such a thing as eminent domain, you know. Think about what would be best for the local economy: a tract of land doing nobody any good, or a new business with job openings."

"Well," I said, infuriated by his cool assumption that he could have anything he wanted and if it wasn't legal, he could make it so. "And what if your *friend in the senate,* Jimmy Ray Mooney, loses the election? What if somebody who is not in your pocket is the next senator?"

"Hah!" he said, delighted at the thought of getting the better of me. "Never happen. I took your advice, madam, and made sizable contributions to both candidates. Just remember this—I never make a move without covering all the bases."

And, leaving me open-mouthed, he walked to the door and left.

Chapter 39

I kept pacing long after Thurlow was gone. I was so edgy and impatient for Sam to get home that I could hardly stand it. I knew—I *knew*—that Sam could never be bought, but I also knew that senators and representatives were constantly being appealed to by constituents who needed or just wanted special exemptions. And many times those exemptions were granted by a beneficent lawmaker who then got his picture in the paper. So I didn't doubt that Thurlow could get done whatever he wanted done, maybe even without having made any campaign contributions at all.

I finally sat down, worn to a frazzle by all the steps I'd taken. But why was I so agitated? We would never know if the requirements of the state cemetery commission could be overruled. Sam would never be asked to interfere on behalf of Rodney or Thurlow, and neither would Jimmy Ray, because it would never come to that point. What belonged to me was going to stay that way, regardless of what Rodney wanted or what Thurlow expected.

Although to tell the truth, I was about tired of hearing about it and could almost wish it was off my hands. So why not, I suddenly asked myself, keep the trailer park as it was and parcel off the rest of it as building lots? All I'd need would be one home built on a nice acre lot with a few other lots staked out, then no elected official would have the nerve to appropriate it in favor of a cemetery. The whole tract would forever be out of Rodney's reach, in spite of having Thurlow's dubious help.

Yet why should I have to do that? It was already out of their reach, although neither of them seemed to understand the word *no*. In spite of their thickness, though, I had every intention to keep saying it until it finally penetrated.

Just imagine, I thought, Sam and I could've been sailing down the Rhine instead of being stuck at home and pestered day and night by the likes of Rodney and Thurlow, to say nothing of Trixie. Too bad that Sam had to get involved in politics—we could've been long gone and far away.

Then I had to laugh. I knew why we weren't on the Rhine, and I knew who'd been the one to turn it down. But if, a few months back, I'd been able to look into the future and see what the summer would bring upon us, I might've jumped at the chance to dangle my feet in that river.

Hearing Sam's car turn into the drive, I hopped up and hurried to meet him. He didn't get through the door good until I had my arms around him and my head on his chest.

"Hey, hey," he said softly, even as he responded by holding me close. "What is this?"

"Oh, Sam, I'm so glad you're home. Seems you've been gone the whole day."

"Just the afternoon," he reminded me. "But it's worth being gone to have a welcome like this." Then he held me back from his chest so he could look at me. "Has something happened? What's wrong?"

"Oh," I said airily, trying to pass off my warm welcome as a normal response to his arrival. "Nothing's wrong, particularly. I've just had visitors all afternoon, so I didn't get the nap I was counting on. The coffee's ready to perk, so why don't you go on to the library and I'll be there in a few minutes. You're probably tired."

"Yeah, pretty much so. But I'm glad Pickens and Lloyd wanted to go with me. I enjoyed having them. That Lloyd is something else. He caught everybody at the door when it was over and made sure they had a brochure and a Murdoch pin to leave with."

After preparing the coffee tray, I took it to the library where Sam was resting with his feet up. I'd already calmed down by that time, telling myself that he had enough on his mind without my adding more on top of what he was already dealing with. I was, therefore, determined to let him talk about the afternoon, his plans for the next few days, and the campaign in general. Too often I was so full of what was going on with me that I didn't give him a chance to say what was on his mind. A good wife makes time to listen, advise, and comfort, which is what I do. Most of the time.

I poured coffee for him, added some cream and stirred it, then put it on the table beside his chair. Then I prepared my cup, sat down near him, opened my mouth to ask how the meeting went, and said, "You won't believe who all came to see me today. First it was Trixie telling me she expected to inherit my estate and asking me to go ahead and give her that tract of land that Rodney wants, just so Rodney won't want to see other people. And then"—I stopped, took a breath, and went on—"then Thurlow showed up telling me I'm standing in the way of progress and economic growth, and when I told him that land wasn't large enough for Rodney's purpose, he as much as told me that he'd paid off both you and Jimmy Ray—just to cover all the bases—so whoever is elected will have a special law passed that will allow grave sites on land that doesn't meet the specifications. And I know you wouldn't do that, would you? And Trixie called me selfish because I told her I wouldn't give it to her and that she wasn't in my will in the first place, and Thurlow called me stubborn because I won't sell it to Rodney. So you see, you've been presumed corrupt, and I've been called uncharitable names, and I'm just waiting for Rodney to add his two cents' worth." I lifted the cup to my mouth, then stopped before drinking and turned back to Sam. "Did you have a good meeting? Who all was there?"

"Forget the meeting," Sam said, putting his feet on the floor and beginning to rise. "Enough is enough. I'm putting a stop to this."

"Wait. Where're you going?"

"To call Trixie and tell her I'm coming over for a sit-down, heart-to-heart talk. And when I get through, she's going to know what a real makeover is—it's called an attitude change. Then I'm calling Thurlow to tell him to back off, and if he thinks he's got a senator in his pocket he better hope Jimmy Ray wins. He won't have this one."

I didn't think I'd ever seen Sam so angry. I knew I hadn't, for in fact I'd rarely seen him angry at all. Sam was generally a live-and-let-live, kindhearted man, but Trixie had been so presumptuous and Thurlow so arrogant that they were more than he could take with his usual equanimity.

"Wait, Sam," I said, putting my hand on his arm. "Let's think about this. Trixie's going to think me selfish regardless of what you say, and she'll think it even more so when my will is read. Nothing you say or do will change that. She's to be pitied for assuming that having that land will hold Rodney for long. And as for Thurlow, he'll get his comeuppance sooner or later. Let him go on thinking he has both you and Jimmy Ray bought and paid for, and let him go on paying you both with contributions. He'll learn quickly enough when you refuse to do what he wants."

"Yes, but I don't like them calling you names. Not even a little bit."

"I know. I don't like it either, but sticks and stones, as they say. It'd be better to just bide our time, let them think what they want to think, and go on about our business. The only thing that would change their minds is if I sell that land to Rodney, or I give it to Trixie, and I'm not going to do either one. Because if I did, mark my words, it wouldn't be long until they wanted something else from me or from you, and we'd be right back where we started."

Sam's shoulders slumped in resignation. "You're right. Nothing I say will do any good, but it'd sure make me feel better." He smiled then, and I knew he'd regained his composure. "You sure you don't want me to tell 'em off?"

I smiled back. "To tell the truth, I'd love it. But right now, it's just not expedient, especially since time is on our side. Let's just rise above the fray. Come on, sit back down and let me rub your back." I drew him to the sofa and eased down beside him. "The doctor told you to get plenty of rest, but you're constantly on the go. I worry about you, Sam. It hasn't been that long since your surgery."

"I'm all right. I hardly know I had surgery by now." He turned sideways so I could massage the back of his neck. "I still think, though, that Trixie would benefit from a good talking-to."

"She needs several, but I sometimes think that all she understands is either *yes* or *no*. Maybe that's all she's ever heard, but as long as she's with Hazel Marie, I don't want to rock the boat. Except for this afternoon with me, she's been behaving herself, and I'm just hoping it'll last through the luncheon tomorrow. It upsets my stomach to think of eating chicken salad with her glowering at me across the table. And," I said, returning to my argument, "think of this. If you did talk to her, she'd likely throw one of her fits and Mr. Pickens would throw her out. Then she'd be back over here with us."

"That clinches it then," Sam said, giving me an over-the-shoulder smile. "No talking-to, at least for now."

Chapter 40

"Etta Mae," I said, calling her the next morning before she went to work. "Sorry to call so early, but I wanted to catch you before you left in case you see Rodney Pace wandering around out there again. I didn't want to bring it up at the luncheon, but you'll be there, won't you?"

"Oh, hey, Miss Julia," she said, almost too cheerily for the hour. "Yes, I'm working half a day, but I'll be there. I have a few minutes now, though. What's he gonna be doing? You want me to watch him?"

"No, no need for that, I don't think. I've given him permission to survey the property, so he'll be bringing some men out. Probably not until the day after tomorrow, though. I wanted you to know so you wouldn't be worried."

There was a long silence on the phone. Then in a dull voice she said, "You're selling it."

"No, I am not. All I'm doing is letting him survey it so he'll have to accept the fact that the land is not adequate for his purpose. That way, he'll have to look elsewhere, and Trixie can't blame me. I don't know why I even care about that, though, because you won't believe what he put her up to doing." And I went on to tell her of Trixie's expectation of my imminent demise and the resultant distribution—even *pre*distribution—of my assets as she'd revealed to me the afternoon before.

Etta Mae gasped. "You don't mean it! I've never heard of such nerve in my life. I hope you told her off good."

"I think I made it fairly plain," I said, somewhat wryly. "She was most unhappy when she left. Called me selfish for not giving it to her."

"What! *You,* selfish? Miss Julia, you are a saint. I can't believe *any*body would call you selfish. Why, you're the most generous person I know."

Of course, I reveled in her words. They were like a balm in Gilead to my soul, but then I felt ashamed of myself. There I was, telling something better kept to myself, just to elicit the response she'd given.

"Thank you, Etta Mae, but I've considered the source and haven't let it bother me. But that's why I'm letting Rodney spend his money on a futile survey. An accurate plat will settle the matter, once and for all."

"But, Miss Julia, what if the survey proves Mr. Pace is right? I wouldn't want to stand in your way, none of us do. I mean, all of us out here would understand if you decide to sell. We might not like it, but," she tried to laugh, "but we know that things happen. So if you want to sell it, we'll find someplace to live."

"But, see, Etta Mae, another survey won't prove him right. I knew the surveyor of that plat I showed you, and if he said twenty-nine and nine-tenths, that's what it is. And even if it's more than that, I promise you, I wouldn't sell it for all the gold in Fort Knox."

Well, I thought to myself, maybe for all the stored gold that's supposed to be there, I would. Just think what I could do with it. I could move all the residents of the trailer park out at my expense, find them a better location, maybe a real park with a playground for the children, maybe even build a house for Etta Mae and get her out of that cramped single-wide, and . . . I almost laughed. When you admit one impossibility into your mind, that's when all the other impossible dreams begin.

"Um," Etta Mae said, "I don't think we're on the gold standard anymore."

"Well, whatever," I said, laughing a little to cheer her up. "How about for all the tea in China? Here's the thing, Etta Mae, the property's not for sale at any price, and it's not going to be. But if you happen to see Rodney out there, I'd appreciate knowing about it."

"Sure, I can do that. He won't be trespassing if you've given him permission, so I guess you don't want me to call the cops."

"No, just ignore him. But when he's finished with the survey, he's done. Those signs will stay up, and he'd do well to take heed from then on out. I've about had my fill of Rodney's big plans."

I was still sitting at the kitchen table having a second cup of coffee while waiting for Lillian to finish with the dishes and join me. I was eager to tell her about Trixie and Thurlow, then to hear her vigorously deny that they'd been accurate in their assessment of me. She'd been unusually quiet as she'd prepared breakfast, but when Lloyd joined us, he made up for our lack of conversation. He told Lillian that he'd come for breakfast because her biscuits were better than James's, and that had made her laugh. "I could've tole you that," she'd said, but soon grew quiet again, barely rising to any of our compliments on the meal.

Sam and Lloyd left soon afterward, heading out to tack up more campaign posters, and still I sat waiting.

"Lillian, you're going to scrub the top off that counter. Get some coffee and come sit down." If she didn't soon finish, it would be time for me to get ready for Hazel Marie's luncheon.

"Yes'm, I jus' got a lot on my mind."

"All the more reason to sit and talk for a while."

Finally she poured her coffee and brought the cup to the table, then sat down with a sigh. "Miss Julia, I want to ast if you would pray for Miz Abernathy, the reverend's wife. She not doin' too good."

"I'm sorry to hear that," I said, and I was. I didn't know the reverend's wife but I knew him, and hated to hear of any trouble he might be having. "Is she sick?"

"Yes'm, been sick for a long time, but she goin' down fast now. Pore ole reverend, he lookin' like he been run over."

"I certainly will pray for her, and for him, too. And for you, too, Lillian. I know you think a lot of them both."

"Yes'm, thank you. We been gettin' together at their house ev'ry night raisin' up prayers. The reverend, he tell us that the Lord answers ev'ry prayer what's put up—it'll be either yes, no, or wait a while. But it lookin' like this be one of them *no* times."

"I am so sorry." I reached out to put my hand on her arm, but drew back when the phone rang. "Stay right there. I'll get it. In fact, why don't you go on home? Leave Latisha with her sitter awhile longer, so you can get some rest."

The phone persisted, and as I started toward it, Lillian said, "No'm, I do better to stay busy. I'm gonna start upstairs." And off she went as I picked up the phone and answered it.

Hazel Marie said, "Miss Julia, you won't believe what happened."

Oh, my, I thought, picturing Trixie on a tear after I'd turned her petition down. She could've ranted and raved, moaned and cried half the night, keeping everybody including the babies up for hours. The girl knew no bounds when she was thwarted. I thought again of trying to track the travels of Elsie and Troy so I could ship her back to them. That's what Mr. Pickens was good at—tracking down fugitives. Maybe I could hire him to find them.

"Oh, Hazel Marie," I responded, "I'm so sorry. I should've warned you, but I was so upset. Then when Sam came home and I told him about it, and about Thurlow, too, he was so angry that it was all I could do to calm him. I hope she hasn't turned your whole house upside down."

"No, no, not really. I mean, I thought she was going to because she came running in from your house, slammed the door, and went straight to her room. Oh, and slammed that door, too. I went back there to see what was wrong, and she yelled at me, screamed at me, actually. Told me that nobody cared about her, and that I was just being a hypocrite for pretending to like her." Hazel Marie paused as if hearing those words again. "I tell you, Miss Julia, I was stunned at that because I don't think I'm a hypocrite. Do you?"

"Of course not. There's not a hypocritical bone in your body. But that's on a par with her calling me selfish—both so far from the truth that we shouldn't let it bother us." I paused to let her agree with me, but she didn't say anything. "So what happened then? How is she this morning?"

"Oh, you wouldn't believe the transformation," Hazel Marie said. "But what happened was that J.D. heard her scream at me, and he was up and out of that chair and walking down the hall before I knew it. He told Trixie to get off the bed and go into the living room and stay there. Then he told me he'd be up in a few minutes to help put the babies to bed. You know how he can be, just so sweet that you want to do whatever he wants."

Well, I did know how he could be, and it wasn't always as sweet as Hazel Marie seemed to think it was.

"So what did he do?" I asked. "Just let her sit in the living room?"

"No, he went in and talked to her. I don't know what he said, but whatever it was, well, it did the trick. She came upstairs and apologized to me. And, Miss Julia, I think she really meant it. Told me how much she appreciated my help and that I'd been nicer to her than anyone ever had been before, and said how sorry she was for being so obnoxious."

"She said that? Obnoxious?"

"She sure did. I'm sure she got it from J.D.—it's one of his favorite words when things don't go his way." She giggled. "He's so funny. But, anyway, I tried to get him to tell me what all he'd said to her, but he said he'd just talked to her, and he was pretty sure nothing like that would happen again. And, Miss Julia, it hasn't. She came to breakfast on time, dressed and made up and everything. And she was just as pleasant and friendly as she could be—even to the little girls. I mean, she was so different that I don't know which one is the real Trixie—yesterday afternoon's one or this morning's one."

"Well, I declare," I said with some wonder. "I'd love to know what he said that turned things around so much and so quickly. I've seen her, Hazel Marie, when she was crying and screaming and so unhappy, and it's not a pretty sight. I think you should push Mr. Pickens to tell you his secret. We might need it again."

"You might, at least," Hazel Marie said, "because she wants to talk to you. She wanted to come see you this morning, but I told her you'd probably be too busy."

"Well, thank goodness. I don't think I could stand another round like we had yesterday. Did she tell you what happened?"

"No, and I never got a chance to ask. And after she had such a turnaround, I didn't want to risk undoing it."

So I told Hazel Marie what Trixie had assumed she'd get just by asking and about the ceiling she'd hit when she didn't.

Hazel Marie was appalled. "I never heard of anybody doing such a thing—even *thinking* such a thing. I tell you, Miss Julia, now that I know how far out of bounds she was to you, the change in her this morning is even more remarkable. We need to find out what J.D. said."

"We sure do," I agreed, thinking that with Trixie, we needed all the help we could get. "Hazel Marie, anybody who can get through to Trixie in one of her tantrums is worth his weight in gold. See if he'll stick around for the luncheon."

Chapter 41

As I dressed in a pastel voile with pearl buttons, slipped on my white Ferragamos, considered then discarded a hat and gloves, I realized that my movements were getting slower as the luncheon hour neared. I couldn't help it. I dreaded seeing Trixie and being in her company for a solid hour or more, expecting at any moment an outburst of temper that would be the talk of the town for months to come. I could just hear LuAnne saying a year from now, "Remember that luncheon for Julia's niece or whatever she was? Honey, let me tell you what happened." Then going on to relate specifics that would keep the incident alive even among people who didn't know Trixie from Adam.

I realized that Trixie may indeed have had a remarkable change of attitude where Hazel Marie was concerned, complete with apologies and getting out of bed at a decent hour in response to Mr. Pickens's oratorical skills, but where did that leave me? Hazel Marie had denied her nothing, but I had. Who knew what anger and bitterness she harbored toward me for thwarting her pursuit of Rodney?

But what did I care? you may well ask. I cared because no one likes to witness a loss of control to the extent that Trixie could lose it. Such a scene can be frightening to onlookers and mortally embarrassing to assumed relatives, especially in a social gathering of ladies, all on their best behavior but eager to have something to talk about.

Sam had warned me before leaving that morning that he would put up with no more rudeness from Trixie. "If she cuts up again, Julia, I want you to come home and call me. I'll have her on a bus to somewhere before the day is out."

I stood before the mirror for some last-minute fiddling with my hair, then decided that it was in as good a shape as it was going to get. There was nothing to do but go on and face the music and hope that Mr. Pickens stayed close.

I drove the four blocks to Hazel Marie's house, figuring it was too hot to walk without turning into a wrinkled frump by the time I got there. Besides, I wanted the means of a quick getaway if one became needed.

Being the last guest to arrive, I knew I'd timed it just right. Everybody was in Hazel Marie's living room, talking and laughing together as James passed a tray of iced lime punch in Waterford stemmed glasses, so I was able to slide in without causing a ripple. Standing in the doorway of the living room for a second before taking a seat beside Mildred, I glanced around the room looking for Trixie, then jumped out of my skin as she appeared at my side.

"Miss Julia," she said softly—no one could've heard her but me. "I'm sorry for the way I acted yesterday. I hope you'll excuse my behavior."

My word, Mr. Pickens has wrought a miracle!

"Why, of course I will," I said, because what else does one do? "Come over here for a minute." And I led her deeper into the hall where we wouldn't be overheard. "Thank you, Trixie. It's very commendable of you to apologize, as we all should do when we regret something we've said or done."

"I hope you won't hold it against me," Trixie said, and I knew she'd been dreading our meeting as much as I had. "I mean, I guess I was out of line, but Rodney . . . well," she mumbled, looking down at her feet, "he wants that land so bad, and I thought that if I could get it for him, he'd be so happy. But now," she said as she looked directly up at me, "I don't give a flying flip if he ever gets it. They's more fish in the sea than him, anyway, and I don't know why I let him get me all wrapped up in a ole funeral parlor full of dead folks."

I blinked at the *flying flip*, which almost left me speechless.

"Well," I finally managed, "well, Trixie, you amaze me. But I'm delighted that you're seeing things with a clearer eye now."

She leaned her head back, closed her eyes, and murmured, "I sure am."

Hazel Marie walked into the hall, saw us, and cheerily said, "Come on, you two. Lunch is served."

I followed her to the dining room with a lighter heart than I'd had since Trixie had called me selfish. Things were looking up, and I was looking forward to a relaxed and friendly meal.

Until I saw what Hazel Marie had asked James to prepare— quiche. I inwardly winced, wondering what Trixie would have to say about such a strange—to her—serving. But one could hope that she would eat the lovely salad on the plate and the blueberry muffins in a napkin-covered basket and keep her comments to herself about the quiche.

Since James already had the filled plates on the table, Hazel Marie quickly placed us as she wanted us. She put Trixie as the guest of honor at the head of the table, herself at her usual place at the foot, Etta Mae on Trixie's right, and Mildred on her left. I was seated at Hazel Marie's right and LuAnne on her left.

"Miss Julia," Hazel Marie said, "would you return thanks for us?"

I have never liked praying in public, always being reminded of those who love to pray standing at the corners of the streets so they can be seen, but I had long ago committed to memory an appropriate blessing for just such occasions when I was called upon.

I bowed my head, murmured, "Let us pray," as Pastor Ledbetter always did when he announced his intent to pray whether anybody else wanted to or not, then spoke from memory, along with a few unspoken thoughts: "We thank thee, O Lord, for friends and family, and for all your blessings (*Sam, Lloyd, Lillian, and so on*). We pray for those among us with special concerns today (*please don't let Trixie throw a fit*), and we thank thee for this food (*even though it's quiche*) and for the hands that prepared it (*thank goodness it was James's and not Hazel Marie's*), and we ask you to bless it to the nourishment of our bodies, and us to your service. In Jesus's name we pray, amen."

A chorus of murmured *amen*s accompanied mine, and Hazel Marie started the small silver dish of sliced lemon for the iced tea, then the basket of muffins and the butter dish.

As spoons tinkled in glasses and forks clinked against plates, Etta Mae asked, "Hazel Marie, where are those darling babies?"

Hazel Marie lit up as she always did when her twins were mentioned. "One's asleep and the other one's being rocked by your Granny. Etta Mae, I don't know what I would do without her. She is a wonder. I asked her to join us for lunch, but she said she'd as soon eat by herself as at a party."

"She's a pistol, all right," Etta Mae said, grinning. Then to Trixie, "I love that color on you. It's so becoming."

I could've hugged Etta Mae for noticing Trixie's mint-green dress that toned down her complexion, and for publicly commenting on it. That was the sort of unsolicited compliment that Trixie needed to give her confidence.

Trixie blushed. "Hazel Marie picked it out for me."

"Miss Wiggins," Mildred said, "Etta Mae, if I may. I understand you're a nurse. Do you work at the hospital?"

"No'm, I'm a licensed practical. I see shut-ins, make home visits, and, well, like that."

"I may be calling on you then," Mildred said. "Ladies, I know this isn't exactly suitable at the table, but I'm having a colonoscopy next week, and I'm scared to death."

"Oh, Mildred," LuAnne piped up. "Don't be such a sissy. There's nothing to it. You'll be sound asleep and won't know a thing about it. I've already had mine, and the worst thing is that stuff you have to drink beforehand. But I'll tell you this," she said, raising her fork for emphasis, "everyone here ought to have one, too."

Only Mildred, I thought, could get away with bringing up such a subject, and only LuAnne would launch into details of the subject. I hoped that both of them would soon get off of it.

"Julia," LuAnne demanded, "have you had one?"

"I don't believe I have," I said demurely, wanting to deflect the conversation.

"Well, believe me, you'd know it if you had." And everybody laughed.

Except Trixie, who glanced around, but who apparently didn't get the humor. I didn't much, either, but I was glad to see that she was eating the quiche—though with small, careful bites from her fork, but doing so without turning up her nose and asking for Doritos.

LuAnne suddenly said, "Did y'all hear about the two high school teachers?"

Everybody turned to her with eager looks on their faces. Except Trixie, who seemed intent on the blueberry muffin she held. She couldn't seem to decide whether to eat it or not, but she broke it in two, put one half on her butter plate, and held the other. She studied it for so long that I wondered if she'd found something besides blueberries in it. She finally began to nibble at it, then, finding it tasty, she ate it all. I declare, though, between visualizing Mildred's colonoscopy and expecting an explosion from Trixie any minute, I can't say that I was enjoying my lunch.

"Which ones?" Hazel Marie asked, drawing my attention back to LuAnne's question.

"Coaches, both of them. See," LuAnne said, scooting up in her chair. "They were at the school—I mean, I know it's summer and they're supposed to be off, but a lot of them have things to do there. Anyway, I guess they thought nobody would be around, but the janitor walked in on them in *the girls' locker room!* And both of them are married, and the woman teaches *sex education*, would you believe! Although they call it something else now—health and hygiene, or something—but she teaches it to *students*. Anyway, I heard they've been reassigned to different schools, but I think they ought to be fired. I mean, right in the *school* where *anybody* could've walked in on them! Have you ever heard of anything so appalling?"

Well, yes, a number of us had, and hair-raising tales of

misconduct on school grounds going back fifty years or more were raised for our delectation. I thought that surely Trixie would be entertained, as some of the stories were quite humorous, so I kept glancing at her. She may or may not have heard a word that was said—she sat at the head of the table, eating small amounts of quiche now and then, occasionally turning her head in the direction of whomever was speaking, but her face was suffused with a peaceful glow as an occasional smile flitted across her mouth. She had the sort of inward look that comes over an infant's face when it smiles at the turbulence of intestinal gas.

I held my breath, hoping that her composure would hold at least until we finished eating. The wonder of it was, though, that whatever Mr. Pickens had said to her had elicited an apology to me and a strident denunciation of Rodney.

I determined to find out what it had been, for I knew a few other people who could use just such a wonder-evoking transformation, even if it proved in Trixie's case only a temporary aberration.

Chapter 42

❧❧

I got home about midafternoon to a quiet, orderly house and sat down at the kitchen table to read a note from Lillian. Apparently Mrs. Abernathy's condition had worsened, so Lillian had gone to help out. *Frid chicken & potatoe salat in frigidair*, she'd written, and I smiled at her thoughtfulness—she knew I was no hand in a kitchen.

In fact, by this time I was worn to a frazzle from the stress of waiting for Trixie to throw a public fit, thereby embarrassing Hazel Marie and proving all her efforts in vain. To say nothing of how such a spectacle would've reflected on me, or what Mr. Pickens would do if he had to speak to Trixie again, or how angry Sam would be if he had to trundle her off on a southbound bus. It was all too much to consider dealing with, so it was with great relief that I had come home without such a story to tell and without having to worry with supper.

Trixie had behaved herself admirably. Well, not exactly admirably unless you knew her background, because she had not been what you would call companionably sociable. She never initiated or continued a conversation, merely responding briefly when someone addressed her. And all the while she'd had that unreadable look on her face, especially when she was left to her own thoughts as the conversation veered away from her, which it frequently did, as her "Yes, ma'ams" and "No, ma'ams" did not encourage further efforts to converse.

I tell you, as relieved as I was that Trixie had behaved herself for two full hours, I was also befuddled as to what ailed her. I mean, Hazel Marie had done wonders with her, no doubt about that, but that glassy-eyed, faraway look on Trixie's face boded trouble in the making. Was she getting sick, and if so, would all the guests come down with the same thing? Was she so upset with Rodney that she'd been making plans to wreak vengeance on him, even as James served meringue shells topped with fruit?

I heard the screech of bicycle tires on the driveway as Lloyd came to a stop outside the kitchen door. Then he banged through the door and smiled when he saw me.

"I didn't know if it was safe to go home or not," he said, grinning. "But I dropped by, and all the ladies were gone."

"Yes, the luncheon is over and it was lovely," I said, saying the expected thing without referring to the tension I'd undergone during it. "Did you see Trixie? What was she doing?" I asked, wondering if she and Hazel Marie were assessing the luncheon—what had gone right, what had gone wrong, and who had said what. Sometimes the debriefing was more enjoyable than the party itself.

Lloyd shrugged, heading for the pantry. "Watching television." He came out with two of Lillian's chocolate chip cookies. "You want a cookie?"

I shook my head. "No, your mother served a wonderful lunch. I hope Trixie had a good time, but it was hard to tell. She didn't have much to say, which was fine because she really didn't know those ladies." I rose from the table. "You want a glass of milk?"

"No'm, I'm okay." He took a seat next to the chair I'd just vacated, so I figured he wanted to talk. I quickly sat back down.

"What've you been doing today?" I asked.

His face lit up. "Helping Mr. Sam get ready for tomorrow. Miss Julia, you wouldn't believe all the people who came out, and every one of them's planning to go with us. You know, for Mr. Sam's Fourth of July district tour. Why, there's so many that he had to call the rental place and cancel the van we were going to use. We're going in a jitney now."

"What in the world is a jitney?" I pictured some bicycle-powered conveyance from the Far East that I'd seen on a public television travel documentary.

"Oh, it's just a little bus, not like a Greyhound, but it'll carry more than a van. You should see the banners we made. They say JOIN THE JITNEY JOURNEY FOR MURDOCH, and we'll put one on each side, so people'll know who to vote for."

Lloyd frowned and brushed cookie crumbs from his T-shirt.

"Except, they say it might rain tomorrow and I'm worried the paint might run."

"Well, let's hope not, Lloyd," I said, wanting to feel him out about the uproars that Trixie had caused in his two households. "I understand that Mr. Pickens had to speak to Trixie after she was rude to your mother. And I want you to know that whatever he said has made all the difference in the world in her attitude."

"Yes'm, I heard about that. I mean, I was upstairs and I heard part of it when she yelled at Mama, and when he told her to go sit in the living room. Scared me to death."

"Oh, honey," I said, reaching across the table to touch him. "I don't know what your father said to her, but he'd never do that to you—you'd never give him reason to."

"Well, I don't know. I might. You know, without meaning to."

"I can't imagine it. Your daddy—as new as he is to the job— loves you. And I'll tell you this: Trixie didn't act scared today. She acted just as a young lady should, and would you believe that she actually apologized for being rude to me? Your father is a remarkable man to have worked such a turnaround."

We sat in silence for a few minutes as I wondered if I'd put any of his concerns to rest. Lloyd had lived so long without a father— the one who'd engendered him had rarely been around, and even if he had, he'd hardly been worthy of a child's emulation. And Mr. Pickens had only recently become his adoptive father. So it was no wonder that Lloyd felt a sense of unease, especially when that new father had just drawn a few lines in the sand.

"Miss Julia?" Lloyd asked. "Can I tell you something?"

"Of course you can. Anything you want." And waited with wary concern for a confession of misdoing that he wanted to keep from Mr. Pickens.

I should've known better, for he said, "I think I know who took down Mr. Sam's campaign signs."

"Oh? Who?"

"Well, I hate to say it, but I think it was Rodney."

"*Rodney!* But why? Why would he do such a thing?"

"I don't know, but, see, I didn't want to say anything because I wasn't supposed to hear it. But late last night, well, it wasn't too late, but it was after everybody went to bed, I went downstairs to get my tennis schedule. I thought I was supposed to teach a class today, but I'd promised to help Mr. Sam and I couldn't get to sleep until I made sure what I had to do. Well, anyway, I didn't turn on any lights because I didn't want to wake the babies, and I came downstairs and heard Trixie on the telephone. And I knew it hadn't rung, so she'd called him. Rodney, I mean, because she said his name, and she was in the den and didn't see me. I didn't want to scare her, so I just sat down on the stairs to wait till she finished, because, see, I'd left my tennis bag in the den." He stopped and looked away. "I know it's wrong to eavesdrop, but it wasn't like I *wanted* to hear, I just couldn't help it. And Trixie was mad, and she wasn't whispering by a long shot. I was kinda surprised that nobody else heard her. Anyway, at one point she said something like, 'You think you can do anything you want to and get away with it. What about when they find out it was you who took down all their signs?' Then she listened for a little bit, then she said, 'I'm not saying whether I will or I won't, Rodney, but you'd just better not cross me again.' And around that time I was already scrambling back up the stairs and didn't hear any more."

"Well, they Lord," I said, just done in at this revelation. "But why, Lloyd, why would he do it? Sam's never been anything but gracious to him. I don't understand."

"I don't either, but he had to be really mad about something. It must've taken him all night."

"Served him right if it did. But it makes me feel bad that he'd go after Sam when it's really me he's mad at. I'm sorry, Lloyd. I know you liked him. You've had a heavy load to bear since hearing that, haven't you?"

"Yes'm, I guess I have, but I feel better after telling you. I didn't know if I should or not, but I figured it wasn't fair to blame Mr. Mooney when he didn't do anything."

"Right you are. Because we'd have gone on thinking badly of Mr. Mooney when all the while he'd been entirely innocent." Well, not entirely, for Jimmy Ray wasn't above finagling a few dirty tricks of his own.

"Will you tell Mr. Sam?" Lloyd asked, picking a cookie crumb off the table.

"We'll discuss it, of course, but if you want to tell him, you can. Sam needs to know, but I wouldn't do it when anyone else is around. No need making the volunteers angry."

"Oh, no'm, I wouldn't do that. In fact, I'd just as soon you tell him. I feel bad about it all because Rodney was so nice and he nailed up almost every one of those signs. I mean, he worked *all day*. It's hard to believe he'd go tear them all down."

"I know, honey. But people can be strange, and it's better to withhold judgment until you know a person well. I, personally, think that everything Rodney has done from the beginning was aimed toward getting that property. And I hate to say it, but I'm including his matchup with Trixie on that dating service, too."

"My goodness," Lloyd said, looking up in surprise. "You think he'd do that?"

"Well, obviously, I don't know how those things work, but I wouldn't put it past him."

Lloyd laughed. "I hope you don't know how they work. Well, listen, Miss Julia, I better get back over to headquarters and see if the jitney has come. I just came home for a snack and because, well, I knew Mr. Sam invited Rodney to go with us tomorrow, and I was kinda worried that he'd show up, and I didn't much know what to do. I bet he won't, though, 'cause he'll be afraid Trixie's told on him."

"I expect you're right," I said, then sent him on his way, thinking as I did so that I could guess what had possessed Rodney to take down Sam's posters. It wasn't something I wanted to share with Lloyd, though, because there was no need to add to the boy's disappointment in Rodney.

But I knew as well as I was standing there that Rodney had not slipped through the night snatching down posters just to get back at me through Sam, but to aid and abet Thurlow's chosen candidate. It was as clear as day to me that with Jimmy Ray back in the senate, Rodney and Thurlow could count on getting a variance if my property proved unsuitable for their grand plans. Which it most certainly would, because how would they get a variance on land they couldn't buy?

Well, but who knew what else Rodney had up his sleeve? If he had no qualms about stripping signs from telephone poles, what would he do next?

Chapter 43

Bestirring myself to get up and perk a pot of coffee, I was missing Lillian's company as I did so, but not because she wasn't there to do it for me. Good grief, even I could turn on a coffeepot. I was missing her because I wanted to know what she'd say about Rodney, now that I could tell her of the anger, resentment, frustration, or whatever emotion it had been that had prompted him to take out his antipathy to me on Sam's campaign posters. And what a petty waste of time that had been. I wondered if he'd felt better after having done it. I hoped not. I hoped he'd felt some shame, except if he hadn't felt better he might think up some other mischief to relieve his desire for vengeance.

Well, a lot of good that would do him, too. But I had about had enough of Rodney Pace and had to smile at the thought of Trixie saying she no longer gave a flying flip what he did. Was that true? If so, it indicated a complete and utter makeover of her attitude and her disposition, the possibility of which I was inclined to doubt. She'd been so wrapped up in him, heeding his every word and allowing him to plan her life, only to suddenly care nothing for him? It seemed highly unlikely to me.

I poured a cup of coffee, lightened it with cream, and returned to the table, wishing again for Lillian. But Sam would be home soon. He would hear me out and offer his sane assessment of the situation, and I'd feel better. For the present, though, whenever I thought of Rodney in a frenzy of frustration going from one telephone pole to the other all over town ripping down Sam's posters, a cold chill ran down my back. But when I thought again of his remark that I was like an old woman with a houseful of cats, I wanted to smack his face.

Realizing that the room had darkened, I got up to switch on the lights and to look out the window. Clouds had rolled in and rain threatened. What a shame, I thought, as I watched a light drizzle darken the driveway, if Sam's Jitney Journey got rained out. To say nothing of all the celebrations of the Fourth, including the expected crowds at every stop, and the fireworks spectacular planned for the following evening.

By the time Sam came in an hour or so later, I had had time to change my shoes, set the table, and put some rolls in the oven. I was slicing tomatoes when he came in, brushing his hand across his hair.

"It's raining," he announced with a grin.

"I noticed," I responded, looking up and smiling, "but the forecast says it won't be heavy. And tomorrow will just be scattered showers. I shouldn't think it'll slow you down."

"Nothing's going to slow us down now. It can rain all day if it wants to. I tell you, Julia, that's a happy, enthusiastic bunch I have. A little rain won't bother us at all."

He was ebullient over the recent response to his senate campaign, and my heart lifted along with his. "What about the fireworks tomorrow night? Will it go on if it's raining?"

He sat down at the table as I brought our plates over. "I think so, yes. Of course if it's a downpour, it might not be as spectacular as they advertise. But they're planning to fire 'em off regardless." He looked up as I put a plate before him. "Lillian go home early?"

"She left early, but I doubt she's home. The Reverend Abernathy's wife is quite ill. I expect she's with her."

Sam nodded. "I heard she's not doing well. I dropped by the reverend's office this morning to ask about her and to see if they needed anything."

I looked at my husband with love and gratitude that he was a man of decency and thoughtfulness. But what he had done was so innately natural to his character that he didn't notice my admiration.

I let him get most of the way through his supper, then asked in an offhanded way, "Did Lloyd speak to you this afternoon?"

Sam's eyebrows went up. "Well, yes, several times. He offered me a Coke about two o'clock and told me he was coming to see you for a while, then, let me see. Oh, yes, he wanted me to check the banner he'd painted, then he asked if he could go inside to use the bathroom. I think that's about all he had to say."

"Oh, Sam," I said, laughing. "You know I meant more than that."

"Okay," he said with that sweet smile of his, "seriously then. Obviously, he didn't tell me whatever it is that's on your mind. What is it?"

So I told him what Lloyd had told me, that he'd overheard Trixie talking to Rodney, that it was a fairly settled fact that Rodney had been the miscreant who'd torn down his signs, that Trixie had said she no longer cared a flip about Rodney, and that she'd behaved herself at the luncheon, except for the distracted, moony look on her face, which I was fairly sure hadn't been caused by having quiche for lunch.

"Well," Sam said, leaning back in his chair with a tired sigh, "I'm sorry to hear that about Rodney. I expected better from him. He's such a go-getter, he could be a real addition to the town's movers and shakers. But not with that kind of anger and pettiness."

"But nobody'll know about it," I said. "I certainly won't tell it around—it was so *small* of him. I'd almost be ashamed to tell it. And you wouldn't, either."

"No," he agreed, "but it'll come out sooner or later anyway. I don't mean that particular act of vandalism, specifically, but it'll come out in other ways."

I nodded, understanding. "I expect you're right. I just wonder what else he's capable of."

We woke to an overcast Fourth of July the next morning, but the clouds didn't dampen Sam's spirits. He ate the big breakfast that Lillian prepared, talked to her about the Abernathys, and joked with Latisha, who'd accompanied Lillian since her usual summer sitter had holiday plans.

As soon as Sam left for his big day, Lillian started apologizing. "I'm sorry I have to bring her, Miss Julia, but she know she got to behave." She gave her great-granddaughter a stern stare, but Latisha paid no attention. She was sitting on the floor surrounded by a pile of doll clothes spilling out of a doll's suitcase, a yellow plastic drawstring bag with a smiley face on it, and a fine-figured, wild-haired doll that needed an appointment with Velma.

"For goodness sakes, Lillian, she's no trouble at all, and she's welcome here anytime she wants to come. Actually, though, I didn't expect you—it is a holiday, you know."

"Not much a one," Lillian said. "They already shootin' off firecrackers up an' down the street where I live. I rather be here where they's some peace and quiet."

"Well, I don't blame you," I said, but wondered that the police hadn't put a stop to fireworks within the city limits. "Latisha," I went on, noticing how intently she was going through the little suitcase, searching apparently for the correct outfit for her doll. "Are you dressing your baby?"

"I didn't bring no baby today," Latisha said in her high-pitched little voice. "I brung my lady doll, an' she sick an' tired of them loud firecrackers. They scarin' her, so I'm gonna bundle her up good so she can't hear 'em."

"Oh, okay," I said and smiled at her imagination. "When she's all bundled up, you can take her into the library and watch television if you want to."

"I jus' might do that," Latisha said. "Great-Granny already tole me she wadn't gonna turn on the one in here, 'cause she don't want to hear that thing all day long."

I laughed, then took myself to the living room, noting as I went that the day was dim with threatening rain. I had wished for a bright, pretty day for Sam's trek around the district, but he had left in great good humor in spite of the dampness. Lloyd and Mr. Pickens were meeting him at campaign headquarters, along with a crowd of eager volunteers. Apparently, they'd loaded the jitney with coolers filled with soft drinks, and some were bringing snacks and, according to Sam, one would bring a guitar and somebody else a harmonica for traveling music. I was just as glad to be home.

But it was a long day for me, as holidays often are, broken only occasionally by entertaining conversation with Latisha. I kept trying to get Lillian to go home, but she filled her time by baking several pound cakes for the volunteers. I finally realized that baking was a comfort to her, as worried as she was about Mrs. Abernathy, and I stopped urging her to leave.

About three o'clock that afternoon, I called Hazel Marie, knowing full well that I should've done it sooner.

"Hazel Marie?" I asked, as one does even when one knows who has answered the phone. "I wanted to tell you how much I enjoyed the luncheon yesterday. Everything was lovely, and it was sweet of you to entertain for Trixie."

"Oh, thank you, Miss Julia, I appreciate that. I'm still not real sure of myself about having the ladies. They do it so much better than I do."

"No one could've done better, Hazel Marie. Everything—your house, the food, the flowers, the conversation—everything was perfect." I deliberately overlooked the unedifying discussion of colonoscopies.

"Well, I'm just glad that Trixie seemed to enjoy it. She did quite well, don't you think?"

"Yes," I agreed, then asked, "but was there anything wrong with her? She seemed, oh, I don't know, in sort of a dreamy state or something."

"*Tell* me about it!" Hazel Marie whispered forcibly. "That's the way she's been acting for the last two days. I don't know what's going on, but she's so agreeable about everything else that I'm afraid to ask."

"Maybe," I suggested, "she's so relieved to be free of Rodney telling her what to do that she now has time to think for herself. Except I'm not sure she can think for herself."

"Well, I'll tell you what I think it is. I think she has a crush on Magnum, P.I."

"Who?"

"Oh, you know. The actor who had that old series. J.D. has all the DVDs, and Trixie came across them the other day, and that's all she's been doing ever since. And, I mean, she's been *glued* to that television set."

"Hazel Marie, he must be as old as the hills."

"Well, he doesn't look it on those shows. Trixie is entranced with him. And you know what? He doesn't look a thing like Rodney. So I hope she's over him for good, and think of this: it doesn't matter how old that actor is, she sure can't get into trouble with him."

That was true, so I decided that a crush on the image of a screen idol, regardless of his age, was healthier for Trixie than the adulation she'd heaped upon Rodney Pace. Besides, I could hardly fault her for being smitten—Magnum, P.I. had certainly been a fine-looking man.

Chapter 44

"Miss Julia," Lillian said as she stood in the door of the library. I had just hung up the phone after speaking with Hazel Marie and had turned to watch Latisha as she rummaged through the myriad doll outfits tumbling out of her tiny suitcase and strewn across the floor, almost covering the yellow plastic sack next to her knee.

"Come in, Lillian. This child has dressed and undressed her doll so many times, it's a wonder it's still in one piece."

"No'm, we got to go. I fixed some barbecue, so all you got to do is heat it up and put it on a bun, an' they's coleslaw in the Frigidaire. You prob'bly didn't hear her, but Ida Lee just run over to tell me Miz Abernathy gettin' mighty low. They want me to come sit with her."

"Oh, I'm sorry to hear that. Of course you must go, but what about Latisha? She doesn't need to be there."

Latisha's head swung from me to Lillian. "That's right, Great-Granny, I be better off here, 'cause I don't wanta go where somebody sick. Everybody keep tellin' me to hush up an' be quiet."

"Latisha," Lillian admonished her, then to me, "I'll have to take her. The lady what keep a few chil'ren in the summer, she gone off to celebrate."

"Then leave her with me," I said.

Latisha instantly perked up. "Okay, that work out real good. You go on, Great-Granny, an' leave me here. Me'n Miss Lady, we get along jus' fine."

"Law, Miss Julia," Lillian said with a slight roll of her eyes. "I can't do that. She run you ragged an' talk you to death."

"No," I said firmly, "she needs somebody to stay with and I need some company. And you don't need the worry. You'll have your hands full, looking after the Abernathys. So you go on and do what you have to do. In fact, it'd be easier for Latisha to stay the night with us. Would you like that, Latisha?"

"I sure would," she said, "an' if Lloyd would come on home, I'd like it even better."

"I'm not sure he'll be staying here tonight," I told her. "He's with Mr. Sam, and they'll be late getting in anyway. But we can meet them at the park and watch the fireworks. How would that be?"

"It be jus' fine." Then turning a frowning look on Lillian, she said, "If Great-Granny don't get all huffed up an' say I can't."

Lillian's eyes definitely rolled then. "I don't think you know what you lettin' yourself in for, Miss Julia, but it be mighty good not to have to take her to the reverend's house. No tellin' what goin' on over there, with people comin' an' goin', some of 'em prayin', an' some singin', an' lots of 'em cryin'."

"It's settled then," I said. "Don't give it another thought. Latisha and I will play dolls for a while and have supper. Then we'll go to the park and be back here for the night."

Lillian hesitated, a skeptical look on her face, but she knew as well as I that a house with a desperately ill person in it was no place for a child. Especially Latisha.

"I guess that be better," Lillian finally conceded, although it seemed to take some effort. But Lillian was between a rock and a hard place, feeling torn between two responsibilities. I was glad to be able to help her for a change. Besides, Latisha was good company.

Lillian sighed and said, "I sure do thank you, Miss Julia. I jus' hope she don't wear you out. Latisha, you mind Miss Julia now, you hear?"

So engrossed with wardrobe selections, Latisha didn't even glance at her. "I see you later, Great-Granny," she said, then stripped her doll naked again.

After an hour or so of Latisha dressing her doll in various outfits, telling me that one dress meant the doll was going grocery shopping, another meant she had a date, and another meant she was going to school to learn something if she paid attention to the teacher. Thoroughly entertained by Latisha's imagination, I almost let the supper hour slip by.

"Let's have some barbecue," I said, getting to my feet. "You want to put all these clothes in your suitcase? I'll help you fold them."

"That's all right," Latisha said, speaking as if I were across the room instead of seated next to her. "She pretty messy, so all I got to do is throw 'em in. She won't care."

I heated the barbecue and spooned it onto warm buns, then put the coleslaw, pickles, and potato chips on the table.

"Well, Latisha," I said, scooting her chair closer to the table, then taking my own. "It doesn't feel like the Fourth of July with everybody gone, but having barbecue reminds us, doesn't it?"

"It would," she said, "if we had us a big ole watermelon and a churn of peach ice cream to go with it."

"Next year we'll plan to have all that, and maybe the weather'll be better and we can eat outside. Won't that be nice?"

"I'd ruther eat in the house, if it's all the same to you. Too many ants and yellow jackets buzzin' 'round outside to suit me."

"You have a point," I agreed. "You want another barbecue sandwich?"

"I guess I better," she said. "I might get hungry if I don't."

As I prepared another sandwich and poured more tea, I sighed at the thought of going out in the drizzle to watch the fireworks. I wondered if Latisha would be as happy as I would be to stay inside and listen to the explosions from a distance.

Doubtful, I knew, for she'd mentioned the fireworks display several times during the afternoon. Perhaps I could find a place to park where we could watch and stay dry at the same time.

By the time we completed our meal with slices of fresh pound cake, topped with ice cream and chocolate syrup, I was getting concerned about Latisha's capacity. When she told me she was about to throw up, I suggested she go lie down on the sofa while I straightened the kitchen.

"I'm not really 'bout to throw up," she said, her dark eyes

sparkling. "I just can't eat no more, an' that's what I tell Great-Granny when she tell me to clean my plate."

"Oh, Latisha, you're such a tease. Here I was about to call the doctor."

"I don't need no doctor. All he say is give that chile a dose of castor oil, an' I can do without that."

I leaned against the sink and laughed. "You and me! I didn't know they still gave castor oil. If you've finished, bring your dessert plate over here, please."

She did and watched as I stacked our dishes in the dishwasher. "What're we gonna do now?" she asked.

"Well, let me think," I said, drying my hands. "It's almost six-thirty, so we have at least two hours before going to see the fireworks. But, I declare, Latisha, it sure looks wet out there. You sure you want to go out in it?"

"Yes, ma'am, I'm real sure. I been waitin' all year to see them fireworks, so I don't aim to miss 'em jus' 'cause it's rainin'. A little rain won't hurt us, an' I got my raincoat an' my rainboots, 'cause Great-Granny's corns was hurtin' this morning so she tell me to bring 'em."

"I guess we better go upstairs and find my rain gear then." And so we did, and as we reached the bottom of the stairs on our way back, the telephone rang.

"Oh, that may be Sam," I said, my heart quickening as it always did at any word from him. "They may already be at the park. Just put that old hat on the table there."

I picked up the phone, answered it, and heard Etta Mae Wiggins. "*Miss Julia*," she said, gasping for breath. "He's back!"

"Who? You mean *Rodney*? What's he doing now?"

"That's the thing—I don't know!" Then her words came tumbling out. "He hasn't been up here where we are at all, and I wouldn't've known he was anywhere around if I hadn't come home the back way and just happened to see tire tracks through the weeds going into the woods."

"Where was this?" I interrupted, trying to picture how any car could jump the ditch that had given me so much difficulty.

"Not far from your south boundary. Has to be the railroad property—the ditch levels out there, so he could drive right in, and at first I thought somebody'd had a wreck, but there was no sign of one. Then I wondered what anybody would be doing out in the woods on the Fourth of July." She stopped, took a deep breath, and went on. "Anyway, when I got home I started worrying about it, so I drove back down there and, going in that direction, I could see the back of a black vehicle with lots of chrome almost hidden in a thicket. It was Rodney's car, I'm just positive. I mean, he's had that thing out here enough times for me to recognize it. And I know an Escalade when I see one."

"Slow down, Etta Mae, and let's think about this. He's having surveyors out there tomorrow, you know. He may just be walking the boundaries so he can show them where they are." I stopped and thought for a minute. "Of course that doesn't explain why he drove off the road and pulled into the bushes, does it? It's a wonder he didn't get stuck, considering the rain we've had. How far from my line was it parked?"

"That's the thing, Miss Julia." Etta Mae's voice was suddenly calm as she gave her eyewitness account. "It was—I'd say about fifteen or twenty feet from the southwest corner of your property. When I went back out to check on what I'd seen, I recognized that blackberry patch we got tangled up in—you remember that?"

"I certainly do."

"And here's the main thing: with all the car tracks and trampled-down weeds where he or somebody had walked, the orange tie on the corner stake was easy to spot. It stood out like a sore thumb, but I didn't see hide nor hair of him. I bet he hides every time a car passes."

"Oh, Etta Mae," I said, fatigue sweeping over me at the thought of beating the bushes for Rodney, especially through a wet blackberry patch. "I don't know what to do. Sam's not here, and I have

Latisha with me. Maybe I ought to call the sheriff." I paused and thought about it. "Of course Rodney could have a perfectly good explanation, then I'd have to come up with one of my own for calling the law on him. What do you think?"

She thought for a minute. "I think that all the deputies will be out at the park directing traffic. By the time a patrol car gets here, he could be gone. So it's a matter of whether you want to know what he's doing or not. And if you do, you'll have to catch him at it, 'cause he won't ever tell you. That kind never does."

A jolt of energy slashed through me because she was right. If Rodney had wanted me to know what he was doing—if he had a good explanation for slogging around in the woods and hiding his car from passersby—he would've notified me before he went. Which meant that he was up to some nefarious activity having to do with obtaining my property for a state-certified graveyard.

"Etta Mae," I said, "are you up for tromping through the woods on a rainy night?"

I could hear the grin in her voice. "Already got my boots on."

Chapter 45

"Latisha!" I called, slamming down the phone. "Where are you?"

"Right here," she said, standing beside me and looking up with wide eyes.

"Oh. Well, look, something's come up and we have to go to Etta Mae's house. I mean, her trailer." I hesitated for a minute. Would Lillian mind my taking Latisha to visit Etta Mae? What if we happened to run into Rodney?

Well, what should I do? Drop Latisha off at the Abernathys and go on alone? Stay home and never know what Rodney was up to? Neither, I decided. I had to go, and I had to take Latisha, and I had to hope Lillian would understand.

"We should call your Great-Granny, but . . ." I pictured Lillian in the turmoil of a grieving crowd of people.

"She won't care," Latisha assured me. "Can I look around that trailer? I always wanted one for my own self."

"I'm not sure we'll have time, but, yes, of course, depending on how things go. But now let's get your boots and raincoat on. We need to get out there in a hurry."

It seemed to take forever for Latisha to get her yellow rubber boots on. She ended up removing her tennis shoes so her sock-clad feet could slip right in. Then, of course, she half walked out of the boots with every step she made. While she struggled into her yellow raincoat, I pulled on my green gardening boots, determined to be prepared for briars this time.

Slipping on a raincoat and a floppy rain hat, I grabbed my pocketbook and Latisha's hand. Switching off the kitchen light, I said, "Let's go, honey."

"Wait!" Latisha turned and dashed toward the library. "I gotta get my sack."

"What in the world?" I asked to the empty kitchen, thinking that it would take her a half hour to stuff the doll and all those clothes into the sack, and, for all I knew, put traveling clothes on the doll. Rodney would be long gone by the time we got there, and I might never know what he was up to until it was too late to undo it. And he was up to something or he wouldn't have pulled that expensive car off the road and into a thicket.

"Hurry, Latisha," I called, following her. "We have to go."

She scampered to me, carrying the yellow plastic sack, lumpy with treasures of one kind or another. The drawstring was wrapped around her wrist for easy carrying. With the hood of the raincoat up around her face, she looked for all the world like a yellow caution light.

At Delmont, I took a left onto Springer Road, then a right into the Hillandale Trailer Park. I'd been tempted to drive on down to where Etta Mae said Rodney's SUV was partially hidden off the road, but thought better of it. If he saw my car, he'd recognize it. Besides, I wanted Etta Mae with me—as a witness, if one were ever needed.

She was waiting under the awning of her single-wide and ran out to meet us when I parked. She was wearing what looked like an army surplus poncho with the hood pulled up over her head. And jeans and cowboy boots, of course.

"Hey, Miss Julia," Etta Mae said, leaning down to the window as I lowered it. "Hey, Latisha, you look like a little yellow duck. Real cute. Miss Julia, I think we ought to walk through the woods. I know it's a long way, but if you want to sneak up on him, that's the best way to do it."

"I'm thinking the same thing," I said, even though I hated the thought of plodding through the woods in the foggy drizzle. "You have a flashlight? I only have the one here in the car."

"Yes'm, I've got a little Maglite in my pocket, but I don't think we'll need them. It won't be full dark for a while. Latisha," Etta

Mae said, turning toward the backseat, "you want to stay in my trailer till we get back? You can watch TV and I have some snacks for you."

"No, ma'am, I don't," Latisha said, quite firmly. "If anybody's going anywhere, I'm goin' with 'em."

"I think we better take her," I said. "I'm not comfortable leaving her by herself."

"Suits me," Etta Mae said. "I just thought she'd rather stay where it's dry."

"Don't worry about me," Latisha said. "Rain or shine, it don't matter." And she unsnapped her seat belt and crawled out of the car.

"What you got in that sack?" Etta Mae asked playfully. "You bring a picnic or something?"

Latisha snorted. "I ain't havin' no picnic in the rain. I got my play pretties in here, an' I'm not leavin' 'em. I might need 'em, an' where would I be if they was settin' back here in the car?"

After locking my pocketbook in the trunk, I turned and looked toward the forested acres we aimed to traverse, wondering again about just driving to the spot and confronting Rodney. I knew, though, that he'd have a ready-made excuse, an acceptable reason for being there, and I might never know the real one—or be able to prove it if I did.

So we wound our way between trailers, detouring around swing sets, plastic cars, and sandboxes, then entered the woods where the walking was easy on the springy pine needles that covered the ground. Easy at first, that is, for I'd kept a fair-sized area past the tree line underbrushed, so all we had to deal with was the rainwater that dripped from the trees and the rain-slick moss on the roots. Latisha led the way, although she didn't know where we were going. But she moved out right smartly, awkwardly swinging her sack with each step.

"Where we goin', anyway?" she called out.

"It's a little way more," I said, "but don't get too far ahead. Stay where we can see you."

It wasn't long before we got into bushes and fairly thick undergrowth, and the going became more difficult. I thought that Latisha would start complaining, but she plowed on through, ducking and pushing aside branches as if she did it every day. We pushed past small pines and went around laurel thickets until I wasn't sure where we were. Water streamed off all three of us, less from what was falling from the sky than from what was dripping from limbs and leaves.

"Etta Mae," I said, "are we headed in the right direction? I'm not that good at dead reckoning."

"We're fine," she said. "Every once in a while when we're in a clear place, I can see the road."

To be walking parallel to the road was reassuring—it'd be hard to get lost with civilization that close. But as the trees became thicker the evening grew darker. Add the rain clouds, and it began to feel as if we were out in the dead of night. Yet it could hardly be much past eight, and if the day had been clear we would've had light until nine, at least. Latisha had noticed that it was getting dark, too, for she put herself between Etta Mae and me, and stayed there.

Etta Mae suddenly grabbed my arm. "Look at that!"

"What? Where?"

"Right over there," she said, pointing. "See it? It's a chimney, looks like. You reckon somebody *lives* out here?"

By squinting through the tree limbs I managed to see the top of a rock chimney. "Oh, Etta Mae, you scared me to death. No, nobody lives out here. Sam said he thought there was an abandoned farmhouse on the place, and I expect that's what's left of it."

"Let's go see," Latisha said, and I had to hold her back from ducking under the limbs and taking off.

"No, we don't have time to explore. You stay with us. Besides, it could be dangerous. There could be a hole where a cellar was, and old boards with nails in them, and . . ."

"Snakes," Etta Mae whispered.

Rain was one thing, but snakes were another. "Give me your hand, Latisha. I want you close by."

"Well," she said, taking my hand, "I'm about to get tired of this. When will we get to wherever we're going?"

"It's not much farther," Etta Mae said. "At least I don't think it is. Actually, though, we might ought to start being more careful. We could run right up on him."

"Yes, and being quiet, too. See, Latisha, we just want to find out what a certain somebody is up to. And we'd like to do it without him knowing anybody's watching. We'll stay in the bushes and see what he does."

Latisha considered this for a second, then used her shoulders to slip between two small shrubs. "You mean," she said, "we gonna sneak up on him, then squat down and watch till he do what he ain't s'posed to do. But *then* what we gonna do?"

Etta Mae started giggling. "Good question, Latisha. Miss Julia, you be thinking about that while I push on ahead. I'll scout things out while you two rest a bit. Oh, and," she said, "turn on your flashlight and aim it at the ground so I can find my way back to you. I'll keep mine off 'cause I think we're pretty close."

Except for the rain dripping off the trees onto leaves farther below, it got real quiet after Etta Mae was out of sight. Covered in that army green poncho, she was like a point man on a raid as she slipped without a sound through the undergrowth. I held tightly to Latisha's hand, noticing that she kept edging nearer to me. I leaned against a tree, thinking how much I longed to sit down. If the ground hadn't been sopping wet, I would have.

"Miss Lady?" Latisha said, her piercing voice mercifully toned down a notch or two. "I got to go to the bathroom."

Well, come to think of it . . . but with an effort of will, I refused to think of it.

"You think you can wait? We'll be back at Etta Mae's trailer before long."

"I don't believe I can. But don't worry, it's just number one an'

I can do that in a hurry." She pushed aside her raincoat and began pulling down her shorts, jiggling a little in her haste.

"Wait, wait a minute, Latisha." I carefully aimed the flashlight around, searching for a clear spot. If I let her crouch down in poison ivy, Lillian would never forgive me. "Okay, right here. Hurry now before Etta Mae gets back."

She did, then looked up at me. "I need some paper."

Oh, Lord, my pocketbook, full of Kleenex, was in the car trunk. I searched through the pockets of my raincoat and came up with a wadded tissue, left over from the time of the last rain. No telling how old it was, but I handed it to her and she used it.

"What do I do with it now?" Latisha asked, still in a squat.

"Just leave it. It'll be all right."

"That's *litterin'*!" she said, and I wondered again what she and Lloyd were learning in school—if it wasn't anti-littering, it was an anti-snack or anti–fast food or anti–something else campaign. Teach them to read and be done with it, I thought.

"Sh-h-h, not so loud, honey. Now, Latisha, we have two choices: you can put that wet Kleenex in your pocket and take it home to be disposed of correctly, or you can just leave it."

"Well, in that case," she said, "I'll just put it under a rock so nobody'll know what I been doin'." Then, with a little help from me, she pulled up her step-ins and her shorts, straightened out her raincoat, then said, "I feel lots better."

Etta Mae suddenly materialized out of the shadows. Latisha yelped, then covered her mouth to stifle the sound.

"We're not far from him," Etta Mae whispered. "Y'all all right?"

"We're fine," I whispered back. "Did you find out anything? What's he doing?"

"I'm not sure, but he's sure working at it. Come on, you need to see for yourself."

Chapter 46

"Everybody be real quiet," Etta Mae said, pulling up her hood. "He's not far, so let's go slow and easy."

She hunched her shoulders and slithered through the undergrowth with me, holding Latisha's hand, slithering right behind her. We carefully pushed aside wet branches, trying to see in the gray light filtering through the trees where we put our feet. We moved cautiously toward what I realized was a strange grunting sound. Etta Mae suddenly crouched down and stopped.

I almost tumbled over her back before pulling up short.

"What's that noise?" I whispered, crouching down next to her. Latisha scrooched up next to me.

"I don't know," Etta Mae whispered, "but I think it's him. Peek through here and see if you can see anything." She parted a few laurel limbs and I leaned forward to look through the gloom.

It took me a minute to focus on the dark shadow that stood out against the gray sky. There wasn't much undergrowth to hinder our vision because most of the weeds and bushes around the area had been trampled down into a muddy mess. Rodney—if it was Rodney—was standing on the edge of the ditch we'd once scaled, and because of his dark clothing, he was clearly outlined against the gloomy sky.

Etta Mae peered through the leaves beside me, and we were both speechless as we watched the shadow lean over, grab on to something, then move back and forth with strong jerking motions, each one eliciting a grunt from deep in his chest.

Some ways away a glow of light appeared as a car approached on the road to Delmont. The shadow threw itself on the ground, lying flat until the car had passed. If that wasn't an indication of a crime of some kind being committed, I didn't know what was.

Latisha edged in closer. "I wanta see."

"Sh-h-h," Etta Mae and I both said. I pulled Latisha down in front of me and let her look through the hole in the leaves.

"What's he doin'?" Latisha said, trying to whisper but not quite making it.

I put my hand over her mouth, as the shadow stopped and looked around. Then, apparently satisfied that nothing was amiss, he leaned over, grasped something near the ground in both hands, and, to the accompaniment of more grunting, began to-ing and fro-ing again.

Suddenly the shadow collapsed to the ground, or maybe it fell down. Whichever it was, it ended up on its bottom. Breathing heavily enough for us to hear, Rodney—and I was sure it was Rodney by this time—sat for a while catching his breath. Then he held up what looked like a long, heavy cane, stuck it upright, and used it to lever himself to his feet. Then, carrying the cane, he walked away from us toward where I assumed his car was parked.

Etta Mae stiffened beside me. "Let's get outta here."

"Wait," I whispered. "I want to know what he's doing."

"I *know* what he's doing," Etta Mae hissed. "Let's move out of earshot so we can talk."

I didn't know how far that would be, but I followed her, helping Latisha along as I went. When we got back near the old home-stead, Etta Mae stopped and, without a thought of the wet ground, sat down. After a second of hesitation, I did, too. My back and my knees were so grateful for the rest that I took no thought of the soaking I'd get. Latisha didn't either, and the three of us gathered on the pine needles for a conference.

"Okay," I said, keeping my voice low, "what's he doing?"

"Pulling up stakes," Etta Mae said.

That stopped me for a minute. *Pulling up stakes* meant leaving a place, but if Rodney had come out on a wet evening just to pick up a walking stick and leave, then he was goofier than I'd thought.

Then it hit me. "He pulled up *a* stake! Etta Mae, he's moving the stakes!"

"That's exactly right. We saw him pull one out of the ground."

"That long thing? I thought a stake was a, well, a stake, a little short thing. What he had was a good two feet or more."

"Yeah, and you saw what a time he had getting it out of the ground, too. But that's what a property stake is," Etta Mae assured me. "They're iron rods, and only a few inches stick out of the ground. The rest of it is hammered in. Surveyors mean for those things to *stay*. No telling how long he's been working to get it out."

"You think he's going to put it somewhere else? Or maybe," I said with a sudden hopeful thought, "he just took it up so the surveyors wouldn't set their sights on it. They'd have to measure the land in its original state with no previous markers to rely on."

"If that's what he's doing," Etta Mae said wryly, "he's got a long night ahead with three more stakes to pull up. But, no, Miss Julia, I don't think so. I think . . ." She stopped, clamped her hand on my arm, and whispered, *"Listen."*

Latisha and I sat up straight and strained to hear what Etta Mae was hearing. Then I did hear it, or felt it, maybe, for it was a dull, rhythmic pounding, sort of like a headache, but not quite.

"What is it?" I asked.

"It's Rodney," Etta Mae said as confidently as if she could see him, "and he's hammering that stake back in the ground."

Latisha, her head swiveling from one to the other of us, chimed in. "He jus' prise it up. Why he hammerin' it back in now?"

"Because," Etta Mae said, "he's hammering it into a different place. And I think he's doing it down near where his car's parked. Which is some ten feet or so from the original corner. Miss Julia, how far would he have to put it to gain a tenth of an acre?"

"I have no idea. But I'll bet *he* does." I was smoldering by this time, ready to spring to my feet and crash through thickets, briars, mud puddles, and blackberry patches to have it out with Rodney Pace. Never in my life would I have dreamed that a lawn cemetery was important enough to warrant lying and stealing—for that's what he was doing—in order to dig a few graves.

But a calmer head—Etta Mae's, for one, and mine soon

after—counseled caution. "Let's think about this for a minute," she said. So we did, and as we did, that dull pounding started up again. I finally figured that Rodney must have put some sort of protective cover over the head of the stake to muffle the sound of metal on metal when the hammer hit it. That made me all the more irate, for it meant that he'd carefully planned every step he had to make in order to steal a tenth of an acre from the railroad and add it to my twenty-nine and nine-tenths.

"See if I've figured this right," Etta Mae said. "If he's doing what we think he's doing, then moving one stake's not going to help him. He'll have to move the one on the opposite corner, too. That would give him an extra, say, ten feet or so all along the south edge of your property. So, we could walk over to that stake and wait for him. We could just be sitting there when he shows up with all his tools. Maybe tackle him and hold him down, or make a citizen's arrest or something."

That's when Etta Mae's calmer head went south on her. If we were going to do that, we might as well do it here and now.

"No," I said, shaking my head, "I don't want to take a chance that he'll get there before us—we're tired, which'll slow us down, and he has his car. And now that he's moved one stake, he'll be faster moving the second one. What I want, Etta Mae, is for that other stake marking the southwestern corner of the property to stay where it is, and this one—the one he's working on now—to be off by however many feet he's putting it. Proof positive, Etta Mae, of a crime interrupted in midstream."

"I gotcha," she said, seeing the wisdom of what I'd said. "That means we gotta do something pretty soon, or he'll really be pulling up stakes."

Latisha said, "I b'lieve he done with that hammerin'."

Etta Mae and I lifted our heads and listened. Those muted thuds had ceased, and I pictured a few inches of an iron stake sticking out of the ground in an entirely new and illegal place. He'd have the orange plastic tie on it, too, just as if the stake had been right where it now was for the past sixty years or so.

How did Rodney think he could explain to his surveyors the discrepancy between the figures on the old plat and the new figures that they would come up with? Claim that their modern equipment was superior to the old? Would they care or would they simply do the job they were hired to do, then move on to the next one?

But the big question was this: how did Rodney expect to get title to the land, even if it had grown in size overnight? I'd told him a million times that I wouldn't sell it. Thurlow Jones came to mind. If there was some not entirely illegal way to force me to sell, he was the one who could find it. He'd already as much as threatened me with a legal seizure of my property on the grounds of the public good.

I shivered slightly, although the air was so heavy with humidity I could hardly breathe.

Etta Mae and Latisha sat waiting for me to decide what to do. Time ticked by, and Rodney would soon be on his way to the next stake. Then we all perked up, for we were hearing a new sound. It sounded like something scraping and scratching against the ground.

"What's that?" I whispered.

Etta Mae cocked her head and listened. "Sounds like he's filling the hole where the stake was. I bet he'll cover it with brush and stuff—maybe even plant a little bush in it so nobody will suspect a thing."

"Etta Mae," I said, taking a firm grip on my nerve, "we've got to do something to run him off, and I don't mean run him off to the other stake. I mean run him off completely. What if we dash out of the bushes, screaming and yelling, and see if we can scare him off?"

Latisha whispered, "I bet I can scare him."

I looked at Etta Mae. "Or do you think I ought to just walk up to him and threaten him with the law? I'd love to tell him he can dig up all the stakes he wants to but he'll never dig a grave on this place."

Latisha whispered, "I know how to scare him, Miss Lady."

I patted Latisha's shoulder, told her to wait a minute, and looked to Etta Mae for an answer.

"Miss Julia," Etta Mae whispered, "you're a brave woman, but he's got a shovel in his hands and we've got Latisha with us. I don't think walking up and threatening him will work. It might make him mad, and we don't know what he'd do."

"I can't just sit here and do nothing," I said, going over the possibilities in my mind, "but I can't put Latisha in danger, either." Fully aware of Rodney's determination to have what he wanted, I was hesitant, even slightly afraid, to confront him so far from public view and first responders.

"Miss Lady," Latisha said, tugging on my sleeve to get my attention. "I know how to scare him. My play pretties'll scare him so bad, he'll run right outta his britches."

"Latisha, honey," I said, "we don't have time for play pretties. We have to think."

"Well," she said, "think about this." And she unwrapped the drawstring from her wrist, spread open the top of the sack, reached in, and pulled out a handful of firecrackers.

"Look at that!" Etta Mae rasped out. "Latisha, where'd you get firecrackers?"

"I got my ways," she said complacently. "But that ain't all I got." She pulled out a long item on a stick and held it up. "I bet this'll fix him good."

"Oh, my word!" Etta Mae whispered in awe. "Miss Julia, she's got a *rocket*!"

Chapter 47

"Yeah," Latisha said, eyes gleaming. "Le's shoot it an' see what happens."

"I tell you," Etta Mae said, running her hand over the rocket, "this thing will do the trick, all right. Miss Julia, you have a match?"

"I don't smoke, Etta Mae."

She started giggling, then grew quiet. "This is ridiculous. Here we have what we need to scare the you-know-what outta Rodney, and neither of us has a light."

"Look in my sack," Latisha said. "I gotta a Bic down in there somewhere."

"What!" Etta Mae grabbed the yellow sack, rummaged around in it, pulling out handsful of firecrackers and, finally, a Bic lighter. "My land, Latisha, you come prepared, don't you?"

"I'm gonna be a Boy Scout one a these days."

"Honey," Etta Mae said, "you're already an Eagle Scout in my book. Miss Julia, what do you think? We could edge in a little closer and set off a few firecrackers and see what happens. If they don't work, we can light him up with the rocket."

"That'd be dangerous, wouldn't it?" I didn't want to damage anything but Rodney's arrogance.

"It's too wet," Etta Mae said, separating the bundles of firecrackers into separate strings. "We won't start a forest fire."

"I wasn't . . ." I started, then said, "I don't want to really hurt him, Etta Mae."

She glanced up from her squat. "I know, and I'm just aiming to scare him. Of course, we're not responsible for anything that happens afterward." She giggled. "He may have to change his shorts."

"Oo-o-o," Latisha said. "You 'bout said a bad word."

"But not quite," Etta Mae told her with a grin. Then she stood up and started filling her pockets and the waistband of her jeans with strings of firecrackers. She looked like a commando preparing for a raid.

Squatting down again, she said, "Miss Julia, here's the plan. We'll sneak up as close as we can, then I'll light a string of fire-crackers and throw 'em at his feet. Not too close, but pretty close. And I'll keep peppering him with as many strings as I can light and throw. If that scares him off, then we're done. But you take charge of the rocket, and as soon as we get there, stick it in the ground and aim it in his direction, but above his head. I'll get the Bic to you while the firecrackers are going off. You know where the fuse is? Right here, see? Just stick it in the ground, light the fuse, and step back. Way back, okay?"

"What about me?" Latisha asked. "What do I get to shoot?"

Etta Mae and I looked at each other. I was already dreading the fit that Lillian would have when she learned that Latisha had been carrying around a sack of explosives, so there was no way I was going to allow her to light even the tiniest of firecrackers.

Before I could say anything, though, Etta Mae came up with the perfect response. "We need a forward observer, Latisha, and that's your job. When I throw a string of firecrackers, I want you to watch where it lands, and while I'm lighting the next string, you tell me where to throw it. You know—a little to the right or not so close or whatever. Can you do that?"

Latisha, a solemn look on her face, nodded her acceptance of the duty.

"Let's go then," Etta Mae said. "Oh, wait. Everybody stay real quiet. No yelling or anything. We don't want him to hear our voices. If he figures out we're women—well, two and a half women—he might come after us. We want him to think it's a bunch of crazy men with guns. Okay?"

That sounded sensible to me. I nodded and watched as she struck off through the brush, Latisha right behind her, then me, clutching the paper-covered rocket, following the two of them.

We crept closer, giving the treacherous blackberry patch a

wide berth. As we neared the small clearing where Rodney was laboring in the mud to cover the evidence of his stake-removal operation, Etta Mae slung out her arm for us to stop. Latisha and I immediately crouched down behind a tree. Etta Mae motioned to us to stay there. We did, but I strained to see where she was going. Her dark form crept to another tree a little way from us and nearer to the clearing.

Peeking around our tree, I could make out Rodney working away, using a shovel to smooth the dirt he'd removed, then, panting heavily, walking back and forth to bring brush and pine needles to cover his spadework.

Etta Mae whispered something to us.

"What?" I whispered back.

Latisha said, "She say are we ready."

"Sh-h-h," I cautioned, and looked to see if Rodney had heard her. Then, anxious to do my duty, I leaned around the tree and stuck the rocket's wooden spike into the dirt, making sure that it was firmly anchored and that the business end was aimed straight at Rodney's head—I mean, straight *over* his head.

A light flared on our left, and Latisha and I both gasped. As Etta Mae lit the fuse, we heard a fizzing sound, then saw her dark form step out and make an overhanded throw, sparks flying. Rodney, alarmed by the light and the noise, jerked upright just as the bundle sailed through the air behind him and landed a few feet away. When it hit the ground, the string of firecrackers went crazy, popping and sparking and jumping all over the place, sounding for all the world like gunshots on a television show.

Rodney dropped like a rock, yelling, "Don't shoot! Don't shoot, there's a person out here!"

Etta Mae lobbed another string of firecrackers which landed a few feet to the right of the first one. It, too, went into a frenzied dance of popping and sparking, while Rodney screamed, covered his head with his arms, and rolled away. He yelped as he went over the side of the ditch, and Etta Mae threw another fired-up string into the ditch.

Rodney scrambled out the other side of the ditch, yelling and clawing his way up, finally gaining his feet and taking off at full speed down Springer Road, yelling, "Don't shoot, don't shoot!" as he went.

Etta Mae scooted over to us. "Here's the Bic. Light it up, Miss Julia."

"Yeah," Latisha said. "We don't wanta waste it."

I stood and watched Rodney run down the road. He'd passed his car, depending on his feet to get him out of the line of fire. Just then, we heard rumbling thuds off in the distance. Thunder? No, the fireworks show was starting in Abbotsville. Rodney didn't notice. He was running flat out down the middle of the road, yelling, "Stop, stop! Don't shoot!"

By this time, Etta Mae had broken cover and was crouching on the edge of the ditch watching him. I leaned over, adjusted the aim of the rocket to send it down Springer Road, and flicked my Bic. The fuse lit right away and began sizzling, sending out sparks like it was on a launching pad. I jumped back, dragging Latisha with me.

I held tightly to her hand, as we watched and waited. Set for a low trajectory, the rocket was aimed, fired up, and ready to go. It just sat there, sputtering.

"Oh, no, Latisha," I said, fearing the paper covering had gotten wet as we'd walked through the brush. "It's a dud."

A loud pop made me jump and I grabbed on to Latisha.

With a sudden whoosh, the rocket came alive. We had liftoff! With its tail on fire, the rocket zipped up, up, and away, whizzing through the air with an ominous whistling noise.

"That ain't no dud!" Latisha cried.

We ran out to the edge of the ditch, joining Etta Mae to watch in awe as that smart rocket followed Springer Road like a programmed missile. With a loud *whump*, it burst overhead and blossomed into a shower of red and blue sparks, lighting up half the railroad's land and Rodney, too. He leapt straight up, legs still pumping, as Etta Mae lit another string of firecrackers. With a mighty effort, she threw it as far as she could to speed him on his way.

Yelling. "Don't shoot me!" Rodney didn't break stride, just suddenly made an airborne left and veered off the road at speed. He sailed across the ditch on the other side and disappeared into the dark.

"He gone," Latisha said.

Etta Mae and I started laughing and couldn't stop. Leaning over to get my breath, I wished I'd gone to the bathroom when Latisha had.

"We did it, Etta Mae," I said. "We ran him off!"

"We sure did," she said, still laughing. "Oh, man, that was something!" Then she straightened up and reminded us that we weren't through. "Listen, he'll come back when he realizes he wasn't being shot at. To get his car, for one thing. And maybe to move that other stake, for another. Let's take these shovels and things with us and get out of here."

"Good idea," I said, as she leaned over to pick up a pickax. I grabbed a shovel, then looked around for more tools. "The hammer. He used a hammer, so it's got to be here somewhere."

Etta Mae said, "He probably left it where he used it. Hold on to this pickax, Latisha, while I look for it." She walked off along the edge of the ditch, searching for the new location of the old stake.

After several minutes during which I thought Rodney might have put the hammer in his car, Etta Mae called out, "Found it," and slogged back through the weeds to us. "Let's go."

Latisha struggled to lift the pickax, then said, "I can't tote this thing through no woods."

"No, it's too heavy for you," Etta Mae said. "Here, let's swap and you take the hammer. Miss Julia, you all right with the shovel?"

Well, no, I wasn't. Not because it was heavy, but because it was awkward. "Carrying these things will slow us down, Etta Mae," I said. "And we need to get you home and Latisha and me back to Abbotsville before Rodney sneaks back up here and finds out who we are."

"Just leave 'em?" she asked. "I don't think you want to do that, Miss Julia."

I smiled. "Yes, I do." Then I whirled that shovel around and let it fly right into the middle of the huge blackberry patch full of briars and thorns and, hopefully, snakes.

"Hah!" Etta Mae said, and she chunked the pickax into the briars too. "Let's see you throw that hammer, Latisha."

And she did. We heard the clunk when it landed on the other tools. "That'll fix him," she said. "He won't be movin' no stakes now."

Even though we'd effectively put a kink in Rodney's plans, we knew we weren't out of the woods yet and a sense of urgency gripped us. Taking Latisha's hand, I hastened back the way we'd come with Etta Mae highstepping it behind us.

We hurried through and around laurel bushes, pushing aside small pine seedlings and avoiding thickets. I kept looking back, fearing to see or hear Rodney hot on our trail.

We stopped once to catch our breath, but none of us wanted to linger.

"What if Rodney goes to get more tools, Etta Mae?" I said, wondering if we'd done enough to deter him on his determined path. "Walmart stays open all night, so he can buy whatever he needs and get back here with plenty of time to move that other stake."

The clouds overhead briefly parted, and the moon gave enough light for me to see Etta Mae grin. "I don't believe he'll make it to Walmart tonight," she said. "Not with that flat tire, he won't."

Chapter 48

On our way home, Latisha fell asleep in the backseat, lying slumped over her seat belt. I had a hard time getting her in the house when I pulled into the driveway. Although it wasn't as late as I'd thought—only a little past ten-thirty—I knew Sam would be worried. He would've looked for us at the park and, not finding us, he probably called home. Being otherwise occupied, I, of course, would not have been where he could reach me. I had a lot of explaining to do.

Surprisingly, though, Sam's car wasn't home, so I figured he and the volunteers, perhaps along with the Pickenses, were having a late supper somewhere in town. Maybe he wasn't worried.

"Come on, honey," I said, unbuckling Latisha and helping her out of the car. "Let's get you to bed."

We stumbled together into the kitchen and, after switching on the lights, I stepped out of my muddy garden boots and began removing her rain gear.

"Well," I said, picking some leaves from her hair, "we missed the fireworks at the park, didn't we? We'll make up for it next year."

"I don't need to make up for it," she said, her voice regaining its usual volume. "We had us a fireworks show better'n anybody else's, an' the only thing wrong with it was I didn't get to light none of them firecrackers."

After getting her cleaned up and into a cotton nightgown that Lillian kept for those occasions when they stayed the night, I tucked her in bed. She'd been half asleep on her feet, so she quickly curled up and settled in.

Looking down at that sweet child, I shivered at the thought of what could've happened if we hadn't discovered that loaded sack she'd carried around and put its contents out of commission. I didn't feel much better at the thought of what Lillian would do when she learned of Latisha's portable arsenal.

The sale of fireworks was illegal in North Carolina, and I knew Latisha had not been to any state where they were legal. And I also knew that Lillian would not have let her buy any, if she had. But *somebody* had, and that somebody had supplied them to Latisha.

I sat on the edge of the bed, smoothed back her hair, and said, "Honey, where did you get all those fireworks?"

Her eyelids fluttered, and she murmured, "I buy 'em."

"You *bought* them? Where did you get the money?"

"Didn't need no money." She flipped over on her other side. "Mr. Nub jus' wanted two a Great-Granny's pound cakes."

They Lord, I thought, patted her shoulder, and took myself downstairs. So Nub Walker had been her supplier. I should've guessed—he walked around with lit sparklers on every holiday, including Halloween. He would have to be spoken to, but not by me. In fact, the sheriff should consider taking him into protective custody to keep him intact, once Lillian found out what he'd done. Poor Nub, he was sweet and trusting and as good a soul as you'd ever want to meet, but he wasn't all there. Well, frankly, he was mentally retarded, and I know that's become insensitive to say, but how else do you describe a forty-year-old man who'd spent five years in first grade and hadn't learned to read to this day?

When Lillian learned that he'd sold fireworks to an eight-year-old child—regardless of the compliment to her pound cakes—she would skin him alive. Even the Witness Protection Program might not keep him safe.

Tired and worn out, but too full of the evening's events to sleep, I prepared for bed, but went downstairs to wait for Sam. He came in a little while later, equally tired and full of his day's happenings. We sat together on the sofa in the library where I could hold his hand and worry about the fatigue on his face.

"What a day, Julia," he said, but not tiredly. He said it as if he were ready to do it all over again the next day. "I've never seen such enthusiasm. Big crowds everywhere, and they clapped and cheered and waved Murdoch banners. I rode in a couple of parades and went to three barbecues and two picnics. Then Jimmy Ray and I were introduced out at the park." He laughed. "They put us between a bluegrass band and the fireworks show—didn't get to say anything but 'I hope you'll vote for me,' or some such, but lots of people were there, in spite of the drizzle." He stopped and looked at me. "The city outdid itself with the fireworks. Did you get a good parking place?"

"As a matter of fact," I began, then went on to tell him that Latisha and I had missed the great fireworks display, but that we'd put on one of our own. I thought his eyebrows were going to disappear into his hair as I told him of Rodney's brazen attempt to enlarge my property and of our successful counterattack.

"Latisha saved the day, Sam," I concluded. "But Lillian is going to thrash Nub Walker to within an inch of his life for selling her a sack of fireworks and a Bic lighter, as well. I think you should talk to the sheriff about him. No telling how many other children he's sold to."

"I will. But, Julia, what in the world possessed you to go out there by yourself? I know, I know," Sam said, holding up his hand to stop my protest. "You had Etta Mae and Latisha with you, but I wouldn't call either of them much help if you'd had trouble."

"Oh, Sam, you wouldn't believe the help they were! I couldn't have asked for better. Why, if it hadn't been for Latisha's sack and Etta Mae's throwing arm, all we could've done was watch while Rodney stole a tenth of an acre. And, speaking of that," I went on, hoping to distract him, "why did he think moving a couple of stakes would do him any good? He knows I wouldn't sell if there were fifty acres out there. And how would he explain the difference between the old plat and what the surveyors would've found?"

"He wouldn't have to explain it," Sam said. "He'd probably have acted as surprised as anyone at the discrepancy. Although most likely the newer survey would stand unless the railroad questioned it. But from what you say, he'd better have a good explanation in the morning. When his surveyors get there, they'll have questions about that stake being so far out of line. Plus," he went on, trying not to smile, "somebody's going to have to explain the evidence of it having been moved. He didn't finish covering his tracks, did he?"

"No, but he'll have the rest of the night to finish it. Except, somehow I don't think he will. His tools are out of reach, for one thing—but ready to hand if we need his fingerprints. And Etta Mae arranged for a flat tire, and, Sam, I didn't have anything to do with that. Didn't even know about it till it was done."

"Okay, but would you mind if I went out there in the morning? I'd like to meet Rodney and his surveyors."

"Oh, Sam, *would* you? I'd be so relieved to have you lay down the law to them all. I'm so tired of Rodney and his mortuary plans, and tired of Thurlow hovering in the background with threats of bribes and political influence and eminent domain for the public good. I'd like to wash my hands of it all, pay my property taxes as I've always done, and assure Etta Mae that her home is safe from gravediggers."

Sam laughed, took my hand, and said, "Are you engaging me as your attorney of record?"

"Yes," I said, smiling, "and for anything else you might have in mind."

Thunder and the sharp flashes of lightning woke me sometime in the night. Scrooching up close to Sam's back, I listened to the pounding of heavy rain and wondered what Rodney was doing. If he'd regained enough courage to try to finish what he'd started, he'd be out there in it, slipping and sliding in the mud and soaked to the skin. Surely, though, he had enough sense not to attempt to move another stake in bad weather. Holding an iron stake in the midst of a thunderstorm would make him a lightning rod the likes of which would put our little fireworks show to shame. Lightning Rod-ney, I thought, then turned over and went back to sleep.

Chapter 49

Sam was up and gone before daylight. Whispering that he wanted to be out on Springer Road before Rodney and the surveyors got there, he said he'd get a bagel on his way and for me to stay in bed.

Gratefully, I did, thinking that if having a gallbladder operation would give me as much energy as Sam seemed to have, I ought to schedule mine fairly soon.

About eight, I went downstairs, dreading every step, to face Lillian. Latisha was already there, having had her breakfast and, from the look on her face, a good talking-to.

"Lillian," I said as soon as I stepped into the sunny kitchen, "I can explain, but first, how is Mrs. Abernathy?"

Lillian turned to me with a big smile. "She so much better, thank the Lord. Miss Julia, I tell you the truth, we all thought she was passin', but the Lord, He hear our prayers, an' He answer 'em jus' the way we ast Him to."

"I am so glad. Did you get any sleep?"

"I doze off an' on, so I'm all right." Lillian cracked an egg on the edge of a skillet, cut her eyes at me, and said, "Latisha tole me what y'all done last night. I guess she need a switchin' for gettin' firecrackers from ole Nub, but, I declare, she don't know no better, an' he don't either. I don't know what I ought to do."

"Nothing," I said, "don't do anything. Sam's going to talk to the sheriff about Nub, and, Lillian, I had no idea that Latisha had a sackful of fireworks, but they couldn't have been put to a better use. I just want you to know that she was never in any danger—I wouldn't have had that child hurt for anything. And we only went out there to see what Rodney was doing—nothing else, just to sneak in and sneak out. It was only when we got there that Latisha called our attention to what she had, and I thought it was better to go ahead and use them in a good cause than to let her keep them." I stopped, wondering how much more to say. "I should've called you, but with Mrs. Abernathy so sick . . ." I trailed off and quit.

"I don't never worry 'bout Latisha when she with you," Lillian said, making me feel both better and worse. Then she laughed. "Sometimes I reckon I ought to, though. Set on down, this egg be done."

Just as I sat at the table, the phone rang. Hurrying to answer it before Lillian fussed about a cold breakfast, I heard Etta Mae on the line.

"Miss Julia? I'm out in the country on my cell, so I might lose you. I have to hurry and tell you that I passed that place on my way to work—you know the one I mean, don't you? The place where we were last night?"

"Yes, I know. Out there on—"

"Don't say it," she said. "No telling who's listening. Anyway, there was a whole bunch of cars on the side of the road and men wandering around above the ditch. And I mean, a couple of cop cars and some other cars, and a wrecker." She giggled. "Guess what they need that for."

We chatted a few minutes longer while I told her that Sam would've been one of the men, and that he knew exactly who and what we'd seen and exactly where Rodney's tools were, in case he needed corroborative evidence.

"As far as you and I—and Latisha, of course—are concerned," I assured her, "we're out of it. What Rodney did is as plain as day, and even more so after that downpour last night, so they won't need any eyewitness testimony. And, Etta Mae . . . Etta Mae? Well," I said, replacing the phone, "I've lost her."

About midmorning, Sam came in looking pleased and slightly sun-burned. "An interesting morning, Julia," he said. "You would've enjoyed it." He sat at the table as Lillian brought over a cup of coffee.

"What happened?" I asked, eager to hear it all. "Tell us every-thing."

"Well, I got there first, as I intended," he said. "Then somebody in what looked like one of McCrory's Lincolns dropped Rodney off. To say he was taken aback to see me is an understatement. He hemmed and hawed, trying to explain why his car was parked in the bushes. He told me he'd been out there the day before looking around so he could point things out to the surveyors, and that his car wouldn't start when he was ready to leave." Sam looked up at Lillian and me. "Why don't you two sit down? This is a long story." We did and he continued. "Anyway, he was fit to be tied when his car really wouldn't start. Not only did it have a flat tire, it was mired in mud from rainwater runoff. Took about an hour to get a tow truck to come pull it out. And, let me tell you, he was one anxious young man. He couldn't stand still, kept snapping his fingers and jiggling around, saying, 'I got to go. I'm late, got to get to work,' and so on. No way around it—he wanted to be gone before the surveyors came.

"But he didn't make it. Two surveyors showed up, and as soon as they crossed the ditch, one of them looked around, saw the footprints and trampled weeds, as well as the mud puddle where the stake had been, and said, 'Uh-oh. Looks like we got us a land thief.' I thought Rodney would faint, but he pulled himself together and got real interested in who could've possibly moved a stake. He even went so far as to discover the new location—just happened to stumble across it." Sam stopped, shook his head, and laughed.

"Well, finally the wrecker got there, and Rodney got busy di-recting the driver on how to do his job until, that is, Coleman pulled up in his patrol car and another came in behind him. Rod-ney was beside himself by that time, talking a mile a minute, saying he couldn't imagine who could've done it, and that he'd been there the day before and somebody had shot at him, and he wanted to report the incident. Well, Coleman perked up at that, asked him all kinds of questions he couldn't answer. Rodney said, 'They shot at me a dozen times, and I'm not ashamed to say I ran for my life. I mean, there must've been five or six of them, and I knew I couldn't take 'em all on.'

"During all this I just stood back and let the surveyors point out the evidence to Coleman. He was taking notes and snapping pictures while Rodney was about to talk himself into real trouble. I finally drew him aside and told him he'd said enough, and that as long as the deputies didn't find any tools with fingerprints on them, they wouldn't know who the guilty party was. He turned white as a sheet and said he hadn't seen any tools and didn't know where they could be. 'I don't doubt that,' I said, 'but whoever shot at you probably has them or knows where they are. My advice to you is to cancel the survey and get out of Dodge.' Well," Sam said, laughing again, "I put it a little differently than that. But he thanked me and said if he'd known there were crazy people roaming around with guns in that part of the county, he never would've considered your property. By that time, they'd pulled his car out, so Rodney gave his card to Coleman, crawled in with the truck driver, and off they went, towing the Escalade behind them."

Lillian and I laughed, and I must say that I did it with a great deal of relief.

"Oh, by the way, Julia," Sam went on. "Do you know what surveyors call the iron stakes they use as markers?" I shook my head and he told me. "They call them monuments."

"*Really*? Well. I declare. Then since Rodney's given up on his cemetery, we'll have something to remember him by."

You would think that with Rodney getting his comeuppance and Sam making sure my property was no longer desirable that, for one day, we'd had our fill of unexpected events. For one thing, I'd begun feeling a nagging guilt for leaving Trixie so long with Hazel Marie. The Pickens family didn't need a permanent houseguest, so it was time for me to take up the burden of that prickly girl again. The time came sooner than I expected, for the day wasn't over by a long shot. I knew it when the mailman came.

Along with the bills, a letter from Elsie was in the pile I drew from the mailbox on the front porch. I stood looking at it, hoping that it would be what I'd longed for, but realizing that, without a return address, it was unlikely to be. I sat in a wicker chair on the porch, tore open the envelope, and read:

Dear Julia,

    You probably don't wont to hear this, but I need for Trixie to come home.

A smile spread across my face and I had an urge to sing the Hallelujah Chorus. Although to be truthful, with Trixie at Hazel Marie's, she had been little trouble to me. The same could not be said for her former gentleman friend to whom she'd introduced us. I kept reading.

    Well, home to us but not to her since she don't know where we are. So you can tell her this is where we are Ocean View RV Park #213 Whisper Lane Daytona, Fla I don't know the zip. We're just renting so dont think we can't afford a house but Troy took a parttime job at a gater farm and got bit. On the leg and it swoll up something awful and he went to the hospital and the doctor says he has to stay off of it, so I need help taking care of him. Troy don't like to be tied to his bed, so he is ill as a hornet all the time. I'm tired of being up and down all night long every night of the week waiting on him hand and foot.

Poor Trixie, I thought, to have to leave the gracious home she
was in and go to a cramped RV, whatever that was, and care for
an ill-tempered patient who would likely undo everything Hazel
Marie and I had done. I felt a stab of sympathy.

> *You'll just have to do without her and so will anybody*
> *else she's taken up with. If she pitches a fit, tell her ab-*
> *sence makes the heart grow fonder and so forth. She's*
> *needed here, but tell her the Ocean View Park is close to*
> *the race track and they's men young and old around all*
> *the time. Some of them even park their million dollar*
> *RVs right here in the park close to us. So let me know*
> *what bus she'll be on and I will meet it.*
>
> *I know you hate to see her go—anybody would, but*
> *maybe she can come back at Xmas if Troy is on his feet*
> *by then. Hope you won't miss her too much.*
>
> *Your cousin, Elsie Bingham*

My heart had grown lighter with each line, although there was
not one word of thanks or a hint of gratitude in the letter. But she
had added, like an afterthought, a phone number at the bottom.
That was more than she'd done in her first letter, which meant
that she was no longer hiding their whereabouts from Trixie or me.

In spite of having received the news I'd been longing for, I had
to admit to myself that I would regret being unable to witness
Trixie's full blossoming under Hazel Marie's tutelage. I comforted
myself, however, by noting the distinct possibility that Trixie had
already reached her peak, and there'd be nothing more to witness.

Chapter 50

After calling Hazel Marie to ask if it would be convenient for me to visit, I started the four-block walk to her house, recalling the phone conversation as I went.

"How is Trixie this morning?" I'd asked, wanting to be prepared for whatever mood she was in.

"To tell the truth," Hazel Marie said, "I'm a little worried about her. On the one hand, she gets up early, dresses nicely, puts on her makeup, and does her hair. And she's pleasant enough to be around, although she acts kind of dreamy-like—like she's off in her own world. But then she goes to the den and sits there *by the hour* watching *Magnum, P.I.,* one DVD after the other. I think that's a little strange, don't you?"

I certainly did, although Trixie had done stranger things than that, so perhaps we should be thankful for small blessings.

I walked up onto the porch, where Hazel Marie met me at the door. "She's still at it," she whispered. "I told her you were coming, but she just nodded and kept on watching."

I followed Hazel Marie into the den, found Trixie glued to the television set where Magnum, P.I., was involved in a fistfight on a beach somewhere in Hawaii.

"Trixie?" I said to get her attention. "A letter from your grandmother just came."

That got her attention. "From Meemaw? What does she want?"

"She wants you to come home. Well, to Florida. Here it is," I said, handing the letter to her. Frowning, she accepted it and slowly smoothed out the folds.

While she read, I picked up the remote and turned down the sound. Hazel Marie and I stood watching, our eyes drawn inexorably toward Magnum, P.I.'s antics, as we waited for Trixie to finish absorbing the letter. With Rodney now out of the picture, I hoped the recall would please her. She hadn't wanted to be sent away in the first place, and it was a settled fact that she'd been miserable in my care. The thought of leaving Hazel Marie, however, might dampen her eagerness to return to Meemaw and Pawpaw.

At that realization, I was somewhat saddened by Elsie's summons, for as much as Trixie had wanted to go home at first, I wondered if she'd be all that thrilled now.

Trixie held the letter long enough to have read it twice or three times over, but finally she handed it to Hazel Marie. Right in front of my eyes, Trixie's face slowly turned a deep red, almost as if she were holding her breath. Then it crumpled up and a single tear ran down her cheek.

"Oh, honey," Hazel Marie said, going to her and putting an arm around her shoulders. "Don't cry. We thought you'd be happy to go home—I mean to Florida."

"I am," Trixie said, sniffing as she ran her hand under her nose. "I guess. Except Meemaw wanted me to find somebody and I have, but . . ." She trailed off, while I stared in surprise.

"Oh, Trixie, you don't mean Rodney, do you?" I'd thought that was over for good. If not, well, I didn't want to think of the resulting complications.

"*No!*" Trixie cried. "I wouldn't have him on a silver platter. I'm talking about a real man, but now it's too late. I have to do what Meemaw wants."

Well, no, she didn't, but I was hesitant to encourage open rebellion. She could be with us forever.

Hazel Marie said, "It'll be all right, honey. She says you can come back at Christmas. Why don't we plan for you to do that? Then we'll both have something to look forward to."

Hazel Marie was undoubtedly the sweetest woman alive, but

I had little patience with Trixie's vacillations. First she'd wanted to go home and now she didn't. Then she'd wanted Rodney and now she didn't. And now she had her eye on somebody else, except, I realized, she hadn't been anywhere to meet anyone. Of course, she hadn't had to go anywhere to meet Rodney, so maybe she'd matched up again with an online stranger. Which I could live with as long as he had no interest in funeral parlors and cemeteries.

Trixie wiped her face and stood up. "I guess I better go pack."

One of the babies screamed upstairs and the other one joined in a moment later. Hazel Marie jumped up and hurried off, saying Granny Wiggins needed help. That left Trixie and me alone.

"I'll call the bus station," I told her, "and find out the bus schedule. But, really, Trixie, there's no reason for you to hurry off. They've been getting along fine without you, so a few more days won't hurt. You'll have time to meet with your new beau and exchange addresses, and maybe make plans to see each other over Christmas."

"Won't do no good," she mumbled, then plopped back down in the leather chair she'd just gotten up from. She buried her face in her hands and began sobbing.

I'm not good in such situations, but I tried patting her shoulder and saying, "There, there."

It didn't help, so I spoke firmly to her. "Trixie, you're old enough to do whatever you want. You can either go to Florida or you can stay here. Well, not *here,* because you've been with Hazel Marie long enough, and it seems to me that she's accomplished a marvelous makeover for you in that time. So if you decide to stay"—I stopped and steeled myself to finish—"you're welcome to your room at my house until you find a job and an apartment." That was the best I could do.

She sniffed wetly and said, "Guess I'll go on to Florida then." Which almost hurt my feelings, but then she pushed back her hair, looked up at me, and said, "Wouldn't do no good to stay. I know that. I'm not dumb. All the makeovers in the world won't change a thing. He don't even know I'm alive."

"But haven't you talked to him?"

She nodded. "We talked. Some."

"Then he'll understand about sickness in your family, and, think of this, you can stay in touch by email and that Skype thing that Lloyd has. You'll be as close that way as you are now, won't you?" I was beginning to lose patience. Trixie was quick to fall for somebody, and just as quick to fall out with somebody. It was hard to keep up with her.

"Not hardly," she said with a little more spirit. Then she looked at the television screen. Magnum, P.I., was now driving a convertible on a street somewhere in Hawaii. "Miss Julia? Do you think I could ask Hazel Marie for just one DVD? You know, to remember him by?"

Stunned that she seemed actually to be in love with a figment of some screenwriter's imagination, I stumbled out a reply. "I expect she'd be glad to give you one. They belong to Mr. Pickens, though."

"I know," she murmured, turning to gaze at the silent but still active television hero. "He never watches them, but I do. If she'd give me one, I could watch him all the time."

I blinked in sudden understanding and almost gasped. That was exactly what she'd been doing. Hiding my dismay and mentally making plans a mile a minute, I said briskly, "Well, that's nice, but you don't have time to watch a show now. Why don't you run on and start packing? There might be a bus heading south this afternoon. I'll check the schedule and call Elsie to let her know when to meet you. Hazel Marie will have some shopping bags for your new clothes, or I might have a suitcase you can have. If you forget anything, I'll send it to you. Run on. Trixie, hurry. We need to get you on your way home."

On the evening of the following day, Sam and I returned from a walk around the neighborhood. We'd spent part of the time talking about his campaign schedule, which would get even busier as November neared.

"How do you feel about the race now?" I said, picking a leaf from one of Mildred's boxwoods as we passed. "Will we be going to Raleigh?"

"I can't tell you, because I don't know." Sam smiled and squeezed my hand. "But it doesn't really matter. I'm having such a good time campaigning that win or lose the election, I'll win either way. I wouldn't have missed this for the world, Julia."

"Not even for a boat trip down the Rhine?"

We laughed, and he said, "Not even."

He released my hand as we stepped up on the porch. "Let's sit out here awhile," he said, pointing to the cushioned wicker chairs behind the wisteria vine that partially shielded the porch from the street.

I smiled, feeling refreshed from the walk, as I always did, especially on such evenings when the day's heat had lifted. Taking a walk with my husband was still new enough to be treasured, and I recalled how I used to feel about couples, young or old, who walked along holding hands. I'd looked at them with scorn, thinking that such displays were unseemly and slightly déclassé. Until I became Sam's wife instead of Wesley Lloyd Springer's widow, I hadn't realized that what I'd felt was not contempt, but envy.

"Think you'll miss having Trixie around?" Sam asked, returning to the main subject of our walk—the Trixie saga. I'd told Sam about getting her packed, missing the bus the day before so she had to spend another night, her determination to spend it at Hazel Marie's house instead of ours, and my concern about her makeover having taken so long that she'd practically moved in with the Pickenses—a momentous mistake in hindsight.

"I had in mind something on the order of a day spa," I'd said. "I didn't expect her to be there day and night for days on end. Knowing what I now know, though, Elsie's letter came in the nick of time."

"Did you tell Hazel Marie?" Sam asked.

"No, and I don't think I will. No need stirring up trouble when the troublemaker is gone."

Sam laughed. "Honey, I don't believe Hazel Marie has anything to worry about."

"Well, that's true," I said, smiling. "Besides, I think she'd already figured it out. I stopped by after getting Trixie on the bus this morning, and Hazel Marie was putting away all those DVDs that had been pulled out. She told me she'd put four of them in Trixie's suitcase as a surprise, which was a very kind and thoughtful thing to do. All I said was that Trixie would be thrilled when she found them. And Hazel Marie smiled that sweet smile of hers and said. 'In his younger years, like he was on these shows, Magnum, P.I., had a remarkable resemblance to J.D., don't you think?' So I think she knows."

"What about Pickens?" Sam asked, thoroughly amused at the thought of such an unlikely triangle. "Does he know?"

I waved my hand at such a notion. "The man is oblivious. But I tell you, Sam, I think that talking-to he gave her when she was so rude to Hazel Marie turned everything around. I think she was so impressed with his firmness and his . . . well, masculinity, I guess, that she realized the difference between a dilettante like Rodney and a real man. I think her crush began right then. In fact, she referred to her new interest as a real man, although I didn't know who she was talking about at the time."

We sat in companionable silence for a while. Three cars passed with bumper stickers for Murdoch on one and for Mooney on two. Not a good sign, but we smiled at each other because there was still plenty of time.

"You know, Sam," I said, musing over the summer, almost in a stock-taking mood, "we've had some interesting events in the last several weeks. First, Trixie landed on us, then you had your surgery—two totally unexpected things, neither of which I'd want to repeat. Then there was my foray into public speaking, another experience I wouldn't want to have again. Then there's been your campaign, which you chose over a boat trip." I smiled at him. "I'm glad you don't regret the choice. Then, of course, there was Rodney. Just think, if it hadn't been for Trixie, we'd never have known him—imagine what we would've missed." We laughed together. Somewhat ruefully, though.

Sam said, "You and Hazel Marie did a lot for Trixie. And, in spite of her disappointment in Rodney, she'll never forget her time here."

"Well," I agreed, "I'll never forget her time here, either. And as beneficial as cosmetics and deportment exercises proved to be in her case, I think that just being here with us wrought a much more important makeover in the way she views the world. If, that is, she can separate it from a television show. But since I find myself missing her just a tiny bit, maybe she wrought one in me, as well." I reached for his hand. "It's been quite a marvelous summer in its way, hasn't it?"